SHOTGUN

By Paul Thomas

Copyright © 2017 by Paul Thomas

This book is a work of fiction. Names, characters, places, and incidents are either a product of the author's imagination or are used fictitiously. Any resemblance to actual persons, living or dead, events, or locales is entirely coincidental.

Cover art by Paul Thomas

1.

Stiller was just another New England factory town on the downside. It had been many years since its 30,000 or so working class people looked to the blue sky with hope. Some were able to gather up the courage to move on to places with more to offer. When asked where they were from, most would simply dodge the question. Being from a nothing mill town was a label they didn't want.

In its prime years, Stiller, Massachusetts, on the banks of a long winding river, was a prolific textile producer. The river rapids provided the juice to run the heavy machinery in the stretches of stark red brick mills. Later, steam power took over and Stiller flourished even more. But now in the early spring of 1969, the town lay in decline, in the silence of abandoned buildings and the drone of the mills still operating. Those remaining businesses faced a constant struggle to maintain a sufficient worker count.

In the middle 1800's, men and women came to Stiller and other Massachusetts mill towns from the northern part of New England and Canada. They worked long hours in the factories and endured tough working conditions. They did it to put food on the table and to keep a roof over their heads in hope of a better life. Immigrants from Ireland and Eastern Europe followed into the early 1900's. Not long after, the textile industry began moving to the south. There, labor was cheaper and more available. As the mills closed in the northeast, unemployment rose in Stiller along with poverty. The morale of its people declined, as many descended into a state of passivity and resignation.

At this time, the war in Vietnam was at its height. There was strong opposition to it by the youth of America and heated demonstrations rose up on college campuses throughout the country. This situation, coupled with the sluggish economy, came to affect the townspeople of Stiller. They walked the gray streets with heads down and hands in pockets.

Although a number of mills were still up and running, there was sparse other industry in the town. The goal of most of the young people was simply to get out and many of them had. But the older folks, set in their ways, stayed on. They faced each new day as best they could. Stoically, as they tried to hold on to some semblance of pride, they watched Stiller continue to sink, drip by drip.

It was then that Jeff Jones, just turned 22 years old, got ready to head south from Lincoln, New Hampshire. He'd given his notice on his job at a lumber yard two weeks prior and now he was done. Jeff had been on the move since turning 18 and had trouble staying in one place too long. The job at the yard was tolerable but he gradually got restless with life out in the sticks.

Finally things came to a head. One of his co-workers had relatives in Massachusetts. They told him that the town of Stiller was hiring help in the factories along the river at a good wage. The co-worker mentioned it to Jeff one day and the notion of moving on took hold with him. After wrestling with the idea for weeks, he finally settled on going through with it. The time to leave the White Mountains region had come.

Jeff Jones stood around six foot one and was thin and wiry. He had straight brown hair. Sometimes it looked like it had been messed up by a gust of wind and that he'd righted it by running his hands through a couple of times. He wore it long more to save money than to be trendy, but it fit him well. Jeff was a good looking guy in a rustic way. However, there was something about him that wasn't quite right. His eyes gave it away to some discerning people; droopy and sad looking no matter what kind of mood he was in. He wasn't the happiest person in the world, but he coped. Jeff's eyes were a window to the hardships he'd suffered throughout his young life.

He was born In Holyoke, a city in the central part of Massachusetts, and left town almost four years ago. Before that, Jeff completed a year at a state college in the area, but dropped out due mostly to a lack of drive and belief in himself. He'd gotten decent grades, but worried too much and had a lot of trouble focusing. A tight money situation sealed his quitting school and taking to the road. Jeff wanted to return to college eventually and get a degree in something, but he had no idea in which direction to go. Although he had a steadfast will to be independent, decisions did not come easily to him. He lacked faith in himself.

Jeff didn't have much of a family. His mother, Meredith, was dead and he hadn't seen his father, Anson since he was 11. He had an older brother Luke who was married with an infant daughter and lived in Annapolis, Maryland. Jeff's mom died of ovarian cancer when he was barely four so he vaguely remembered her. However, his one clear memory was of her funeral. On that day, young as he was, Jeff understood clearly that she was gone to him forever. He felt a horrible sense of loss in the following weeks and months. Right up to the present, that feeling had never completely left him.

Jeff's dad was dependable and a good provider as a heavy equipment operator up until after his wife's death. It crushed him and he slowly resorted to the bottle. It took many years, but Anson Jones ultimately developed into an irresponsible alcoholic with periodic bouts of violence. He just could not handle the job of raising his boys on his own. Older son Luke did his best to help his father and Jeff chipped in what he could too. But they were dealing with a state of denial like a stone wall. Their dad flatly refused to seek help. The nightmare continued on.

Things finally came to a climax in the summer of 1958. Anson Jones, hung over on the job, fell off his tractor, which then damaged a building. He came out of it with a concussion and a broken wrist. The construction company fired him and that proved to be the tipping point. Shortly after, he went on a binge and disappeared, leaving his sons flat. Anson was never heard from again other than possibly one sighting. On a busy street in New York City, a family friend, from his seat on a bus claimed to have seen a bum sleeping on a bench who resembled him. A few other people who knew Anson well speculated that he may have done himself in. But nothing ever turned up and he remained missing.

There were relatives in Pittsfield and Williamstown, Massachusetts, but none of them had the financial means to take in Luke and Jeff permanently. They had their own troubles. The boys eventually became wards of the state and spent some time in an orphanage. Then, for the next few years they bounced in and out of foster homes. Eventually, they were separated.

Luke was four years older and was able to fend for himself first. As soon as he turned 18, he left foster care and enlisted in the U. S. Air Force. He spent the next year at the Lackland base in San Antonio, Texas. Luke did three more years between a base in England and some deployment in Vietnam, during which he serviced fighter jets.

After his military time was up, Luke returned to Texas. He resumed a relationship with a special woman he'd been involved with while stationed there. They later married, moved to Annapolis and had a daughter. His military training paid off in that Luke was doing well working as a flight mechanic. He was more strong willed than Jeff and better able to rise above the tough hand they'd been dealt.

When Luke entered the service, Jeff, already separated from him was left even more on his own. He was still living in foster homes with little stability. Jeff was somewhat more passive than his brother but he didn't like being pushed around. A few times, he lost his temper and scared the people whose care he was under. But he was quick to apologize when he knew he was wrong and was always able to move ahead.

Jeff learned to survive in the foster situations which generally weren't too bad. But still, he was wary and untrusting of most people. However, he was able to cooperate with the social workers assigned to him and even came to trust one particular woman who went out of her way to help him. Jeff did his best to handle each move that came along. But nobody could get close to him, not even her. He'd been through too much and had a strong wall built around himself.

After he quit college, Jeff left his final foster arrangement in Holyoke and drifted around New England from job to job. He was a survivor, able to

8

deal with each situation in finding lodging and work to support himself. He'd considered staying with Luke and his wife in the beginning. They wanted him and offered several times. But Jeff had a solitary nature and felt more comfortable as a loner. Plus he didn't want to be a burden to his brother and his family.

Jeff wasn't lazy or undependable. He took whatever job he was able to nail down seriously no matter how mundane it might be. But he was just too antsy. He couldn't last and put down roots anywhere.

Now Jeff was ready to go again. He loaded all his gear, which were only the bare necessities, in the Air Force backpack that Luke gave him and in his carry bag. Jeff walked out the rooming house door into the fresh air of a new day. It had actually been a decent place to live but he was done with it. He had close to a thousand dollars saved over the last few years. Jeff always lived within his means, and having a considerable amount of money stashed gave him a feeling of at least some security. It was plenty of cash to tide him over in case things became tough in finding a new job. He tried to look ahead with hope.

2.

It was a bright spring Sunday morning. Jeff's car blew a cylinder the week before and he sold it to a junk dealer. So he was without wheels and decided to hitchhike south since it was many miles to a bus station. The sun felt good on his shoulders as he stood on the side of the highway. "Man, it's nice to be alive and free," he said to himself taking a deep breath. "And moving on. I'm going someplace new and I call my own shots. Thank God at least for that."

He was out there ten minutes before an old Ford wagon stopped ahead of him. Jeff broke into his hitchhiker's trot, stowed his gear in the back seat and slid into the front. The cargo bay was loaded with luggage and some small furniture. He looked across at an attractive young woman. She had long auburn hair, straight and parted in the middle, which fell just past the loops of her faded jeans. Her skin was smooth and tanned. Although her clothes were loose fitting, they couldn't hide a healthy womanly figure.

"Peace," she said holding up the V sign. "What's your destination, man?"

"Umm…destination unknown. Just kidding - Stiller in Massachusetts. Due south around a hundred miles or so."

"Yeah – I know that town," she said with a chuckle. "It's right off this interstate. We'll be going past there – I can take you all the way. I do believe it's your lucky day."

"I'll say," Jeff smiled.

The girl adjusted her sun glasses, brushed back her hair, and accelerated back on to the road. Jeff relaxed and glanced over from the corner of his eye. There were flowers and arty designs sewn into her jeans and she wore moccasins with no socks. "Hippie flower child", he thought. He was kind of interested in the counter culture movement but had never talked at length with a full blown hippie.

The girl looked over at him and broke into a wide grin. "What's your name, dude? I assume you have one."

"Jeff – Jeff Jones."

"Nice name – nice flow to it."

"That's what they tell me – the two J's do it," he laughed.

"I'm Crystal – pleasure to meet you."

"Same here."

"Big day for me today, Jeff," Crystal said enthusiastically. "First leg of a cross country trip to San Fran. Finally headed for California, man – finally headed for the west coast. Blows me away!"

She had such an easy way about her that Jeff found himself surprisingly relaxed. Normally, he'd be a little nervous around such a hot woman. Not this time.

"Cal', huh? Cool," he said rubbing his chin. "Brings to mind this friend I had when I was a kid. We were pretty tight but one day he and his family packed up in a camper and moved out to Pasadena. Never saw them again after that…it was almost like my childhood ended on that day."

"Dig, I can relate," Crystal said, again brushing her hair back. "Kind of a drag but that's interesting, man. I hear you. Sometimes one event can change everything – like a disturbance in the field, you know?"

"Never thought of it like that but I'd say there's some truth to it. I missed them for a time but after a while it faded away – like everything does eventually I guess. So what's out there in Frisco for you? You're a hippie, right?"

A smile rose from deep within her. "Yeah – I guess I am. It's the revolution – Cal's the home of counter culture – the rucksack revolution."

"Rucksack revolution?"

"Haven't you ever read 'The Dharma Bums', man? It's going down in California – dropping out – communes – an end to all wars – peace and love. Screw all these phony politicians and their capitalist funky jive. It's the beginning of a new way of life - people sharing and living together in harmony instead of always competing with and screwing each other. The movement is all about young people who reject the establishment's rules and see a better way – a peaceful way. Gonna be just one in a commune of many, man. I'm all in for it, you know?"

"Yeah? That's pretty far out. Tell me more."

"Sure I will," she beamed.

Crystal went on to describe the scene in San Francisco: the Haight/Ashbury district, Grateful Dead free concerts, the Jefferson Airplane, the Doors and other hot bands in the city, and the hippie settlements out in the wine country and the desert. She was picking up a

11

friend in Bayonne, New Jersey. They already had a commune lined up to join in the hills around 50 miles outside of the city.

Crystal continued to explain how everybody in a commune contributed to the health and well-being of the group. There were no private possessions. Everything belonged to everybody. They farmed the land, made some of their own clothes, and built and maintained their own shelters. In general, the hippies turned their backs on the establishment. "Dropouts just temporarily," she emphasized. "In time, our lifestyle will be the norm and the bastardization of this planet will be reversed for all time."

"You really believe that?" Jeff asked pensively.

"Of course I do. The revolution is brotherhood and sisterhood, man. The whole damn world's going to get caught up in it. White, black, yellow, red – it doesn't matter what color you are. No more war. We're going to live in peace like it was always meant to be. See - I just met you today and I love you already 'cause in the end, we're all brothers and sisters, man, don't you know? Love your brothers and sisters – all animals – nature, etcetera. Peace - not war – peace. And that's the bottom line truth, dude."

"Phew," Jeff sighed, "heavy – real heavy."

She sold it pretty well and was convinced of it. What Crystal described sounded almost too good to be true to Jeff but her story did spark his interest. Still, he could only imagine how much things would have to change for the counter culture to have a chance to make it.

They rode on and talked a little about their pasts in between Crystal's steady pumping of the movement. She was positive it was going to work. "Like a Rolling Stone" played on the radio as the late morning rays framed the horizon. Spring warmed down on the passing landscape, fueling the light green of rebirth. Jeff sat back and appreciated the tranquil moments, feelings few and far between for him.

In time they neared Stiller. Jeff darkened at the prospect of the ride's end and the uncertainty ahead. His stop came up. Crystal slowed the car and pulled over. She brushed back her hair and looked him up and down.

"I like you, Jeff – I really like you. You're a nice looking guy and you have an honest vibe. Why don't you join us? Come to California with Amber and me."

"Really?" Jeff said, surprised.

"Of course."

"Well, let me think about it a minute."

She meant what she said. It was a tempting prospect and Jeff turned it over in his head. He looked over and saw the soft skin of her braless breast between the buttons of her shirt. If he went, he'd surely get a shot with her at some point. That alone might be worth it. But it was too much too soon. It wasn't in him to act fast like that right on the moment. Way too risky.

"Man – I don't know what to say," he finally began. "Awful nice of you to make the offer, Crystal – especially not even knowing me and all. But see, I have to get a job and get ahead a little more than I am right now. Can't just change my whole game on a dime – you know how it is. Going to renege this time, but thanks again for asking."

"That's cool," she said acceptingly. "But take this just in case you change your mind." She wrote something on a slip of paper and gave it to him. "At the very least, if you're out to Cal, come by and check us out. We can put you up no problem for as long as you want."

"I sure will."

"Let the sunshine set you free, man," Crystal said with a big smile as Jeff got out of the car. He smiled back and gave her the peace sign. Then he watched her drive off. He looked at the slip she gave him. It said:

Crystal Farlow

P.O. Box 3125

San Francisco, CA

Jeff thought about the day's events so far. Then he looked to the ramp on which he was about to begin walking. Clouds had moved in and the sun was gone. A ripple of anxiety ran through him as he wondered what lay ahead.

3.

It wasn't far to the center of Stiller. Heading into town, Jeff walked by rows of triple-deckers, all with long front porches. They were old structures, mostly white or gray, with peeling paint, grimy windows, and banged up doors. On some of the platforms kids yelled and played games, running this way and that. Through the windows, he noticed a few adults inside some of the buildings. Some just sat and stared out absently, as if they were in jail.

From a second floor porch, one kid, a little guy only four or five, watched the stranger with the big gray backpack pass by. "Hey Mistur, hey Mistur!" he yelled down, "yer got a dime fer a cup uh cor-fee – or 15 cench?"

Jeff looked up and smiled but said nothing back. He moved ahead and reflected back on Crystal, and if maybe he should have joined her after all as he looked down this ragged street. "What's done is done," he told himself, "don't look back."

Before long he was out of the slums and on to Water Street, which was the main drag of Stiller. The sun filtered through again in spots and things began to look a little better. The wide avenue was alive with the hum of traffic and the beat of pedestrian footsteps.

Jeff figured the best place to stay for the short term was the local YMCA. He approached an old woman with her back to him leaning on a lamp post to ask for directions.

"Any idea of where the town YMCA is, Ma'am?" he asked after he tapped her shoulder from the side.

He stiffened when she turned and faced him. She was wrinkled and weather beaten, wearing a jacket and a long tattered dress with nylons balled up at her ankles. She flashed a gaping smile. Her false teeth didn't fit right and he could see the top edge of her denture.

"You talkin' to me Sonny – you sayin' somefin tuh me? Why...you know - that friggin mutha fah 'bout an hour ago - he tied to steal my pockah book...I should've kicked his fat flabby ah – a - aaarse...!"

She barely finished the sentence and her breath just about melted him. Then, her upper denture dropped out of her mouth but she caught it before it hit the ground. Jeff took a couple of steps back.

"Just take it easy, lady," he said facing the palm of his hand to her. "You just get yourself together and I'll find somebody else to ask."

The woman put the teeth back into her mouth. It surely wasn't the first time she'd dumped them. She went back to leaning on the post and mumbling to herself. Jeff quickly moved on up the street.

He shook his head. "Of all the people to ask, I have to pick the town bag lady," he said to himself. "What the hell is wrong with me? I've got to learn to think more before I act." Then, he walked a ways up the street. In the distance, he saw a big YMCA OF STILLER sign far past the traffic lights. In a few minutes, he was up the steps and through the glass doors.

4.

It was a big old red brick building, much the same as most YMCA's built across America in the early 1900's. The floor creaked as Jeff walked toward the front desk and took in the layout. To his left was a spacious area with a large television set on a high stand. In a semicircle around it were a long couch and stuffed chairs plus some foldouts, all sitting on a braided rug that spanned far and wide. On the right was reading space with more chairs, tables, a couple of sofas, and racks of newspapers attached to long wooden binders. At the far end was a glass enclosed room with four heavy-legged old style pool tables. And to the rear, stairs and double doors that lead to the gym and the pounding steps of a basketball game in progress.

An older man sat behind the desk. Heavy set and with half glasses sitting on the tip of his nose, he looked up at Jeff and smiled. "What can I do for you, son?"

"Looking for a room to rent, sir."

"Okay – now let me give you the spiel. Ten dollars a week in advance. Cleaning woman once a week, common area television 'til eleven, and a quarter for use of the gym and pool if you want to, which covers one full day. How long do you plan on staying, son?"

"I'm not really sure right now but a few weeks at least. Going to be looking for a job in those textile mills along the river. Any suggestions which?"

The man removed his glasses and rubbed his eyes. "You'll have no trouble on that end. Tough places to work but they're always looking to take help on, at least the ones that's left here. You might want to try Warburton Textiles down on Abbot Street. They're the best of the lot. I hear they're still doing pretty well too. Here you go. Room 22 for as long as you need it. We're glad to have you with us, son."

Jeff dug out the ten dollars and put it on the desk. "Thanks – I for the help," he said.

The man nodded, pointed to the stairs and directed him to his room. Jeff was relieved. He was a nice guy and it seemed that finally he'd made a good move. He figured in time he'd get to know some of the boarders. For now, this was going to be home.

Jeff went upstairs and found Room 22. It was bigger than he anticipated, with a high ceiling and one large window that looked out to Water Street. The rest was a bed, dresser, a couple of chairs, and a wash basin. He put his gear down, walked over to the window and pulled up a chair. For a minute or two, he looked out and listened to the drone of the afternoon traffic, allowing himself to unwind.

"This place is no palace but it could be worse," he thought to himself. "At least I have a little more privacy than I did back in Lincoln. I'll find a spot for my hot plate and it'll be just like home."

Jeff then unpacked his gear and sat down on the bed. He noticed the clock above the dresser. It was three thirty. He figured he'd get a nap and then go out and get some supper. Maybe he'd take in the TV room after that, then hit the hay early. He wanted to start fresh the next day to look for work.

He got back up and threw some water on his face at the basin. Jeff took a peek at himself in the mirror. "Wow - my eyes look sunken in and I've gotten too damn skinny," he told himself. "I've got to make sure I eat better and get enough rest – and get right back into my exercise routine. The last thing I need is to get sick and not be able to work. Then I'd really be screwed."

For the next couple of minutes Jeff felt down and lonesome. But he tried not to let those feelings linger. He lay down on the bed, which creaked loudly with his weight. In minutes was asleep. Jeff was a dreamer. Sometimes he had two or three a night that he could remember. He had an active subconscious that didn't miss a trick. It had filed everything away from day one.

Strange happenings surfaced in Jeff's dreams, many times in absurd settings with him in some kind of jam he can't get out of. Often, he'd be trying to make a phone call to deal with some emergency, but would be unable to get the number right. He'd scratch his head in the morning to try to make sense of those crazy situations he could recall.

After he'd slept awhile, a dream surfaced that he had periodically in one form or another. It usually came up when something happened in his life that caused stress. In the dream, Jeff is a little boy. His mother is alive but not yet sick. He's in the kitchen of their apartment in Holyoke standing on a stool, trying to get a snack from a dish on the counter.

Just as he gets his hand on one, Jeff loses his balance and falls in slow motion to the floor. He begins to cry but settles when he hears his mother's soft footsteps. He looks up and is struck by her figure, a golden angel's aura around her but her face is blurry. She's in a white gown leaning forward and appears weightless, although her toes are just on the floor. Jeff feels a calmness as he reaches out for her. But just as his fingers touch hers, she comes into clear focus, smiles, and then disintegrates into dust. A wave of fright passes through his body and then everything fades into a fog.

Jeff woke up in a fit and nearly fell off the bed. "That nightmare again," he said shaking his head. "Am I going to be haunted for the rest of my life? I probably should see a shrink."

He lay back a minute and looked to the ceiling. In the corner, a black spider was tending to its web. It motored back and forth focused; spinning here, connecting there, simply doing its thing. For a series of seconds Jeff was mesmerized by it. He thought of swatting it down but its work ethic got to him.

"That little insect," he said to himself, "nah – it's not an insect – what's the word...arachnid? Guess I learned SOME-thing in college. Well, whatever the hell it is, it's just trying to get by - just like me and the rest of the poor slobs in this world. Just trying to carve out a little space, that's all. What gives me the right to snuff out that life however small it might be? Nah - no way."

Then he spoke out loud. "Black spider," he said, "we're kindred spirits for as long as you'll have me."

The spider continued on oblivious to Jeff's words. He shook his head and figured now that he was talking to spiders, maybe he was finally losing it. Then his thoughts returned to the dream. He knew he'd have trouble sleeping through the next night or two as that was the routine after having it. He thought his mother must surely be in Heaven; she looked so beautiful each time before she vanished. She just had to be.

He got up and stretched. At the basin, he splashed cold water on his face again and felt better. It was five thirty. Time to clean up and get something to eat.

Jeff looked around the room and saw there was no shower or toilet. He got his stuff together and went out in the hall to look for the common lavatory. Passing by Room 20, the one next to his, he heard someone playing a guitar. Jeff was a big fan of the instrument. Whoever it was had some serious chops. Jeff made a mental note to stop by soon and introduce himself.

Near the end of the hall, he saw a confused looking man of medium height in a sleeveless T-shirt. He looked to be in his 40's. The man was bent to the side holding on to his foot. His hair hung wildly and a lock fell right at the top of his nose. Jeff thought of Alfalfa of the Little Rascals and had to stifle a laugh. The man straightened up and with a quizzical expression, looked over at him.

"How goes it?" Jeff said.

"Terrible, and you?"

Jeff smiled. The man started talking before he could answer.

"See, I dropped my damn glasses and broke 'em five minutes ago – everything's a dang blur now - like when you get your bell rung In a scrape. Anyway, I banged my toe on the chair over there – it is a chair, ain't it? Hurts like a basted. Nah – I'm just busting your chops, pal – it's not really that bad. But...aww – I mean...what's the use?"

"I get it," Jeff laughed. "But by the way, I'm looking to get a shower. Do you happen to know where they are?"

"The wash room? Sure, bud – way down the end of the hall. That's where I'm going. Just foller me. Name's Creecher – Harley Creecher. Glad to know you. Just call me Creecher - that's what I go by mostly."

Jeff introduced himself and they shook hands. As they slowly walked along, Creecher talked nonstop. He told Jeff he was from Boston and worked for the Globe for many years. Two years ago, he got laid off, and at the same time, his wife left him "to find herself" as he said it sarcastically. There were no kids so it was a clean split. But he fell into a downward spin and was homeless for a time. Somehow he'd landed in Stiller, was driving a cab for a living, and had straightened himself out. They turned into the wash room and stood at the sinks.

"Yeah – I'm just driving a hack and trying to figure what to do next, Jeff," Creecher said. "But I'm okay. You never know what kind of hand life will deal yah next, right bud?"

"I hear you – believe me I do."

"Like it almost ended for me yesterday," Creecher continued looking to the ceiling. "I should be friggin dead. You got a minute?"

"Sure."

Creecher leaned on the sink and collected his thoughts. "Well, I picked up two old ladies from the Stop and Shop with around 20 bags," he began. "Put 'em in the trunk of the Checker and I take the ladies to this big three decker at the top of Argyle Street. Shift the cab in PARK on the hill and I get out to let the ladies out. Didn't pull up the hand brake. Cab's runnin', ladies are still in back. Get the picture?"

"Got it."

"So, just as I'm opening the door for them, I hear a clunk, and somehow the cab's back in NEUTRAL and she starts rolling down the goddamn hill. I'm standing there frozen for a second – looking at two heads in back and nobody up front."

"Wow!"

"You bet your life. Then I snap out of it and run like hell after the cab. Luckily the hill's not too steep and it's not going fast yet. I catch it as it's swerving toward the curb near a big tree. I get the door half open, slide my foot in, and slam on the brake. At the same time I feel something close around my head. The door's gone and jammed against the tree and my skull is pinned like a walnut in a cracker. Just firm and it don't hurt, but another inch or two and my brains'd be splattered all over the road."

"What the hell did you do?"

"Somehow I didn't panic. Ever so easy – my hand trembling – I reach in, shift the cab in REVERSE, and let the car back up just a little bit. Then I'm free and not even a scratch! No damage to the cab and the ladies said they were okay. I get the shift to NEUTRAL, quickly pull the handbrake up and it's over. But I'm so shook up, both my hands are shaking and I can't even calm down enough to back the cab up to the house.

"Finally I did. The ladies took it pretty good considering it all. After I helped them with the bags, they insisted on giving me the fare and a good tip over it. But I couldn't take no money after what I put them through. They couldah been hurt real bad. Gave 'em a free ride and knocked off after that. I kept my hand on the shift and limped back to the garage even though I never stopped shaking completely – my whole goddamn body. Still not over it yet, Jeff. Now I got to get my glasses fixed before I can work again."

"One heavy trip, Creecher," Jeff said.

"For gun-damned sure. I'm just lucky to be standing here talking to you."

Creecher felt some relief having told the story again. It was about the tenth time. He laid out his shaving gear and directed Jeff to the showers.

"Wehhyll, I just have to move on, I guess," Creecher concluded almost singing the words. "That's what I'm gonna do - move the hell on down the roderreo. Shave, then hit the hay early. Tomorrow I'll walk down to the optomerrrist or however the hell you say it, and I'll fix them spectacles. That's the plan, my friend."

Jeff smiled and nodded. He told Creecher to have a good night. Then he walked into the shower area. As showers go, it was a good one. Plenty of hot water and even a fresh bar of soap. He lathered up and felt better as he rinsed off the grit of the day.

5.

Back in Room 22, Jeff got himself organized and then headed downstairs. He walked by the TV room where a number of men were camped out. They were mostly middle aged, plus a few old guys here and there. Some watched television while others passed the time quietly, smoking, reading the newspapers, or just gazing absently out the windows.

Jeff exited the building and looked down Water Street. He saw a sign in the distance that said EAT AT JOEY'S and figured it would be as good a place as any. He walked over to the small restaurant and took a seat at the counter. He looked around and saw there were only two other people in the place; a young couple in one of the booths. A big guy in a blue t-shirt sat facing a thin woman wearing a halter tied around her waist. They were arguing back and forth about something.

Jeff ordered a chicken salad sandwich with a side of fries and a coke from a tall slender waitress. She wore her long black hair in a ponytail. The young woman was striking, but more sexy than pretty. The food came and he went at it. He was starved. As he ate, he noticed that the disagreement between the two in the booth was getting more heated.

Then the big man got up in a huff and stormed to the counter. The woman followed, fussing at him. He slammed the slip and some money down so hard that it knocked Jeff's coke over. "Damn!" Jeff said as he pulled away and the drink went all over the floor. A little spilled on his pants. The waitress, who saw the whole thing, came over and handed him a rag.

"What the fuck'za matter with you, Biz!" the woman said to the man. "Are you fricken stooooopid or sumthin? Look what you done!"

"Yeah," the waitress said, "just calm down – relax, will yah dude?"

"Aww, shaddup yah dumb broads – and I don't need no crap from no nuthin waitress!"

The waitress looked at Jeff and rolled her eyes. The man's girlfriend took on an expression of utter disgust. She teed up and smashed him right on the nose as hard as she could. Stunned, he tripped over a stool and fell on the floor. In a second, she was on top of him. Jeff and the waitress froze momentarily. Then both of them ran over. Jeff grabbed the man's arm and tried pull him away but he had gotten on top and shoved him away. The man then pinned the woman to the floor by her hands. She squirmed and screamed blue murder at him.

"Joey! Joey! Out front! Out front!" the waitress yelled to the kitchen. The owner, even bigger than the big guy, came flying out.

"What the...! Get the hell off her!" he yelled as he strong armed in and separated them. Jeff got in front of the woman, who was back up quickly and ready for more. The man also got up. Then, surprisingly, the two of them came to their senses and calmed down. As quickly as it started, it was over.

"All right – out – out right now – OUT! Before I call the cops!" Joey yelled as he pointed to the door.

"SHE started it," Biz said dismissively tucking in his shirt.

"I don't give a crap who started it or who ended it – GET OUT and I don't ever come back here – neither one of youse. And did they pay up, Nikki?"

The waitress nodded, gave them their change and they walked to the door. No tip. Biz flipped back the bird as he slammed it behind him.

"Goddamn lowlifes," Joey said shaking his head. "Come in here and make trouble out of nothin' - no regard for nobody else. You okay buddy?"

"Yeah," Jeff said. "No harm done. But what kind of town is this? Haven't even been here a day yet. First person I talk to is a psycho bag lady and now this jam."

"Bag lady?" the waitress said. "Must have been Skid Row Sue. She's always hanging out on Water Street – usually pan handling. Harmless old lady but she's totally insane."

"Yeah – I figured that."

"Look bud," Joey said. "Your meal is free – and get him another drink if you would, Nik, and a cup of java too. This ain't that kinda joint, pal. We don't take nobody for granted. We want your business. Stiller really isn't that bad a town."

"Thanks, I appreciate that," Jeff smiled.

Joey went in back and returned with a mop. He cleaned up the spill. Jeff sat back down and wiped his pants off with the rag he was given earlier and his face with a napkin. He simmered down. The waitress cleaned off the counter and gave him the coke and coffee. Jeff finished the sandwich and fries which had survived the ruckus. Then, he and Nikki Ford exchanged names and talked a little until a few other customers walked in. She turned out to be a pretty nice girl. His appetite satisfied and mind reset, Jeff left her a couple of dollars and walked back to the Y.

6.

The TV room was now about three quarters full. Jeff took a chair at the far corner. A ways down he spotted Creecher, who was talking to a crooked man with a big red nose. He noticed Jeff and waved, pointing him out to the man and saying something to him. Jeff relaxed and began to feel semi-comfortable, at least for the moment.

Somebody was smoking a pipe and the cherry aroma hung in the dimness of the big room. The old carpet was worn to a lighter brown in some places from many years of heavy traffic. Photographs from times gone by hung on the walls along with a few paintings, not one of them level. It looked like they'd been there since the very beginning.

Jeff looked over to the reading area with the newspapers on sticks. A solitary old man sat to the side. He squinted through his glasses to scan the Boston Herald Traveler and it took a lot of effort. On his face was the ingrained scowl of what he'd become; the record of all those years and now days of aches, pains, and just plainly coping with a situation that wasn't going to get any better. For him, it was simply a matter of accepting his reality. Jeff thought of just how that must be. To sit in that old man's shoes.

His attention moved over to the billiard room. Two men were playing a game of nine ball. Jeff, a pool player himself, got up and walked over to watch for minute or two. One of them was clearly better than the other and he executed the grooved stroke of a seasoned pool veteran. A teenager sat nearby and studied them, focusing mostly on the good player and noting every facet and nuance of his game.

The man was in the process of running the table for the win. He pocketed the six, seven and eight, and then left himself a dead shot on the nine. He smiled at his opponent and said, "I wish I could help yah, Charlie, but what can I say?" To which Charlie only glumly frowned and shook his head. As the man made the final ball the teen smiled, all the more captivated.

Jeff went back to his seat and began to watch the 7 PM evening news with the others on the new color television. Frank McGee was reporting on the war in Vietnam. Jeff was lucky not to be there on the battlefield just at that moment. He'd made it so far without being drafted. But if it did happen, he'd go to Nam. He wasn't crazy about the war, but even with the changing times he was pro USA. It wasn't in him to defect to Canada.

Film footage showed soldiers in camouflage advancing through the jungles – explosions of brilliant reds and yellows in the distance – helicopters darting in and out amid the thunder of jets in the background – the cracking booms of bazookas and the blistering rattle of machine guns. Then, body bags. Jeff watched and couldn't help but think of what a waste war was.

A man sitting to his side tapped him on the shoulder. "I'll be damned – I'll be gawd damned if I know what we're fighting for, pal," he said. "This war has to be the craziest fiasco I ever heard of. I mean most of our boys over there haven't even tasted life and they're getting their arms and legs blowed off. What the hell for? My son is there and I haven't heard from him in over a month. Scares me that I might get one of them goviment letters."

"Well, I guess…"

The man cut him off, still all wrapped up in his thoughts. "It's hell to be a father sometimes. I assume you're not married, bud – my advice is to THINK before you do and THINK before you bring kids into this crazy friggin world. There's a whole lot more to it than shows on the surface – believe me."

"Right," Jeff said. Then something occurred to him. "You know, a teacher I had once told me something I never forgot when I got in some trouble. She said you have choices and consequences. 'Think before you act,' she told me. 'Every action you take has a consequence.'"

"Damn straight, kid – damn straight. She tole you the plain truth."

The man then sat back in his chair and exhaled like something weighing heavily on him had lifted some. He felt relief that someone, even a complete stranger, had the patience to listen to him.

"I don't get what's behind our part in Vietnam either," Jeff added. "I read somewhere that the trouble started with France over there sometime after World War Two when Vietnam was a colony or something, and it's been growing ever since. Isn't it all about stopping the spread of Communism?"

"Aww, yeah, but no offense, bud, I think some of that's a load uh hoss shit. Don't get me wrong - I'm no Commie sympathizer, but it ain't none of our business. Plus there's got to be other reasons – maybe strategic crap – the goviment never levels with yah. Nuttin can be worth tens of thousands of kids being killed for something nobody even can get straight! I wish my boy had gone to Canada now, pal – never ever thought I'd say it."

It ended there. Both turned back to the television. The program had moved on to other topics and they took a break from the problems of Vietnam. Jeff closed his eyes for about a minute and let his thoughts settle. During that time, a young woman walked by, checked in at the desk and went upstairs. It was Nikki, the waitress from Joey's Restaurant earlier.

The Evening News came to an end. The man who lamented about his son got up to leave, patting Jeff on the shoulder as he moved away. One of the viewers went over to the set and flipped the channel to "The Three Stooges". The group clapped with approval. Jeff smiled. He was a long-time fan of the comic trio.

In the first short, the boys were infiltrating the Confederate army as Union spies. In one scene, they're observing three southern belles preparing cakes for baking. "I baked a cake once," Moe remarked, "but it fell and killed a cat." That got a rise out of the audience.

Then Curly tried to get next to one of the girls. "Can I help yah?" he said to her. "I used to work in a bakery as a pilot." "A pilot?" she asked. "Yeah," Curly answered, "I used to take the bread from one corner and pile it in the other." Thundering laughter from the group.

In the following scene, he remarked that he quit the job at the bakery. After she asked him why, he said, "Oh I got sick of the dough and thought I'd go on the loaf." More laughs.

In the next short, the Stooges were cleaners in a doctor's office. Curly got shoved, fell, and ended up with a fishbowl full of water on his head. After Moe and Larry popped it off, Curly complained of a tickling feeling in his stomach. With a clunk on the head from Moe using a mallet that just happened to be handy, Curly was sedated. Using a nearby X-ray machine on him, Moe and Larry observed a gold fish swimming around in his stomach. With a spool of string, a safety pin, and some bait provided by Larry, Moe began fishing down Curly's throat.

The audience now was now fixated and laughing harder. "He's goin' after it – he's goin' after it!" Moe said. "I think I got him!" He gritted his teeth and pulled on the fish, but suddenly the string spun back, and he yelled with anxiety, "He's gettin' away!"

Finally, Moe pulled the fish out of Curly's mouth and held it up proudly. Then Curly came to, and said, "Hey – have you got a fishing license?" And to Moe's perplexed "No..." he exclaimed, "Then gimmie back my fish!"

That line brought the house down and the place rocked. Jeff roared along with everybody else. For the first time since he got to Stiller, he was able to relax and plainly enjoy himself. The program ended and the group fell back into doze mode. Jeff's eyes became heavy and he figured he'd call it a night.

He took another look around and soaked in the small time scene. Men of different ages, backgrounds, and dreams most probably gone down the river. All roads intertwined and intersected at this point, together at this stop along the trail, peacefully sitting among one another. Some maybe just for this one night and others in an endless string of nights, but all under shelter and protected from loneliness and the uncertainty of the outside. At least for the present. And at this moment, they had each other. Though most would never say it, they all knew it.

7.

As Jeff got up to leave, a bum stumbled through the doors and wobbled up the steps. He had spittle on the side of his mouth and mumbled under his breath. The man wore a shabby black jacket that hung on him like clothes on a scarecrow. The scally cap tilted sideways, the pants were stained, and the fly was open half way. The face was yellowed; the cheeks sunken and unshaven.

"Textbook wino," Jeff thought as he looked over. Then he was suddenly troubled and felt his eyes droop. He thought of his father who he hadn't seen in years. His dad's ruined life if he even was still alive. Where was he? What was he doing? Was he in the same boat as this poor soul Jeff was looking at? A denizen of the streets and gutters? Standing by a park bench eating popcorn off the ground with the scavenging pigeons? And during the cold nights, sleeping under a bridge with the river rats?"

Jeff shook his head and tried to blunt those thoughts. He turned to see the man at the desk rush over to the bum and catch him as he was about to fall.

"C'mon, Barney," he said, "You look like hell. You can't stay here t'nite like this. Come over to the bench, now – I'll call up the shelter next to the hospital. They'll come over and pick you up. You'll get a nice clean bed and you can dry out the next couplah days. They'll take care of you."

Barney looked up at him like a little boy would who knew he'd goofed up. But he couldn't understand much and barely made it to the bench.

"Yaaah, yaaah," Raymen – sheltah," he moaned. "I'm a friggin saint! I yain't been canonized yet but I'm a friggin shaint!"

"Okay, relax now – we'll get you took care of."

Barney Ebersol had been a recurring figure for several years at the Stiller YMCA. He generally lived on the streets but sometimes, he was able to sober up and get a little money together doing odd jobs. During those times, he'd get a room at a boarding house or at the Y. But it wouldn't last as he was prone to binges. Before long, he'd be back to the boozing routine and on the streets. It was a spiral that cycled down a tick lower each time, until one sorry day he'd find what he really longed for. The relief of death.

Barney plopped on the bench like a dead fish. Raymond looked down at him and shook his head. Then he got on the phone and made arrangements with the shelter.

"Hey buddy," Barney yawped to the old man in the reading area, "gimmy the paypuh – I wanna see the obishiearries – see if I died yet."

Jeff still had not moved. Then he felt a hand on his shoulder. It was Creecher standing next to him.

"Jesus, Sonny – I mean Jeff. You okay? You look like you seen a ghost."

"Yeah," Jeff answered softly. "Don't worry, I'm good. Just got a little shook up at the sight of that sorry guy. Poor bastard."

"He's not the only one, Jeff," Creecher said shaking his head. "There's others just like him around Stiller. Barney is a sight at that. Guess we're all so used to him we don't much notice any more. You see what the stuff did to him. Let it be a lesson to you to steer clear of it. I know it firsthand."

"Me too...in a different way."

Creecher nodded. He then sat down in a nearby chair and lit up a small cigar. He looked to the TV but was unable to concentrate. Creecher had beaten alcoholism from a time back when he too was on the streets. Cold turkey. But painful flashbacks of that awful period in his life still lived in the recesses of his mind.

8.

Jeff made his way upstairs and headed for his room. The door to Room 20, the one before his, was half way open now. The music was going again and there was also an aroma in the air. Jeff glanced in as he walked by. He saw a guy around his age facing out to him, sitting on a cushion on the floor cross-legged and playing the guitar. A woman sat to his left with her back to Jeff. The guy smiled out at him and continued to play. The woman turned to the side and caught sight of Jeff. He waved but didn't get a good look at her. Jeff continued on to his door. Then he heard a shout.

"Hey Jeff – Jeff – come over here – come on in."

"Man, who the hell would know my name in this place?" Jeff thought. He walked back and looked in curiously. It was Nikki the waitress talking. She smiled at him.

"Small world, huh? C'mon in and join us for a little bit."

"Okay," Jeff said as he stepped in and looked around. The room was the same as his but in much better shape. The walls were a bright blue and the floor looked like it had been varnished. There was a wide braided rug in the middle and every article in the room, the bed, the bureau, the night table; they all had a fresh look. To cap it off, there were a couple of vases full of rustic straw, and strawberry incense burned off to the side in a sea shell. It was like walking on to a stage.

The guitar player finished, put the instrument aside, and stood up. He was tall, six foot two, and lean but strong. He had long black hair and a full beard - a show beard - cut features and classic good looks. He wore a Villanova University t-shirt, faded jeans, and a pair of sandals. One look at him and Jeff sensed there was something unique about this dude.

The guitar player smiled broadly and extended a hand. "What's happenin' my man? My name's Tom Slade. Just call me Slade – most people do."

"Or Shotgun," Nikki added laughing.

"Shotgun?" Jeff asked.

"Like Shotgun Slade – the old TV western. Get it?" she chided.

"Oh yeah - sure."

"I answer to that too," Slade smiled. "There's worse nick names. But don't worry – I don't carry a sawed off shotgun around with me."

They shook hands in the thumbs up hippie style.

"Jeff Jones – just moved in next door this afternoon," Jeff said. "How'd you score such a nice room, man?"

"Oh I've been here for like...five months or so. When I moved in, the room was like a jail cell, you know? Dank and dreary. I told them downstairs I'd fix it up if they'd pay for the materials and they agreed to it. Took me a week or so but it suits me now. I like a bright clean pad and I get that great morning sun. Sets the right tone. Dig it?"

"I do. I heard you playing earlier and just now when I walked by. Pretty damn good, I have to say."

"Yeah, I like to come by and hear Shotgun play, Jeff," Nikki said. "He IS a good musician. Jeff's the guy I told you about earlier who got dragged into the incident at Joey's, Tom."

"That sounded like an interesting trip," Slade offered. "And thanks to both of you for the compliments on my music. A ton of lessons went into it but there's a million guitar players better than me. Well, Jeff, sit down and join us awhile. Since we're gonna be neighbors, I might just as soon be neighborly. So what brings you to beautiful downtown Stillborn?"

"Stillborn?" Jeff laughed, as he and Slade took a seat along with Nikki. "I like that."

Jeff went on to explain about his last job in New Hampshire plus his plans to look for work in the mills along the river. Slade perked up when he got to that part.

"That's interesting," he said. "I drove a truck for the Stiller Sounder newspaper over the winter dropping off paper route bundles. But I wasn't getting enough hours and I quit last month to join a paving crew which paid a lot better. We did driveways and parking lots, stuff like that. But it was a drag, man - worst damn job I ever had in my life. Like being on a chain gang. Don't care how cold it was, we all still sweated like pigs. And some days, the fumes — like I was in the twilight zone, dude. My clothes got beat to hell too — stained with tar and grease. Like, you know, I always hate to quit a job when I don't have another one lined up, but I couldn't hack much more of that scene. Four weeks is what I lasted. Luckily for me though, the owner was a good guy and understood it wasn't my thing. He set me free without any hard feelings and said he'd give me a good recommendation if I needed one."

"I can relate. Been in that boat more than once, man."

Slade nodded and stretched his arms. He was relieved that his days on that crew were over. Nikki got up, walked over, and massaged his shoulders.

"Poor Shotgun," she said. "We'll have to find you a job in some nice air conditioned place for the summer. Want to work with me behind the counter at Joey's?"

"Don't think so," Nik, he answered. "Thanks, but dealing with the public day in and day out is not my line.

"Okay, just a thought," Nikki said as she returned to her seat.

"But by coincidence, Jeff," Slade continued, "I was planning to walk down to Warburton Textiles tomorrow morning to apply for a mill job. Saw an ad in the paper that they're hiring and the dough is pretty good, plus as many hours as you can stand. I need to save some bread. I hear that people come and go like the wind in those mills. I mean surely they're no par-ey-dise. But anything beats the hot topping racket and I have to support myself, right man?"

"Sure," Jeff agreed. "How about if I go with you? The guy at the desk mentioned that place to me. That fits right in with what I was figuring to do."

"Deal."

The three talked another half an hour or so. It was a lively and engaged conversation. Jeff learned that Nikki was 25 and divorced with no kids. She lived with a roommate in an apartment above Joey's. Tom Slade was 23 and grew up in Pennsylvania in a town near Philadelphia. He enlisted in the army after high school wanting to see the world. But he flunked the physical with a phlebitis issue, which he still disputed.

Slade worked in a book binding factory for a year-plus after graduating, while also playing lead guitar in a rock band. Although he'd gotten high grades in high school, he explained to Jeff and Nikki that he just didn't want to get locked down to college, at least for a while. There was a healthy dose of nonconformist and free spirit in him.

Eventually, the urge to move on was too much for him to resist, Slade went on to tell them. He leveled with his parents, left home, and became a free spirit drifter as he liked to think of himself. He talked about gradually becoming fixated on finding some kind of universal principle or truth that he felt was somewhere out there. Then he could get his future in order. He'd put down some place, stay a while, work, observe and learn, and move on when he felt the urge for going.

Slade had seen much of the northeast and a bit of the south in the past few years. He was comfortable in his lifestyle although he knew it wouldn't be permanent. He did feel that each new place brought him closer to an understanding how to approach the rest of his life. He was certain he'd eventually find that...thing, he explained with emphasis to Jeff and Nikki. His time in Stiller was just another stop along the path to it.

Jeff was slightly overwhelmed by the philosophy material but he did at least get the main idea. After Nikki talked a while about studying dancing as a young girl, Slade took the stage again. He went on to describe his family. His dad was a draftsman; a regular hard working guy. But conversely, his mom was an art teacher and a prolific painter with her own studio. It was more from her that he felt he got his creativity and sense for adventure. He had an older sister Jodie who married her high school sweetheart after graduating from college. She and her husband continued to live in their Penn home town of Drexel Hill.

Slade explained further to Jeff and Nikki about his leaving home. At age 20, he told his parents that he was taking to the road to find himself. Surprisingly, they understood and encouraged him.

"My dad told me I had character, a good work ethic, and that he had faith in me," Slade told them. "My mom agreed. She just told me not to forget about college somewhere along the line and to stay in touch at least once a week. Support like that fueled me – it was the best thing they could have done for me. And I've never failed to do what my mom asked with letters, phone calls, and I try to get back there on holidays. What about your folks, Jeff?"

"Well...you paint an interesting picture, Slade," Jeff answered, stalling a little. "You're a tough act to follow. I have a brother in Maryland and...that's all I want to say for now. See, it's a long story that I couldn't even begin to start. Maybe someday when I'm in the right mood."

"That's cool. I get you," Nikki nodded.

"Yeah, when you feel like it," Slade agreed.

"Well, boys, it's late for me and I have to work early in the morning," Nikki said getting up. "Now don't be a stranger, Shotgun – keep in touch with me. You too, Jeff. Drop by the diner when you feel like it."

"Just might do that – thanks."

"See you around, Nik," Slade said. "And try to stay clear of trouble at that wild eatery you work at."

Nikki smiled and walked out the door. When she was out of hearing distance, Jeff turned to Slade.

"If you don't mind my saying," he said with a grin, "I mean...I take it you two are just friends from the conversation. But man, Nikki sure looks good walking away, if you get my drift. And she's got a nice personality too. She took good care of me after that jam at the diner."

"I don't mind your saying at all. You're right – she's not my girl. I'll tell you though, Nik...she enjoys everything there is about being female. That's for sure. And she was about the first person I got to know a little in this town – always has been kind and helpful to me. She's good people."

"No doubt," Jeff agreed. "By the way, what's the policy for having women in the rooms? Some Y's don't allow it. They didn't tell me anything about it when I checked in."

"You can have them up in your digs but they have to sign in. And you can hang with them out front too – this is a pretty liberal joint. There's a ladies room for them downstairs. But they're supposed to be out by eleven o'clock. I've seen a few guys stretch the rules and I can't say that I haven't. Long as you're quiet and discreet about it, the powers that be look the other way."

"That's good to know," Jeff said. "Nikki seems interested in you, Slade – I picked up a little vibe. Think it might develop into something down the line?"

Slade brushed back hair from his forehead and then stroked his beard. "Nah – I doubt it. I'm too unsettled for a relationship right now, man. She's just a good friend like you said – drops by here every so often just to talk. And I stop in to see her down at the restaurant off and on. That's as far as it goes.

"Guess she likes my guitar playing. Hey – I'll admit it – she gives me a kick. I like her. I dig the attention she throws my way and she's got some ammunition – no question about that. But I haven't made any moves on her, at least as yet. Me, dude? I am a one man show right now and I like it like that. Get it?"

"Yeah – fair enough. Takes some will power, though, doesn't it?"

"Sure, and I got plenty of that! Hey, here's an idea. I got a fresh bone over there in the drawer. What say we take a couplah hits over by the window. I do it all the time and blow the smoke out. Nobody's questioned me about it yet."

34

Jeff was open to sharing a joint when the opportunity came his way. "You don't have to ask me twice, friend," he said. "You only live once."

"Ain't THAT the truth?"

Slade fetched the roach and they sat down. He lit up and they passed it back and forth as they rapped. When they got to the end, Slade inhaled the last hit, looked to the ceiling, and whispered, "sike-ey-del-ic."

Jeff pointed to the guitar. "Feel like playing a little something, man?" he asked.

"Sure thing," Slade said. He picked it up and got right in to a familiar rhythmic piece, his head moving side to side.

Jeff was feeling it. He relaxed in his chair and listened with pleasure.

"I know that from somewhere," he said as Slade finished the song with a smooth fade. "What is it?"

"'Green Onions' – by Booker T and the MG's - from the early sixties. Has a jazzy feel that I always liked. One of the really great instrumentals."

"Cool – do you sing too?"

"Yeah – for fun sometimes. I do some Bob Dylan and Neil Young – and a few songs by Tom Rush, local guy from New Hampshire. He's a hell of a song writer. Buddies with Joni Mitchell who is like a goddess to me. She's written songs for him. But I lean more toward instrumentals with a little improvisation from the jazz study I did. Chord and melody solos they're called in musician jive."

"I wish I could play the guitar," Jeff said. "Never had the chance to study an instrument."

"Well, we should be hanging at this place for at least some time. I'll show you - I'll get you started."

"Far out."

Slade put the guitar aside and then rubbed his thighs. "Sometimes my damn legs fall asleep when I play," he laughed.

Jeff was feeling high and his tongue loosened up. "Hey - Shotgun...I know we just met but is it okay if I call you that?"

35

"Of course it is."

"Now I don't mean to be nosy or anything, but I see the long hair and the beard. You look kind of like a hippie, man. Are you a for real one by any chance? On the way into town this morning, I hitched a ride with this...flower child I guess. She was heading out to San Fran to join a commune. Are you into that trip?"

Slade clasped his hands behind his neck and thought a few seconds. "Oh wow – I feel all right," he said, peacefully buzzed. "Interesting question. Nah – I'm not a freak. But I'd say I'm a rebel to some degree and there's stuff I like about the movement. But I'm not one for blind faith and giving my freedom over to a cause. I don't have enough trust in the dropout agenda in general to go off, cash everything in, and commit to some commune where I don't go my own way. I don't operate like that – I like flying solo. But my mind's always open. One thing I've learned is to never say never. Still, the drug part of it isn't my bag either. Now don't get me wrong. As you can clearly see, I like to smoke grass every now and then. But it stops for me right there. Life is challenging enough without getting hooked on something dangerous."

"I can relate," Jeff said. "'If it feels good, do it,' – I hear it a lot but that's a scary idea to me. I've thought about it some since the ride this morning – the idea of maybe dropping out. I'm not so big on the establishment and how it's affected me in my life. And this wacked out war it's gotten us in to. That girl who picked me up – her name was Crystal - she painted a beautiful picture. She surely did. Dude, she looked like an angel – and she asked me to join her. I was stunned. Never really considered it and – well – here I sit now. But it hangs in my head, you know?"

Slade paused and then let out a big laugh. "Sure – I get it," he said. "You sure are an honest cat. I like that. We're going to get along great – I know that from the get go. Well, how about if we just let that topic simmer for now. I suggest we get some sleep and hit the pavement to Warburton Textiles tomorrow in the AM. We can have breakfast here in the building and get down there for around nine. It's only about a 15 minute walk."

"You got it, friend," Jeff said standing up and stretching his arms. "Think I lucked out crossing tracks with you, Slade. Always cool to meet decent people when you're new in town."

"Destiny, my man - destiny. See you in the morning."

36

Both smiled as they shook hands. Jeff then walked out the door and closed it behind him.

9.

Back in his room, Jeff propped up the pillows and lay still on his bed. He looked out the window and listened to the traffic pass, the rumble of the motors and the drone of the tires. Then his mood took a dip on a dime, as it often did. He felt like he was nothing – a grain of sand on a stretch of beach in a world that snowballed forward with no conscience. That whatever became of him or the lonesome guy or girl on the street wouldn't matter in the end. That if he up and died right there on the bed, only a few people would care and his memory would fade like newspapers fluttering down an alley in the wind. And everything would just go on. In the end, nothing really mattered at all. Nothing mattered. Nothing.

He shook his head and closed his eyes but those thoughts hung on him like glue. The harder he tried to get rid of them, the more they seemed to linger. Then, he just lay there, didn't move a muscle, and made himself focus on Crystal the flower child. After several minutes, the anxiety lessened and calmness returned. He opened his eyes and looked to the ceiling. The spider was out again, reworking the web in the solitude of its desire to continue to live. It ignored the surrounding dangers and even instant death if Jeff got the notion. But that was its lot. That was the raw truth. The spider accepted it and lived it every day.

"Good example for me and everybody else," Jeff thought. "The spider faces it and grinds it out – does the best it can to make it. That's all anybody can do. That's what I have to continue to try to do."

The next morning, Jeff was up before his alarm, showered and dressed by quarter to eight and ready for the new day. He sat in a chair with his feet propped up on the window sill and relaxed. At eight on the nose, Slade tooled around and rapped on the door three times.

"C'mon in, it's open."

"Mornin'," Slade said, walking in and standing to the side. "What a guy – up and ready to rock and roll. There's a little grill downstairs, Jeff – Shorty's – where we can get a cheap breakfast. Good food and the best coffee in Stiller."

"Lead the way."

They walked down the hall by a couple of bleary-eyed unshaven men headed to the latrine, and down the stairs to Shorty's. It was a small establishment deep within the heart of the old building; a counter with ten stools and eight booths along the wall. A diminutive balding man labored behind the counter. Shorty himself.

"Whoah – ev'rybody stop what you're doin' – Shotgun's entered the premiceeys," he said smiling. "What's with you being here so early?"

"Hey, Shorty, what's the good word?" Slade said rapping the counter. "Well see, me and my friend over here are going out to look for gainful employment this morning. We need a fresh start with some of your famous flapjacks – you know – to give us the strength to face that jungle. This here is Jeff Jones. He just came into town yesterday and is gonna be with us for a while."

"Glad to know yah, kid – welcome."

"Thanks."

They drew two mugs of coffee at the urn and sat down in a booth. The coffee was strong and rich. It hit the spot. The pancakes came with a side of bacon and they were great, just as Slade said. The sun pushed through the windows and the place warmed to the day. It was a bare bones joint but it had a certain feel that Jeff liked. All its own.

He kicked back and talked with Slade and several other customers that Slade knew. He seemed to know just about everybody and was very popular with the crowd. The food settled in well. Jeff and Slade got more coffee before getting ready to leave, both wondering what lay ahead at Warburton Textiles.

10.

They hit the streets to the mills. There was a haze in the air and it was going to be hot for an early spring day.

Slade wiped his forehead. "This deal shouldn't take long," he said. "We'll be back before 11. Maybe we can take a dip in the pool after to cool off."

"Yeah - the guy at the desk did mention a pool. Where is it?"

"Deep in the bowels of that old building, man."

They got to the end of Water Street and took a left into Pickford Street. Now they walked along the banks of the river and the wide turn it cut to the east. They looked out to the water, hard brownish-yellow and murky in spots. Still as death in others. They could see the outlines of fish in the shallows; carp and eels foraging along the bottom. An old tire here, a refrigerator door there, the fish made their way around all kinds of dumped junk. Near shore, on a walkway down river, a man briskly walked his dog.

"Man, that dude's hair sure is white," Jeff remarked glancing over at him.

"Like the pure driven snow," Slade agreed.

"Jimmy, Jimmy – wait for me," they heard a woman call to the man from a distance.

"But you know what, Shotgun?" Jeff remarked looking ahead again. "That river looks sickly - like a person who's been abused over and over. How do you figure it ever came to this?"

"Well...that IS the truth. Just think that probably a hundred years ago, before the industrial revolution, that river was probably clean and strong – loaded with fish – bass, shad, salmon – you name it. Bet there were plenty of red-tail hawks and bald eagles around too. Now, all that can live

39

off of it are those carp and slimy suckers you see there, eating up the scum off the bottom. That river is like a beautiful thing gone sour, man. I mean look at the lines it cuts – wide, deep, majestic - but the whole thing is ravaged and polluted. The Indians fished it and respected it in the old days. Bet they'd tell us a thing or two now. You know, sometimes I think about it, and I'd take living back then when things were a lot purer and bottom line. Either you made it or you didn't, and everybody died young, but it was more like abiding by some kind of binding code that overrode everything. A natural balance I guess."

"Well said – 100 percent," Jeff agreed.

Jeff looked out further on the river expanse as they moved along closer to the mils. As was his habit, began to project in his thoughts. The river was kind of like old Barney the wino from the other night. Both were once clean and pure, at least Barney was when he was baby, and now this. "Choices and consequences", he thought again. The weight of it all, the risks and the aftermath. Reality. Damaged goods. The river would go on in the end but not Barney. He was toast. Did a guy like him ever really have a chance at all?

Jeff shook his head and got a grip on his day dreaming. They turned in to Ledge Road and looked ahead to the mills in the near distance. There they stood in stoic bleakness, smokestacks pointing skyward and ladders climbing to the tops. Along the street were tenements like those Jeff saw coming into town. The same kids running up and down the porches. The same steely-eyed, never-smiling mothers. And at one place, an agitated father in a t-shirt with a big pot belly. Slade took a look at him yelling at his kids.

"Scary scene over there," he said turning his head away from it. "Sometimes I see people going the way of a herd of cattle – you know – just acting on instinct. Go with the flow even if it leads to a bog of quick sand. They get cemented into a situation like that with no way out, man - no escape. And gradually, they just let themselves go. You have to kind of feel for them, don't you?"

"I have no feeling one way or the other," Jeff responded. "I'm just glad I'm not one of them, at least not yet. That deal scares the life out of me. I have enough trouble taking care of myself, dude. If I ever get stuck in a thing like that and you're around, please shoot me and make sure I'm dead."

40

Slade liked that remark. They both laughed and continued on.

11.

It did become warmer and a little uncomfortable as they approached the entrance to the red brick facade of the Warburton outfit. A couple of workers hacked away at dead brush at the front of the main building. They had the hang dog look of years and years spent in and around the mills.

It crossed Jeff's mind that this could be the first day of the rest of his life as a mill worker. Again he began to obsess about what-ifs and what-might-happens. He knew it was a waste of time but sometimes he couldn't help it. Was he going to be one of those guys cutting grass 20 years down the road? He shook that off. Then he pivoted to the positive. He'd just take things a day at a time, save some money and maybe someday take another shot at college. "Nobody knows what the hell's going to happen, nobody," he reflected. "Why the hell worry about it?"

They walked over a small bridge above a canal, and through a set of tall green doors into the employment office. The hard wood floor was warped enough that they had to watch their step. Four large windows looked out to dense bushes and glimpses of the river. A few applicants sat hunched over desks filling out forms. One, an older woman with hair pulled back tightly, looked sideways at Jeff curiously.

He turned away and focused on the receptionist at the desk. There sat an attractive young woman. With wavy blonde hair and blue eyes, she wore a low cut blouse. She fooled around with her hair as she took care of some paper work, a little smile at the corners of her mouth. Slade took her in right along with Jeff.

41

"Wow," he whispered as they walked toward her. "Get a load of the clerk – nothing better than the sight of a great looking woman in the morning sunlight. Gurls, man - they're the livin' end, aren't they?"

Jeff nodded. Slade said it softly enough that she didn't hear him but the receptionist sensed he was talking about her. She glanced up and smiled. Jeff looked to the side. Slade grinned straight back at her. She brushed some hair behind an ear and addressed them.

"Good morning gennelmen. Welcome to Warburton Textiles. How may I help you?"

"Well we…,"Jeff began. Then he got a tickle in his throat and began coughing.

Slade gently nudged him aside. He smiled and said, "What my friend means to say is that we're looking to work here – to apply for jobs. And I don't mean to be forward or anything, but you look awfully nice today, Miss. Purely a compliment – nothing more – nothing less."

Jeff exhaled and smiled sheepishly. "Sorry, sometimes I get a little congested," he said. "But I second that remark."

"Thank you very much – so nice of both of you to say that," she said.

The woman then leaned to the side and dropped a pen to the floor. In bending forward to pick it up, the cleavage line up top was further exposed, drawing their eyes down and then straight back ahead as soon as she sat up again. She gave them their forms.

"If you two will take a seat over there and fill these out, then I'll get them to George Sheppard, our personnel manager," she told them. "He'll come over to talk with you. You probably know we're hiring, but right now it's only for the third shift. If everything checks out okay, he'll probably start you tonight if that's doable. Does that work?"

"Sounds okay for me," Slade said.

"Ditto," Jeff agreed.

"Thank you very much."

They sat down, entered the information and gave the applications back to her. In a few minutes, George Sheppard, an older gentleman, walked over. He introduced himself and sat facing them, the forms in his hands.

42

"Harumph...hmm...hmm – looks good, boys – everything looks good here. Now you guys are aren't gonna wimp out on me, right? It's a tough go in there – they don't call it a sweat shop for nothing. Lots of noise and no air conditioning, but we'll pay you well. Hard night's work for a hard night's pay, right boys?"

"Right."

"Okay, Jill said you can start tonight, correct?"

"Yes."

"Good. The shift goes from 11 PM to 8 AM. You get an hour for lunch which we don't pay for. Come in all five work days for the week and we give you an eight hour bonus. See, we're trying to create incentive to rectify uhh...attendance problems. The work you'll be doing is mainly unskilled. It won't take much time to get you up to speed. Any questions, boys?"

"Two I can think of," Slade said. "What's the pay rate and is there much overtime?"

"Good questions," George smiled. "How could I forget an important thing like hourly wage? Two fifty an hour but no piece work on your jobs. You can work an overtime shift on most Saturdays if you choose to. Time and a half - sometimes double if we're really strapped. Of course that's optional. Anything else?"

"What does rectify mean?" It was Jeff.

George and Slade both laughed. "It means to correct," George said. "I just like to sound important, I guess. Welcome aboard, boys – you look like a couple of decent guys. At least you're both tall – good for reaching on the job you'll probably be doing. Be at the main building, the one next to this one, at 11 tonight, fourth floor. And make sure you get some sleep in the meantime."

They shook hands and George walked back into his office. Out the door and on to the walkway, Slade and Jeff pointed north back to the Y.

"I think that went pretty well," Jeff said. "Feels good to have a job again and regular dough coming in. And the pay isn't too bad – a lot more than I made in the lumber yard."

43

"Right, and I like the overtime option," Slade agreed. "I really do need to save some jack. I got a good vibe from that George cat. He laid it straight out to us. I'm kind of looking forward to seeing just what this mill gig is like. We're probably going to learn something that'll help us down the line."

"Maybe so," Jeff agreed. "Hey, that woman behind the desk – I give her a solid ten. And what you said went over pretty good with her. She gave you a look, man."

"I'll say this," Slade said. "She had a wonderful pair of inflated footballs. When she bent over, I felt a little... avocado in my pocket."

"Huh?"

"I think you know what I mean, dude. But to be honest, I wasn't giving her the business or anything. I meant what I said. Maybe she took it as a come on – I can't control that, but I don't think so. I believe in being straight with people, you know? She tries to look good and she does look good. Why not tell her without being a jerk about it? It's a good vibe, right?"

"I haven't known you very long, Shotgun, but I can tell you mean it. Just admiring her beauty and having the balls to say so. Sure, I get it."

"Nothing more, nothing less – just like I told her."

"Cool," Jeff said. "But getting back to what just happened back there. We got those jobs just like that. On the other hand, it makes me wonder just what kind of hellhole that place might be. I mean we're just a couple of warm bodies off the street and they reeled us right in. Do you think we might be in for some tough sledding?"

"Maybe, but it couldn't be much worse than some of the jobs I've had over the past few years - prime example the paving crew. I'm not worried. Like we'll make the best of it whatever the hell it turns out to be. If it's a total drag, we can quit and look for something else. It's as simple as that."

"Simple as that."

Slade took a peek at his watch. "Ten thirty now and we have to be in for 11 tonight. What do you say we do something to get us tired so we can get a nap for a few hours in the afternoon like George said? Otherwise we'll be fighting off sleep at around two in the morning. I've worked the graveyard before – take it from me. Do you play basketball, Jeff?"

"Sure do. I played two years of varsity in high school."

"Great. We can hit the gym and play for an hour before the business crowd shows up for pickup games at noon. Maybe take that swim after that."

"You got it."

"Oh, and one other thing," Slade grinned,

"What's that?"

"I didn't know what 'rectify' meant either."

12.

Back at the Y, they paid their quarters at the desk, got passes, and went upstairs to change. Jeff didn't have gym clothes so he wore a t-shirt and a pair of cut-off shorts. He felt like a farmer. But Slade, clad in a basketball jersey and a pair of sweats, was the kind of guy who looked right in whatever he wore. He led the way to the gym. At the bottom of a stairway to the lockers sat a man in a caged booth. One of his hands had only a thumb and a finger. He scowled at them as they approached him.

"Passes, passes, PASSES!" he yelled.

"Okay, Pangy," Slade said rolling his eyes as he and Jeff produced the passes. "Do you mind if we breathe first? Now how about a couple of soft fluffy towels?"

"Don't get smahht, Mistah Slade, or I'll report yah to the desk!"

It sounded bad but there was a twinkle in Pangy's eye. Slade winked back at him. He was a man who'd seen hard times. His hand was blown apart in action in World War Two. But now he was just a curmudgeon who got his kicks out of giving people a hard time. A scrooge. Slade knew it and always played along with him.

Pangy placed two towels on the counter and said "have a nice day" wryly. Then he looked the other way. Slade grinned at Jeff as they walked away.

"What a negative pain in the ass," Jeff said as they took a couple of lockers and hung up their towels.

"Just a gasbag of hot air," Slade smiled. "Probably bitter about ending up a jailbird sitting in that cage. But once you get to know him, he's kind of funny. He'll push you to the edge where you're ready to strangle him. Then he'll say 'Calm down, buddy – I'll buy you a coffee.'"

"Really?"

"Absolutely - I get a rise out of that bugger."

Jeff followed Slade up a staircase to the back of a handball court with windows at the rear wall. Two men were having a furious match. Jeff had never seen handball played before and was impressed with the movement and athleticism involved with the game. Whack – plop – whack. They whipped hard clean swats through the ball with either hand and bounced back into position off the walls.

"Phew – look at them go," Jeff said as they watched a minute or two. Slade nodded. Then they walked through a slider into the gym. It was empty just as Slade predicted. There were weights on pulleys along the walls and a few rows of benches on the right side. Above the floor at the next level was a running track that encircled the perimeter of the room. Jeff felt good being on the court again; it had been a while. He breathed in the heavy air; the smell of sweat that's the same in all gyms across America.

Slade found a basketball and bounce-passed it over to him. "Here you go – shoot around a couple of minutes. I have to limber up." He sat upright on the floor, stretched, and rubbed his legs up and down.

Jeff took a few layups and jump shots around the perimeter. Slade then joined him and they picked up the pace with dribbling and feeds to the basket. Jeff could see right away that Slade had the stuff of an athlete.

"Are you ready?" Slade said holding the ball. "A little one-on-one action?"

46

"Ready as I'll ever be."

"Okay – the way they do it around here is winners out. You make a hoop and keep the ball 'til you miss, then the other guy gets it. One point for each hoop – 21 points to win and you don't have to win by two."

"Sounds good to me."

Jeff took the ball out. He faked left and drove hard to the right, slipped a little, but still sensed he had half a step. He went up hard at the basket but at the top was cleanly rejected. Slade dribbled out to the foul line to clear and waited for Jeff to get back on defense.

He drove left and stopped on a dime at the baseline, double faked and got Jeff to commit, then easily laid it in. Jeff could see that he had his hands full. With an array of jump shots, layups, and a near dunk, Slade racked up eight points before Jeff saw the ball again. Jeff was impressed with how good his opponent was with both hands. He could not find a weakness to exploit.

Although he was a little overmatched, Jeff had some game too and enjoyed the challenge. He hustled, got his points, and worked up a good sweat, as did Slade. Whatever Jeff scored, he earned. The final total was 21 to 15, Slade's favor. Perspiration dripped to the floor as they sat on the bench and rested.

"What's with you, man?" Jeff laughed. "Where'd you get that timing and control? And you can jump like a friggin kangaroo. You must have played high school ball too, right?"

"State champs of Pennsylvania in 1963," Slade said matter-of-factly. "But I wasn't the man. I was actually the number three option. We had a kid from Yugoslavia – funny name - Danlod Losneivka. We just called him Downtown Danny. He could shoot the lights out, Jack. His range was off the charts. But the 'man' was a black dude from South Philly – Leon Choate. Six foot six and he could jump out of the building. Great skills and a really nice kid. The whole team revolved around Leon."

"Leon Choate – that name rings a bell."

"Yeah, you probably heard of him. Leon went on to play at Pepperdine and became a pretty well-known college player. Not NBA material but he was good enough to play in Europe after that. He might still be there. And

Danny went on to be a bench guy for Providence College. I actually got a couple of scholarship offers to smaller schools but I just wasn't into it. Maybe it was a mistake – I don't know, but I had to go with what was in my heart. No regrets, man, but I'll tell you, there's nothing like being on a championship team. It's was an experience I'll take to my grave."

"Unfortunately, I can't relate," Jeff offered. "Both teams I was on didn't even play 500 ball, but I did start my senior year. I will never know that feeling. Oh well - ready for round 2?"

"Let's do it."

Slade and Jeff played for another half an hour. As both tired, play got a little sloppy but they got the exercise they wanted and more. They walked off the court and to the showers with that satisfied feeling after a good workout.

13.

Slade was spent and opted out of the swim. He retired to his room for some shuteye. But Jeff wanted to try out the pool and decided to go ahead with it. He asked at the desk and was told he could use it for no charge since the quarter he'd paid earlier covered the day. His pass was on the board in the cage.

"I have no bathing trunks," he said to the man at the desk, a different one from the night before. "Can I wear a pair of shorts?"

"Pal, all you need is your birthday suit," he was told. "The pool don't have a filter – everybody goes in necked, that's the rule. Take a shower beforehand and use the toilet if you need to take a leak, okay?"

"No trunks? Really?"

"Yep."

The man smiled. Jeff walked back to the locker room. To his surprise, Pangy gave him no static when he asked for another towel and directions to the pool. He just laid it down and pointed to some steps and a door at the end of the locker room. Jeff stripped down and took a quick shower. Then he put the towel around his waist, went up the steps and opened the door.

Green pool, green walls, a big white ceiling, and echoes all around if you said anything. Jeff watched a couple of older men swim by, their bare cheeks bobbing in and out of the water. He couldn't help but turn his head and chuckle, it looked that funny. He dropped his towel on a bench and dove in. Jeff was invigorated by the cold water. He also got sort of a freeing feeling, like weightlessness being naked in the deep end. Jeff was a strong swimmer and cut through the water with clean strokes. After a couple of laps, he treaded water out in the middle.

"Hey Sonny," one of the men yelled to him from the side. "You a nuwcomuh? Haven't seen you 'round heyah before."

Jeff swam over to them and shot the breeze for a couple of minutes; explained how he'd landed in Stiller. He also mentioned his new job. After he brought that up, the same man who first spoke, the smaller one, held the pool edge and looked up at him.

"Sonny – I don't wantuh rain on your parade or nuttin, but you're not likely to like them mills much I don't theenk. Not that the work is so haahd, but the place is a sweat box'z what I hear – a hot, greasy oven as you get into summah. My bruthah worked at the Souther Mills for a couple of years in the 40's. He could tell yah some stories, pal."

The other man laughed out loud. There wasn't a tooth in his head.

"I know what you're saying," Jeff smiled. "The guy who hired us even said it was a sweat box. If it's the pits, then I'll just tough it out awhile and then look for something better. And I do have company. A friend of mine is starting with me. Hell, I'm not gonna worry about it – doesn't do much good anyway, right?"

"You got that right, Thonny," the toothless man said. "Worryin' ish like rockin' in a chair – thomethin to do but it gets you nowherz."

"That's pretty good," Jeff remarked. "So I assume you guys live here. How'd you end up in this place?"

49

Both talked of having run into hard times in their lives and finding themselves alone. Jeff noted to himself that it seemed to be the standard story of many of the boarders. Now retired, the Y offered these men cheap lodging and companionship, which both agreed was important, especially as they aged.

"The best thing 'bout the place is that you ain't alone," the smaller man said. "You got people 'round you facin' the same problems. There's strength in numbiz, bud, and there's dy-versions to keep you occupied — newspaypuhs, TV, books, and so forth."

"Pluth thafety," the toothless man added. "It's a thafe place to be."

"Good stuff," Jeff said, "and I like what you said about worrying and the rocking chair. I'll remember that one."

"You bethcha, Thonny."

In time, the men had enough of the water and climbed out slowly like a couple of turtles. With the pool all to himself, Jeff stayed in another 20 minutes and swam laps, up and down in a relaxing groove.

14.

After he finished and got dressed, Jeff got a hamburger and a root beer at Shorty's. Then he hung around the TV room and read the Globe and the Sounder. At around two thirty, his eyes glazed over and he went up to his room to sleep awhile. It was stuffy like a greenhouse. He opened the window for a little air and pulled the shade down. It was old and faded and didn't darken the room enough. Jeff found a blue sheet in the closet and doubled it up over the window. That killed the daylight.

He stripped to his boxers, lay on the bed and looked above. The spider hung over him on a string of silk and then quickly ascended back to its lair. "Live and let live," Jeff reminded himself as he drifted off to sleep.

Next door, Slade had been sleeping for over an hour. He could fall asleep on demand, any time, any place. But on this day he slept lightly. In the haze of the ending of a dream, he felt a presence and opened his eyes. He was startled as he looked to the side and saw Nikki sitting on the easy chair, looking straight at him. He pulled down the covers and sat up.

"Hello, Shotgun?" she said smiling.

"How - how did you get up here, Nik?" Slade said rubbing his eyes. "You scared the bejesus out of me." Then he realized he was only in his shorts but figured the hell with it.

"I got the afternoon off and was kind of antsy — thought I'd drop by. By now they know me around here pretty well. I told them you were expecting me and they checked me right in. The door was open. I was going to wake you up in a minute or two. Sorry if I imposed — didn't mean to."

"Not a big deal," Slade said settling down, "but next time, Nik, please knock first. Nobody likes to be surprised when they're sleeping. You made my heart jump a beat."

"Yeah — sorry about that, chief," she said with a wink. "But if the tables were turned, I'd have no problem with it. Know what I mean?"

"Is that so?"

"Yes, it's so."

She walked over and sat next to him. Slade took a deep breath and then a long exhale with a whistle. Then he looked at her and grinned.

"And just what might be on your mind, Nikki Ford?"

"I think you know."

Slade paused for a few seconds. "Well, now," he began, "you know I've told you before that I'm a one man show — no commitments — no ties. I do have principles and I generally stick to them. And I don't use women or anybody else for that matter. At least I try not to."

"I'm understand that. Likewise with me."

"Plus I never know when I'll be moving on," Slade continued. "You're an attractive woman, Nik, but if we do anything here and now, it's got to be with that understanding. And I assume you don't have a boyfriend, 'cause if you do, the show stops right here. You've never mentioned anybody." He moved closer and stroked her hair.

"Free as a bird. I'm a big girl. It's 1969 for God sakes, Tom. I get it," she smiled. "I'm on the pill – last thing I want to do is get pregnant. You know what the hippies say – 'if it feels good, do it'. I'll be honest – I need some male attention – right now. And, I've been pining for you for a long time...Shotgun."

"If it feels good...yeah, I've heard that phrase before. Well that's awful nice - I'm pretty damn flattered and I guess lucky too. I'll admit you've crossed my thoughts more than once too."

Then, feigning a serious look, Slade added, "But Nik, I don't know if I can live up to my nickname."

"Oh, I think you'll do just fine. What say we just give it little a try?"

"Nothing ventured, nothing gained."

They both paused and then laughed out loud. Slade pulled Nikki close and kissed her long and smoothly. Both felt it from the get go. He got up, pulled the curtains and lit a stick of incense. Then he opened the drawer to be sure he had a skin handy. He took no chances. There was no way he was ever going to let himself get in trouble and locked into anything. He had too much ahead of him to see and do.

"Such a romantic," Nikki joked.

"Yes, I always like to get the atmosphere just right. Now, one more thing."

He put an LP on his portable record player – Blind Faith. Nikki reclined on the bed.

"I think we've covered all the bases, beautiful," he whispered as he lay beside her and gently kissed her on the neck. "I think this is going to be special."

"Glad fate has brought us together – for however long," she responded.

"Me too, but remember where we are – we've got to be quiet."

The next hour or so was definitely special and it wasn't exactly quiet. They'd go a few more rounds before the summer was out.

15.

Tom Slade had to be continually thinking about moving on to the next experience; that was his bottom line. See new places, meet new people, learn new things and grow and develop like a spreading sapling. Get closer to that main idea; that eternal constant to live by. Mistakes weren't necessarily bad, he figured. He'd made plenty, learned from them, and always felt he came away a better informed person. And Slade was beginning to understand the cut and dried reality of life; that the road was long, winding, and full of hairpin turns. The more he learned, the more he realized just how much he didn't know.

In high school, Slade was one of those guys who had it all: good looks, exceptional athletic ability and above average grades. However, by choice, he wasn't much a part of the in-crowd or any kind of jock. He saw himself more as an outsider and gravitated to that element, finding he could better relate to those kids on the periphery. And they in turn valued him as a guy who could be popular on the other side, but also had the depth to understand and appreciate what they brought to the table. Slade looked further to something deeper than the jock scene.

Although he'd decided to put off college, he continued to read and learn. Slade was a big Jack London fan and had read many of his books and short stories. He was especially taken with the rawness and adventure of "The Sea-Wolf" set on the Pacific high seas. Slade also explored the realm of philosophy, having familiarized himself with the works of Rene' Descartes and in particular, the enlightenment writings of John Locke.

When he first met Jeff, Slade sensed the tenseness and insecurity about him, although Jeff did a good job of hiding it. But before long he also could see the goodness and potential in him. He knew if they became friends that he could help Jeff with his issues. And like Slade, Jeff was a drifter. They were cut from the same mold.

Most every day, Slade thought of this far reaching quest for "the way", as he often termed it in his mind. Sometimes he figured it might be some insight that would set life straight for him. Eventually, it could all shake down to something simple but profound and lasting. It was out there. Somewhere. He really liked the idea of it.

Slade also believed that there was some kind of higher power that ruled the show. What exactly it was he didn't know but still he was certain of it. All he needed to do was to observe the beauty and wonder of nature around him to feel its presence. But his approach to a concept of God was far more spiritual than religious. Slade was more into seeking the best way to approach things based on the here and now; learning to live the right way. Whatever came after, he'd hope to move closer to it by living as cleanly and resolutely as he could. In searching the land, he was solidifying his soul.

Jeff Jones conversely took a more bottom-line view on things. He focused on food, shelter, and keeping out of harm's way much like a wild animal would. Unlike Slade, he feared doom somewhere out there, maybe just around every corner, which he had to dodge at all costs. His background had contributed heavily to that attitude and he knew it. But still, reality was his motivation: to save money, settle himself on level ground, and somehow get a little more ahead and stable. Above all, stay healthy, make a few friends along the line, and just let things ride. Let them ride into the sunset.

Contrary to Slade, Jeff's reasons for moving on were usually either money related or just to escape boredom. He had no grand visions. Get to the next job, find a cheap place to live, and make things just a little better. Relationships? Marriage? Kids? They hardly crossed his mind. Just simply staying above water was his first goal every day. Jeff lacked Slade's sense of wonder and idealism. But he would become interested in both in the coming weeks, as he got to know Slade better and became more tuned into his views.

16

Ten thirty rolled around. Slade and Jeff walked to the Warburton building feeling the snap in the cool night air. In the parking lot, spring bugs flew in frenzied loops beneath the spotlights. The gray factory stood before them like an enduring monument from a past era. Only the third and fourth floor lights burned in the facade, the home of grave yard shift.

Climbing up the staircases, the pungent drift of oil and dye hit them. It was the kind of smell that you never get used to. A baritone hum rose from the heart of this structure, from deep within its aged soul. The sound conjured up the image of tired blood still being pumped through an old body, its remaining days clearly numbered.

They stepped into the fourth floor cafeteria and took a couple of seats at one of the tables. A slew of second shifters, done with their work, sat and talked absently, waiting to punch out. For the most part, the older ones looked worn out just like the building, with the same passive expressions cemented into their faces. Everybody wore drab clothes, all seemingly in shades of green or brown in the dimness of the cafeteria lights. Some workers were covered with a fine coating of lint. A few heads turned to Slade and Jeff and back, much like cows in a meadow to somebody who passes by.

Third shift workers gradually filtered in and bought coffee that was steaming hot from the Servomation machine. It was as strong and bitter as could be but they were used to it. At the table beside Slade and Jeff's sat a couple of women. The younger one leaned forward and tapped Slade on the shoulder.

"You guys look new. Are you just starting tonight?" she asked.

"That's right," Slade said.

He and Jeff turned to look at her. She was of medium height and light skinned with a few scattered freckles. Her natural blond hair was long and tied back off her shoulders. One of her front teeth was chipped just a tiny bit, but she had full lips and her face featured a classic symmetry. Probably not much older than twenty, the woman had a certain beauty that was accented by a distinct edge hardened into her features. It was the result of the hard work she'd done night in and night out at Warburton for several years.

"I'm Lynne," she said, "Lynne Charland. And this is my Aunt Hattie. Welcome aboard, boys. Welcome to hell on earth."

They all laughed. Slade then introduced himself and Jeff.

"Almost starting time," Lynne told them. "C'mon and follow us out to the floor. You need to see Sam, our new shift foreman. He'll show you the ropes."

"Thanks," Jeff said.

The four of them walked out together, Jeff and Slade trailing behind. The two in back took in Lynne's assets. They already noticed she had a first class rack and now they admired her curves from the rear view. They looked at each other and nodded. Her jeans fit her nicely and she walked with just a hint of a swagger. Lynne was every bit as hot as the receptionist from the morning, but in a different bottom-line way.

"Sam – Sam!" she shouted to a figure far in the distance. "Couple of new guys here need to see you."

"Be right there."

Talk to you later, guys," Lynne smiled. Slade and Jeff watched her walk in the other direction before turning toward Sam.

"Stiller may be a pit," Jeff whispered, "but man, between Nikki, the secretary, and that chick, it's got some smokin' babes."

"I'll bet she's dangerous after the sun goes down," Slade added with a grin.

"You got that right."

"And she looks a little like my girl Joni Mitchell, doesn't she?"

"She does at that."

A tall man who looked awfully young to be a boss approached them. He had an odd look about him, as if he was unsure about what he was doing. Sam Burnside, 30 years old but indeed younger looking, had only been on the job for three weeks. He was still finding his stride. He'd managed

56

people before but didn't know much about the textile business. Over and above that, Sam was a nice guy and the night crew liked him. He looked at the new employees with tired eyes.

"Thomas Slade and Jeff Jones, right?" he said.

"Yessir."

"Sam Burnside - nice to meet you guys. Welcome to the company. Here – I've got a couple of punch cards for you."

He reached into his back pocket and gave them the cards. Then they walked over to the clock. Jeff and Slade punched in and inserted their cards in the rack. It was now official. Sam then turned and scratched his head.

"Man, I still can't get used to these hours," he said. "Hope you guys adjust better than I have so far. Anyway, I'm gonna put you on as creelers to start with, and you'll work on the floor up the ramp there."

"What's a creeler?" Jeff asked.

"Hang with me boys and I'll try to explain it – see, I'm new here too. Well, that floor up the ramp there is full of knitting machines that weave fabric. The girls – knitters – run them for the most part – usually eight machines each. The fabric comes off in rolls that go downstairs to be inspected and dyed, but that doesn't concern you. Let's walk up to the machines and I'll explain what a creeler does."

They entered an enormous room with rows of bright ceiling lights and supporting posts. It was split by a wide aisle. On both sides were lines of knitting machines, each around six feet high and bolted fast to the floor. They looked like squat trees, flattened on top to an expanse of branches supporting a collection of spools, bobbins and threads going in every direction; everything somehow connected to everything else. Each machine held eighty or so spools of yarn, in twos, one atop the other. In their caged hearts were large spindles that wound the end-product fabric.

All was quiet now with the change of shifts. The knitters, Lynne Charland one of them, tended to their machines, checking to see that everything was ready. They oiled here, greased there, and squinted to read starting numbers to monitor their piece work. The more production, the more money for them. And they checked the boxes along the aisle for yarn supplies, flicking on a green light for the floor man if they needed more.

Sam wiped his forehead and grimaced. "You know, boys, I'm embarrassed to say that I still can't remember some of these people's names. Anyway – to describe your jobs...the thing of it is...those spools up there – see them?"

"Can't miss them there's so many," Slade said.

"No doubt, Tom. Well...now bear with me. There's one on top of the other like you see there. And there's a string at the start and end of each spool, see? The string from the bottom of the top spool has to be tied to the string from the top of the bottom spool – so that once the top spool runs out, the line flows to the bottom spool and the machine doesn't have to stop. Are yah with me boys?"

"I think so," Slade said. Jeff wasn't so sure but he kept quiet.

"So...the thing of it is...now...when it gets to where the top spools are out and the bottom spools are beginning to run low, we gotta stop the machine and set up all new spools on the bottom, and put what were the bottom spools on top, and tie each of them together, see? That's called creeling the machine and you guys are creelers – the guys that do the setups." He paused for a couple of seconds and ran it back over in his head to see if it made sense.

"Yeah – I think that's right," Sam continued. "Probably sounds confusing but you'll pick it up pretty fast. You just have to tie the knots very clean so the strings don't jam on the transfer. The knitters will show you how. Normally, it takes around 45 minutes to creel a machine when you get a little experience. And the faster you are, the more the knitters will like you."

Now both Jeff and Slade were slightly overwhelmed but they got the general idea. Sam went on to add more details. He told them that a knitter usually ran seven machines with one down and being creeled. Sometimes, only six with her creeling one too if that was needed. As soon as a machine was back up and running, the next one that needed work most would be attended to. Creeling typically went on constantly throughout the shift, with breaks given here and there.

Occasionally a machine would jam up and shut down on its own, he explained further. Little red lights came on to show where the trouble was. First, the knitter would try to repair it herself, but if she was unable, she'd flick on a yellow light in the aisle. In a minute or two, a fixer would show up; somebody more skilled with the machines to repair breakdowns.

"Creeling can be tough in the beginning, boys," Sam finished with. "To get up high enough to work, you have to use a spool roller." He pointed at one. "You can see that it's a stepladder on wheels with a bin that holds 30 or so spools of yarn. The goal is to get the roller close enough to the work area so as still not to disturb the machine. It's tricky, especially for the hard-to-reach inner spools. Basically, you load up and move from perch to perch atop, like monkeys in the canopy, I guess - with your eyes focused on tying those clean little knots."

Both Slade and Jeff smiled at the monkey analogy. His spiel completed, Sam patiently answered a few more questions. Then he introduced Jeff to his knitter, Simone Ledoux. She was a middle-aged woman with the pallor of a ghost. Simone shook his hand and managed a smile upon seeing a new face. Jeff nodded back.

Slade was led over to the next group of machines to meet his knitter, Dina Fantozzi. She was in her early thirties and thin, probably didn't weigh a hundred pounds. But Dina was wiry and tough, with an olive complexion and a couple of biker tattoos on her arms. She was a bottom-line type of person and a hard worker. Dina had an edge to her and a twinkle in her eye. She looked up sideways at Slade, smiled, and said "nice to have you with us, handsome." He liked her from the start.

The knitters demonstrated the jobs and then began starting up the machines. In 10 minutes, both Jeff and Slade were atop their spool rollers and actively trying to creel. Jeff felt a lot of pressure at first and nearly fell off his perch twice during the first hour. Both times, he looked around and saw that Simone took little notice. She was too focused on the machines and taking care of business. And she was good at it.

In little time, Dina next door had seven machines running and spinning out production, Slade creeling the eighth. He got the hang of it a little quicker than Jeff did and was able to find a groove. Dina walked by and cracked a few jokes like she'd known him for years. It gave him a settling feeling and took the edge of any first night jitters.

59

Before long, most of the machines on the floor were running. It was like the room was alive, humming in a steady drone, cylinders spinning and churning out the fabric. The women tended their machines like bees to a field of flowers; touching, checking, craning necks to look up, and bending backs to check below.

Jeff's mind began to wander in the wrong direction again. Was this going to be the story for him? Would he be a factory drone the rest of his life? He looked around and locked on some of the older workers; long timers - long suffering people with crooked backs doing jobs that they did for no other reason that everybody has to do something just to get by and live.

"Cut it out, man!" he scolded to himself. It didn't have to be him too, he thought alternatively. This was just a stop before moving on to the next thing. He'd find his way. And he'd be damned if he'd let himself end up like his father on the streets or even dead before his time. Whatever it took, that's what he was going to do. Still, his depression persisted.

"Sad deal," Jeff thought as he paused to look out to the floor. "They're kind of like robots. They run on automatic — do what they have to do — then get sick and die — maybe from what they have to cope with each night in a place like this. Almost like a slew of ants in a big colony — this factory. Christ — I think too much — just stop it, man — stop it!" With that, he was able to get his head back on straight and refocused on his job.

Alongside him in the next group of machines, Tom Slade was calm and upbeat. He had a different take on the situation. He saw things in a broader way without himself at the center. Slade was intrigued with just who these people were. Dina, for example, had a hardness from her years as a mill worker but seemed to accept things and approach her job with a smile. Slade imagined she had problems and responsibilities like everybody else does, maybe more than the average person, but it looked as if she kept them in line. "You can't always control what happens to you, Tommy, but you can always control your attitude toward it." His mother told him that many times. It stuck with him. "Always do your best with what you have," he thought. Dina was a good example of that.

17.

That night came to an end — the next night — the night after that — and a string of nights that all seemed pretty much the same. In a few weeks, Jeff and Slade were up to speed and into the third shift flow. They'd gotten to know most of the workers and were an accepted part of the crew.

One guy they got a special kick out of was a character named Lew Masterson, better known as Beans. He was a short person, only about five foot four, and in his late forties. Beans was a floor man, one of the guys whose job it was to keep all the knitters supplied with yarn and to remove the finished fabric rolls.

Beans had a crew cut and usually wore a flat cap gangster-style, with a cigarette out the side of his mouth. At times, he walked around like a tough guy. But as soon as you got to know him, it was clear that Beans was really a gentle soul with a good heart. He was also very funny. Plus he had a way of spinning terms. For instance, if he was describing somebody as cheap, he'd use the word "thrifty" instead with a sheepish grin.

Back on the second night Jeff and Slade worked at Warburton, during a break, Beans spotted the new guys and walked over. He looked straight up to the six foot two inch Tom Slade and said curiously, "What's your name? This is just a question."

Slade looked down with a straight face and said "Shotgun — this is just an answer." Beans took a step back and smiled. He liked the comeback. Then he introduced himself. Slade smiled back and they shook hands. Jeff, standing to the side, chuckled, told Beans his name and did the same. There began a solid friendship between the three.

"How'd you get the name 'Beans'?" Slade asked him a week later, sitting with him and Jeff in the caf during a break.

"It's my real name...bah hah hah!" Beans laughed. "Nah — just kidding. Has nothing to do with pork and beans like you might think — I hate 'em. See, when I was a kid, I took a liking to jelly beans. I was always bugging my mother for more jelly beans. She started calling me 'Beans' and that's who I been ever since...bah hah hah."

"Man, that is one unique laugh," Jeff said pointing his finger at Beans.

"Never heard another one like it," Slade agreed.

"I was born with it."

Beans was like a character actor right out of the movies. His job was fairly easy and on many nights he had time to kill. He was always hanging around the knitters, creelers, fixers – whoever would listen, telling stories, making jokes, or constantly complaining about the company. He'd spent all of his life In Stiller and every street and gutter was ingrained into his look and actions. If you threw a dig his way, Beans was sharp with the retorts. One time Dina yelled over to him, "Hey Shorty – I need some yarn over here ASAP!" "You know, I used to be tall, Dina," he yelled back with a smirk, "I didn't like it."

Beans claimed that in his younger days, he was connected to the local mafia and worked for them as a collector, or as he preferred to say, an enforcer. He also bragged that he had a black belt in karate. Everybody in the building knew that five foot nothing leg breakers were hard to come by. He probably knew a few shady people and maybe did a correspondence course in martial arts, but nothing beyond that. Even Beans knew he was stretching the truth to put it mildly, but he liked that image enough that he probably let himself believe it. It gave him an identity that he needed. And he dropped enough names to give the impression that he knew something about the local crime business so as to give him a shred of credibility. Sometimes at the end of one of his tall tales, he'd go into a karate stance as an exclamation point. It always broke everybody up.

One Friday night, during the lunch break, Beans was in especially good humor. He got into a story about something that happened to him many years ago while night-fishing in the river. His audience was Slade, Jeff, and a tall young fixer who was known around the company as Rails.

"Think it was in the summer of 1960," Beans began, finger to his chin. "My cousin Ernie and me were up on the north part of the river - near the town line, a mile before the falls where the current runs slow. We'd caught pickerel up there before where the water's cleaner with no junk. We had a lantern with us but that was all – no moon out – dark as tar. I'll admit I was a little shall we say, ascared. But Ernie and me, we stayed put where we was, casting out our lures and reeling them back in. We were both thinkin' 'let's bail' but neither one of us had the balls to say it."

He paused and grinned, then rubbed his forehead. "So the moon's out and water's still and smooth as glass – like the calm before something bad happens – you know – like in a horror movie."

"Now you got me," Rails said. "I'm officially interested."

Beans smiled widely exposing a missing front tooth, scratched the stubble on his chin, and looked side to side. "And I'm getting more nervous with every minute that goes by, and more pissed off at Ernie for talking me into coming along at night time. Then, I cast out my line, begin reeling it, and there's something on it, but it don't feel like a fish – more like something I snagged, maybe a log. But it's heavy – really heavy."

"Here it comes," Jeff said.

"Well...it took a couplah minutes, but when I finally get it in close where we can see it – it's a friggin corpse floating face down – a woman in a dress with real long hair all twisted around her head! My heart stopped for a few seconds – couldn't say nothin' - could hardly even breathe. I didn't know whether to shit or go blind. Ernie seen it and let out a yowl "YEEEAAAAHHHHH!! That snapped me out of it. We left everything there and screwed – fast as I ever ran in my life. What are the odds of that, Railsback? Reeling in a stiff?"

"Outah sight, Beans," Rails said and they all laughed. Beans broke up so hard that he almost lost his breath. "Bah ha ha ha!"

"So what was the outcome, bud?" Slade asked. "Who was the body?"

"Well, we got back to my house and called the police - tole them what happened. We had to go down the station and fill out a report. Turned out it was a young woman who was missing a week or so, and they questioned us like we was suspects! But we were cleared pretty fast and in the end, the finding was that she was drunk, fell in the river and drownded. No foul play."

"Good story," Rails said.

"This is true," Beans agreed. "And just for the record, I've never fished at night in that river since then – nine years and counting."

63

18.

More time moved on. As Slade and Jeff got to know most of the mill people they worked with better, they developed a rapport with some of them other than Beans. The girl they met on the first night, Lynne Charland, liked them both and the three quickly became friendly. She'd been working at Warburton since she was 17, following in the path of her mother and aunt. Lynne had become the most skilled knitter on the floor. She was fast, focused, and productive. Lynne was able to grind out a pretty good salary each week.

Because he worked next to Lynne's machines, from his perch atop his spool roller, Jeff often was in a position to observe her routine. There was an elegance and grace to her that oddly blended in with the factory background. Jeff marveled at her movements when she helped her creeler, Melissa Palmer, a shy youngster a year out of high school.

Lynne's slender body always looked alluring even in the most awkward positions around the machines. Her long hair, when not tied back, sometimes fell gently over the strings, almost caressing them. Maybe she was a little hard at the edges, but Lynne Charland was a beautiful 22 year old woman with a sexuality that could not be denied. On those mornings after work, lying in bed, when Jeff's tensions got the best of him, Lynne was fantasy number one.

There were several foreign students working their way through the local technical college on the third shift. All of them had day classes and would be taking summer courses. Peter Swenson was one from Sweden. Hawsitu and John Yan Yin Kang were Asian students, both quiet guys and skilled ping pong players, at least according to them. Arun Bakare was a good natured student form Pakistan. And Ravi Mohan was an older student from India, who generally kept to himself and did as little work as possible. They all mixed in with the older workers scattered across the mill who'd been there seemingly forever.

Young Ed Collins worked the floor with Beans. He was a wiry Stiller street kid, just turned 21 and aching for some kind of change. At about five foot ten, with floppy dirty blond hair, he looked a little like James Dean.

Ed was easy going and liked to joke around. A skilled amateur boxer, he had won a Golden Gloves welterweight title. He got the nickname "Fast Ed", from a trainer named Archie Lloyd for his slickness in the ring. "Eddie's there, and then he ain't there," Archie would say about him. But after winning the title, Ed abruptly quit boxing. He'd had his bell rung once or twice and realized that getting punched in the face for a living didn't have good long term prospects. There was a thoughtful aspect to his personality.

Ed sometimes walked the floor with a tough sneer throwing karate chops but it was all just a put-on to mimic Beans, who he got a real kick out of. He was a good natured kid and always up for anything.

The only black working on the third shift was Curtis Fitz, a 19 year old ex-high school tailback. He'd learned how to repair machinery and worked in the third floor machine shop, which often had a skeleton grave yard crew or just one person on. He was good at it and a valued employee at Warburton.

Curtis had some small college scholarship prospects and was taking post graduate courses to get his grades up to qualify. He was a quiet introspective kid, but if you approached him the right way, he'd let his guard down. Sometimes he was good for a wry remark that got everybody laughing. Slade knew just how to get him out of his shell.

Finally there was Steven Railsback, Rails to just about everybody. He worked as a fixer. Twenty three years old, Rails was very tall, close to six foot four, and lanky. His hair was long and sandy brown, and he had a fumanchu that would make Frank Zappa proud. Smart and serious looking, Rails usually walked around as if he had something interesting on his mind, which he often did, but also with sort of an underlying grin at the corners of his mouth.

Rails grew up in a little town in upstate New York called Oriskany Falls. He'd attended college at Boston University and graduated with double majors in English and Journalism. He was an exceptional student, but like

65

Slade, Rails had a rebellious streak in him. He now lived in a studio apartment by himself in Stiller. He hadn't worked in his field yet; Rails was taking time off to gather life experiences to use as material for a novel. That was his reason for working a blue collar job at Warburton other than to pay the bills. He was fascinated by the lot of the long time mill workers.

Steve Railsback had seen himself as a writer from a very young age, when in grade school, his stories were so good that they often were displayed on the principal's bulletin board. He had the calling and the talent. Rails was eventually going to make it as a writer. He was certain of it. In his mind, it was only a matter of how many experiences he would gather, and how long it would take to get a book together and break out. He always carried a pocket note pad and could often be seen standing to the side jotting down his observations. He loved Beans as a character and already had a load of material on him.

The college students, Rails, and Jeff were the only people in the mill with any higher education. The rest of the lot were high school or less. But most everybody was impressed with Rails' college credentials and they took his ambitions seriously, even if some didn't really understand them. No one ever thought to make fun of him or his note taking. Something about Rails was special and to be respected. There was a gleam in his eye; a deepness within him. Jeff, Slade and Ed Collins too would come to be very interested in Rails; his views on current events and life in general. His was a voice to be reckoned with around the fourth floor.

19.

It was now into late May. Jeff and Slade had successfully adjusted to the weekly factory grind and didn't find it so bad that they couldn't hack it. They'd put in some overtime and the money was good. Both were able to put a little on the side weekly for whatever the future might hold.

Simone gave Jeff fifteen minute breaks here and there throughout the night. She was very good to work with and Jeff felt lucky he'd been assigned to her. During those breaks he'd usually walk over to one of the big open windows, sit on the sill, and look down on the dark river waters. The pulse of the rapids was settling and almost hypnotizing. The water brought on soothing sleepy thoughts, so that at times, Jeff felt he was one with the river and pointed toward his own inner peace. He did have brief brushes with serenity.

One night, Jeff was at a window, eyes closed and in that kind of state. A touch on his shoulder from a smooth set of fingernails drew him out of it. He opened his eyes to see Lynne standing next to him, her body silhouetted against the bright lights behind.

"Did I scare you Jeff?" she asked playfully. "What were you doing – meditating or something?"

"Your guess is as good as mine," Jeff smiled. "I was in a zone, I guess. What's up?"

She sat down beside him and looked down to the water. "I don't know. Well...I was bored and thought I'd wander over. Many nights I see you here by yourself and I wonder what the deal is. It IS kind of calming, isn't it? Sort of slows you down. Is that it?"

Lynne eased back and put her hands behind her neck, pulled her hair pony tail up and let it fall down again. Jeff felt a little charge go through his body.

"Yeah – I guess you could say that," he agreed.

"Too bad that river's such a sty, though," she continued. "Some days it even smells. I get a better feeling when I go out to the ocean – so clean and powerful. I went out with a guy a couple of years ago who took me to Ogunquit Beach up in Maine once. We walked for two hours – all the way out to a jetty and back. It was one of the best times I ever had."

"Nice," Jeff said. "Actually, Slade and I talked about that a while back – what you said about the river being polluted, I mean."

Lynne stood up and leaned against the wall. "Yes," she said. "Hey, maybe sometime we can get a group of us together to take a ride up to Ogunquit for a day. We have the whole summer ahead – anything to get a little relief from this hole."

"I've never been to that place – never even heard of it."

"You'd like it, Jeff," she continued. "Well, let's put that on the back burner and keep it in mind. Now there is one other thing. I know some people who are renting a cottage out at Wells Beach the week of the Fourth of July. It's a little further up the Maine coast. They're planning a party and they invited me – said I could bring along a few friends. Melissa said she'd go. Would you be interested?"

Jeff paused for a few seconds. "You're asking me if I want to go to a beach party?" he finally replied.

"I think that's what I said, Jeff," Lynne smiled.

"Well...then, I accept. And thanks for the invitation. Only thing is I don't have a car."

"No problem – we'll go in my car. I talked to Tom Slade earlier and he agreed to come too. You and Slade are such nice guys – it'll be fun to spend some time together on the outside. Just a little get together, that's all. It won't be for a month or so but it's something to look ahead to."

"It sounds like fun."

"Great," Lynne said. "Well, duty calls. I have to get back. Talk to you later, Jeff."

"Okay – and thanks again."

Lynne walked off happily. Jeff sat back again and thought about what he'd just heard. A minute later, Slade, who had watched the whole thing from his perch nearby on his spool roller, came over and sat down next to him.

"I'll take a wild guess and say Lynne invited you to the party at Wells Beach."

"You would be right, my friend."

"What did you tell her?"

"It took me by surprise but I agreed to it. And she told me you were in the fold too. Man, I'd have a tough time ever saying no to her no matter what she asked for."

"I hear you. You know, once you get past that tough exterior she sometimes puts on, Lynne's a nice girl. Surprisingly intelligent. Plus she's a hard worker and actually has a little class over and above the situation in this place. And some depth too over the average mill girl. You know what? I think she asked us just because she likes us and thinks we're good people – no other reason. I really do."

"I agree with all of that. You did a nice job of describing her. Rails would be impressed."

"Thanks."

"But she almost...scares me sometimes, man," Jeff added. "I mean that's a whole lot of woman - too much for me, I think. It's like if I ever had the stones to ask her out and she turned me down, I'd probably want to throw myself off the building. Know what I mean?"

They both broke up laughing.

"Power, Jeff, power," Slade said emphatically. "A hot woman like Lynne can have a ton of influence over a guy and you always have to be aware of that. Don't get me wrong, though. I wouldn't say Lynne is the type to hold anybody to the fire, but some women know they have it and they wield it like a shotgun – no pun intended. You get hooked and it's like you're in this spell. You know you're acting crazy but you can't help it. You can't get her out of your mind even if you know it's a bum deal in the end and you're gonna get scalded. I've been through it and believe me, even when you know it's no good, it's still a bitch to finally break free."

"Really? I've never been in any kind of long term thing with a girl. Never experienced anything like that."

"And I hope you don't, pal. It can be a living hell. Just always use caution when it comes to hot babes. But like I said, Lynne seems to be above all that crap. At least I hope so."

"I wouldn't mind finding out."

"Maybe you will one day my friend. I think she kind of likes you. You never know. Just be careful."

"Careful is my middle name, man."

Jeff thought about it off and on for the rest of the night. He decided to follow Slade's advice; to stay grounded and not let his thoughts go wild over Lynne Charland.

20.

As the days passed into the latter part of June, the coworker group got tighter. A core of Jeff, Slade, Rails and Ed formed, with the much older Beans sometimes on the periphery. They turned over many topics during breaks and lunch, usually introduced by Rails or Slade. Sometimes, Rails just threw something out and eased back once the conversation got going, pulling out his note pad and taking material down.

More than once he brought up the hippie movement and the counter culture philosophy. He was intrigued by it; the principles of love and brotherhood that it seemed to be built on, and that possibly the country could really take a severe turn for the better. However, Rails was also a realist. Because of the firm hold of the establishment, he figured chances were small. But still, it was something for young people to consider and his generation was igniting it.

On a night when a thunder storm raged outside, the topic came up for discussion at the hour lunch break. Jeff, Slade, Rails, and Ed were sitting at a corner table. They'd finished eating and were talking over coffee.

Slade leaned back and stretched his arms. "Gonna be time to move on before too long, boys," he said, "I'm starting to get just a little itchy, you know?"

"Getting restless already, Shotgun?" Rails said taking a sip of coffee. "You've only been on for a few months here. Aren't you jumping the gun a little?"

"Not really, Rails. I've already been in Stiller longer than I hang in most places. See...I'm on a mission, man. Got to keep moving from place to place when the urge says to go. There's something important ahead out there for me – somewhere way past the horizon. An enlightenment – an epiphany – a satori – call it whatever you want to."

"Interesting words," Rails said leaning forward. "I even know what a satori is. Have you ever read 'On the Road' by Jack Kerouac, Slade?"

"Can't say that I have but I've definitely heard of it more than once. I've been meaning to pick it up."

"Oh wow – phew!" Rails exhaled getting the full attention of the others. "You've got to read that book immediately, my man! It's YOU, only on a larger scale. Two guys in a Hudson driving back and forth across America, just continually moving and digging all the people - and searching for the truth...as you say, enlightenment. They referred to that...thing you talk about as 'it'. And the prose is written in a jazzy style. Some of the paragraphs are like improvisational phrase solos. Kerouac was a big jazz guy. When I finished it, I was stunned it was so good. I've read it cover to cover three times."

"I've heard that Kerouac name before," Jeff said. "Isn't he from somewhere in the area?"

"Born and bred in Lowell, Massachusetts, a place he wrote about in several of his other books, particularly 'The Town and the City', his first one. You know, he's the guy who got me started with the note pads. He used to go around doing prose sketches of any scenes or people he found interesting. Always had a note pad on him."

"The truth spills out," Jeff joked.

"Tell us some more about 'On the Road', Steve," Slade said with interest.

"Well, Shotgun...that book ignited the Beat movement – remember the beatniks in the early sixties? Bohemians, coffee houses, poetry readings to jazz in the background – all that cool stuff. And he wrote another book after 'On the Road' called 'The Dharma Bums'. It was all about embracing Buddhism and rejecting conventional society - departing to the frontier and living off the land. He talked of an exodus of young people out of civilization to the wilderness and simplicity. He actually...like prophesized the hippie movement."

"Wait a minute," Jeff said. "That rings a bell. The girl who gave me a ride into town – you remember, Shotgun, that flower child I told you about? She mentioned 'The Dharma Bums' and something she called, what was it, uh…the ricksack revolution, I think.

"That's rucksack, Jeff," Rails smiled, excited about the topic. "And 'The Dharma Bums' is the hippie handbook. In fact, here's a quote from it that I memorized." Rails closed his eyes and looked up, "Let's see…'I see a vision of a great rucksack revolution of thousands or even millions of young Americans wandering around with rucksacks, going up to the mountains to pray, making children laugh and old men glad, making young girls happy and old girls happier…all of them Zen lunatics who go about writing poems that happen to appear in their heads for no reason and also by being kind and also by strange unexpected acts keep giving visions of eternal freedom to everybody and all living creatures.'"

They all leaned back for a few seconds. Slade was intrigued and took a deep breath. Ed wasn't too up on the subject but he got the drift. The whole idea of it sparked something inside of him. Jeff was fascinated by the clear-as-day connection to the counter culture, and the fact that Rails had that long quote nailed to the wall.

"How do you memorize that stuff so well?" Ed asked with awe.

"I just care about it. It means something to me."

"Far out," Slade commented. "That Jack Kerouac is one deep cat. I'm going to go out and get that book first thing tomorrow. 'It' – I feel that - I get that. I've probably had 'it' on my mind for a very long time, man. My mom always told me there's some kind of 'it' thing out there although she didn't use that word. The idea kind of worked its way into my head almost like a calling. Been all over the northeast the past few years – maybe the next thing is to broaden the horizon – head cross country like those characters you talked about. Got to think about that one – let it develop awhile."

Ed's eyes widened as a thought occurred to him. "Shotgun – I've heard of…yew-tow-pee-yer somewhere – I think that's how you say it. Like a perfect world, man – Eden. That's not 'it', is it?"

"Umm - that's pronounced Utopia, Ed," Slade replied. "Nirvana might be another word for it. But no - not exactly…but it is, like…I think, related. Look, I'll give you guys my ideas on this but just bear in mind that it's only

72

my view. Just take what you like and leave the rest, dig? I mean I'm no TV preacher trying to shove some jive down your throats."

"We're hip. Shoot," Jeff said.

"Well, I mean, you don't have to kick the bucket to see signs of the existence of God around every day if you are just aware, see? Like being able to step outside of your own thing. Think of a horse without the blinders. There's little clues all around – like the dales of yellow straw in the rolling hills outside of Stiller and the way they sway in the wind at the end of the day. The smiles I get from some of the nice people I meet wherever I go. Stuff like feeling the morning sun on your shoulders – touching a wild flower by the side of the road – looking to the huge sky and clouds like a beautiful painting. Things like that show me the existence of something powerful and great that's behind all of it, man."

"Yeah," Ed said with wonder.

"A lot of that stuff goes right over many people's heads who do the same dull routine day in and day out." Slade continued. "That's a part of 'it', I think – developing that awareness, just like practicing on an instrument, you know? Getting good and continuing the practice to stay sharp and get better. Even the colorful sounds I get out of my guitar some nights when I'm by myself and its quiet. It's like the thing is alive in my hands and responding to my soul, dig?"

"Yes…I get it. Kind of feel like I'm back in college listening to a philo' lecture," Rails laughed." But you know, I can relate to what you say, Shotgun. It makes a lot of sense. Like the other morning when I walked out of work, there was this beautiful white cat sitting on the roof of my car. I walked up to it and put my hand out. It looked straight up at me – with the most piercing green eyes - and it moved its head into my palm. I was stunned for a couple of seconds – and I felt something – like a beautiful connection between me and another species. Sounds crazy but I'm dead serious."

"That's a good example, Rails," Slade smiled, "and you were aware enough to sense it. That's the key. That's exactly what I'm talking about." He shifted forward in his chair. "And here's one thing I've learned in my travels over the past few years. It's important to do positive things outside of yourself, man – send out good karma – 'cause you know, it comes back to you. I'm serious - you do good and good comes back to you. May take a while, even many years, but it all eventually comes back. I really believe that. Giving a buck to a bum on the street, feeding a stray dog, or even just being kind and friendly in general. Stuff like that – doing what you know is right. You get in the habit and you're on track to that 'it' thing. You're a better person because you're thinking outside of the box. Now - everybody please get down on your knees and pray."

There was a pause and then Slade flashed a wide grin. They all had a good laugh.

"Had you going, didn't I?" Slade remarked. "But seriously, I meant what I said. That's how I try to live."

"Well, it does get you to thinking," Ed said. "I'd say it's a pretty good way to go."

"I agree, especially the way you put it, Shotgun," Jeff added. "Powerful."

"Thanks guys," Slade said sitting back in his chair.

"And one final thing about believing in something bigger," Rails offered. "Not to be a downer but let's face it, we all have to deal with the end at some point. You don't want to face it alone, right? You don't want to be on your death bed thinking it's only you and there's no help – no guidance – nothing beyond. Imagine how scary that would be. You've got to believe in something."

"Tell you what," Ed added. "Last year my uncle Ted was really sick in the hospital with congestive heart failure. I went to see him the day before he died. He could barely talk, but he told me not to worry about him – said he saw where he was going in his sleep the night before – and it was all good."

"Really?" Jeff said running his hands through his hair. "Heavy, man. That sure makes you wonder. But all I can think about right now is that beautiful hippie chick again – what was her name...Crystal – yeah Crystal. That girl keeps flashing back to me. She talked just like what you guys are saying. Think all that, like...idealistic stuff is what the hippies are looking for?"

"Sure - at least that's a big part of it," Slade said. "But you know there's one thing about movements where they think they have it all worked out and everybody's all in. I'm cagey about them. You've got to be careful.

74

Intentions can be great but there's always stuff connected that isn't so good that's overlooked – an underside, you know? You have to be aware of that. Like all the pot they smoke and the psychedelics they do. Hey, I like some weed every now and then, but everything in moderation, dude. They seem to worship those acid trips. That ain't MY bag."

"That's true," Rails agreed. "They like to get blasted most of the time."

"Now, here's a for instance," Slade added. "You guys may have heard about a big concert coming up in August at a farm somewhere in New York. I think they're calling it something like 'The Woodstock Music and Arts Fair'. I read a long article about it in the Globe. It's supposed to go on for three days and I hear many of the big bands are going to play. I thought about going, but it's not a cagey move for me, man, at least as I see it right now. Weird things can happen when you got a hundred thousand pot heads and druggies in one place for three days. I'll just sit back and observe a while from afar. It will be a hell of a long time before I ever join any movement."

"It's in Bethel," Rails said. "Yasgur's farm in the hamlet of White Lake. I know all about it. I grew up around a hundred miles north of there. But about what you just said, Shotgun, on the other hand, if you never take a risk, you'll never know. If I get a chance to go to that gig, I'm down, man. But I do hear you. And I agree what you said about 'it'. I'm glad I heard that. Could be 'it' happens more often than you think. You just have to be tuned in at the right frequency, right?"

"Oh yeah," Slade said pointing straight at him and smiling. "Just get tuned in, brother!"

The two-minute buzzer sounded and it was time to return to the floor. The four walked back to their stations all turning thoughts over in their heads. It had been a deep discussion. Beans approached Jeff and tapped him on the shoulder.

"What was you guys talkin' about over there in the corner?" he said. "It looked like a goddamn debate."

"T'was a meeting of the minds, buddy – a meeting of the mill rat minds."

"I don't need to know no more – I knew enough to stay clear. Don't think so much, Jonesy – just live for Crissakes!" He chuckled and walked off. "Bah hah hah!"

75

Ed Collins felt like he'd been doused by a big wave as different ideas passed through his mind. He felt a new connection with Tom Slade and his words, and the same for Rails and Jeff. Ed decided at that point that if he got the opportunity to one day travel with Slade in a group cross country as he had mentioned, he'd jump on it. It didn't matter when or where.

Rails thought about Slade's quest for "it" from a writing standpoint. He began to consider using the theme in the book he was trying to get straight in his mind before sitting down to write it.

Jeff loaded up his spool roller thinking about Crystal and the hippies out in San Francisco, plus the Woodstock concert too. He even thought about maybe going. He knew Jimi Hendrix would likely be there and maybe the Jefferson Airplane. Grace Slick had that million dollar smile and an energy about her that really did it for him. But no, he thought, not at this stage. Three days in that situation was way too much. Like Slade, he was more an observer than a believer. At least for now.

The night droned on as if time had slowed just a few ticks. The hum of the factory was down an octave; the place like a bee hive late in the day. Jeff looked out at the dank aisles, the dusty boxes, and the vibrating machines. Like a flash storm, another low set in. His spirits dropped - way down. He was attacked by feelings of hopelessness and despair, feeling doomed to live in misery until the inevitable end. No way out. And one day a crooked old man like Barney the YMCA bum, just looking for a place to fall down and die – die – die.

Jeff's spirits fell further. His father's image took hold and focused clearly in his mind. Where was he right this minute? Was he even alive? Jeff shook his head and paused for a minute. He'd reached rock bottom. There was no way to go but up.

Then he thought again about what Rails said about believing. He knew something about that. He closed his eyes and asked for that great something, much greater than anyone could imagine, a higher power that he knew was all knowing – to lift it...lift it – please lift it! "Help me let it go – help me let it go," he said over and over again to himself. Then, gradually, it did begin to let go of him. Jeff got back to focusing on work and the darkness cleared. After a while, the low was gone and he felt right again.

Lately, it was getting easier for Jeff to get back on track after one of these bouts. In the past, he'd been involved with a special young social worker for a time back in Holyoke, Sharon Jensen. She educated him on the 12-step program and how it was key to kids with backgrounds like his. He'd attended a support group regularly and over time, it made a difference.

It wasn't cast in cement, but Jeff eventually came to believe in something like Slade had described. An all knowing higher power. Exactly what it was he couldn't be sure but he believed in it anyway. When things went sour, he leaned on that belief more and more. Since he'd made the commitment at, least to some extent, each time he felt at the end of his rope, that he couldn't go on for another minute, and even got on his knees and begged for help...he got it.

"The glass is half full," he told himself. "Think positive – don't give in to negativity. You have food – you have a roof over your head – you have health – you have a few friends you can trust that you didn't have before. You're lucky, man – be grateful. Remember what that old guy said about worrying that time in the pool – gets you nowhere. Like they used to say in program, have an attitude of gratitude."

Jeff put the episode behind him and in its place. "Do positive things outside yourself," he remembered. Slade's words. He'd be sure to try and work them better.

21.

Jeff and Slade continued to have regular one-on-one basketball matches two or three nights a week. Usually they played between the hours of nine and ten PM before heading for work later, after most of the gym rats had gone home. That was Slade's idea. Jeff asked him about it, wondering why Slade didn't want to go up against better team competition in the earlier full court games. He just smiled and shrugged; said it didn't matter much to him and that he was happy with things as they were.

Like the first time, the games were always spirited and competitive. Jeff managed to win occasionally, but only when he hustled and played really well. He always got a rise out of knocking off such a good athlete. Slade kind of liked that. A glimmer would show in his eyes when it happened. It gave him a feeling of satisfaction when he knew he'd brought out the best in somebody.

Jeff sensed it and sometimes wondered about Tom Shotgun Slade. Did this guy have any faults? How did he manage to be so smooth and unruffled all the time? How was he so at peace with who he was and where he was going? How could he be so in tune with the moment all the time and what was happening around him? Then Jeff would stop right there and laugh it off. "Listen to Beans, don't think!" he'd often say to himself shaking his head.

22.

On the following Saturday night after the 'it' discussion, Jeff and Slade were hanging around the TV room reading magazines. Both were kind of bored.

"Feel like a little game of stick?" Slade asked.

They hadn't had the chance to play pool at the Y. The room was closed for a complete do-over since the week after Jeff came into town. For some reason, work had started and then stopped. The room laid locked up and dormant.

"Yeah – but where can we go? Any place nearby?"

"Sure – Roscoe's Rec Room. Down Back North Street – maybe a mile walk."

"Okay, I'm in. But hey, by the way, Shotgun, I've been meaning to ask you something. You've been around here awhile and have made a few bucks. Why don't you own a car?"

"Good question," Slade answered, then pausing a couple of seconds. "Well, I haven't had a real need for one since I got into town last November. My last car, a VW Bug, fizzled out down on Cape Cod a month or so before I cleared out. I was living in Wellfleet at the time. I didn't get another one since I was short on cash. When I left, I hitched up here to Stiller. I got that job at the Sounder right away, which is just down the street from this place. And I had a regular ride to the paving job after. Now, we work within walking distance to Warbs. No need for a car, right?"

"Check. Come to think of it, I don't have wheels probably for the same reason. But I've been thinking about getting some lately."

"Right. So to continue, after I ditched my car, I got used to hitching and taking busses from place to place when I needed to. And I got to like it, you know? I mean all the new people you meet and the stuff you hear. It gives you a better feel for where you are and what's going on. Although I do dig driving, I don't want to be tied down to a car right now unless I really have to."

Jeff shook his head and smiled. "You ARE the ultimate, no connections - free spirit."

"And that is the best compliment you could give me. That is exACTtly who I want to be."

"So be it. But I'd like to get myself some tread before too long."

"I wouldn't rush into it," Slade said. "Wait a while and see what develops. You never know what might come your way."

They walked down Water Street to Roscoe's, a small place on the second floor of an old business building called the Halifax. The room contained about 20 tables. They were all close enough to each other that it was easy to interfere with somebody else's shot. Most of the players looked to be local hoods, some wearing caps angled down low with shirt sleeves rolled up and cigarettes dangling from the corners of their mouths. It resembled a scene from an action movie.

79

Jeff and Slade got a table at the far corner of the room. The pool tables themselves were in rough shape. Some had tears here and there a few with splotches from spilled drinks. Slade looked at a spot on theirs and frowned.

"I'll tell you," he said in a low voice, "pool's a great game but some people in joints like this don't respect it. Spill drinks, rip the felt, and jump up on the sides to screw up the level of the slate bed instead of using a bridge. Hard to play the game right on a table that isn't level, man. No conscience – none at all."

"I hear yah," Jeff said. "Now I don't mean to brag, but I think I know my way around a billiard table pretty good. In my misspent youth, I was a pool rat at the boy's club in Holyoke. One of the older kids there was a really good player and schooled me. I learned a lot from him."

"I'll take that under advisement," Slade smiled. "My best friend in high school had a table in his cellar – a ping pong table too. There were four of us. All we did through the winter was shoot pool, play ping pong, and have marathon penny poker games. Those were the good old days."

"I should have known," Jeff laughed. "I figure now that you're a pool shark too, Shotgun. If I keep looking hard enough, maybe someday I'll find something I can beat you at."

"Never say die, my man. Don't forget, you do win occasionally at basketball. And that's legit."

"That I do," Jeff smiled.

After they warmed up a few minutes, Slade racked the balls and suggested a game of straight pool to 50, one point per ball, all balls fair game. Call the shot and pocket. Jeff agreed to it.

They played along a while, both at a high level and looking to be evenly matched. Jeff was thinking he could maybe take charge until Slade got into a rhythm and turned it up. Before long, he was tuned in and all Jeff could do was sit back and watch. Slade played with a locked in focus, able to pocket his shots and control the cue ball to break up clusters along the way. He made a couple of long runs, setting up perfectly to break into the next rack on one of them. And when he missed, he didn't leave much for Jeff to clean up. He jumped out to a comfortable lead.

"Isn't there anything you're not good at?" Jeff said shaking his head.

"Off hand, no," Slade laughed. "Just kidding. But you're no slouch either, Jeff – I can see that. See, when I take up something I like, I try to get as good as I can. Say with guitar, pool, basketball – whatever it is. I read up on pool and practiced hard and long. And I got someplace. You know, you try to develop whatever talent you have. I believe in that pretty strongly. And of course, the better you get at something, the more fun it is."

"I get it. Easier said than done though. But nothing of any value ever comes easy – I think I've at least learned that. You have to commit to it just like you said."

"You get out of it what you put into it. It's as simple as that."

Slade focused back on the table and continued to pile up points. But Jeff was able to break in here and there and made a few long runs of his own. Both showed enough game to get the attention of a few other players in the room. They fell into their various type bridges smoothly and made shots with precision, using English when needed, and controlling that round white rock. It was a battle and Jeff came on strongly at the end. But Slade prevailed to win by eight balls.

"That was a good match," he said. "Our levels are pretty close. And I love straight pool. You have to put your mind through a workout to play it well, especially against a good player like you who will make you pay if you screw up. Forces you to think – not only make the shots but to stay in position and break up trouble, and leave just enough angle so you can control the cue ball. Just like you see them do it on television."

"And in the movies too," Jeff added. "Jackie Gleason comes to mind in 'The Hustler' as Minnesota Fats, man. You must have seen it. Remember what Eddie Felton said about him off to the side while watching him play?"

"Of course. 'Look at that fat man move – he's like a dancer!' My favorite line. And Gleason was a pool player in his own right. He made all his own shots in that movie."

"Really? I didn't know that."

"'Dat so, Slick?" It was a voice from the next table. After he pocketed a shot, one of the hoods approached them. He was tall, thin and steely eyed; had a pack of cigarettes rolled up in his sleeve.

"Dey call me Smoke," he said. "Youze guys look like you got a little game. Want a little...ahh competition? Say a game of eight ball for maybe a twenty spot? Either one of you – don't make no difference to me whose money I take."

Jeff didn't like this guy from the get go. But he held back and didn't answer.

Slade turned his head and looked at Smoke. "Thanks, but we only came by here to kill a little time. We're not looking for any action."

"Oh I understand perfect," Smoke grinned. "Flashy players but no balls. I see it all the time." His playing partner, a big Puerto Rican, looked over from the other table and smiled at Slade.

"I don't take kindly to talk like that but we'll give you the benefit of the doubt, bud," Slade said back, now facing Smoke, who stiffened a little. The Puerto Rican then walked over and took a chair at the corner of the room from where he could watch. But he said nothing. Jeff felt his pulse begin to step up.

"Well, what's it gonna be?" Smoke said. "Is one of youze on or do I look for another sucker?"

"I think you need a couple of lessons in how to act, pal," Jeff said stepping forward. "Talk to us in a civil tongue or don't talk at all." He and Smoke locked eyes. Slade sensed trouble and cut in between them.

"Hold on guys – don't get your water hot," he said. "Tell you what, Smokey – let's see what you bring. I'll play you one game of eight ball for the twenty – one game and then my friend and I are going to split. No trying to win money back for either one of us – agreed?"

Both Jeff and Smoke stepped back. Smoke then gave a little smile. "Sure, man," he said. Then he glanced at Jeff. "Think you can keep your boy under control?"

"I'm not anybody's 'boy', buddy," Jeff said getting irritated again. "But we'll let things slide for now. And good luck – you'll need it."

82

"Okay, Slick," Smoke said looking to Slade again. "You must think you're can actually beat me. That's a laugh. But I kind of like your style, I have to say. We'll do like you want – one game for the twenty. Flip for break."

Jeff leaned against the wall and calmed down as both put their money down on the side. Smoke flipped a quarter and won. He blasted the balls with a crack as if the cue ball was shot from a cannon, pocketing the five and leaving a wide open table, save for one group of three, all striped balls. The solid colored balls were all spread out cleanly and having already made one, he chose them for himself.

Smoke went about his business. Plunk, plunk, plunk...he pocketed everything but the six and eight. But he left the cue ball a little out of position and had to make a tough cross bank to make the six. This left him at a bad angle on the eight and a possible scratch to lose him the game. Rather than take the risk, he ticked the eight ball off the bank out in front of the corner pocket. That way, he could make it from anywhere on the table on his next turn after Slade missed. Plus he blocked the pocket to limit Slade's options. Slade had to run out or lose.

Smoke stepped back and smiled broadly. "Got'cha by the gonads, Slick. Now let's see what CHEW got."

Slade zeroed in and took a lot of time before lining up his first shot. "That's the trouble right there," he said pointing out the cluster along the side rail, which Smoke purposely hadn't touched. "If I can break up that bunch somewhere along the line, you never know what might happen. You never know."

"We'll see."

Slade made his first two balls and nearly clipped the group on the second shot. Then he stepped up to a side pocket shot on the 12, snapped middle right spin into the cue ball, made the shot, and sent the cue ball dead into the cluster. It spread the three balls off the rail. He looked Jeff's way and gave a little wink. Jeff nodded back.

Having only to put stop action on the cue ball the rest of the way, Slade made everything and set up for an angle shot on the eight. No chance for a scratch. He buried the ball, brushed his forehand across his forehead, and then smiled.

"You know what Yogi Berra always says," he said looking over at Smoke. "It ain't over 'til it's over."

"Bullshit!" Smoke retorted hotly, and he walked to the side and picked up his twenty. "That was an ugly ass setup if I ever seen one. Stick it where the sun don't shine, man – nobody hustles me!"

"What the HELL are you talking about, you skinny piece of crap?" Jeff said incredulously, stepping toward him. "YOU'RE the one who was trying to come over here and hustle US! You had the game won if you didn't screw up that last leave. Now he sticks it up YOUR ass and you can't take it? C'mon, man!"

"Fuck you!" Smoke said, but he didn't make a move toward Jeff. Something switched in Jeff's head, something nasty, and in a second he made a beeline at him. Slade saw it and at the last instant, caught Jeff before he got to Smoke, who had backed away.

"Take it easy, man – no need for any trouble," he said pushing Jeff back. "Just calm down a minute."

Slade paused a couple of seconds to be sure Jeff wasn't going to do anything. Then he turned to Smoke. Suddenly Slade was on him. He grabbed him by the collar, shoved him forward, and held him up against the wall. Jeff looked over at the Puerto Rican who remained seated.

"Now, are you gonna do the right thing," Slade said not raising his voice, "or am I going to take you out back and kick your ass all over that alley? 'Cause I got no problem doing it."

Smoke felt how strong Slade was and knew he meant business. He said nothing but dropped the twenty on the floor. Slade let him down and released him. Keeping his eyes straight on Smoke, Slade crouched down and picked up the money. The Puerto Rican then got up and stood but stayed out of it. Jeff remained where he was. Smoke got himself together and walked to the side, defeated. The whole thing happened so quickly that hardly anyone in the room paid it much notice.

"Let's go, Jeff," Slade said.

He picked up his own ante as Jeff got the balls together. But as they walked by, he paused, crumbled up Smoke's twenty, and threw it on the vacant table next to him. Slade stared back at him for a second but said nothing. Smoke didn't know what to think. Then Slade and Jeff paid their time and walked out to the street. Neither one looked back.

"What was THAT all about?" Jeff said as they headed back to the Y. "Why'd you toss that scumbag's money back on the table?"

"Well...first of all, the dough didn't mean anything to me," Slade answered. "I don't need that punk's money so long as I got mine back. I was going to take it but at the last second, I thought that would be like...the cliché thing to do, know what I mean? The cooler thing would be to throw it back – show him no respect at all – even his money's no good. He'll remember that."

"Yeah, but you won that dough fair and square, man," Jeff countered. "It was yours to take."

"I know. But there's this other thing that's always in the back of my mind too. I think you'll understand it. Ever hear of the western novel 'Shane'?"

"Huh? Shane? Hmm... Yeah, I know it was a movie with Alan Ladd in it but I never saw it. Didn't know it was a book too."

"It is – and a good one," Slade continued. "I had to read it in high school. It was just a short book but it blew me away. It was set in the old west sometime in the late 1800's. This guy Shane was a gunman trying to move on from his past, but situations always kept coming up where he had to hold himself back not to revert to what he'd been. Like he was trying to be a regular guy and put all those dudes he'd killed behind him, working as a ranch hand to help out a homesteader. But bad guys would challenge Shane and each time, he'd handle it in the classiest, coolest way – always taking the high road. Until the end of the book where he got even with everybody and they got what was coming to them. That was by far the coolest thing of all.

"I was really impressed. And the whole book was told by a kid in the story, the homesteader's son, who was only around 11 years old. Bob was his name and he was in awe of Shane, the ultimate quiet hero. From the time I read that book, I promised myself I'd remember Shane's approach whenever I got into a scrape. Leaving the twenty was something he'd definitely have done."

Jeff was fascinated. "Wow, you are some kind of thinker, Shotgun," he remarked. "Knowing you as I do now, I do kind of get it. I don't think

Smoke's going to change much, though. But you know, you didn't have to jump in. I was going to get right in his ugly face no matter what he said."

"I know, but It was my fight," Slade said as they neared the building that was home to them. "I was the guy he was trying to screw. Plus I saw that look in your eyes. It scared me a little. I didn't want us to get into a big jam right there in the pool room and have them bring in the heat – get us arrested on assault charges or something. I knew deep down that guy was a coward and he wouldn't stand up. It was just one of those split second reactions. The only thing that worried me in the back of my head is if he might have been packing a shank or even a small gun."

"Yeah, I never thought of that," Jeff said. "But that guy's just lucky you didn't take him out back and mow the grass with him. And you know what? You're right about that look. I've never said much about my...background, Shotgun. I don't like to talk about it. But I will tell you now that my brother Luke and me, we had a pretty rough time growing up. Somewhere along the line, I developed this thing – I guess maybe a trigger point. If I feel I'm getting screwed enough, I can snap - go off the rails. I got in trouble more than once because of it. But thank God I'm aware of it now and I can usually keep under control."

"I figured you'd seen some tough times," Slade said thoughtfully. "It's hard to hide that. Tell me a little about them if you want to. It'll give me a better idea where you're coming from."

"I will – but before I do, I'm still wondering about one thing from what just happened back there. Why did his buddy just stand by and do nothing?"

"The big guy?" Slade said. "That wasn't his buddy I don't think. I'd been to that place before you came into town. The Puerto Rican is sort of a bouncer there and was just playing a game of pool with Smoke. I'm pretty sure of it. I'd seen him with other people and talked to him a few times. I know he remembered me and he's a pretty good guy. He didn't see any need to do anything."

"Good for us. He was a large human being."

"Oh – and one final thing," Slade said. "Your line about – what was it – 'now he sticks it up your ass and you can't take it?' That was a classic, man. I'd have died laughing if things weren't so heated at the time." They both had a good laugh.

"But what gets lost in the shuffle is what you pulled off in that game!" Jeff exclaimed. "He had you on the ropes and you knocked him out with one last flurry. That was awesome, man."

"I looked at the leave and I knew I could do it," Slade said. "I just had to keep my focus and not get ahead of myself. And with the way the situation was, you can't imagine the high I felt when I made that last ball. I love it when it's all on the line. It was definitely special."

"I won't forget it." Jeff agreed.

For the rest of the walk and for a few minutes outside the Y building, Jeff filled Slade in a little on his past. He didn't go into any great detail and Slade mainly listened, making no judgements or suggestions. But when he finished, Jeff felt a small load come off of his shoulders.

23.

Back in April, several weeks after he came into town, inspired by Slade's guitar playing, Jeff took a walk down to a nearby music store to look for an instrument of his own. The owner of the business, Johnny Goodrich, was an accomplished guitarist. He took a liking to Jeff right away. After Jeff told him he was a beginner, Johnny went in back and got a used Guild folk guitar for him to look at. It was in good condition and concert sized to make it easy to handle. The instrument was strung with light gauge strings; easy on the fingers for somebody just starting out.

"This little girl will be perfect for you," he said. "I did a setup on it the other day and everything came out spot on. She practically plays herself."

Johnny played a few arpeggios. Then he plucked a chord and melody solo, finger style, which traveled all over the neck. It demonstrated the guitar's good intonation and resonance, plus Johnny's virtuosity. Jeff was impressed. He fell in love with it right then and there.

"How much?" he said.

"You can have it for 40 dollars." Johnny said. "This guitar sold for a buck twenty five when it was new. And I'll throw in a soft case and a chord book for nothing – plus half a dozen picks."

"Deal," Jeff said." It was about what he planned to spend, but he was getting a much better instrument than he figured on. "Where'd you learn to play like that?" he asked.

"He's been playing since he was nine years old." It was Johnny's wife Shira, slim and arty looking, who had just walked out from the back room. "When Johnny was a teenager, he used to sleep with his guitar next to him!"

"Really?" Jeff said.

"She speaks the truth - I was a guitar geek," Johnny laughed. "No doubt about it. I even became a jazz snob for a time. Joe Pass and Wes Montgomery were my heroes. Today, it's the English guitarist, John McLaughlin who blows me away the most. Many years of lessons, bands, and a lifetime of teaching. Best thing I ever did was to pick up a guitar...check that, second best thing." He looked over at Shira and they shared a laugh.

Johnny slid the guitar into the case and got the other items together in a bag. He and Jeff made the transaction and they shook hands.

"I have some good teachers downstairs in the dungeon if you're ever interested in lessons," Johnny suggested.

"I'll keep it in mind. But I have a friend who plays really well. He said he'd get me started."

"Sure thing," Johnny said, "but let me say this and I'm serious. This is a special day for you, son. It's the beginning of a beautiful relationship."

"I hope it is."

Both he and Shira smiled at him. Jeff gratefully thanked them. He felt a warm glow as he walked out of the store carrying his first guitar.

Back at the Y, he showed it to Slade, who spun it through a few scales and modes and then played a couple of pieces. He gave it his seal of approval and showed Jeff how to tune it.

"Fool around with that chord book for a few days," he said. "I'll check a few off for you to work on. When you get comfortable, we'll start with some lessons."

The next night at work, Rails got wind of the situation while shooting the breeze with Jeff and Slade. "I have a guitar that was given to me," he said. "Hardly ever tried to play it and it sits in a closet in my apartment. Any chance I can join in on the lessons, Shotgun?"

"Of course you can," Slade said. "Just take it to the shop first and have it adjusted so that we're sure the thing is playable. It's always cool to turn people on to guitar – I consider it my mission in life. Especially good people like you two cats. You know what Eric Burdon says, don't you, Rails?"

"No – what does Eric Burdon say?"

"You want to find the truth in life? Don't pass music by."

"Heavy stuff," Jeff remarked.

They agreed to meet for an hour on Saturdays in Slade's room at around 5 PM. It became a regular thing. It went well for both Jeff and Rails, who had similar talent levels. Both were interested and practiced faithfully. Several times they offered to pay Slade for the lessons but he wouldn't hear of it.

Slade was a patient and thorough teacher. He made sure they were solid on the basics before he moved them ahead. In a short time, they each knew a major scale pattern and five chords. Jeff and Rails were thrilled with their progress. Jeff was further dazzled the first time he made it through "Knockin' on Heaven's Door" without having to stop.

Rails was a natural gatherer of information. Like Slade, when he took on something new, he tried to learn everything he could about it. He went to the library and took out a few books on the guitar. Rails read up on the history of the instrument and influential performers. He also became interested in Slade's development as a player.

"How'd you get into it, Shotgun?" he asked at the close of a lesson.

"My mom started me out on accordion when I was 11," Slade began. "I studied that for a couple of years with a teacher – a nice older guy – and I learned how to sight read music pretty well. But I began to notice that

89

there weren't any accordion players in rock and roll bands. And he had me playing polkas like I was in training for the Lawrence Welk show or something. It just wasn't cool, you know? And I got some ribbing from my friends too. One day I just stopped – told my parents that either they get me a guitar or I was done with music."

"And?"

"They got me a Fender Bullet the next week – nice little axe. And they hooked me up with Nick Beshekis, this cool young dude who had a degree in performance from Berklee College of Music up in Boston. He had a jazz background and I soaked everything up like a sponge. He taught me some theory and how to read a jazz chart – helped me a lot with learning basic composition. I was with him for three and a half years 'til junior year in high school when I got recruited into a garage band and started doing weekend gigs. Nick was a big influence on me."

"Groovy, man. What was the name of the band?" Jeff asked.

"Night Hawk. It fit us. We were pretty edgy and did about half original stuff. I wrote some of it. But in every gig we did, we always started off with our cover of 'Jenny take a Ride' by Mitch Ryder and the Detroit Wheels."

"Why that song?" Rails asked.

"'Cause it kicks ass, man, why else?" Slade laughed. "We had a hell of a time – I'm really glad I had that experience. I played with Night Hawk right up until when I hit the road in 1966."

"That's pretty cool," Rails said. "You know what, Shotgun? I've been doing a lot of reading on guitars and the history of the instrument. Ever hear of a guy named Andres Segovia?"

"Sure – he was the father of classical guitar," Slade answered. "What about him?"

"Well, I was boning up on Segovia and what a big influence he was in getting the guitar taken seriously as a solo instrument. He made an interesting observation that I know you'll both like."

"Hit us with it," Jeff said.

"I haven't committed it to memory yet, but I have it right here," Rails said. He fished a note pad out of his pocket and flipped through it. "Okay, I got it. Here goes. 'You know, the guitar has feminine curves, and this influences her behavior. Sometimes it is impossible to deal with her, but most of the time she is very sweet — and if you caress her properly, she will sing very beautifully.'"

"That's pretty nice," Jeff said.

"The man definitely had some insight," Rails concluded. They all smiled and nodded.

"Tell you what," Slade added. "That line rings a bell. Where did I read it, now? I think it was in 'The Catcher in the Rye' senior year in high school. Great book. A line something like, 'A woman's body is like a violin, and it takes a terrific musician to play it right.' Similar idea, huh?"

"Yeah, sure is," Rails agreed. "But you know, there IS one thing. The flower child hippie girls would have no problem with those observations. But that stuff was said way before the woman's movement — feminism. It's coming on strong, man. Today, some women may see it as like — objectifying them. Dig?"

"I do see it," Jeff agreed.

"Maybe so," Slade said. "But I really think that those blurbs were meant in the best way — you know - to celebrate the beauty and complexity of a woman more than putting them out there as sex objects. That's the bottom line I figure."

"Leave it to Shotgun to tie it all up onto a nice neat package," Rails smiled. "Well said, buddy."

"You know what?" Jeff said snapping his fingers. "It just came to me — I remember this line in a blues song I heard on the radio the other night. Something like, 'the highway is like a woman — soft shoulders and dangerous curves.' The guy just kept singing it over and over again."

"That might be the best one of all!" Slade laughed.

24.

In the weeks that followed the pool room jam, Jeff didn't go out a whole lot. He took it easy in his spare time and just hung out and relaxed at the Y, which had become more and more like home. Sometimes he watched television or read in the TV room, in the company of boarders or people off the streets. Many times Slade, Creecher, or others he'd come to know were there to keep him company. Once In a while, bums like Barney Ebersol found their way in, and they were always given relief and treated kindly. Jeff would sit back in his easy chair and think that at least guys like that had someplace to go when things got too tough on the streets.

Observing scenes like that, it sometimes crossed his mind that they might be somehow connected to that concept of "it" that Slade and Rails talked up. Maybe a small part of "it". The YMCA was a relief stop for the downtrodden. Jeff wasn't a drunk but he had his issues, and it had given him safe haven too. Everybody had different baggage but still they all fit in; there was a common thread that ran through all of them. Some even talked about it. They all got along well. There were never any fights or trouble. Misery loves company? No, not that, Jeff thought. Just something more than that. Compassion, kindness..."it".

Most every night before work, Jeff ran a couple of miles on the track that hung on the next level over the gym. Slade often joined him. Jeff also lifted regularly in the adjoining weight room for 15 or 20 minutes after. He had established a regular routine and gained some weight since his arrival at Stiller

Jeff learned long ago that being in good shape helped him handle things better. The vibe; the repetitive thump, thump, thump of sneakers pounding the floor as the laps piled up seemed to fuel strength within him.

In the weight room, Jeff usually did repetition lifting to try to work all the muscle groups. "Strong mind, body, and spirit"; he'd heard that so many times in 12-step meetings. It had taken hold.

There was a short muscular man around 30 years old in there often who Jeff came to recognize. He worked out on the weights as if it was the most important thing in the world. The man always said hello and gave Jeff a friendly smile. This guy lifted, squatted, and sweated hard. He was pretty ripped. It was as if he was working the toughest problems in his life, back and forth, up and down, through the weights. He was rugged and strong jawed. One night, he approached Jeff while he was resting on an incline board.

"Hey, what's happenin'?" he said toweling sweat off his brow. "I see you putting in the laps pretty regular and lifting too – getting in good shape huh? Best thing there is."

"I try my best," Jeff said sitting up on the board.

"Mickey – Mickey Bantom," the man said extending his hand and shaking firmly.

"Jeff Jones – glad to know you."

Mickey took the next incline board and did sets of leg raises with deep inhales and exhales. Jeff continued with his crunches and rest periods. In between, they talked a little. Like most of the boarders at the Y, Mickey went into a little soliloquy about how he landed there.

"I'll make a long story short, Jeff," he said, catching his breath and looking to the ceiling. "Dumb ass that I am, I got married at 19 – had to - didn't have a friggin clue what I was doing. Got my girl in trouble and you know how things were then. You had to get married or face a firing squad. Anyway, of course, I wasn't in love with her, nor her with me. But I guess I was horny, man – and STOOPID too. We had the kid and I got her pregnant again not long after!"

"Oh wow," Jeff said. "Talk about being stuck in the mud."

"You frickin said it. So, of course we couldn't cut it, and after ten years of pure misery, we got a divorce. Now I have a son and a daughter who I don't see as much as I'd like to, but at least I do have regular visitation. But you know, it's all for the best, Jeff, cuz all my ex-wife and I did was fight. Things are smoother now that we're not together and we get along a lot better. And I support my kids. I have to admit that she's a good mother too, thank God. Hey – I'm grateful for my kids. Things aren't so bad."

"Right on," Jeff said. "Seems like a lot of the guys who live at this place here have stories like yours, Mickey."

"Oh yeah – everybody has their tale of woe. If you have it all together, then you don't live here, man."

Jeff smiled. "True, but like a lot of the guys I talk to, you have a good attitude. That's something I've kind of learned along the way. No matter what happens today, tomorrow is a new beginning."

Mickey paused a few seconds and then smiled broadly. "Tomorrow's a new beginning – that's beautiful. Did you think that up yourself, Jeff?"

"Nah - I must have heard it somewhere. I'm not too good at coining phrases." They shared a laugh.

"Well," Mickey said. "I've been here since not long after she threw me out head first – and there's worse places to be. Cheap living so I can afford my child support – that's the main thing. Last thing I want to be is a deadbeat dad. And I can work out every night. Keeps me strong and gets me too tired to worry. I sleep like a brick every night."

"As you should, man – as you should."

25.

Time moved on into late June. At work, the heat became more oppressive as summer took a firm hold. Many of the mill workers took salt tablets to better cope with it. And No Doz if they had trouble staying awake through the shift's end. The place was like a sweltering prison on some nights.

And when those shifts ended and quitting time came, it was go home, have a little something to eat, and then try to get some sleep. Shades drawn tightly, blankets tacked over them, fans turning, and phones off the hook. Five or six hours of sleep if they were lucky, then getting up and never feeling fully rested. Nobody on third shift was ever 100 %. That's just the way it was. Accept it or move on.

Rails was keenly aware of this reality. He described it in his journals along with many other mill observations. He wrote spontaneous entries on how the long time mill workers went about coping with their lot; painted them with their words, postures, expressions, and attitudes. Rails sometimes referred to them as mill rats or lint heads as a group, terms that had been used for many years. He included himself as one of them. The names weren't meant to be insulting. They were just the truth as he observed it. The people were grinding out a living in a tough environment, the same as rats do in a junk yard or a subway pit. Doing what they had to do.

On a Tuesday night, Rails, Slade, and Jeff, were eating lunch away from the cafeteria. They sat on the big tubs of yarn stacked below the ramp in an open area. Beans, cap angled low and a smoldering cigarette in the side of his mouth as usual, wandered over and joined them. Jeff noticed that his face was scratched.

"Get in a fight with a mountain lion, buddy?" he asked.

"Nooo...nobody likes a smart guy, Jeff," Beans answered with a smirk.

"Well, then tell us the truth." Rails smiled. "Unload, my man - you'll feel better."

"I don't know why I hang with you guys, especially YOU, Railsback," Beans said sarcastically looking over at him. "There's gotta be SOMETHING better. Okay – I'll tell yah what happened – just don't laugh too hard."

"Can't promise you that."

Beans frowned at him. "Well, now I shouldn't after that snide remark...but I'll tell yah's anyways. I was sitting in my chair at home, see, and the dog wanted to play. I got a big dog who is a psycho. He jumped up on me – and got a little too – what's the word – rambunkshis?"

"And he scratched your face?" Slade said.

"Correct. Now my wise-ass brother in law, Todd Morley - he stopped by the house about an hour after it happened. He asked about my face and I told him what the dog did. And what do you think that joker said to me?"

"I'm afraid to ask."

"He says, 'next time you bang the dog, Beans, face him away from you.'"

There was a second of silence, then whooping laughter from everybody.

"Hoo hoo hoo hoo – that's nasty!" Rails exclaimed catching his breath. "He thought of a great line like that right on the spot? That guy's quick, man."

"He is," Beans agreed. "Actually, Todd's a good egg - a retired prison guard. He's seen it and heard it all in his 20 years in the big hotel. And that Todd - he can talk – a very convincing dude. He could talk a seagull off a french fry."

"Not many people can do that," Jeff chuckled. "Well, give that man our compliments."

"I certainly will...like hell I will!"

"John Wayne would like that line," Rails added. "But allow me to change the subject if I can be so bold. I have something on my mind. Beans, you've been here a long long time. What's the deal with the average...you know – your basic mill rat?"

"Huh? Well I ain't seen any up here," Beans replied. "But last week I saw a big one downstairs in the dye room."

"No, no bud – I mean the people. You know the term - the committed workers here. Like once you're in this place awhile, you're a mill rat I figure. Myself, Jeff and Shotgun – maybe we're rookies, but we're all rats just like you are so long as we're here. But you're a long timer, Beans my man. It's in your bones – the way you stand – the way you walk – everything about you."

"You're an odd dude, Railsback," Beans said looking at him quizzically. "Maybe that ain't a strong enough word."

Slade smiled and thought for a few seconds. "I think I know what Steve means, Beans." he said. "Jeff and I talked about this a little before - I mean people being wired into a lifestyle until they retire or die."

"That idea has occurred to me more than once," Jeff agreed. "It scares me a little."

"It's probably not so bad for guys like us three," Slade continued, "because we know we're not here for good, at least we hope not. But you,

96

Beans – what's it been – 15 or so years? Do you figure this is it? I know a lot of the others – the true mill rats – the factory drones – they know it deep down. I'd look just like they do if I came in every night and knew this was it for me."

"Okay, wait a minute. Just remember this," Beans said turning serious. "You guys are young. When you get older, you'll see things different and you'll look different too. Think I looked like this 20 years ago? Me? I look at it this way. I got a steady job that gives me enough dough to eat and live pretty decent. Me and my wife raised our daughter on it. Somewhere along the line, I had to accept what I was and make the best of it. You settle – that's all there is to it. Everybody hopes for something better and you never want to give that up, but you settle. Everybody's got to settle. Your day will come."

Rails nodded and pointed his finger at Beans. "That's one of the most thoughtful things I've ever heard you say. I can dig that. But it seems to come on so fast. Maybe you're young like us – and you're thinking that in time, you'll move on to what you really want to do – if you can figure out what that is. But before you know it, if you don't act, the years have gotten behind you and it's too late. You're stuck in quicksand."

"I have definitely thought about that too," Jeff said nodding his head. "Yeah, the quicksand deal."

"It's a fair point," Beans conceded. "But a lot of these people here – I don't think it much crosses their minds, me included. They are what they are. They live their lives. They don't think too much. Thinking can get you in big trouble. You know that, right, Jeff? Maybe they know it too."

"Could be, Beans," Slade said. "Brings to mind something my grandfather – Pop - used to talk about. He'd say something like, that as some people get older, whatever dreams they have drop off one by one. They lose their drive to take risks and go out less and less until they just stay home, sit and look back. And one day it's all gone by like they were standing still."

"Just like we've been saying," Rails noted.

"But on the flip side," Slade countered, "he'd tell me, others reject that. They continue to try new things and keep getting off the mat if they don't work out. They never stop trying. And even if they find themselves in that situation where they have to give up and go another way, they know they tried, and that gives them peace. 'Always fight that urge to give in, Tom –

97

fight it as long as you live,' he'd say. Pop lives like that. It made an impression on me."

"Wow – that's pretty good," Rails said.

"Yes, Pop is a groovy dude," Slade added. "Full of wisdom and sage advice. And one other thing he told me that's always stuck with me. 'Tom,' he said, 'nothing can ever kill your spirit – unless you let it.'"

"Man, that's deep," Jeff marveled. "It's gonna stick in my mind like glue."

"Profound for sure," Rails agreed. Then he pointed out to the floor. "Now, consider Simone walking out there back to the machines." he said with emphasis. "I'll bet she was pretty good looking back in the day. If you look closely enough and imagine hard, you can still see it. But here she is now, bent over and all wrinkled up - getting more crooked every night – locked into it because it's all she knows. It's not like most of the mill rats ever had much of a choice, though. A lot of them were just born into it. Maybe sort of programmed to be here."

"Yeah – it's an interesting thing to think about," Slade said. "You're a pretty keen observer, Steve."

"But way over the top," Beans added firmly.

"Jesus, I hope Lynne doesn't end up like that," Jeff said shaking his head.

"That would be a terrible waste," Rails said leaning back and wiping a little sweat from his nose. "But I don't think so. Lynne's got too much on the ball. She'll find a way out of here.

"So...to sum it up, I figure many of these mill rats never had much of a chance even while they were young and hopeful for something better. Never clued in on the bigger picture – the broader deal, man. It's a cycle that just keeps on repeating, generation after generation."

"Railsback, you make it WAY too complicated," Beans cut in. "When it's all said and done, who gives a flying...you know what. My wife is on me to stop cursing. Just live, dude, LIVE! You can, what...analyze stuff until you go nuts. And there's one thing you guys can't see now but you'll understand when you get to be my age. Life ain't black and white – its grey – GREY! Once you get that, things go along a lot smoother. You don't expect everything to go perfect all the time."

Jeff could only tilt his head up and consider what he was hearing. He couldn't come up with a thing to add but he was impressed with Beans' wisdom. It surprised him. The conversation stoked his thoughts.

"Old Beans has got something there," Slade said. "It's all in how you look at stuff – what attitude you take. And to put it another way, you can always say…no matter how bad things get, they can always be worse."

"Oh, that gives me a ton of hope," Jeff deadpanned from his silence. They all laughed.

"Just a little levity to break the tension," Slade said catching his breath. "But it's not their fault – the people - that they get stuck. Just reality, man. Beans, you're in a different place than us. Hopefully we can learn from you and understand the deal better as younger guys just starting out. We can look at it from the outside, chalk up the experience, and then move ahead and beyond it. It's just up to us. It's a free country – you can always do better if you want to work at it."

"This is true," Beans nodded, moving down to sit on a lower tub. "But there's no shame in the people out there on that floor who's locked in like you say, Shotgun. And for sure, I'm one of 'em. They're making a damn living, staying off the dole and keeping clear of trouble. I respect anybody who works. Nobody should ever be ashamed to do any job."

Rails looked up and scratched his neck. "You both speak the truth," he said. "But it's never easy to accept when we see it live night after night with some of the wasted older crew, present company excluded. Beans. You're not wasted – at least not yet – you're just short. It like moves me, though. That's why I write about it. There's something compelling in them that just hits me – like they're tragic heroes in their own obscurity. Get it?"

"I think now you're getting a little too deep for me," Beans scoffed. "'ObSKEWwrity? I don't even know what that means. We're in a factory, Railsback – not a lecture hall. And I know I'm short – I don't need YOU to remind me."

"Sorry, man - just yanking your chain a little. I know you can take a jab or two. Time for us to get back out to the floor anyway. Good conversation, boys. Don't be surprised if some of it shows up in my writing."

"God help us," Beans said wryly. "And just remember this in your book. Life has a board for every behind, yours included!"

Beans looked up at Rails and grinned impishly. Rails chuckled, got out his note pad, and jotted down that remark. The others also got a rise out of it as they got up to go back on the floor. Then, as he began to get off the tub he'd moved to, Beans felt something shift underneath him. The box had already been partially opened.

"What the fuh...HOLY HELL!" he yelled as he jumped off as if he was on fire. He fell on the floor but scrambled quickly to his feet. "There's something ALIVE in there – and it's big. So help me God, I felt it move!"

Jeff stepped back. Rails and Slade, who had taken a few steps toward the ramp, stopped and turned around.

"What is it?" Slade said. "What's the matter, bud?"

Now a distance away, Beans wiped his forehead and collected himself. "In there – in that tub," he said. "Something alive – might even have tried to nip my ass – I swear it!"

Slade grabbed a broom and approached the tub cautiously. He reached out with it and slowly turned up the flap. There WAS something thick and black against the white of the spools. Then a rumble, spools falling, and there it was. Out of the box, it fell to the floor, coiled up and faced them.

"My God!" Jeff yelled. "That's the biggest snake I've ever seen - it's got to be ten feet long!"

"Okay – easy guys," Slade said. "I'll hold it off with the broom – just be calm. Somebody go and find Sam."

Jeff took off to look for him. Rails grabbed another broom from against the wall and doubled up with Slade. Beans stood off to the side, frozen.

"Shotgun!" Rails exclaimed. "That yarn is from Brazil – and so is the snake - a stowaway. Could be some kind of Amazon snake - a constrictor or even poisonous. We've got to be really be careful."

"I know – I know," Slade said as the snake made a strike at his broom. "WOW!" he yelled, "that sacred the crap outah me. Easy – easy fellah."

100

"It's just protecting itself, at least I hope," Rails said. "Probably it's scared and not out to hurt us. Let's just keep it tied up here 'til Jeff gets back with the boss."

"Right."

Jeff returned with Sam, who took one look at the snake, whitened, and fainted. Jeff caught him before he hit the floor.

The snake saw that and became more agitated with the confusion. It landed a hard shot into Rails' broom. That jolted the hell out of him. Ed Collins heard the ruckus from the floor and got on the scene.

"Damn!" Slade yelled. "On top of all this, our boss has to lose it. Jeff – get Sam over to the office and dowse him with water or something."

Sam revived groggily and Jeff helped him away. Ed picked up a spool that had rolled near him and gunned it at the snake, just grazing it. He didn't think. He just did it. The snake then charged at them and everybody was in full retreat, brooms flying. Now there was a group watching from atop the ramp and a couple of the women screamed and ran.

But of all people, the snake took off in Beans' direction. It cornered him to the fire escape door, which Slade had opened for air when they first came over. Beans tripped on the stoop and fell to the iron grates. The snake slithered right by him and dropped clear over the edge four stories to the river shore. It was over.

Slade and Rails ran out to Beans who hadn't yet moved, whose hands were melded into the steel. Others came over and stood by the door.

"Beans – Beans – you okay!" Slade said. "Did it bite you?"

He could only shake his head no as they helped him up and walked him back in the building. The adrenaline rush was too much for him. Finally he managed a few words.

"When that thing came at me..." he said voice shaking, "it was like my life was passing before my eyes. It was worse than when I hooked that stiff in the river."

That line cut the tension and everybody around them laughed.

"The whole thing happened so damn fast!" Rails said. "One minute we're having a quiet talk and the next were face to face with something really dangerous. Unbelievable! You just never know."

"Curtis from downstairs told me about a snake they found in a yarn box last year," Ed said. "It was dead and nowhere near as big as that one. But if you think about it, a snake like that can go for a month or more without eating or drinking. It's not that big of a surprise we got a live one."

"And why the hell did you throw that spool, Ed?" Slade asked. "You almost got the poor bean man killed."

"Yeah – what the hell was you thinking, Collins?" Beans demanded.

"I had the best of intentions, Beans – you know that. Sometimes you just react and it ain't the right move. I'm really sorry – but I'm glad you're okay."

"Forget about it, kid – no harm done in the end. So long as I don't stroke out later."

Back in the office, Jeff was taking care of Sam, who had recovered. He explained that he'd been sick the past few days. He felt that when he saw the snake his blood pressure took a dive. This type of thing had happened to him before when excited by something. Dina checked in and told them what happened after Sam blacked out. Within an hour, everything was back to normal.

For the next few days, it was the big story on all three shifts. The principal participants did their best to handle the 15 minutes of fame and were asked many questions. They also took some heavy needling for high tailing it when the snake charged. Poor Beans was hounded at every turn. But they all laughed right along with the jabs. Nobody was hurt and all was okay in the end. Ultimately, something different and exciting happened to break the monotony and boredom of the third shift. The mill workers savored it and held on to it for as long as they could.

26

Although it was due to a physical condition, Sam Burnside was more than a little embarrassed over his fainting spell. He did his best to stay low until it blew over, which took some time. A few workers took advantage of him not being around as much while things were still hot. One in particular was Ravi Mohan. He took the opportunity to create his own personal job.

An older college student from India at 29, Ravi had a tough engineering summer course load. On many nights, he came in wasted from studying, labs, and sleep deprivation. He was next to useless. Ravi was short and pudgy, balding, wore horn rimmed glasses, walked kind of bent over, and looked a lot older than his age. He was a funny looking character even when he was rested and right.

Some wondered how he got by in college since his English was broken and he had a hard time understanding instructions. He'd look bewildered and it seemed that any job was too much for him. But others knew better. Ravi had an angle. Play dumb and ignorant, but do just enough to not get fired. He had it all figured out.

Sam tried hard to get him up to speed as a creeler as had the previous boss, but he was slow and clumsy. None of the knitters wanted to be saddled with him since he lost them money. One night there was an incident with one in particular and Ravi was done as a creeler. So on each shift following that, Sam found odd jobs for him easy enough not to screw up. But after the night of the snake incident, the boss lost patience and didn't want to be bothered with Ravi for a while. "Get a broom and keep the floor clean for the time being, Ravi," Sam told him, "'til I think of something else for you to do."

And that's what happened from that moment on. All Ravi did was sweep lint buildup, night after night after night. He actually did a good job and Sam figured at least he was doing something positive. So he let it go and Ravi became the permanent night sweeper – PNS as Slade named him after watching the movie "No Time for Sergeants" - with a few cat naps in between. Everybody was happy.

But an unexpected side benefit that came out of the arrangement was comic relief for the night crew. The workers would watch Ravi pass up and down the aisles in his nightly sweeping routine, doing figure eights in and around the machines like a streetwalker in a daze, and walking a short-stepping waddle like Wimpy of the Popeye cartoons. Nobody gave him a hard time, but Ravi Mohan provided them with a good chuckle most every time he passed by.

27.

In the days that followed, Jeff thought about the mill rat discussion from time to time. Regardless of the points that were made, more than once it occurred to him that everything in life might be predetermined and there was nothing you could do about it. Even reincarnation crossed his mind. Maybe they'd all done wrong in a previous life and this was payback. He still was prone to sometimes going sideways on crazy tangents.

But something he saw watching television with a few others out front one night really got his wheels spinning. It was a PBS show that contrasted the lifestyles of different animals with humans. It focused on getting a steady food source, establishing territory, and procreation; how it all boiled down to the same things for humans too only at a higher level. The animals lived day to day, did what they had to do to keep alive, got old if they survived what confronted them, and finally died. On automatic? Just like the long time mill rats as he'd thought about before? He wondered about that.

The program went on to show a thousand or so male penguins on a vast Antarctic expanse of ice, which they claimed as breeding grounds since no predators save for leopard seals could stand the conditions. They stood like frozen statues, each over a single egg its mate had laid before going to sea for a couple of months to fatten up. Nailed to their spots in the blurring fury of a blizzard; maybe moving only a step or two every hour, with the eggs remaining warm underneath.

If they left their eggs even for a couple of seconds, the developing chicks inside would freeze to death. No food until the females returned. Just

104

standing there, days and nights on end. They reached deeply within themselves and faced it because that was how it was. Survive it or die, along with the next generation. For a few seconds, Jeff focused on a single penguin in a throng of stiff-standing bodies. It was him. Once again he felt worthless. He was nothing. He was going nowhere. His life was a joke. It meant zero.

But again, he snapped out if it quicker than he used to. Since he'd come into Stiller, befriended Tom Slade and the others at Warburton and at the Y, downers like these had lessened. They didn't control him like they once did. With the help of this new support group, he'd learned how to accept and handle them as part of his "stuff". Everybody had their stuff. A state of restlessness and a new confidence was beginning to take hold in Jeff Jones. The time was coming to break out of the old mold and move on - to something exciting and brand new.

28.

The July fourth weekend was coming up and with it, Lynne's party at Wells Beach. She, along with Jeff, Slade and her creeler Melissa, made plans to drive up in Lynne's car. Melissa, or Missy as most knew her, was a tall willowy girl, not beautiful but there was something innocent and genuine about her.

Lynne's friends rented a cottage close to the beach for a couple of weeks. Neither Jeff nor Slade ever visited Wells Beach before. Both looked forward getting out of Stiller for a day or two. The group decided to leave right after work on Saturday morning and sleep for a few hours during the day at the cottage. Lynne arranged for this with her friend Jessica. That way, they at least could be awake to later see the area and not be nodding off at the party.

Lynne made plans with Jessica for them to stay over one or two nights. Jeff told Lynne beforehand that he only wanted to stay the one night and return on Sunday. He didn't like having to work the next day right after a trip, particularly if he got back late. It took him time to get settled again especially with the screwy sleeping hours. Slade agreed and Jeff added there was no pressure for her to take them back if she and Melissa wanted to stay another day. It was a straight shot hitchhiking back to Stiller and would be no trouble. Lynne understood and everybody was on board.

Saturday arrived and with it the end of the work night. The early morning sun danced on the hood of Lynne's Chevy Bel Air as she, Slade and Jeff approached it. Lynne carried with her a cooler containing sandwiches and cans of soda that she'd stored in the fourth floor refrigerator.

"Well, boys," Lynne said, "Let's go places and eat things."

They stopped beside the car and Jeff tapped her on the shoulder. "Was that a Three Stooges line I just heard from you or did I not hear right?" he asked.

"Of course it was," she smiled. "I think I've seen just about every episode they ever did. I always quote them."

"Let me get this straight. You're a girl and you like the Three Stooges?"

"Sure – what's the big deal?"

"Oh, nothing," Jeff answered. "Only that you're the first female person I've ever come across in my LIFE that likes the Three Stooges. I'm stunned."

"Jeff, I think we've stumbled on the perfect woman," Slade added.

Lynne loved it. She grabbed them both and they all had a good laugh.

"Hey, by the way," Jeff said. "Where's Missy? Isn't she coming with us?"

"Oh – about Melissa. I forgot to tell you," Lynne answered tapping her head. "She backed out last night. You guys know how shy she is – and Missy's only just 19 and still lives at home. She told me her father wasn't too crazy about the idea and put the kibosh on it."

"I can understand that."

"Too bad," Slade remarked. "Missy's a good kid. We'd have looked after her. But you never know at a party – a lot of people are going to be loaded, I expect. Probably it's for the best."

"I think so," Lynne agreed. "And if anything happened, they'd probably blame me. I have enough drama in my life as it is."

They laughed as Jeff and Slade threw their gear in the trunk. It took them a few tries to get it to shut. Lynne's Chevy was an older car and many things were finicky in it.

"Who wants to drive?" Lynne said. "I'm a lady – ladies get driven."

"I'll be glad to take the helm," Slade said. "Haven't been behind the wheel for a while. I've missed it."

Lynne placed the cooler on the floor in the back. They all sat in front on the bench, Lynne in the middle. She wore a yellow sleeveless t-shirt with cut-off jeans and sandals. As the car gained speed, her blond hair flowed gently around her neck in the breeze from the vents. Jeff couldn't help but admire her from the side.

"Glad you guys agreed to come along," she said with a smile. "Especially you, Jeff – sometimes you're a tough nut to crack. But I think you'll both have a good time. Wells is a nice place – a long clean beach – lots of people from all over New England and even Canada. Just a cool scene all around."

"I'm hip," Jeff said. "If nothing else, we escape the sweat box for a couple of days."

"Roger that," Slade agreed.

As they traveled along the highway, Slade looked all around and took in the scenery. With no car, he realized he hadn't really been far out of Stiller for several months. It did feel good to be out on the road and moving again. The stripes rolled on, a lazy breeze rustled the trees, and the sun massaged the landscape. Jeff and Lynne stretched out and relaxed. And for both Slade and Jeff, having an attractive young woman sitting between them added a little extra to the atmosphere.

It was only 90 or so miles up the coast from Stiller to Wells. Still, it further fueled an "urge for going". That was something Slade had begun to feel a month or two earlier, and Jeff more recently after the dream about the penguins. The whole idea was gaining strength; to move on to a new a new chapter.

Slade had gotten a copy of "On the Road" not long after Rails encouraged him to. He finished it and was reading it again. He was impressed by the book; the perpetual go – go – go, the energy, the power, at times the hope, and the outright coolness of experiencing that "huge raw bulge" that is America as only Jack Kerouac could describe it.

A similar trip was taking firmer hold in his mind. Not just him alone, but Jeff too, and hopefully Rails and Ed Collins as he had mentioned to them before. A foursome of destiny is what he felt it would be. But he had to think about it more and work out all the details before presenting it to them. Tom Slade didn't fly by the seat of his pants. He liked to be prepared for everything from every angle.

There were a few minutes of silence as they moved into New Hampshire. "Sheesh, it got awful quiet all of a sudden in here," Lynne remarked. "Are you guys in deep thought or something?"

"Yes," Jeff said. "We're working out all the problems of the world."

"Well, that's not MY bag," she laughed. "Do you mind if I borrow your shoulder, Jeff?"

"It's all yours."

She snuggled against him and closed her eyes. "I'm going to take a little nap maybe – or at least rest my dreamy eyes."

Slade took a peek to his right and nodded. Jeff smiled and looked ahead. In the past, he thought he might have picked up a vibe or two from Lynne every so often. There were times when their eyes locked for a second too long. Often she touched him when making a joke or a remark. But he always passed it off as no big deal. Now, at this moment, Jeff felt as if he'd died and gone to heaven. There HAD been something to it. A warm glow passed through him, head to toe.

29

Across the long bridge, over the Piscataqua Tidal River and into the state of Maine, they breathed in the salty air of the ocean water. It was like a B-12 shot. **WELCOME TO MAINE – VACATION LAND** the sign said. They travelled along Route 1 North through Kittery and into York. They drove by the York Corner Gardens farm stand, with colorful crates of fruit and vegetables on display out front. Further on, motels and cabin rentals hugged the roadside here and there, plus a couple of clam shacks. Tanned teens on bicycles and motor scooters rode the shoulders to a day on the beach. The three passed by the Ogunquit Summer Playhouse, a stately white building with green shutters surrounded by immaculate grounds and rows of neatly trimmed shrubs. The marquee out in front said:

NOW PLAYING

BYE-BYE-BIRDIE

STARRING BETSY PALMER

"That looks like a happening place," Jeff said. "Betsy Palmer's a pretty big name in show biz."

"Right," Slade agreed. "I've seen her many times on 'What's My Line'. That playhouse is well known across the country. Actors and actresses do summer theater there to keep their chops up. A guy I knew in high school saw Lloyd Bridges in a play there once. And he said he even met him and his son Jeff down at the beach. Plays are a lot more demanding than movies, you know. It's live on stage – you don't get to do retakes."

"Really?" Lynne said opening her eyes and looking out the window. "I've never seen a play but I guess you're right, Tom. They must rehearse it 'til their blue in the face, but they only get that one shot."

"Oh – they goof up, no doubt," Jeff commented. "Nobody can get all those lines perfect. But they adlib through it and nobody in the audience even knows the difference."

"Still amazes me how they memorize all that material," Lynne said.

"True, but it's their job," Slade added. "They have to be prepared or else. And if the play has a long run, they might do it every day for a month or two – sometimes twice a day. Probably it becomes routine."

"You guys have a lot of knowledge about different things," Lynne remarked.

"If it can't make you any money, then I know something about it," Jeff laughed.

They slowed and came into the center of the Ogunquit village. At a four way intersection, they sat at a red light.

"How about if we take a right and go down Beach Street just for a quick look at that big ocean?" Lynne asked. "I was here once before. It's a pretty special view."

"Okay by me," Slade said. "What about you, Jeff?"

"Certainly we should. And maybe we can get a cup-a-caffey and take a little break. I need to stretch out my creaky bones."

"Then it shall pass," Slade said.

They turned down Beach Street and saw some beautiful old-style cottages, upscale and nicely kept. Passing the Lobster Barn on the right, they crossed a bridge over a tidal basin on to a lengthy island of dunes and beach. There was a row of restaurants and motels on the left and a spacious parking lot on the right. They pulled in to it.

Ahead of them appeared the serene blue Atlantic and a horizon larger than life. Slade parked the car pointing straight out to sea and they got out and stood for a few minutes. Multi-colored umbrellas dotted the long strip of shore along with hundreds of bathers in the water and out. And walkers so far out in the distance that some were barely visible. The waves crested in a steady rhythm and splashed to shore making the distinctive sounds of the sea. On this day, the panoramic sky was painted powder blue.

"Man, every time I come back to the ocean, it's like I'm seeing it for the first time." Slade said. "You think of all that water – how far it goes – all the life out there in the deep – the awesome power of it all. Blows me away each time."

"Definitely gives me a buzz too," Jeff agreed. "You look out, and whatever troubles you have, they seem to shrink away. You feel almost like you're closer to God."

"I like that, Jeff," Lynne smiled touching his shoulder. "Closer to God."

Jeff looked at her and nodded. They walked over to the Beach House Snack Shack along the side. There, they bought hot coffee and doughnuts at the window from a smiling young man. He was tall with curly black hair and a wide moustache. Then they headed over to the rows of benches sitting under a green and white canopy facing the sea. There, they sat down among parents, kids, grannies, grandads, and several little old ladies who looked like spinsters, in flowered dresses, wearing dark sun glasses and licking ice cream cones. Looking north past the Norseman Hotel, with the tide out, the expanse of beach stretched far and wide.

"Awesome," Jeff said sipping his coffee. "What a beautiful place. Never even heard of it before today, Lynne."

"I had, but I never made it up here either," Slade said taking a bite out of a cruller. "Definitely a post card scene kind of town. Reminds me a lot of Cape Cod."

"See those two black dots way out there past the waves?" Lynne said. "They're harbor seals."

"Far out," Jeff marveled.

"And those people way up there walking on the side of the hill," she continued pointing out to the right. "They're walking the Marginal Way. It's a trail that goes from the center of town about two miles to Perkins Cove where all the fishing boats go out from. The path hugs the coast line – post card scenes up the yin yang, Shotgun."

"Cool," Slade said. "Maybe we can hit that trail on the way back from Wells."

"I'd like to do that," Jeff agreed.

They finished their coffee and savored the scene for a few more minutes from the benches. Then they walked down to the shore. They looked north and got a more complete view of the beach. It extended at least a couple of miles to a jetty that was barely visible.

"I remember you telling me you walked out to that jetty," Jeff said. "Got to come back some time and walk this beach – or better yet, run it," Jeff beamed. "It goes on and on and on."

"For sure it does," Lynne agreed as a wave made them retreat backwards. As it began to recede, Slade cupped some water in his hand and tasted it. Lynne gave him a funny look and he smiled at her.

"Just a force of habit, LC," he said. "Got to taste the salt water each time I come to the ocean – does something to me."

"Nothing wrong with that, Shotgun," Jeff said. "We all have our...excentricities."

"Remind me to check with Rails to see if that's a word."

Lynne got a kick out of that banter. On the way back to the car, they noticed a candy store and Jeff suggested they buy some for the people at the cottage. It was a quaint little shop run by an old woman with white hair tied up in a ball on top of her head. She told them that all the products were homemade. The sweet aroma of everything was intoxicating. They bought a couple of pounds of milk chocolate, fudge, penuche, and toll house cookies.

"This ought to get us in tight with the party crowd." Jeff said. "Always like to make a good impression."

"You only get one shot at it," Lynne commented.

Back on to Route 1, it was only another five miles to Wells. They passed the Village Inn on the left in the town of Moody; an old boarding house with a crow's nest room pointing straight up in the middle. Out on the grass were several hippies. There were three guys, all with beards, bandanas, and a couple of girls wearing love beads. Both had long hair parted in the middle. One wore cut-offs and the other a granny dress. All five of them were barefoot. One of the guys was playing a guitar and seemed to be off in his own world, his head rocking side to side. It was clear they were all just hanging out, in no rush to go anywhere or to do anything. Simply living in the moment and not worried about a damn thing.

"What do you figure their bag is?" Jeff said as they drove by. "They look pretty mellow."

"They're freaks," Slade said, "and I don't mean that in a bad way. Last summer, before I moved on to Stiller, I lived in Wellfleet down on the Cape for a time. I think I told you that, Jeff. There were some what I'd call authentic hippies living outside of town – on a real commune – genuine believers...and there were the freaks."

"What's the difference?" Lynne asked.

"Well, the freaks...I'd call them drifters like Jeff and me but way less structured. They usually do their own thing and don't work unless they're really desperate. They act more like the hobos of the 40's and 50's. Total free spirits who reject the system and just want to go their own way wherever it takes them – with no connections or responsibility – no plans for the future. All that matters to them is 'now', man. Longhairs tanned with cowboy hats and beards – and cute chicks with hair down past their waists just like the ones we just saw. The girls hook up with the dudes with positively no strings. The freaks play by no rules, see? I knew a few pretty well out in Wellfleet. Work was like a horrible word to them. If you mentioned it, they'd freak out – the freaks would freak."

Jeff and Lynne cracked up laughing.

"It's true," Slade continued, laughing with them. "They had no problem begging or even stealing food from variety stores or super markets. One guy I knew, Earl Ross, was an expert at it. He'd walk out of stores with boiled ham packages in his jeans. I never liked that, but otherwise he was a cool cat. Earl was the kind of character that Rails could focus a novel around."

"I'll bet he could at that," Jeff said.

"For the most part, they were all peaceful, the freaks," Slade continued. "Never any yelling or fighting. Most were aspiring musicians, painters, writers, poets, or even no-talent wannabees. One guy named Paige Dalporto I knew pretty well – Nice gentle kind from West Virginia. Paige used to practice on the guitar and sing most every day at a boarding house we lived at. He was a bad player and a worse singer. But he kept on keeping on – said he only wanted to make am meager living at it someday. Yeah, they all seemed to have some connection with the arts and expressing themselves. Interesting products of the times, I guess."

"Then that settles it," Jeff said. "That's my kind of bag. I aspire to be a freak as of this minute."

113

"Hoo hoo!" Slade laughed. "You have a wry sense of humor, dude – you got to work that more."

"Thanks…I think. But anyway, you're a pretty observer, Shotgun. Rails would find what you just said very interesting, I believe. You have to tell him."

"Steve Railsback," Lynne sighed, "he's one dude I just don't get. "A nice guy but he's so intense all the time like he's wired or something. What's the deal with him?"

"Rails is a born artist, Lynne," Jeff explained. "He sees stuff others don't see. Once you get that straight in your head, you can understand him better. He's got that creative bent, you know? Just don't expect him to be rational all the time."

"Really? You two are such thinkers," Lynne sighed. "I'll have to let that one sit for a while."

Both Jeff and Slade smiled as they turned down Sanford Road and passed a field of trailers near the end. Wells was more of a working class type resort than Ogunquit. About 500 yards ahead, they could see grassy bluffs and the ocean showing between them. Lynne directed Slade to take the next left down a narrow street of cottages all with the same sized yards. They stopped at number 73.

"This is the place," Lynne said as they got out. "Same one they had last year. Let's get our stuff inside and we can get some sleep."

A sunny young blonde greeted them at the door. Behind her stood a tall thin man with hair down to his shoulders. He was slightly balding with a drooping stash like David Crosby's. The man looked to be in his late twenties. The woman was pretty, with freckles on her nose and an upbeat disposition. She wore a tie dyed shirt and jeans, no bra and no shoes. Although she was dressed, she oozed of nakedness. She smiled and hugged Lynne, who introduced Jeff and Slade.

"Welcome, guys," she said. "I'm Jessica - and this is my friend, Dusty."

Dusty seemed like he was in a trance for a couple of seconds. After she elbowed him, he came out of it and shook hands.

"Pleased to meet you, dudes."

"Likewise, Dusty," Slade said. Jeff nodded.

Then something occurred to Dusty and he perked up. "Got to go out and score a little weed, my friends, if you'll excuse me. A man's gotta do what he's gotta do."

Jessica frowned at him. "Must you be impolite?" she said. "You just meet somebody and you have to leave – right now?"

"No big deal, we get it," Slade said. "Go ahead, Dusty – first things first. We'll see you later."

"Peace, men." Dusty smiled. He tosseled Jessica's hair and was off in his jeep.

"Sorry about him," she said as they walked inside. "Dusty means well but sometimes he doesn't think. I swear – he smokes so much dope, I think it's affecting his brain waves. Anyway, I know you worked all night and have to sleep. Want something to eat or drink before you hit the hay?"

"We had a snack on the way up," Lynne said. "Maybe something to drink and we'll sack out wherever you say, right boys?"

They both nodded.

"And here's a little contribution to the party," Lynne added. She placed the tub of fudge and cookies on the table.

Thanks, Lynne. Oooh, they look great," Jessica said peering into the box. "Now, there are three mattresses laid out on the floor for all of you in the next room. No beds in the place yet. Sorry, Lynne but the other bedroom is occupied – one of Dusty's friends is sleeping off a bender."

"Oh, we'll manage somehow," Lynne said. "But why no beds?"

"Well, the new owners, Brian and Karen Perry are friends of mine. They used to rent the cottage every summer before buying it last month. Brian's a really nice guy and Karen is just the most beautiful person both inside and out. I love her. Anyway, the old beds were falling apart. Brian threw them out, but he kept the mattresses until he gets new beds. He hasn't gotten around to that yet. So like I said, Lynne, you'll have to bunk with your two friends. But you will have your own private mattress at least."

"That's fine, Jess," Lynne laughed. "I'm a man's woman anyway."

115

"We're actually the Perry's first renters, "Jessica continued, smiling. "And we're getting a big discount. So we can live with things the way they are. How's about a little Boone's Farm apple wine to make you drowsy?"

"You talked us into it," Slade said.

They sat at the kitchen table, had the wine and talked for around 15 minutes. Then Jessica showed them the bedroom. "Welcome to the boudoir," she said with a laugh grabbing Jeff's forearm. She then excused herself to go out and do some party shopping. The mattresses were spread abreast on the floor. After they got their gear sorted, Lynne surveyed the layout."

"Looks like I'm going to be sleeping in between a couple of tall handsome studs," she laughed. "Now...no funny stuff."

"Studs? I'm liking that," Jeff joked.

"I can think of worse arrangements, LC," Slade grinned. "But you can trust us."

"And I do," Lynne said thoughtfully. "Not that I couldn't handle things if I didn't, but I do because you've both earned it. I don't think we've ever had two nicer guys at the sweat box and I've been there since senior year in high school. So many jerks hit on me. Look now, I'm not bragging but I see how some guys react to me. It gets hard at times because I know what they want and that's all they want. I don't know...you two just handle that stuff better – you know? Act right and keep things where they should be. I really like that."

"It ain't easy sometimes," Jeff said before he had time to think. After a pause, the three of them roared laughing. Lynne went over to him and gave him a push as Jeff cringed and faked a look of embarrassment.

"Well, all I can say is that you're one great broad if you know what I mean, Lynne," Slade said testing out his mattress. "I knew that from day one when we first saw you in the caf at work. What did you say - something like 'welcome to hell on earth'? I thought right then – here's an 'in there' woman who has an edge. And I was dead right."

"I remember that night like it was yesterday," Jeff said, "and those were your exact words, Lynne."

"Really? I said that?" Lynne exclaimed. More laughs.

"You sure did," Jeff continued. "And to be serious for just a minute if that's possible, we've been around you what, now...maybe four months? Shotgun and I see how you handle things at the factory. You have the skills and you bring it every night no matter how you're feeling. That takes character and don't think it goes unnoticed."

"Thanks a lot, Jeff. Nice of you to say that. And you too, Tom. I'm so glad I met both of you and that we're friends."

"That calls for a group hug," Slade said. "C'mon, let's go." For about five seconds they rocked and held tightly. Everybody came out of it with a little glow.

"Well, I'm just going to sleep in these clothes I'm wearing," Lynne said walking to the window and drawing the shade. "We can figure out the rest when we get up later."

"Right," Slade said.

"What do you think your mother would say about this arrangement, Lynne?" Jeff asked.

"My mother died when I was 18, Jeff. But she was pretty looo...well, let's just say she liked men and they liked her. If she was here, she'd probably flip a coin with me for dibs on you two."

"Sorry to learn about your mom passing," Jeff said. "But no way on the coin flip."

"Way! My dad and mom divorced when I was ten. She got plenty of male attention after that, believe me. And she loved it. My mother was very attractive."

"I have no doubt about that," Slade said. "The apple doesn't fall far from the tree – I mean looks-wise of course. But I'm sorry to learn that your mom passed away too, Lynne."

"Thanks, guys," Lynne smiled. "I put it all behind me a long time ago. But I like men just like she did. I like to think I just handle them better."

She got out a brush, combed her hair back and tied it into a ponytail. Then she removed her sandals and lay down in the middle mattress, pulling the sheet over her. Jeff and Slade, now tired from the trip and the wine, took off their shoes and took positions on the ends.

117

"It's about eleven thirty now," Lynne said. "I have my little alarm clock here. I'll set it for five. That will give us time to have something to eat and maybe hit the beach for a while before the party starts."

"Check," Slade said. "Damn, my leg is falling asleep again."

"You mention that pretty often, man," Jeff remarked. "Maybe you ought to have it checked out some time."

"Nah, it's nothing. A little rub down always does the trick."

After some stretching and massaging, Slade was out like a light. Lynne soon followed with slow steady breathing. It took Jeff a little longer to find sleep, being anxious in a new place and lying right next to a woman who he was desperately attracted to. It took a bit of restraint to keep his thoughts on the right track but he managed. In the kitchen, Dusty had returned and Jeff could hear him and Jessica squabbling about something. Dusty didn't exactly seem like the most above board character and for sure, his crew would be at the party. Jeff wondered what might be in store for the upcoming night.

He slept lightly on and off and was awakened once by of all things, a few snores from the lovely Lynne. He noted that both she and Slade slept soundly. Jeff looked at her closely; how she slept on her back, mouth slightly open, with the most feminine little exhaling whistles. He then lay back and closed his eyes, drifting into wondering how things would be different for Lynne had she been born into a stable family with money. Her parents would have fixed that little chip in her tooth. She'd have gone to college because it was clear she was smart, and she'd be a little more refined. With her looks and figure, she'd have her pick of successful men. But it was just the luck of the draw. Instead, here she was, lying between a couple of guys who had not put down any roots and had no immediate plans to.

Then, as he neared sleep, Jeff imagined Lynne as a little girl. Pretty, innocent - in a faded dress - her hair flopping in the wind – playing with friends in the courtyard between housing project buildings – the wash flapping on lines strung from one to the other. And her mother watching from the second floor window with a toddler or two at her feet. Her now deceased mother – then alive - husband long gone. With the eyes – the steely sad eyes of resignation to her lot in life, just like eyes of the long time mill workers. Jeff faded off with those eyes staring him down.

30.

Slade woke up abruptly with the clangs of the alarm clock. The other two followed drowsily.

"This place is like a hot house," he said sitting up and rubbing his eyes. "Where's the shower at?"

"Down the hall on the right, I think," Lynne said. "Well, the three of us slept together – we might as well take a shower together."

Slade and Jeff both turned and looked at her. They could see by her smirk that she was just joking.

"Oh sure," Slade said, "That would make a hot topic for the party tonight."

"It does sound interesting," Jeff added groggily. "But I doubt we can all fit in the stall."

"Seriously now, guys," Lynne laughed, "the beach is just down the street. How about if we go for a little swim – then come back and shower. And I'll bring the cooler with us. It's got a carry strap. We can have a picnic."

"How ordinary," Slade joked. "But I'll go for it."

"It will be a different kind of threesome," Jeff joked getting to his feet and stretching.

"Okay, give me a minute to change."

It was around five thirty when they got to the beach. It had pretty much cleared out. They took off their foot gear and walked barefoot in the warm sand. It felt good. They passed by a beautiful young woman by herself on a blanket in a blue bikini. She was tanned to perfection, with eyes closed, listening to a transistor radio. A couple of young men in cut-off jeans sat up on towels about 20 yards north of her, admiring every aspect of her being, but neither with the courage to even think of approaching her. She was the type of woman who loved passive attention.

The three found a good spot on some flat volcanic rocks in the damp sand area where the water washed up and receded. Lynne broke out the sandwiches and cans of soda, plus potato chips she'd also packed. They relaxed awhile and ate. There was no need to talk. They inhaled the salty air, watched the plovers and terns scour the shore line, and admired the stoic postures of the gulls who stood nearby hoping to score some handouts. They ate and listened to the song of the sea. Being away from the grind of the factory and in such a nice quiet place was stimulating to all.

They finished the food and relaxed a while more. "Well," Lynne said after a few minutes, "no time like the present – let's hit it."

Jeff and Slade, both wearing shorts, took off their shirts. Lynne stripped down to her two piece. Great curves just like Jeff expected, even better that he had imagined so many times. When they waded into the water, Jeff was surprised at how cold it was and pulled back. But Lynne moved right on past him and dove straight into a wave.

"Whew!" she exclaimed, her head popping out of the surf. "Now I know I'm alive! C'mon, guys – you have to just do it – wading in is torture!"

"She's right," Slade said and he followed suit. Jeff hesitated, took a deep breath, then moved ahead and took the plunge. It was so cold that it even hurt his sides a little. But he stayed with it, standing in water up to his shoulders, and gradually adjusted. The tide was coming back in and the ocean rocked with powerful waves. The three of them swam out a ways, treaded water and rolled with them up and down, enjoying the awesome strength and rhythm of the sea.

"Invigorating is not the word!" Slade exclaimed. "Nothing beats the ocean!"

Lynne swam over to Jeff and ducked his head into the water. Then she let herself float out some distance and faked that she was drowning. They laughed and ignored her. Slade then swam out far out past her so that his head disappeared when a high wave passed him. After a few minutes, he moved back in near Jeff and Lynne. They goofed around a while longer when suddenly Jeff began to feel sick.

"I have to go in," he said. "Something's going on in my stomach – I don't think that tuna sandwich agreed with me. I need to go back and use the bathroom. I'm really percolating."

"We'll go with you," Lynne said.

"No – no need to," Jeff said, now standing in the shallows. "You guys stay and enjoy it some more. I'll be okay. I'll see you back at the house."

"You sure, man?" Slade said.

"Positive."

Back at the cottage, Jessica showed Jeff to the bathroom. As soon as he got in there, he dropped what felt like a quarter of his body weight down the pipe. Two courtesy flushes later, he felt a lot better. Then he took a shower and put on the fresh jeans and t-shirt he brought with him. It was now around seven o'clock and about a dozen people were already there. Music was playing and things were getting started. Jessica spotted him. She walked over and grabbed his hand.

"C'mon with me and I'll introduce you to a few people, Jeff," she said, giving him a can of beer. He said hello to several faces, most whose names he forgot as soon as the next person was introduced. They all seemed like okay people, though. Jessica smiled, rubbed Jeff's shoulder, and excused herself to put out more food in the kitchen. There was energy between them that he clearly felt.

He grabbed a chair and shot the breeze with the three or four of the people he'd met. One, Pat Raymond, was all the way from Madawaska in northern Maine. An impressive guy, he talked about life out there in the sticks among the potato pickers. Pat was also a basketball player on the U Maine Fort Kent basketball squad. He and Jeff got into some heavy sports talk.

Over to the side, Jeff noticed Dusty talking loudly with a guy and a girl. There was a lot of slurring and arm flailing. "He's stoned already," Jeff thought, and he wondered how tight Dusty and Jessica were. She hadn't called him her boyfriend earlier.

The woman next to Dusty stood close and leaned on him at times. She seemed to be high on something. She touched him a lot and he pinched her rear end a couple of times. Not far from them, Jessica had returned and was sitting on the lap of some guy on the couch, laughing and swapping jokes and digs. Dusty didn't seem to care and neither did she about what he was doing. Jeff got the drift that this was going to be a very loose crowd.

Beatles music picked up in the background as the party gained strength and the white noise increased. "The Magical Mystery Tour is coming to take you away..." By now, Jeff was on his fourth beer. He moved around and talked with some other people here and there, and was also content to relax, blend into the background, and observe. But as night fell and the alcohol began to take hold on the crowd, he sensed a dark cloud slowly rolling in.

As more new people joined the party, Jeff recalled that Lynne and Slade hadn't yet come back. He wondered if they slipped off somewhere or if maybe something happened to them. "Whatever", he said to himself and decided to let it go. He moved to the kitchen for another brew. Jeff was feeling a good buzz by now. As he took a can from the refrigerator, he slipped on a wet spot and accidentally grabbed the knee of a young girl sitting on the counter in breaking his fall.

"Sorry," he said.

"Oh – don't worry about grabbing my leg, man" she said. "I'm used to guys doing it all the time."

She was a cute little thing. The girl had long brown hair, light skin, and a wispy figure in tiny little shorts. Her nipples pressed out from her Old Orchard Beach shirt. She was very sexy but looked to be around 15 at the most. The smell of weed was strong in the kitchen. The girl took a joint from an ash tray next to her and took a hit.

"Toke?" she asked.

"Huh? Okay," Jeff said, feeling a little unsteady. "But how...how old are you anyway? I mean...aren't you a little – like young to be smoking at all – let alone grass?"

"Old enough to know better. You sound just like my old lady. Never trust anybody over 30, man. She tells ME not to smoke weed and then her and

122

her pot head boyfriend do it right in front of me. All right for them but not for me? Fuck that. I been smokin' since I was 12 and I just turned 17. This ain't my first rodeo, budyroo. I know the score."

"No way you're 17 – no friggin way."

She reached into her purse and showed him her license.

"Okay, you got me there," Jeff said trying not to slur his words. "But let me ask you a question – uhh...if you don't mind. Well then - why...? Nah...I should stop right there. What you do is your business. You're over 16 – it's your affairs – doesn't concern me."

"What the hell are you talking about?"

"Huh? Well see – it's like...aww, never mind. I mean...maybe I'm out of line, but the thing of it is..." He breathed in and stifled off a burp. "Where was I? Give me another hit of that." He inhaled deeply and continued. "See...the thing of it is like I was saying – those shorty shorts you got on – umm – I mean shorts. You have a lot of ho...horny guys drinking and getting high all over the place in here, right? Am I right? It's...that's like a signal to them – green light – come and get me, boys, I'm good to go. Get it? I mean you're a very attra...aww – I can't go any further – I'm too spaced out – I can't make any sense even to myself."

She took his wrist and looked at him closely. "I know you're trying to be nice and you mean well," she said softly. "But see...I look at it this way. God gave me this booty and it's mine to do what I want with it. Fuck what anybody else thinks."

"Okay – you're the woman charge," Jeff said. "I uhh...I just hope you don't learn the hard way. Sorry...I shouldn't have said that."

"Don't worry. It's okay. I already learned the hard way a long time ago."

Just then, a big armed guy wearing a black t-shirt walked in. On the front of the shirt were the words, DON'T BLEEP WITH ME. And on the back, it said, GOODBYE – YOU WON'T BE MISSED. Jeff took a look and couldn't help but laugh. The guy grinned and nodded back at him. He then focused on the girl and a sigh of relief passed over his face. He swooped her off the counter and draped her on his shoulder.

"Leanne! Where the hail have you been?" he said. "I get up to take a leak – next thing I know you was gone!"

123

"I just needed a little air. I went outside and then lit up a joint in here, Corey. Now please, put me the fuck down!"

"Well, you're with ME t'nite, babe and nobody else – remember that!"

"Oh, all right for crissakes. Put me the fuck down I said!"

Corey kept her where she was and carried her off like a sack of potatoes. She rolled her eyes and made a face to Jeff as they left. As he watched them go, he thought of how dumb his lecture must have sounded. Jeff moved back to the living room as the noise got louder and the area seemed to shrink. He then realized he forgot his beer in the kitchen but it was too much trouble to go back.

Jeff noticed a cooler full of ice and beer nearby that somebody had brought in. DIG IN said a sign attached to it. He grabbed a can. Then he sat down in a big easy chair. With the combination of pot and beer, Jeff was really feeling it now. His mind began to race around with strange thoughts which he had a hard time shaking off. He couldn't help himself from picturing that girl – Leanne – naked – and him making it with her, going all over that alluring little body and closing the deal with a big rush.

"Get a hold of yourself, man," he said to himself. "I'm getting too screwed up. This has to stop right now. Get the hell up and go talk to somebody now."

He happened on a couple of guys and a girl he'd met earlier. He immediately forgot about what he said to himself, shared a joint with them, took a shot of anisette, and in a couple of minutes, downed another one. Bad move. He knew it shortly after he swallowed the second shot. It didn't sit right. But what was done was done. Now, he needed to hit the head – immediately, and drunkenly excused himself. The trip to the bathroom was a wobbly struggle to stay upright. Shuffle, bump, shuffle, bump, and finally in the door.

"I'm in big trouble," he said to himself as he tried not to miss the toilet. Then, a fumbling flush and stagger back to the living room where one of the girls was passed out on a chair. Now the music seemed to be blasting – the song "Helter Skelter" – boom – Boom - BOOM – people dancing wildly all around – glasses and bottles clanking and a one falling to the floor. Jeff danced around a little by himself. Then he found a spot at the end of the couch and crashed there. Off in the distance, he heard somebody slur, 'One drink won't suffice, dude – better make it three!'

Plop. Suddenly a female was beside him with her arms around his shoulders. She murmured "mmmmm, I dig you" in his ear and kissed him on the neck. Then she settled with her head up against him. Things were beginning to spin around and Jeff couldn't focus clearly, but he could see well enough to figure out who it was. Jessica – and she was hammered.

"Me too," he managed to say, putting his arm around her.

Jeff was too loaded to even think about Dusty and figured to hell with it. He turned to her and she closed in. They got into an extended make out session like he'd never experienced. Hers was the most searching tongue he'd ever encountered. Even though she was drunk, or maybe because of it, she was super sensual and passionate.

That lasted roughly 15 minutes with some drunken whispering mixed in. Then somebody from outside yelled for her and just like that, Jessica was gone. For Jeff, things then settled as if they were slowed down to 33 RPM. He talked to some people nearby, but it was as if he was outside of his body watching himself talk, slurring, laughing at nothing, being bombed and stoned all at once. In fact, just about everybody was in the same boat; either getting drunk and high or staying drunk and high. He was just one of them. And in the morning, they were all going to pay for it. That, even in the state he was, he knew for sure.

Jeff got up to go outside but made it only half way. He lost his balance and fell into a chair. Suddenly, things sped up again and his mood took a nose dive. He began to feel like he was going to die, that he'd surely die that night. His brain felt like mush, the slop shifting every time he moved his head. Everywhere he looked, the place took on angles like in a fun house, the floor seemingly on a skid. His stomach turned and on top of everything, he began to feel like he wanted to vomit.

Now Jeff realized just how drunk he was and that he could be in some serious danger. But he'd lost control of himself. It was what it was, he figured in his twisted mind. "It's not so bad," a voice in his head said. "One more – that's all you need. One more for the road."

He got up and made it to the cooler for another beer. Then he sank into a corner on the floor and drank. "Maybe I'm dreaming this whole thing," he told himself. Then he thought again of Lynne and Slade. "Got to find them – got find them – get the hell up!"

Easier said than done. He put the can aside and took him all of three tries. Finally he was up and stumbled toward the hall way, which seemed to be alive and moving right along with him. Then he was down again like he was shot, tripping over a threshold that he thought had to be a foot high. But he hardly felt the fall. His body was as soft as jelly.

"What the fuck! Where yah' goin' dude – you're smashed!" Those words came from a guy standing over him who helped him to his feet.

"Thanks, man," Jeff said. "Ju…just got to get outside. I can't br…breathe in here."

"That-away," the guy said. He pointed Jeff in the right direction and gave him a gentle shove. Jeff went straight ahead like a wobbly bowling ball. He forgot all about Lynne and Slade; just focused on getting outside. He slowed down and saw two doors in front of him. Jeff went for the one on the left.

It was the wrong door. He opened it half way and for a few seconds, was blitzed sober at what he saw. It was the door to other bedroom, not the one he'd slept in. There, on one of the mattresses on the floor was Leanne having sex with Corey, the big guy who carried her away earlier. And to the side, a couple of other people – a guy and a girl – sitting there and watching as if it was a porno flick being filmed. Eyes closed and head to the side, Leanne looked so drunk that maybe she didn't even know what was happening to her.

Jeff had never seen anything like that and had no idea what to make of it; whether it was consensual or if Leanne was so blitzed that she was being raped. But in his condition, there wasn't a thing he could do.

Somebody yanked him aside and slammed the door shut. "Get the hell outah there, mother fucker!" he said. "That's none of your business!" Then he let Jeff go and walked off.

Jeff stumbled down the hall and back into the living room. Then he fell into something that caught him square in the groin. The arm of a chair. But luckily for him, it was padded. Still, the pain came in a rush and he slid down the side of the wall. From deep within him, a sobering voice came and said, "You're at the end of your rope now. Find someplace out of the way to fall down in and sleep it off."

Jeff knew this voice spoke the truth. He made it back up and then melted into the chair he'd tripped on — felt he became one with it — even imagined his clothes changing color to match the upholstery. This was it, the end of the line. He wouldn't be moving again until morning unless by some outside force. Whatever would be would be.

Jeff felt safe for the time being. But there was a dangerous air in the place that was heated and still rising. Some hoods had crashed the party earlier and they had issues with people already there. It was going to go down. It was just a matter of time.

Now the music raged. "Five to one, baby — one to five...no one here gets — out alive!" Jeff's head was spinning and the room was as well each time he opened his eyes. It scared him. For a couple of seconds, he was able to focus on one of the crashers at the far end. He was shaking a woman by the shoulders.

"You fucken whore!" he yelled straight into her face. "What'd you do with my yellow sunshine? You copped my shit, bitch! I KNOW you stole my acid. Get my mother fucken dope back — NOW! Or I swear I'll knock your teeth out!"

"Go FUCK yourself, you ugly piece of shit!" she yelled and blew a clam straight in his eye. Enraged, he let her go and gave her a backhander. She went down like she was shot. Then, the woman got to her knees, grabbed a bottle, and heaved it at the guy. It sailed past his head and exploded on the wall. The wall behind Jeff's chair. A picture dropped and a spray of glass and beer fell on him.

Fear gripped Jeff as the two of them wrestled on the floor not far from him. Others joined the fray and a donnybrook broke out. The place went absolutely nuts, bottles flying and people screaming. Jeff never felt more helpless. But all he could do was sit there and hope he didn't get hit.

He motioned to raise his hand and brush the glass from his hair but the effort was just too much. It fell back by his side, dead. "God help me," he thought to himself. "I'll be lucky to get out of here without getting hurt really bad."

Another fight broke out in the kitchen and there was trouble going on outside. The floor shook with people yelling, fighting and falling. Others attempted to break up the fights. Jeff tried to make himself as small as he could, be calm and accept the situation. If a bottle was ticketed for him or he got kicked in the teeth, then so be it. There was no way out. He was just too drunk and sick to defend himself. From far off, he heard the sirens of cruisers. He then felt something smack him on the side of the head near his eye. But luckily, whatever it was didn't hit him squarely and glanced off. Then, ever so gradually, a calmness came over him.

All the noise and violence became muted. Jeff felt safe and sealed off from it, as if a protective bubble had formed around him. His eyes closed, he focused on the beautiful splotches of color at the back of his eyelids, rolling in like fireworks with their brilliance intensifying before they crested like waves and were gone. In time, he was sealed off from all the mayhem and one with himself in the realm of spectacular color.

They didn't come all at once. They just sort of snuck up one by one. Zipped in and zipped out. Within the inner theater of his eyelids – gruesome faces – horrible leers - pointy teeth – twisted bodies...demon-like. Gradually more and more until the colors were only burning reds and yellows around the parade of ugly shooting mugs. With each one Jeff wanted to scream but he couldn't. This was far worse than just being loaded. Too frightening and real to be a dream. It was the most fear he'd experienced since he was a kid. Gruesome hallucinations. The delirium tremens.

In between Jeff saw flashes of his mother dead and stiff on a stretcher, his father drunk in an alley and beaten to a pulp, and finally at the end, a Satan-like figure. It was all ablaze, leering and extending a claw with sharp talons. He felt the flash of an icy grip on his ankle. His heart seemed to stop. All went to black. He passed out.

31.

Jeff tried to open his eyes. They were caked with mucus and it took some rubbing before he could see anything. The sun fought its way through the early morning fog through the two living room windows. Both rolled around in slow circles as Jeff struggled to focus sideways. Spread eagled on the floor, stomach down, head to the side at a 45 degree angle. That was Jeff's position. His cheek sat in a little pool of saliva. He felt as if he'd been out for a week.

Ever so slowly, Jeff twisted around, sat up and checked himself out. He felt a big welt on his thigh and was very sore around his right eye. Everything else seemed to be okay. He figured he must have gotten kicked after he passed out, but only vaguely remembered being hit in the head. The important thing was that he'd made it through. Jeff rolled his tongue around in his mouth and the taste was vile. He exhaled into his hand and his breath almost knocked him over. He felt along his neck and realized he'd dribbled a little vomit down into his shirt. "I must have barfed in my sleep," he thought to himself. "I'm lucky I didn't choke to death on it."

He sat there awhile, opening and closing his eyes and continuing to clear them. Things began to slow down and come into focus. Scanning around, the room looked like it had been hit by a hurricane. The furniture was all over the place, chips and nuts scattered on the floor, beer splotches on the carpet and a few tears showed in the wallpaper. One chair had half the stuffing ripped clear out of it. It had been a bad, bad night.

Jeff sat up straighter and now began to feel the full extent of his hangover. There was dizziness, mild nausea and throbbing pain at both sides of his head. He noticed that he wasn't alone. There was somebody passed out on the couch. Jeff recognized him as a guy he'd talked to early in the night before he got loaded. One leg was hooked up over the back of sofa and one arm was turned sideways around his neck. His head was jammed into the corner. But he was breathing.

"I can't believe – I cannot BELIEVE I'm sitting in this place," Jeff thought. "And alone – what the hell happened to Lynne and Shotgun?"

But he wasn't mad at them. Whatever kept them away was their business and they had no way of knowing what would develop at the party. The more he thought about it, he was glad they'd dodged all the trouble. But he hoped nothing bad happened to them.

"I have to get it together and get out of here," he told himself. "Got to move on from this. And the sooner the better."

But there was no Lynne, his ride back to Stiller. And he had yet to even stand up. Still, the thing to do was to get straightened out and split as

129

soon as he could; put the nightmare behind him. Even if Lynne's car was out there he wasn't going to hang around. He'd catch up with her and Slade later. Get out – now. He focused on that thought alone.

Getting up off the floor took some effort and Jeff gave it a lot of patience. He wanted to be sure he could make it without falling. In the meantime, he noticed that the guy on the couch had woken up and was on his back staring at the ceiling. They locked eyes once but neither said a word. Too much trouble. Nothing to be said. The scene said it all.

As carefully as he could, Jeff finally stood up, swayed a little, and then leaned over against the wall. His head was chiming but not so bad that he couldn't take it. He used the wall to steady himself to the bathroom and dowsed his face with cold water over and over. The dizziness lightened a bit and he felt a little better. Then he got a jolt when he looked in the mirror. One eye was bloodshot red and bruised all around; a world class shiner. His shirt was torn too. And he looked exactly how he felt. Wasted.

Jeff ran water through his hair and combed it with a brush he found in the medicine cabinet. Then he took a belt of Listerine and blasted it out into the sink, the medicinal taste jolting him down to his toes. He washed off his shirt, tucked it in, pulled up his pants and tightened his belt. "I'm on a roll," he said to himself.

More steadily now, he walked back onto the living room. Oddly, nobody else was around other than the guy on the couch, who continued to look straight up. The door to Jessica's bedroom was closed but he could hear snoring going on from there and also the other bedroom. Jeff looked at the clock in the kitchen and it was only eight thirty. He figured anybody who had stayed the night was likely still sleeping it off.

The blasting music, the chaos, the screaming, the fights and the fear he felt. It all began to come back to him as he looked around, his faculties gradually sharpening. He remembered Leanne and what he saw. Did that poor girl get raped? He'd never know and frankly didn't want to.

Jeff walked to the bedroom where his gear was. The door was half way open and he slipped in. He saw four people spread out on the three mattresses at odd angles, all crashed and out, and one snoring like a Grizzly bear. As quietly as he could, he got his stuff and snuck out the back door. He never looked back.

Jeff was surprised to see that Lynne's car was still parked outside the cottage. But he walked right by it and into the salty air of the Sunday morning by the sea. It was a mile and a half out to Route 1. His head was hot and his feet were cold but the walk did him a lot of good. Jeff survived the night and was taking care of business. It was a positive thing, he figured. Within 10 minutes he hitched a ride all the way south to Kittery, getting dropped off at a truck stop. There, he got a large black coffee and a couple of slices of toast. It was a deal changer. Jeff began to feel more like himself.

At the counter, he hooked up with a trucker headed south to New Jersey. Jeff got a break and was taken all the way to the exit to Stiller. The driver was a great guy and after hearing Jeff's story, had him stretch out in the sleeper for the rest of the way. Finally Jeff's luck had changed. Walking the last mile to the Y, he was never so happy to see an old red brick building in his life. He was home.

It was Sunday and he didn't have to work that night. Jeff took a long shower and then spent the rest of the day, fortunately a cool and comfortable one, in bed. His fan was on slow speed and he had soft music playing in the background on his portable radio. After what he'd been through, it was like heaven. He slept peacefully. By five, Jeff was up and felt much better. He even had an appetite. It was time to hit Shorty's for some chow.

Jeff cleaned up and headed downstairs. As he took a seat at the counter, Shorty walked over and gave him a puzzled look.

"Jonesy! What in God's name happened to you?" he asked with concern. "That's one hell of a shiner. Did you get into a fight?"

Jeff managed a smile. "Yeah, but you should see the other guy. Nah, not really, Shorty. I was at a party that got way out of control. I had a couple too many – try about half a dozen. I was already close to passed out when I got hit so I don't know how it happened. I'm lucky a black eye and a sore thigh's all I got."

"You hung over too?"

"Yeah, but I'm a lot better. I could barely get up off the floor this morning."

131

"Well, I got just the thing for yah, Jeff," Shorty said snapping his fingers. "Homemade chicken with rice soup left over from lunch – from Connor's market down the street. It'll go down nice and easy. And black coffee. You've been a good customer and you're a good kid. All on the house, Jeff."

"Yeah? Then bring it on. And thanks."

"Ole Shorty'll take care of yah – fix you right up, son."

"You're a good dude."

Jeff went over and drew a cup of coffee. He then noticed Creecher having his supper and reading the paper off in the corner booth. He took his coffee and walked over.

"Want a little company?" Jeff said.

"Of course."

He took a seat opposite Creecher with his back to the entrance. Jeff then explained the black eye and told him a little about the party as Shorty brought the soup over. It was just the thing, as he'd said. Jeff was getting to the meat of the story when Creecher looked up and saw Tom Slade walking toward them, whistling Yankee Doodle Dandy.

"Creech, my man – what's happening?" Slade said. Jeff turned around and looked at him.

"Jesus! Jeff – you made it back!" he exclaimed. "What a relief. We looked for you all morning. Wow - look at that eye. What the hell went down, man?"

"Have a seat, Shotgun," Creecher said. He moved over and Slade slid in opposite Jeff.

"What went down? More like what didn't go down," Jeff finally answered.

"Oh, Lynne and I got the skinny on all the trouble in the morning," Slade said. "Had to be after you split that we got back to the house. The cops had been up there and arrested three people – one for assault and battery and the other two for possession of drugs. We heard it was the blow-ins who wrecked the house. I was worried about you, man. Glad to see you're in one piece."

Jeff took a sip of coffee, put his hands behind his head, and collected his thoughts. His face took on a puzzled look. Creecher set his paper aside and moved forward in his seat.

"But the burning question," Jeff began, "before I talk about what happened to me...is what happened to you and Lynne? I never saw you after I left the beach. I had to face that freak show alone, dude. I'm not ashamed to say that I was in fear for my life, man. But knowing both of you, I'll bet the house you had a good reason. It couldn't be just that you got lucky. C'mon now, hit me with it."

"Yeah – hit us with it, Shotgun," Creecher said poking Slade's shoulder.

Slade paused and then let out with a laugh. "Nooo – I didn't get lucky. That chick has eyes for you, not me, Jeff, and you know I'd always respect that. But we were involved in an incident too. It actually could have been a disaster a lot worse than what happened at the party."

You were?" Jeff asked incredulously. "Then give us the story behind the story."

"Okay, here's how it all developed. Lynne and I swam around some more after you left, but as we did, the surf got rougher and Lynne drifted out further than she should have. Then she put on what I thought was that phony drowning routine again. I yelled out to her that she might as well get it over with and drown because I was getting cold and wanted to get out. But in a couple of seconds I realized that she was serious and in trouble with the undertow. She was really drowning!"

"Holy crap!" Creecher gasped.

"I yelled for the lifeguard and I swam like hell for her. He had just packed up and was leaving but thank God he heard me. I saw her head go under once and I was really fighting it to get to her. Then I got worried that I might be in trouble too, but I reached her and got a hand on Lynne's arm. The guard was right behind me on a paddle board. Between the two of us, with all the power we could muster, we got her to the beach."

"Man!" Jeff exclaimed. "Is Lynne okay?"

Slade stroked his beard and continued. "She took down some water and was out of it on the sand for maybe a minute. The lifeguard did CPR and she came to and was coughing up water pretty quickly. I never felt so relieved in my life. But she needed medical attention and the guard radioed in for an ambulance. I rode in back with her and spent the night on a couch in the waiting room of the hospital in Sanford. Lynne checked out okay in the morning and they released her. We hailed a cab and got back to the cottage at around 10 – cost us a fortune but we had no choice. You must have slipped out like a fox before then. We asked around but nobody saw you leave."

"That's because they were all bombed and sleeping it off save for one sorry dude besides me. But wow, that was pretty edgy. I'm glad Lynne pulled through. You saved that girl's life, dude."

"Not really. I don't know CPR. If the lifeguard wasn't there it might have been a different story. But there's more. I saved the most interesting part for last."

"Give it to us," Creecher said. "Shotgun, you've rescued me from another dull day in Stillwater."

Slade smiled and paused for a little added drama. "Okay, now I have to put this tastefully. Well see...somewhere along the line, Lynne's top came loose and went out to sea. Just briefly, she was topless on the beach. I won't go into detail but let's just say God was very generous to her. Only the lifeguard, a few bystanders and I witnessed it. Somebody contributed a towel and Lynne was exposed only for I'd say - less than a minute. But like you mentioned once a while back, Jeff, she IS lot of woman. And I had the presence of mind to remember to grab her stuff and mine before we left on the ambulance. The woman from the ambulance helped her get dressed."

"Beautiful – bee-you-tee-full!" Creecher smiled.

"So that was two shockers for one night," Jeff reflected. "I didn't think it was possible, but your story tops mine. Hey – look, I'm just glad Lynne's okay, and you too. Knowing her, I don't think losing her bra is any big deal. I mean she isn't exactly shy about her body."

"Nor should she be," Slade agreed. "Right you are, Jeff. We even laughed about it on the way back from the cottage. She's just glad to be alive, man – that part didn't faze her much. Just one thing, though. Keep it between the three of us. She'd rather that it doesn't get around, especially at work.

"Of course," Jeff agreed. Creecher nodded.

134

"But she's still nerved up about coming close to kicking the bucket," Slade continued. "I think she's going to take a few days away from work. So the bottom line is that we're all okay – the three of us. Thank God for that. Now - I gotta hear your story. Lay it on us."

"Yes, and start from the beginning again," Creecher said.

"Sure I will, Creech. But before I do, I have an announcement to make."

"Oh, this oughtah be good."

"No joke, man – I'm serious. You heard a little about what happened to me before Shotgun got here. And it was all because I was so wasted that I couldn't think straight or let alone even move. I thought it over in bed today. I'm done with alcohol for a long, long time. Done. It's like...over. That kind of thing is never going to happen to me again if I can help it. It ruined my father and I'll be damned if it's going to take me down. You know from experience, Creech, and now I do too. Oh, I'll still smoke a little grass, but any kind of beer or booze? I'm through."

"Good for you, Jeff," Creecher agreed. "If you keep to it, you've turned a bad experience into a positive."

"Commendable," Slade added, "And I know you mean it."

"I do. My mind's made up. So now that that's established, here's my tale of woe."

Jeff spent the next 15 minutes painting the night from front to back, not missing one detail that he could remember to a captive audience. The narrative completed and all questions answered, he got up and helped himself to a second bowl of soup. Getting it all out kind of put a cap on things. He'd learned from it and was looking ahead. Jeff slept well that night, as did his friend Shotgun.

It wasn't until Thursday of the new week that Lynne returned to work. Physically, she'd gotten back to normal quickly but the mental part took a little longer. Lynne was shaken by the whole thing and concerned about Jeff and what she'd gotten him into. She got to work late but searched him out the first chance she got. She found him out on the floor loading up on spools.

"Jeff, Jeff!" she said approaching him. He turned her way and she stopped cold when she got a good look at his face.

"Oh my God!" she gasped. "I talked to Shotgun on the way in and he told me about your eye – but seeing it – oh my God!" She darted forward and pulled him up against her.

"It's no big deal, Lynne," he said rubbing her back. "I've had shiners before. Doesn't even hurt now – getting better already. And I can even see fine out of it. Don't worry – it's my badge of honor."

"Well, it makes me feel better to hear you joke about it," she said as she released him and stepped back. "I'm so sorry, Jeff. We were having such a good time before you left the beach. Then everything just fell apart and from what Jess told me, it was all from those jerks who crashed the place. She told me one guy was going around spiking drinks with tabs of acid. I felt so bad about what happened to the cottage. We're all chipping in to help Brian and Karen pay for the damage."

"I'll be glad to contribute to that," Jeff said. Then he had a revelation. "Wow…then that explains it!" he exclaimed. "He must have dropped LSD into one of those shots I took - I'll bet that was what triggered the bad trip I went through! I was having bizarre visions and everything else you can think of. But I was already loaded by then, Lynne, and I acted like a jerk too. I could have done things a lot differently and I learned a good lesson, I'll tell you that. For all that went down, it might have been a lot worse. I'm just glad you're okay. Slade told me the whole story. You battled through some serious trauma, girl."

"I don't even remember half of it, but thanks. I know you mean it. You know, Tom probably saved my life – I'm so grateful. But I promise I'll never put you in another situation like that, Jeff – never again!"

She collapsed into him for another hug and cried just a little bit.

"I do mean it," Jeff said holding her close. "Your being okay is the most important thing. Now don't give it another thought. We're both good and it's over. Time to move ahead."

Lynne stepped back and wiped the tears. Then she looked up at Jeff straight into his eyes. "I already thanked Shotgun a hundred times for what he did for me. Now I feel better that you and I have talked. I'll make it up to you, Jeff. I don't know how right now, but I'll make it up to you."

"No need to," Jeff smiled holding her shoulders. "You just keep being Lynne Charland and don't you dare change one thing. That's all I need."

136

"You're a great guy," she said with the hugest smile. "I can go on now!"

Jeff brushed back her hair and they both laughed. Lynne walked back to her machines, greatly relieved.

32.

The summer took its sweet time and moved on into late July. On a Saturday afternoon, Jeff and Rails were just finishing up with their weekly guitar lesson with Slade. They both committed to it like he urged them to and were rolling along at about the same speed. They'd just played a simple two part etude by sight reading single melody lines and it sounded really good.

"Man – I almost feel like a guitar player after that," Rails beamed to Jeff. "Great job, bud."

"First time I've been able to get through a whole song without screwing something up," Jeff said. "It's a milestone."

"Both of you are doing really well," Slade said. "You know, I did some teaching in a little music store back in Penn before I hit the road. Mostly it was kids and a lot of them would come in not having practiced. Sometimes it was a big waste of time and I'd get on them for it. So much easier with you two. Even when you struggle, I always know you've put in the time. Keep up the steady work ethic and you'll both be good someday. Guaranteed."

"Coming from a guy who can play like you – that's inspiring, Shotgun," Rails said.

"And we appreciate what you're doing for us," Jeff added. "You've opened up a whole new world."

"Pleasure's all mine, gentlemen. And remember this. That axe is your companion for life. Think of it as your soul mate. Whatever happens, she'll always be with you, and she'll never talk back."

"Another nugget, Slade," Rails said shaking his head. "You're full of nuggets. It's settled, dude – there's gonna be a character modeled after Tom 'Shotgun' Slade in my book."

"That will be an honor," Slade offered. "I mean that you'd find me interesting enough to write about, Steve. And one final thing. May I impart a little sage advice as you guys continue to improve?"

"Impart away," Jeff laughed.

"Nick Beshekis, my former teacher, once told me this and I never forgot it. He said the better you get, the more humble you should be. When you're good, you don't tell people – they'll tell you."

"Heavy," Rails said.

"Listen, before you guys split, got any plans for tonight?" Slade asked.

"Nuttin," Jeff said.

"Hadn't even given it a thought," Rails added. "I fly by the seat of my pants."

"Well, I got a pretty cool tip this afternoon over at Joey's when I was rapping with Nikki. That new movie that came out a couple of weeks ago – 'Easy Rider' – you guys must have heard about it?"

"Of course," Rails answered."

"Anybody seen it?"

"Nope."

"It's playing at that drive-in up on Coburn Street by the river. They must have gotten it so soon 'cause it's a low budget flick. I've heard it's pretty good. Are we in?"

"In," they said together.

"What's it about?" Jeff asked.

"I don't know any of the details," Slade answered. "But I do know it has to do with a couple of young guys on choppers who travel across the southwest. That alone is enough for me to want to see it. I'm not sure what the movie's supposed to say, though, aside from that it deals with the hippies and dropping out. Pud told me about it – my mareejeewanna connection. He said it was a real trip and it kind of documents the movement that we talk about from time to time. I figure it's a must-see for us.

"Definitely," Rails said. "I'm going to go back to my apartment to take care of a couple of things I need to do. The show up there usually starts just after dusk. How about if I pick you guys up say around eight?"

"Oh yes," said Slade. "You're the key man, Railster – the ride."

"Always knew I was good for something."

It was a nice summer evening with low humidity and a red setting ball on the horizon. Rails picked them up in his 61 Ford Galaxie 500. It was very roomy inside. Slade and Jeff got a kick out of making fun of it.

"Hey Shotgun," Jeff said. "I hear a strange noise. Better go down to the engine room to check it out."

"Nah – no big deal," Slade said. "Just the tail gun turret rattling."

"Okay, you guys are funny," Rails said laughing with them. "But consider that you're sitting in the ultimate drive-in car. Ever see sight lines like this?" He spanned his hand across the windshield in a wide arc. "Panorama, baby."

Not far along the way, they saw a familiar face on the sidewalk. Ed Collins was walking along absently, hands in pockets. They pulled over and Jeff yelled out, "Hey bud – you got any spare change?"

Ed smiled. Jeff then asked him if he wanted to join them to see the movie. He was all over it and practically dove into the car.

Ed leaned forward from the back seat and grabbed Rails' shoulder as they neared the drive-in. "You guys are in luck," he said. "Keep your money in your pockets. Steve – just park in back of the pizza joint next door – there on the right."

"What do you mean?" Rails asked as he pulled in.

139

"Well, a couple of my friends and me have been watching movies here for free here all summer long. We hacked a path through the bushes out back and dug a hole under the fence. Just wait a little bit - until twilight and we can pull it off. It's a sure thing."

"But once we get in, where do we go?"

"Way in back at the end – at the speakers nobody ever uses. There's even a mound on the ground if you want to lie back."

"You sure it's okay?" Jeff asked. "We don't need any trouble with the law."

"Guaranteed. Once it's dark and you're in, you're in. Nobody checks on anybody."

"Let's do it then," Slade said. "They make plenty of dough – they won't miss a couple of bucks. Plus, I'm curious to see Fast Ed's secret path. Lead the way, my man."

"Okay – let's just wait a little longer 'til dusk ends and it's darker."

They sat awhile, listening to WBCN progressive rock on the radio until night began to fall. Then Ed walked them far around the back into some thick growth and brush. He guided them along the path as the crickets began to sing. Ed led the way like a pioneer as the going got denser with burrs and thorns. Then they had to get on all fours just to reach the fence. Down and under, they were in the drive-in confines. Back up on their feet, they navigated the last of the bushes and saw the big screen light up in the night sky.

I don't know if that mission was worth it," Jeff said picking burrs out of this shirt.

"Not for wimps," Ed laughed. "Just remember the key word, Jeff – free. Anything for nothing is always better. Forbidden fruit, you know? Even if the movie sucks, you walk away knowing you didn't have to shell out any bread. Follow me, men. I'll show you the final resting place. Wait a sec' – I have to get our uhh…seating."

Ed stepped back into the thicket and came out with a big sack stuffed with something. Then he showed them to the spot and from the sack, removed four cushions.

"Very nice," Slade said. "Didn't expect hospitality like this."

"All the comforts of that beautiful brick building you and the Jeffster live in. And the bag's waterproof so the cushions never get wet."

"Like Moe would say, I'm beginning to think you might have a sliver of a brain, Steady Eddie," Jeff laughed poking at him.

"Soitenly!"

Slade went over to the concession stand and bought a couple of tubs of popcorn. Then they settled in as the coming attractions ended and "Easy Rider" began. The anthem "Born to be Wild" played as the camera focused on the two bikers. "Like a true nature's child...we were born, born to be wild...we can climb so high...I never want to die!" The four of them were drawn in immediately to those lyrics and the action that followed.

For the next hour and a half, they watched Wyatt (Captain America) and his partner Billy made the trek on their choppers from Los Angeles to the Mardi Gras festival in New Orleans. The bikes were cool, their duds were cool, especially Billy's buckskin jacket and bushman's hat, and what they were doing was cool. Everything was cool.

The group were so into the movie that few words were spoken throughout the entire thing, save for a sprinkling of "groovys", "far outs", and "outah sights". Slade and Rails especially liked how Wyatt and Billy so casually passed through towns of the southwest and interacted with the town folk, whom they seemed to dig for the most part. The two did their thing with no drama or urgency, and no set schedule or goals. They just moved ahead and lived each day, experiencing the land and its people.

Jeff was particularly interested in the hippie commune that the two main characters spent some time at. It was his first tangible connection to what that lifestyle was really like. He thought back to the flower child Crystal from the spring and pictured her there. To him, the hippies were like throwbacks to the pioneers; grow your own food, build your own shelters, no technology or medicine. He thought to himself, "Man – they're believers – dropping out and giving up everything for the new cause."

The four of them took note of the scene at the commune. Like the group Jeff and Slade saw in Maine, all the guys had beards and long hair. Some wore Australian hats and bandanas. The girls were in jeans or granny dresses to the ground – all kinds of patches and artwork sewn in - none of them wearing bras – some with love beads around their necks and others dancing around like gypsies. They did what they damn well felt like doing. And all were willing to get naked at the drop of a hat. So uninhibited and far from the constraints of conventional establishment life.

Ed, the youngest of the group, mainly enjoyed the choppers and the pure adventure of the film. But he also sensed that the underlying message went further. He wasn't sure just what it was. Hanging out with the other three over the past months had stimulated Ed's sense of wonder and curiosity. He looked forward to talking with them about "Easy Rider" after it was over.

The others related to the movie on a somewhat deeper level. For Slade and Jeff, it was like a broader version of the lives they'd lived the past few years, but with a ton more action and excitement. Rails saw it more as a statement of a genuine movement, and material well worthy of winding up in his writing.

It was as if they all were there in spirit, on choppers too, riding along with Wyatt and Billy. They felt the gunshots at the end with the bikes aflame and the main two characters dead, as the camera panned up to the big southern sky.

With the movie over, Ed stowed the cushions away and they walked out the main entrance without any hassles. On the way to a Denny's restaurant across town, they went over their impressions of "Easy Rider".

"Pud was right – it was dynamite," Slade began. "That was one of the coolest things I've ever seen on the screen, man. Just the way they shot it and how it kept moving all the way to the end. And that was our generation right there on film, gentlemen – an expression of our generation."

"It was...authentic," Ed said. "That's the word – authentic."

That term sparked something in Slade and he laughed. "Ed – this big time director," he said. "I think his name was Wilder...yeah, Billy Wilder. He once said something like, 'You have to be authentic in the movies. You have to be sincere. And if you can fake that, you've got everything.'"

"I don't get it."

"I do," Jeff laughed. "You know, Ed – faking being sincere – the contradiction in it. But I really liked the part about the hitchhiker and the commune. I learned a little something – just how the whole thing is supposed to work. Remember that line one of them said – 'simple food for our simple taste'? And that prayer they said I think before eating - 'to make a stand'?"

"Yeah - all in tune with the counter culture philosophy, my friend," Rails cut in. "Another line that stuck in my head was when the hippie hitchhiker tried to get them to stay at the commune. He said something like 'Stay with us – the time is now.' And Captain America comes back with, 'I'm hip with time – but I just gotta go.'"

"I could relate," Slade said. "No way either one of them could commit to something like that – not considering the kind of guys they were. What struck me is that even though you like...reject society and drop out, if you commit to a commune, you give up something big in the end. Your independence."

"That's true – that's a good point," Ed said. "But that dude who played George – man – he was great. What was that line he said when they offered him the bone?"

"I remember," Jeff answered. "He said something like it leads to harder stuff and he didn't want to get hooked. The dude was already a committed alcoholic." They all chuckled over that line.

"That guy's name is Jack Nicholson," Slade said. "I saw him in a B movie called 'Little Shop of Horrors' a couple of years ago. I think they shot it in two weeks for about fifty grand. He played a nut job who loved pain at the dentist's office. The guy was a riot and the movie was far out, man. The cast had the most wacked out names – like for example, Hortense Fishtwanger, a big wig reporter from 'The Society of Silent Flower Watchers of Southern California'. I don't know why I remember weird stuff like that but I guess I liked the names. Sorry about the digression, boys – sometimes I just can't help myself."

You got one hell of a memory for trivia, Shotgun," Ed said, "Hortense Fishdwanger!" They all roared. "But getting back to the movie, what about the ending – can anybody explain that to me?"

"That's 'twanger', man," Slade laughed. "Sure think I can explain it. They screwed up – they blew it like Wyatt said. Think about it. They smuggled coke from Mexico and made a big score in LA. Bad karma, dude. That's what financed the trek they were able to take. In the end, they paid for it with the bad LSD trip In New Orleans. The drugs wrecked the whole thing is the way I see it. Maybe it was even kind of an omen for the drop out and turn on philosophy."

"So explain them both getting shot at the end." Jeff said. "Was that part of karma too?"

"I think that kind of made a broader statement," Rails answered as they pulled into the restaurant. "Like Captain America and Billy were symbols of the disillusioned youth of America and the movement. The rednecks represented the narrow minded establishment – you know - using violence to deal with something they couldn't understand or didn't want to."

"Wow," Ed said. I'd have never figured that out in a million years."

"You're a little younger than us, Ed," Slade smiled. "Just keep on listening and asking questions like you've been doing the last few months. You're growing, man. But I'll tell you guys, that flick just lit a burn under me. I've been considering doing something big like that trip they took for some time now, actually since that first time we talked about Jack Kerouac's books. But I know I have to accumulate more of a cash reserve before I take anything on but I'm getting there. How about maybe the four of us? Doing something like what they did but minus the drugs. I'm just planting a little seed right now – I have to think it through more. Let the idea roll around over the next month or two – see if it germinates. We have plenty of time 'til the weather gets cold. What do you say?"

"Absolutely," Rails answered enthusiastically. "It's rolling around already. What an opportunity that would be for writing fodder."

Jeff and Ed nodded their heads. The four spent the next half hour in the restaurant over burgers, cokes, and coffee, rehashing every detail of "Easy Rider".

144

33

More than a month now after she almost drowned, all was back to normal for Lynne Charland. As a result of the experience, she'd become tighter with Jeff and Slade, particularly Jeff. She liked them both as friends she could trust as she'd told them. But as Slade had long since noticed, she had a special little something going Jeff's way. Occasionally, she got just to the edge of openly flirting with him with touches here and rubs there. He sensed it pretty clearly now.

But as much as he thought about Lynne, Jeff just couldn't see a way to ask her out. He didn't even own a car. He had nothing for her at this point besides himself. Plus he considered the fact that they worked together. If it didn't go right between them, there would be major awkwardness after. He didn't want any part of that drama. Still, for sure, it was there between them. He felt it for her too.

Now into the second week of August, the dog days of summer took hold. Each night in the factory seemed hotter and stickier than the one before it. Even the bugs flying around the lights sometimes appeared exhausted. But it came with the territory and you just had to stick it out. The long timers knew it well. Face it and be patient; nothing was forever. It wouldn't be long before September and relief.

Just as Slade and Jeff had finished work after probably the hottest night of the summer, they were walking toward the time clock. Rails approached them.

"You guys look like you just ran five miles," he said. "Your shirts are saturated."

"As do you, buddy," Slade said. "But at least you don't reek."

"Yeah, but you're not downwind. Never mind about that. Stop here for a second. I have a little surprise for you two gentlemen – and of course, I use the term loosely."

"Oh boy," Jeff said rolling his eyes.

"For a change, I'm serious, Jeff," Rails said. "Let's see. Well, a couple of my college buddies called me and said they had a seat on the van for me – one last seat."

145

"Van?" Slade asked. "Going where?"

"Woodstock, dude. An Aquarian exposition as they're calling it now. Three days of peace and music at Yasgur's dairy farm – Bethel, New York – about 90 miles north of NYC. Remember that night we talked about it a while back? I said I'd be in if I got an opportunity. Well, they asked me to go and I jumped at it. The dates are August 15th, 16th, and 17th."

He showed them a flyer for the event depicting a dove sitting on a horizontal guitar neck.

"Groovy," Jeff said. "You're just the guy to be there with all the stuff you want to write."

"Exactly why I'm going, Jeff Jones, master of perception. I'll be taking a sheet-load of notes. I'd ask you guys to come along but unfortunately, there's no room."

"No prob'," Slade said. "I'm still not into it enough to go all that way – plus I don't like being in...like big masses of people if I can help it. Makes me a little jumpy, you know? But like Jeff says, you're the guy. Plus I know we're going to get a real detailed report of what goes down. I look forward to that."

"Me too," Jeff added. "I'm glad at least one of us is gonna be there."

"Right, but listen," Rails said reaching into his back pocket. "I have something for the both of you in lieu of that. Two tickets for a show on Saturday night the 16th in Boston that I can't use now. Shotgun, my gifted teacher - and Jeff, my fellow guitar student, they're yours."

"Thanks, Steve," Slade said taking the tickets. "Who's the headliner?"

"A kick ass band from San Fran," Rails answered excitedly. "Cold Blood – I was out there last summer and I saw them at the Avalon Ballroom. They're a rhythm and blues group with a side horn section. They set down a mean groove – jazz/blues with just the right amount of funk mixed in. And the lead singer is this outah sight chick – Lydia – a five foot tall dynamo. She has all the vibe of Janis Joplin but with a better voice and she's significantly hotter, man. I actually got to talk to her for a couple of minutes after the show. She couldn't have been nicer. The band is just a cut below hitting it big like the Airplane or the Dead. Now is the time to see them. And a real gone group called Frijid Pink is the opener."

"Catchy name," Slade said. "You got me sold, bro."

"Dig it," Jeff agreed. "Like Fast Ed says, you can't go wrong with free. Where are they playing at?"

"Jungle Jim's — that underground club on Tremont Street near the common. Just take the train into North Station and its four or five stops on the subway."

"Done," Slade said, examining the tickets and tapping Rails on the back. "Thanks, pal — should be a cool night. And we'll be thinking of you grooving out at Woodstock."

"Oh yeah, you got that right, Charlie!"

34.

The next week and a half flew by. On Thursday, August 14th, Rails and five of his pals left in a van for Bethel, New York. Saturday night then came around and both Jeff and Slade were psyched for the show in Boston. They got a cab over to the depot where they bought the Globe and the Record American for the ride, plus a couple of large coffees. In about ten minutes their train arrived and they were on board.

"Doesn't get any better than this, my man," Slade said as they took their seats next to one another. "Nice wide bench — hot coffee — the news of the day — and even cup holders. What more could a humble man desire?"

"Nothing more," Jeff agreed. "Doesn't take a hell of a lot to please me as you probably know by now. And check out the opposite facing benches. Pretty cool."

"Yeah, the backs are reversible," Slade said. "If you have a little group you can have a conversation facing each other. You know, trains these days

147

are like that cab we came in on, though – crappy and they might smell a little. But at least there's always plenty of room."

"Like Beans would say, this is true."

There were only a dozen or so people scattered throughout the car. Jeff and Slade put their cups aside in the holders. They dug into the newspapers as the train got up to speed. Jeff glanced up a few times and noticed a couple of girls sitting one block up in the opposite row, facing them diagonally across the aisle. They were talking absently but twice he made eye contact with one of them. The second time she laughed a little and Jeff sensed they were talking about him and Slade."

"Shotgun – a couple of live wires at two o'clock," he whispered to him. Slade nonchalantly looked over. One of the girls smiled at him.

"I see what you mean," he said putting down his paper. "Not bad. This looks like it might have some potential. What do you think?"

"I think they're both good looking for sure," Jeff answered. "And they look older than us too – maybe we can learn a little something. You're the man who can think on his feet. Why don't you go over there and see if you can strike something up?"

"Right – there are times in life when you must act and this is one of those times. And you know what? I have a real edgy line that I've never tried yet. They look like the types that won't be offended. Maybe I'll lay it on one of them – what have we got to lose?

"Absolutely nothing."

"Okay, I'm going in. Now remember – you're my wingman. Be ready with something clever if I get them to come join us."

"Oh, I'll be ready!"

Slade got up, took a deep breath, and as smoothly as he could, approached them. He but his hand on the backrest, leaned In, and with a smile said to the closest one, "Excuse me – can I buy you a drink or do I have to sleep with you first?"

There was a pause for a couple of seconds and then both girls broke into a big laugh. "That's the first time I've ever heard that one!" the girl he addressed said.

"Just kidding, of course," Slade said smiling. "Now seriously, my slightly lonesome friend over there pointed you two out and begged me to come over. He's too shy, you know, but a very nice guy. And I figured I just had to say hello to two great looking sophisticated women like yourselves – you know - for his sake. And I thought you might appreciate something different for an approach...get it?"

"You figured right, stranger," the other one said. "You can really shell the bull out. I like that! And what might your name be?"

"They call me Slade."

"Well, I'm Tina, Slade, and this is my sister Tress. Actually, we're twins but not identical. Do we look like each other?"

"You sure do," he answered. "I figured you were sisters. Twins, huh? That's cool. Tina and Tress – would you like to join me and my pal Jeff over there? He's not really lonely – maybe he's a little shy. But see, he's the guy who sent me on this mission. I know he'd like to meet you. All joking aside, we'd dig some company for the ride."

"The twins exchanged looks. "Don't mind if we do," Tina said. "You may escort us."

Both girls were short; five one or two. They weren't knockouts but attractive and very fit. Tress, the smaller one, had a first class curves and Jeff's eyes focused on her. Tina was an inch or two taller, and a bit thinner with more of a model type of build. Slade's cup of tea. Both had long auburn hair with a lot of bounce in it. They got comfortable on the opposite bench as Slade introduced everybody.

"Nice to meet you, ladies," Jeff said smiling. "My friend here told me he was going to try out a new line on you. Mind cluing me in on it?"

They told him and he faked being taken aback. "Slade," he said. "You have some kind of nerve!"

"A little crude, maybe, but effective," Slade laughed and the girls along with him.

"Where did you ever think of an approach like that, Slade?" Tress asked.

"I'll make it quick. I knew this good looking cat on the cape when I lived there. All the girls dug him but he was kind of warped. We'd be in a club and he'd scan the floor for the really hot chicks who were turning down all the average looking guys for dances. Then he'd go up to one and he'd say, 'Would you like to dance?' When the girl said 'Sure', he'd say, 'Maybe the next one', smile, and he'd walk away."

"Eww," Tress said. "I don't know how I'd react to something like that."

"He only did it to the really stuck up prima donnas, Tress," Slade said. "Kind of like a mercenary type of attitude. Nice girls like you and Tina wouldn't be fair game for him. But Gary – that was his name – Gary Colvin. He's the one who gave me that line. He told me to be sure to use it wisely, though, which is what I did."

"Interesting," Tina said stroking her hair. "You tell a good story, Slade."

"One of his many talents," Jeff agreed.

As the train moved along, the four of them hit it off like they'd known each other for years. The girls had been at a dealership in Stiller looking at used cars and were returning to their apartment in East Boston. Both were LPN's at the New England Deaconess Hospital and 26 years old. As they neared North Station, Jeff was feeling good about the situation and decided to take the lead.

"Do you guys have any plans for tonight?" he asked.

"We're going to Zack's in Cambridge," Tina said. "It's a great club and we're regulars there on Saturday nights. You're both welcome to join us if you want to."

"Sounds good but how about one better? We have tickets to see Cold Blood at Jungle Jim's. I'm sure we can buy a couple at the door for you. On us – cool with you Slade?"

"It would be an honor."

The girls looked at each other and both gave a nod. "Funky," Tress said. "We can skip Zack's for one week. We're in."

"Great," Jeff said.

He sat back and felt a feeling of satisfaction. Slade had done the heavy lifting but he'd come in at the right time and chipped in. Not only were they going to see a good show, but now he and Slade had a couple of hot babes as company to add to the mix.

150

Just as Rails told them, the club stop was a snap from North Station. In about 15 minutes, they were out of the subway and on to the platform. At a busy spot near the stairs sat a street musician on the long bench. He was alone and playing a classical guitar. Beside him was some sheet music, a mug and a thermos full of coffee.

"Hey, guys," Slade said. "We're early. How 'bout we give that dude a listen for a couple of minutes? Jeff and I are aspiring musicians."

"He's not aspiring," Jeff smiled. "Slade's the real item – my teacher. I'm aspiring to be aspiring."

They all laughed and Slade guided them to a side spot. "Not a good thing to stand in front of a solo musician," he told them. "We should let the guy play with no distractions."

"You have the knowledge," Jeff said.

The man was middle-aged with a big stash and long gray hair. He had a peaceful air about him. They listened to him finish a familiar classical piece and then play all the way through a catchy blues instrumental that Slade recognized. He was very polished. Finished with the song, the musician then paused. He took a sip of his coffee, looked up and said hello to them.

"Interesting stuff," Slade said to him. "Classical, then right into the blues. What's the name of that first piece?"

"'Jesu Joy of Man's Desiring,'" the man said. "Some just call it "Joy".

"Oh, that's a Bach composition, isn't it? Wasn't that written for the piano or harpsichord?"

"That's right – harpsichord, I think," the man said nodding his head. "It's a tough go on guitar. But it was played on the organ at my father's funeral eight years ago. I was so moved by what a great piece it is, I went out and got the sheet music. I learned an advanced arrangement for guitar in G major. It's a long composition and it took me a month or two to get it to performance level. But it was worth it. Whenever I play it now, I just close my eyes and my dad comes alive in my mind."

"That's nice," Jeff said. "I never much thought of music in that way."

"Oh, a lot of people have that one song that does it for them, Jeff," Slade said. "I always get a special kind of feeling when I play 'Green Onions'. And I know the other one you did - 'Mean Streets', right, man? Been wanting to learn that."

"Yeah," the musician answered. "It was the final song in a blues book of 15 total that I got all the way through. Memorized 'em all. 'Mean Streets' was the hardest one. Never thought I'd get it down to be able to perform it. Still gives me goose bumps sometimes."

"I can relate," Slade said. "I know how hard it is to finish all the music in those books."

"You don't look like a lot of the musicians we see in the subways," Tina remarked. "My sister and I live in Eastie and ride them a lot. You seem a little more together than some of the guys and girls we see performing down here."

The man turned to the girls and smiled. "Thanks," he said. "Guess I have to do a little more work on my disguise. See, I'm not your standard street performer. I actually was a professional writer in the high tech field before I couldn't take it anymore and quit early last spring. Six years of that grind was enough for me. I'd had it with the treadmill – it just wasn't my thing at all. But luckily, I had some savings and began substitute teaching to fill in the money gap."

"What kind of books did you write?" Jeff asked.

"Reference manuals, user guides, data sheets – dry stuff like that. It was like studying boring material eight hours a day and then generating huge term papers over many months that nobody wanted to read. Got paid very well but it was misery every Sunday night, man, knowing that Monday morning and torture was looming. Many of us in the field really longed to be creative writers and I was one of them. I actually completed a couple of short novel manuscripts on the side but I haven't been able to break through as yet."

"That's interesting. What led you down here?" Tress asked.

"Well, I'd had about ten years of private guitar lessons over my life and accumulated a big repertoire of diverse material. I was never the greatest, but I had some chops and played in a few bands. Also worked with another guitarist in a duo for a time. After I left the job, I did some solo coffee house gigs where I could find them, but there was nothing steady. Summer vacation came and I picked up part time work to survive. But I needed more cash.

"One day, I read an article about the Boston subway musician scene. I got the idea to come down here and play regularly on my days off – to fill that income gap while getting in practice. I did it a few times and made decent money, tax free of course. Then it hit me that this unique experience is great material for a book. You know, sort of a documentary on what it's like to be a working street musician in Boston. Been at it since June and I've written about 50,000 words up 'til now. I'd say I'm about half way to being done, I think. It's coming pretty well."

"That's close to home," Jeff said. "We have a friend who's a creative writer. He's at Woodstock right this minute gathering material. He'd be blown away to talk to you."

"That's great," the guitar player said. "You know, besides playing down here myself, I've gotten to know some of the other performers at different stops. I move around a lot and I've interviewed a few of them for the book. Many Berklee music students play underground regularly to refine their material in public. One guy I know of actually recorded an album down here. And I've also rapped with a number of street people who sometimes come and sit with me. I hear some compelling stories from them. Plus interesting folks like you stop by and talk. Maybe you four will find your way into the book."

"I hope so," Tress said, "How much do you make on a good day down here?"

"Between fifty and a hundred in three or so hours, sometimes more," the musician said. "It takes time and some days I come out with a sore butt, but there's an art to it once you get comfortable and can connect with the people. And don't forget, there's a brand new audience every ten minutes or so."

Anybody ever give you a hard time?" Jeff asked.

"Not once," he answered. "That's what really surprised me. Boston people are very appreciative of the arts and are respectful. Many tell me how nice it is to listen to live music while they're waiting for their train."

"Cool stuff," Slade marveled. "I'm really glad we talked with you, man. Our buddy Steve, the writer, is going to love hearing about this. We've got to split now – we're on our way to a show. What's the book going to be called?"

"The working title is 'The Underground Scene', probably with a subtitle I haven't come up with yet."

"Perfect - stick with that," Tina told him. "We'll be sure to look for it."

"Sometime next year, I hope," the musician said taking a sip of coffee. "Provided I can hook up with an agent who believes in it. We'll see what happens."

"And what's your name?" Jeff asked.

"Ken – Ken Roberts."

"Smooth name for a smooth musician," Slade offered. "Best of luck, Ken."

"Thanks, man."

They all shook hands with him and each left a dollar in the open case. Up the stairway, they breathed in the invigorating air of downtown Boston on a summer night. They all smiled.

35.

Tremont Street bordered the Boston Common. Tina looked over to it and got an idea. She tapped Slade on the shoulder.

"The show's not for another hour, right?" she asked.

"About 45 minutes to be exact," Slade said checking his watch.

"And the place is down just a couple of blocks. That gives us plenty of time. Do you guys get high by any chance?"

"Does it get dark at night?" Slade answered with a grin.

"Well, I happen to have a rather robust roach rolled up in my purse. What say we find a nice out of the way place and share it – you know…to get in the right mood to really enjoy the show."

"This has to be a beautiful dream," Jeff said. "But it's got to be a safe spot. Getting busted would be a serious drag."

"For sure it would," Tress said. "But Tina and I have done this before. We know where to go. It's only a five minute walk."

"Then what the hay-yul, let's do it," Slade said. Jeff nodded in agreement.

The girls led them to a dense area bordering the swan-boat pond. They cut through some bushes to a small clearing surrounded completely by cover, but still lit well enough by the Common lamps to see. There they sat. Tina produced a thick joint half the length of a number two pencil and lit up. They passed it around and after only a couple of hits, all felt an unusually strong buzz.

"Wow!" Slade said. "This is some dynamite green. Got to be hash, right?"

"Yes it is," Tina said. "I've got a great connection – an aide who also works at the hospital if you can believe that. He only gets the best hayseed."

"I'll say," Jeff agreed. "Hooooo!"

Tina laughed – then Tress laughed – then everybody laughed together – about nothing in particular – they all just laughed and laughed – for a minute until they were out of breath. Then the joint went around a couple more turns.

"We'd better hold off now before we get too spaced out and don't want to even move," Slade said coughing a bit.

"Right," Tina agreed. "One more toke all around and we'll save the rest for later. There's still half left."

With that, they were back up and out to the street, a little unsteady at first but all feeling on top of the world. It was one of the cleaner highs either Jeff or Slade had experienced. All Jeff could think of was how much better this was than getting bombed. By the time they got to Jungle Jim's, with the interesting conversation with Ken the street musician and then getting high, they were all cruising and primed for the show.

The club was down some stairs below street level; a big room that could hold 200 people. The place was all painted up in bright slanting colors with psychedelic artwork all around. A long bar sat at the rear with rows of tables and chairs all around it. A dance floor was to the left of the stage and a standing area at the front of it. The stage itself was only two feet above the floor. It was positioned such that you could stand near the monitors and almost be right with the band.

The opening act were beginning their set as the four got a table and were approached by a waitress in a miniskirt. The girls ordered a couple of screwdrivers, Slade a Budweiser, and Jeff, true to his declaration, a glass of orange juice with a lemon slice. That was the new normal and he was sticking to it.

Frijid Pink, a blues/rock band from Detroit, hadn't made it big yet but they'd been together for a few years and knew how to get it going. They had a catchy sound and the musicians jived well together. The band established a nice groove and before long, the dance floor was full. Slade paired up with Tina and Jeff with Tress – it just fell in naturally like that – and they went up and danced several times. Both of the girls could really shake it with no inhibitions. And each was one of those kind of young women who look better and better with each hour that passes.

Back to their table for a break, the four sat and listened as Frijid Pink finished with a cover of "House of the Rising Sun". It was their big single and had gotten air play across the country. At a slow tempo but with sustained power chords underneath, the band clearly put their own stamp on a tried and true blues standard. The crowd loved it and the group got a nice ovation when they finished.

As they left the stage, a balding older man ran onto the platform and grabbed the mic. "I cain't sing and I cain't dance!" he said with a wry smile, "but I can lick every sun-um-bitch in this joint!" The crowd roared laughing as one of the bouncers escorted him off stage, both of them smiling.

"That dude's a real hoot," Slade said. "And that was a pretty good opening act too - Frigid Pink. Our friend Rails, the guy who gave us the tickets said that Cold Blood was the headliner, which of course they are. But I noticed on the poster on the way in that Frijid Pink got pretty high billing too."

"I think the bands are pretty close in popularity," Tina said. "Neither one has made the big time yet. But what I really liked about Frijid Pink is that they could get it done live. I mean I've heard 'House of the Rising Sun' on the radio by The Animals many times, and also the version they do which is totally different. Most times bands suck when they do their hits live — the singer can't hit the high notes — the tempo's too fast — and the musicians blow. Almost every time. But not them. It sounded just like the cut on the radio — maybe even better."

"You're right," Jeff said. "I've heard the song before too. I agree completely."

"Besides being beautiful, you're also quite astute, Tina," Slade added putting his hand on her shoulder. They all laughed.

They relaxed and talked some more as they waited for the Cold Blood set. Another round of drinks; a steady spacing between to feel good but not be bombed. Jeff didn't need alcohol to still be in a nice groove. And as he and Slade expected, the girls were mature and uninhibited. Nobody felt nervous or awkward. Everything was smooth all the way.

In about 20 minutes, the roadies had all the equipment set and five band members were on the stage getting tuned up. There was a bass player, guitarist, keyboardist, drummer, and a brass section consisting of a trumpet player and a tall black man on tenor sax. The lead singer, Lydia, the performer that Rails talked about so much, was nowhere to be seen.

"They're almost ready to go," Slade said. "How 'bout if we go up to the standing area in front?"

"Sounds good," Tress said

With that the four got up and moved over there. They staked out a good spot. The background lights faded down and a strobes lit up the stage in bright reds, yellows, greens, and blues on the grey facade in back. The band began with just the bass and drums; a steady 4/4 tempo like a Ferrari idling and getting ready to rip. The four spectators swayed with the beat as did the crowd that had gathered all around.

Then the organ cut In with some funky chords and the guitarist, on a Strat, kicked it with a familiar lick. DA- DA-DAAA....DA-DA-DA-DA-DAAA....DA-DA-DAAA....DA-DA-DA-DA-DAAA....

157

Slade recognized the song right away. "'I Just want to Make Love to You' – Willie Dixon." he said. "That song absolutely kills me."

"Yeah!" Jeff yelled, as the band began to gain power and the drummer laid down a thunderous beat. "Dig the cat on percussion," he said excitedly. "Can he bring it or can he bring it?"

"Yes!" Slade agreed. "And check out the dude on lead guitar – laying out that killer lick over and over again – setting the whole thing up but not overdoing it. There's an art to it. I tried to be that guy in Night Hawk. You want to be on the side and not take over but still stick it hard and true at the same time – like subtly. That man gets it."

"Oh, I'm digging this!" Tress said as both she and Tina rocked from side to side. The brass joined in and the band gained more strength. As the drummer added some bawdy accents on the cymbals to further make the point, one thing became clear to all. Whether you liked it or not, this band was taking over. It continued that way for a minute or two more; the band cranking, grinding, and revving that motor to just the right RPM.

"Are you ready to kick some ass?" the P/A man finally shouted over the music.

"YEAH!!!"

"Then let's hear it for... LIDDEEYAAH!"

Still another 20 seconds passed. The band had the audience worked up like a mob ready to explode. Then, from the side, grooving to the beat, out she walked. Feeling the vibe – swaying, smiling – comfortably in her element, she moved to the microphone, looked out to the crowd, and then grinned side to side at the band. She felt it - cemented to the moment – right now! A five foot tall dynamo – blond hair – in black tights and a gold top – black stilettos with gold laces; a stunningly radiant young woman who couldn't have been older than 21 or 22. She continued to move to the beat around the mic, feeling the groove until the band found that cruising level. "It". Then she grabbed the stand with a choke hold and pulled it toward her.

"I don't WANT you – to be no slave...

I don't WANT you – to work all day...

I don't WANT you 'cause I'm – sad and blue...

158

I just want to make LOVE to you!"

The crowd cheered and Jeff fixated on Lydia. He couldn't take his eyes off of her. Although he hadn't had a drink, he was still on a high from the hash they had done earlier. Watching Lydia perform, it was as if he'd never seen someone so beautiful and talented. Slade and the girls were right into it too. The entire group in the standing area became fused like one huge rocking mass.

Slade looked over at Jeff, grabbed his shoulder and smiled. "You okay?"

"For the first time in my sorry life, I'm in love at first sight," Jeff laughed.

"Oh – she IS the balls!" Slade agreed.

Cold Blood moved into their next few songs, all up tempo, without even a pause. The standing area was now so packed that if you fell down you might never get up. And the dance floor was jammed too. The place was rocking at full tilt. Finally, the band slowed it down and played a nice ballad that showed off Lydia's pipes and range. The couples paired up and slow-danced right there in the standing area. Slade and Jeff got to experience Tina and Tress up close and personal.

Then the band kicked it up with "Back Here Again", a power funky tune that got everybody rocking. Again Jeff was mesmerized with Lydia and every move she made. He even thought she might have smiled directly at him once or twice, but passed it off just to being high.

The band hit the bridge in the song and then went into a long improvisational segment where each instrument got a long solo. Lydia took a swig of soda, moved to the side, and grooved to the beat. Then, about midway through as the organ ripped in, she jumped down, grabbed Jeff's hand, and yanked him up to the stage. For a few seconds, he was dumbfounded and had no idea what to do.

"C'mon, man!" she shouted in his ear. "Feel it! Boogie with me!"

Something beautiful came over him and any inhibition he might have had flew straight out the window. He got right into it with her, smiling, with the beat leading him on like a driving locomotive.

"All right!" she shouted to him as they moved around in sync and she fed off the vibe. With an assortment of jukes and twirls, she absolutely kicked ass, just like the P/A man had said. Jeff stayed in step and complimented

159

her surprisingly well. It lasted a couple of minutes before the bridge neared completion. Lydia then applauded Jeff, gave him a hug and led him off the stage.

Jeff was keenly aware through it all, as if he was on acid but on good trip. He was able to drink in the lights, the crowd, the band around him, and the sexy lead singer who was his alone for those moments. It was maybe the most spectacular spontaneous feeling he'd ever had in his life.

Lydia kissed Jeff on the cheek as she left him back with the group and returned to the stage; right on time to finish the song as the band locked back into the head. Then she tossed an album his way, which Slade caught. The crowd didn't fight him for it and everybody around Jeff gave him gave him pats on the back. When the song ended, Jeff wiped his brow and pointed to the table. He needed to sit down and collect himself after all that happened. Slade handed him the album and the two couples made their way through the crowd.

"You were great up there!" Tress said into Jeff's ear as they got seated. "And what a cool thing she did – and so unplanned, I'll bet." Slade shook his hand and Tina rapped him on the back.

"Awesome," Slade said as he passed Jeff the album. "You pulled it off, man – it was so good that I'll bet half the crowd thought you were a plant."

Jeff paused to get his breath. He was still all caught up in it.

"I was in...like another world up there," he began. "I was nervous at first, but then this feeling came over me and it all was like a beautiful dream. That's the only way I can describe it. Like it was me and her up there and the whole rest of the world just froze. I will never forget that experience for as long as I live."

They sat and talked through a couple of songs but before long, slithered their way back in to the standing area. There, they just plainly got down with the mind blowing groove that the band continued to hammer out. Moving, grooving, slipping, sliding; the whole nine yards plus. The applause was deafening as the set ended. The crowd demanded two encores, clapping, stamping their feet, and pounding the tables. Cold Blood delivered with "You Got Me Hummin'" and finally "I'm a Good Woman!" "Such a gooooood woman – so treat me right!"

Then the show was over and the band gave their final thankyous to a thunderous standing ovation. Slade, Tina, Jeff and Tress went back to their table and ordered a round for last call. They basked in a state of euphoria after witnessing a great performance.

"That might be the best live gig I've ever been to!" Tress said excitedly. "I'm so glad we ran into you guys – thanks so much!"

"Our pleasure," Slade said. "Sometimes the stars line up and things work out just right. Tonight is one of those times."

"Kismet," Tina agreed.

Jeff examined the album cover in his hands. It showed a picture of Lydia in a thoughtful pose with her hand supporting her chin, surrounded by bright red. COLD was written on top and BLOOD on the bottom. And it was also signed by Lydia.

"No offense, ladies," he said, "but as Slade recently described a mutual female friend of ours, that Lydia is one great, great broad. And I'll include the two of you in that category also." Tina and Tress nodded and smiled.

"Hey, I lost track of the time," Slade said. "It's almost twelve thirty. I hope we didn't miss the last train."

"Only by about an hour," Tina said.

"Wow – I never gave it a thought!" Jeff exclaimed. "A cab will cost a fortune back to town. Have we got enough bread to cover it, Slade?"

Before he could answer, Tress cut in. "Fear not, boys," she said calmly. "Come stay with us for the night in our luxurious East Boston villa. The jets flying overhead every ten minutes are like a lullaby. You can get the train in the morning."

"Are you serious?" Slade asked.

"Sure we are," Tina said. "You guys did us a good deed. The least we can do is return the favor. Just keep in mind that we're respectable girls and you've earned our trust. Now don't disappoint us."

"You picked the right two guys," Jeff said gratefully. "Don't worry. We'll be perfect gentlemen."

"And that's the truth," Slade agreed.

"Then it's settled," Tress said. "Now let's go get something to eat. I'm starved!"

They exited from Jungle Jim's and walked back up to street level. A block a way they saw a pizza joint and headed straight for it. To cap off the night, it was one of those great pizzas – chewy and gooey with pepperoni and a generous helping of extra cheese.

The girls had a second floor apartment in an old building on Bremen Street. It was a two bedroom and everything about it was huge. It had a high ceiling, enormous windows, and the longest couch maybe ever manufactured.

"Who lived here before you," Slade asked looking around, "a family of giants?"

"No, but I think maybe Bill Russell and his girlfriend," Tina laughed. "And don't talk too loud – the echoes can rattle the building. What say we watch a little TV and finish that giggle weed?"

"You mean the fatty boom blatty?" Slade asked smiling widely.

"I don't mean anything else!"

"Oh, man," Jeff laughed. "I love the way you two have that roach lingo down pat."

Tress turned on the television to the Late Late show and the four of them sat down on the couch. The horror movie "Frankenstein" had started earlier. Tina lit up the joint and passed it around. A couple of tokes each and they were all high again. Soon it came to the part in the film where the audience gets its first look at the scientist's creation.

"I've seen this movie a bunch of times," Jeff said. "Check out the filming work coming up. This is cool."

The camera focused on a big door in the laboratory that was closed. As the door slowly opened, the creature stood facing in the opposite direction, only it's back side in view – seven feet tall, stiff as a board, top-heavy and hulking. Slowly it turned around – a quick body front body shot, and then ZOOM - right to full face – scars, neck plugs, and a scary questioning expression filling the screen.

"Wow!" Tina exclaimed. "I've seen this movie before but never when I was high. That was chilling."

"That's just first rate cinematography." Slade said. "I've seen this flick before too. Can you imagine the reaction of the audience in the 1930's when they first saw that on the big screen? I mean things were so reserved then. I'll bet they all shit a brick."

"1930's?" Tress said. "I didn't know the movie was so old."

"Yeah, it's old all right – and I think I have that timing pretty close," Slade said.

"1931 to be exact," Jeff added. "And this far out cat James Whale directed it. The sequel "Bride of Frankenstein" too. He was right on with both movies."

The film moved to a scene where the creature was calm and sitting in the middle of a large room next to the laboratory. Dr. Frankenstein slid open a panel in the ceiling and it saw light for the first time. It stood and raised its hands trying to touch the rays, like a child reaching for God.

"Check that out," Slade said nudging Tina. "See – even though the creature never speaks in the movie, Boris Karloff had to be scary, but innocent like a baby too. I mean, big and gruesome as it was, the creature was just born like a day or two ago. The whole world is new to it – he doesn't know really anything yet."

"Karloff is the guy who plays the monster, right?" Tress asked.

"Check."

"This is a coincidence, gang," Jeff said, "but one of my last acts in my fabled college career, the one year that I lasted, was a research paper on Mary Wollstonecraft Shelly. It was for a Brit Lit course and I learned all about how Frankenstein came to be."

"I was wondering how you seem to know all the facts," Slade remarked.

"After that paper, I'm like a Frankenstein fiend, I have to say," Jeff said excitedly.

"Who was Mary Whatever Shelly?" Tina said.

163

"The author of the book the movie was based on," Jeff answered. "It was called 'Frankenstein or the Modern Prometheus'. And she was only 19 when she wrote it. Is that far out or what?"

"Really?" Slade said with added interest. "I knew there was a book but I never came across it. You mean a teenage woman wrote a first rate horror story like that?"

"Would I lie to you?"

"Perish the thought, dude. Well, now then – seeing that you're 'the source', you must tell us more."

"Be glad to," Jeff said, feeling no pain and getting off on talking about something he had a passion for.

"Go!" Tina said. "But wait - let's get comfortable first."

She got up and turned down the volume of the television a few notches. Then she grabbed a couple of blankets from the bedroom and everybody got nice and comfy.

Jeff adjusted his side of the blanket he and Tress shared and collected his thoughts. "Well, let's see. It was like...umm. It was the summer – 1815 or 16 – sometime around then. Mary Shelly was in Switzerland with her lover Percy Shelly – her last name was, uhh...Wollstonecraft Godwin then. Percy Shelly was a big time poet. They were living together at a cottage near Lake Geneva, and another well-known poet type, Lord Bryon; he was a friend of theirs and came to stay with them for a while. And I think there was one other person who visited off and on, but I can't remember who it was. But I don't think he was much involved in what I'm going to tell you."

"The scene is set," Slade said.

"Anyway, it rained just about every day," Jeff continued "They stayed in a lot and talked to kill the time. One afternoon, the three of them were sitting around the fire reading ghost stories and discussing them. Byron threw out the idea that they all write a horror story to see who could come up with the scariest one."

"For real?" Slade asked. "You're not putting us on, are you, my man?"

"No way," Jeff said, taking another long drag from the roach. "I really dug the subject and did a ton of research. I spent hours at the library on it –

included footnotes in my paper - a bibliography, the whole deal. Everything I'm going to tell you is the truth."

"Then please continue," Slade said taking a hit. "And pardon the rude interruption. I don't know what came over me!"

He just about choked the last sentence out and they all laughed for about a full minute, just like they did earlier at the Boston Common. Finally Jeff caught his breath and got up another head of steam.

"Okay – so a few days go by and Mary can't come up with a damn thing. They're sitting by the fire again one night and now they're talking about the principles of life – like if anybody could ever reanimate a stiff – cool stuff like that. So it gets Mary's imagination stoked up and she has trouble staying asleep later. She has what she calls a waking dream."

"I know exactly what that is," Tress interrupted. "Like being between awake and sleep – you're conscious but kind of dreaming too – almost like a mini trip. I've had it many times."

"Me too," Slade said.

"You described it just right, Tress," Jeff agreed. "So, in this...waking dream, she sees a scientist kneeling beside this ugly thing he's put together on kind of a stone slab. But there's no electricity or gizmos like in the movie – whatever animates it he's already done. The thing comes to life and opens its eyes – moves its fingers. But unlike in the movie, this creator dude is repulsed by what he's done. The thing is so gruesomely ugly that he can't even look at it. The yellow in its eyes – I remember that - like grosses the hell out of him so much that he wants to puke. He feels as if he's defied all mighty God or something and...he flips out and splits."

"Far out!" Tina exclaimed.

"So the creator runs out of the laboratory and up to his bedroom – hoping the thing will die or just go away. He falls asleep but before long, he feels something on his arm, wakes up, and sees it – standing over him, peering down at him with like...those yellowed curious eyes he can't stand."

"Jesus - that gave me goose bumps," Tina said.

"There's more – much more," Jeff continued. "Mary wrote up a short story the next day based on that waking dream. Percy Shelly and Byron both read it and were...totally stunned by its power and potential. 'Mary –

165

this is dynamite – you've got to flesh it out into a novel – like immediately!' they told her. Well, not in those words but you get the idea. And that's exactly what she did. She worked on it for the next year or so and called the book 'Frankenstein or the Modern Prometheus' like I said before. Most people think Frankenstein refers to the thing the scientist created, but Dr. Frankenstein was the creator. The creature was never given a name in the book, but I think it called itself 'thy Adam' once or twice - like in Adam and Eve."

"It talked?" Tress asked.

"Oh yeah, and a lot besides that – I'll get to it."

"So obviously you read the book," Slade said. "How true was the movie to it?"

"I read it twice," Jeff said. "Good as the movie was, no – it wasn't that accurate to the real story. The creature doesn't even talk in the movie. In the book, it's abandoned and lives on its own. It survives in the forests like a wild animal. But it's intelligent and sensitive too. Every time it comes across people, they like - recoil in horror and run away. That bugs the hell out of it because he wants to be accepted.

"So for a year or two, it lives undetected in this unused boarded up hovel built flush against a cottage – sleeps during the day and hunts for food at night. It survives on mostly nuts and roots. The thing is super strong and tough – really good at coping like a lone wolf. None of the people in the cottage ever know it's there because he keeps quiet and knows enough to cover up his comings and goings."

"A smart monster? Crazy!" Tina exclaimed.

"Exactly!" Jeff agreed, taking another hit from the diminishing joint. "Intelligent and sensitive too. A lot of time goes by. It watches the cottage people day by day through a crack in the wall after it wakes up. In time, it learns French and even how to read through observing one of the adults giving a kid daily lessons. I think somewhere along the line it must have stumbled on some books too, but I can't remember.

"Then, probably after a year and a half or two, one day it works up the courage to show itself. The people take one look and run for the hills before it can hardly say a word. That pisses him off to no end, man! You know, being rejected by people it respected and admired. Not long after, he burns down their cottage and commits himself to terrorizing all of mankind, who won't accept him."

"Awesome," Tress said, now higher than a kite.

The roach came around for a final time. Jeff hissed up a big toke, exhaled, and shook his head. He was on a roll now and nothing was going to stop him. His audience, equally high, were glued to the couch.

"Then, a few weeks later, Dr. Frankenstein's younger brother is murdered in Geneva," Jeff continued. "He goes out to the crime scene and catches a glimpse of the monster, who sees him and takes off. It can run like the wind. Dr. Frankenstein puts two and two together and figures the thing killed his brother to get even with him for being abandoned. He commits himself to find the monster and to have it out with him."

"Man – this thing goes pretty deep," Slade remarked.

"You wouldn't believe how well thought out and detailed the book was," Jeff agreed. "So in time, he does catch up with it, but the monster convinces Dr. Frankenstein to listen to its story before he does anything crazy. Lucky for the doctor - he'd have gotten creamed in a fight. It gets him to sit down in its hut over a fire way out in the wilderness - and tells him his whole story – soup to nuts. And in this – what's the word...eloquent way. Almost like a long soliloquy - with a bunch of thous, thees, and thys. That's how they talked then. The creator is like – taken aback with the monster's sincerity and the case he builds in the story."

"What case?" Slade asked.

"Oh, the coolest thing," Jeff answered. "At the end, after describing all the shit he's been through, in like a lawyer's concluding statement, it says to Dr. Frankenstein something like, 'Since you created me and caused me all the misery I've just described, make me a female like me so there'll be one more of my kind that I can relate to. Then the two of us will go off and stay in the mountains where nobody lives and I'll have nothing more to do with humans. Otherwise, I'll strike fear in mankind and commit murder whenever the mood strikes me.'"

"So what then?" Tina asked. "Did the doctor make a female like In 'Bride of Frankenstein'?"

167

"He agreed to, but in a few days he chickened out. He figured they might have kids and create a whole new race of zombies or something. When the creature found out, he flipped out in a big tantrum. I think the first thing he did was to kill Dr. Frankenstein's bride – on their friggin wedding night!"

"Oh my God!" Tress gasped.

"Hairy," Slade said. "The thing really knew how to strike where it really hurts."

"It had a steel set of balls," Jeff shot back. "Sorry, girls – sometimes I get carried away. Now, to continue. So Dr. Frankenstein was filled with rage over it and dedicated himself to hunting down and killing the monster from that day on. He chased it all over Europe for like the next year or two. But the creature was real savvy - always staying a couple of steps ahead, committing murders here and there when he felt like it, and scaring the crap out of everybody in its path."

"Wow," Slade marveled. "So much more than what was in the movie. But that's the way it usually is. The book is always better than the movie. How'd it end up, Jeff?"

Jeff sat back and closed his eyes. He had to think hard to remember.

"I…umm…okay – now it's coming back," he began. "Let's see - I think that Dr. Frankenstein had chased the fiend – that's what he called the creature – the fiend or the demon…or the wretch - out to the frozen seas somewhere up near the Arctic Circle – might even have been the North Pole. I remember sled dogs, ripping winds, whitecaps – all that kind of stuff. Yeah. Then somehow, Dr. Frankenstein gets stuck on an iceberg that breaks off and he's stranded adrift. He almost dies but is saved by a ship, which for a while, also gets stuck in a frozen part of the sea. But it eventually breaks free."

"A 19 year old girl thought up all of this?" Tress asked incredulously.

"That's what blows my mind," Jeff answered. "What an imagination! So to sum it up, after they get the ship righted, Dr. Frankenstein tells the captain the whole story. Then he begs him to allow him to take a lifeboat so he can continue the chase to do in the creature. But the captain says no, he can't spare the boat. Not long after that, Dr. Frankenstein loses his mojo, gets sick, and dies on the ship."

168

"It ends like that?" Tina said.

"Oh no," Jeff said. "Now I remember the ending clearly. Shelly had a final shot left. A day or two later, the captain hears something in the room where Dr. Frankenstein's body lies. He peeks through a crack in the door, and it's the creature – all seven feet of him or whatever, draped over the body – mourning the death of its creator, weeping like a baby."

"Wild!" Tina exclaimed.

"Of course the captain is probably shitting his pants," Jeff continued, "But he stays – watches undetected and listens. The creature is all caught up in remorse and talking to itself – saying stuff like Dr. Frankenstein's death brought him no peace and that the crimes he did only brought him more misery. He closes with vowing to burn himself to death and then quietly leaves the room out the opposite door. The captain rushes out on the deck and watches the creature drift away on an ice raft, never to be seen again. The end."

Slade, Tina and Tress all stood up and clapped. Then Jeff stood up and took a bow – and the four of them fell back into the couch like they were shot. Plunk.

"A cool resolution," Slade said. "That was great. Way to tell a story, Jeff."

"Terrific," Tina agreed and her sister gave a thumbs up.

"Thanks," Jeff said, feeling comfortable in his own skin, which used to be rare for him. "Could have never done it if I wasn't high I don't think. That hash just kills any feelings of – you know – of listening to what you're saying and judging it. You get up a head of steam and go, man!"

"Well, you really painted a hell of a picture," Tress said. "Still can't believe such a young woman could achieve something like that. Even though I know the story now, I still want to read that book."

"Just look in the Classics section of any bookstore or better yet, the library," Slade said. "They'll both have it".

"Just a few more things about Mary Shelly I remember from the research I did," Jeff added. "Her mom died when she gave birth to her. And that book and her success were like - kind of a curse. She had a miscarriage and almost died, and had at least one other kid who died very young. I think both Shelly and Byron were killed in a storm out to sea, at least I

169

know for sure Percy Shelly was. And she was also blackmailed later in life several times, got sick, and was paralyzed before she died at maybe 50. But man, she created something so good that it will live through the ages, right?"

"She sure did," Slade agreed. "And may I ask what grade you got on the paper?"

"A-plus. The professor went ape shit over it and she even read sections to the class. The only A-plus I ever got in my life."

"It was well deserved," Tress said.

Tina then reached over and turned out the light. The room was now lit by the television only. They sat back, pulled up the blankets, talked a little more, and watched the final scenes of the monster burning to death in the windmill. Then they simply vegged out. As the station signed off and the screen went to a white dot, Tina cuddled up to Slade and Jeff pulled Tress in close. The only light was from the street lamps through the windows. There was some kissing and above the waist action, but everybody was too mellow and just plain tired for anything further. Plus Slade and Jeff had given their word and both meant it. Before long, all four fell into a deep and peaceful sleep. With a ton of room still left on the couch.

Morning came and a strong sun warmed the apartment to life. In the background were the traffic sounds of Bremen Street and the booming thrusts of jet takeoffs at Logan Airport. When Jeff and Slade awoke at about the same time, it was to the aroma of bacon sizzling on the stove and the pulse of coffee bubbling in the urn. The girls were up well ahead of them and working on a first class breakfast.

Slade sat up and rubbed his eyes. "Oh wow, he said, what a nice drift there is in this place."

"Oh yes – that IS a beautiful smell," Jeff said removing the cover. "You girls are the damn best."

"We take care of company," Tina smiled. "But both of us have to be at the hospital for work at 10 so we don't have a lot of time. Breakfast is on the table in a few minutes, boys."

"We'll be there with bells on."

170

Slade and Jeff threw some water on their faces in the bathroom. Both had slept well and felt good; no after effects from the hash they'd done. They sat down to a New England breakfast of waffles, bacon, toast, home fries, and hot coffee. A good combination to cap off a great time. There followed a flow of conversation about the show the prior night peppered with jokes and laughs.

After finishing breakfast, everyone got organized and left the apartment together. The girls walked Jeff and Slade to the subway station, at which they exchanged phone numbers and hugs as the cars pulled in.

"Guys – we had a ball – thanks for everything," Tina said.

"You have our phone number – now be sure to keep in touch," Tress added. "We mean it. And any time you're in town, stop by and see us. Just show up - no notice needed."

"We had a blast," Slade said. "We will – and once again, you girls are the greatest."

"My faith in human kind is fully restored," Jeff said, saluting them after more hugs, as he and Slade stepped on to the subway car.

They took their seats and looked back out to the platform. Jeff's eyes focused squarely on the girls, watching the two of them smiling and waving. He waved back, as did Slade.

The girls were young, attractive and full of spirit. Maybe they were at their peaks. Both might never look better in life than they did right at that moment. That scene clicked in Jeff's mind – ZAP – like a photograph taken. And it was quickly filed away to some remote address in memory, saved to flash back periodically until the day he'd die.

36.

171

At North Station, Jeff and Slade caught the 11:25 train back to Stiller. Settled in their seats, they rested back. For a while there was a peaceful quiet. As the train got to cruising speed, Slade thought of Rails and Woodstock.

"Hey, man – last night was such a gas that I completely forgot about the Railster," he said. "The event should be close to over now – I wonder how it went. We'll have to check out the news on TV when we get back."

"Definitely," Jeff said. "But you know he's going to give us a full rundown. I'll bet he took so many notes that he ran out of those dime pads he always carries."

"Well, we've got to be grateful to that guy. He turned us on to a super show and a couple of groovin' girls. Rails was nice enough to give us those tickets. We owe him one, don't you think?"

"Nah – maybe I owe him but you don't, Shotgun," Jeff said pointing his finger at Slade. "You've given us months of music lessons for nothing. Steve really appreciates it and so do I. He told me on the side that it was the least he could do for all you've taught us."

"Really?" Slade said thoughtfully. "Thanks for telling me that. It gives me a nice feeling down deep, you know what I mean? But leave me aside – let's talk about you. You were…THE MAN last night! First the smokin' lead singer picks you to go up on stage where you both kill it – and then you tell that awesome Frankenstein story back at the sisters' pad. I'm still thinking about that fascinating complicated creature you described so well. They dug it and so did I. You knew that material cold, man. It was great to see you so – like – in your element."

"Element? That's interesting. I never figured I had an element."

Jeff smiled at saying that and glanced out the window at the passing trees and houses. He collected his thoughts for a few seconds before he spoke again.

"Thanks, Shotgun…but I have to tell you something," he said.

"Uh oh…"

"Nah – it's nothing so bad. I just want to level with you about…my stuff."

"Stuff? Okay, hit me."

172

"See, maybe I hid it pretty well," Jeff began, "but I was kind of a mess by the time I got into town last spring. I'll admit now that I was depressed a lot of the time up there in Lincoln – maybe I had too much time to think. It wasn't so bad that I couldn't work and support myself, but I looked on the bad side a lot. You know – what if this happens – what if that happens – what's the use anyway – negative crap like that. I had headaches all the time. The only peace I had was sleep at night, and even then, I had these friggin nightmares two or three times a week."

"Sheez...I remember you talked to me about your issues a while back but you didn't get into any detail. I never figured it went that deep."

"Oh yeah, it goes that deep all right. I didn't want to lay too much out on the table then – I didn't know you that well. But I'll be honest now and say that more than once I was so low, I thought seriously about doing myself in – ending it – like death would be the escape from all my misery – escape that I had to have. Relief, man – eternal relief. But you know what? I could never get up the stones to do it. Plus I knew from the time I spent in 12-step meetings that it was all part of the game for kids of alcoholics. That took the edge off a little but I still couldn't stifle those thoughts sometimes."

"Wow – and you were all alone with it."

"Yeah, but that was my own choosing. You want a laugh? The main reason I didn't kill myself was the fear that I might screw it up like I felt I did everything else. You know - live through it and be paralyzed or something - like I wouldn't even be able do that right." There was a pause and then both of them broke into a laugh.

"I'm serious!" Jeff gasped catching his breath. "Sometimes I even laugh to myself today thinking about it."

"Please continue on," Slade said, admiring Jeff's honesty.

"Well, I was just spinning my wheels up in the White Mountains and I knew it was either move on or things would get worse. So after I got a tip about work in Stiller, at least I made a decision and acted. And it was a good one, finally. The situation lifted just a little bit on the day I left, beginning with that ride I hitched with the flower child."

"I remember. It was one of the first things you talked about."

173

"Yes. And that first night at the Y – when I bumped into you and Nikki – man, it was like an enlightenment. As if I walked in on a prophet playing the guitar - you! I'd found a peaceful place with good people where I could kind of reset and get pointed forward. Can you dig what I'm saying?"

"I hear you loud and clear."

"I figured then that the Y would be just a stop gap until I found something better. Never thought I'd be still be there now."

"Same goes for me," Slade agreed. "I found out pretty fast that there's strength in the group in that place. That's why I fixed up my pad and settled in."

"Yeah. So in the what – five or six months I've been in Stiller, thanks to you, Creech, Shorty, some of the other good dudes in the hotel – and Rails, Ed, Beans, and a few of the other guys at work – and of course Lynne, and I'll throw Nik in there too...I'm in a better place, man. I'm a lot calmer and the nightmares are pretty much gone now. I hardly ever get those migraine headaches that I used to have like every other day. I know the Y is just a temporary stop, but for the first time – just about as far back as I can remember – I feel like I fit in someplace. Like I have a home to go to where I can get support."

"For sure," Slade reflected pausing a few seconds. "And when you come down to it, most people are pretty good after all if you just give them a chance. That's really cool that a place like the Y, the last resort for some, can give young guys like us strength and hope like you say."

"It does," Jeff agreed. "The place has been huge for me. I was on the phone with my brother Luke in Maryland the other day and I told him what I just told you. He was like – ecstatic, man. He's always wanted me to stay with him and his wife but I'm stubborn and had to go my own way. I know he worries about me. Luke's a good guy and he really liked the way I sounded."

"That's nice, Jeff. Now you have something really special. Like a strong insight that you can stow away and keep with you for the rest of your life. 'Enlightenment' like you said – that's a good word for it."

"Agreed. And the best thing is that I'm kind of excited about the future because I feel a lot more able to handle things now. You know, stronger and more resilient. I know change is coming but it doesn't scare me like it always used to. I kind of welcome it."

"Too bad your parents aren't around," Slade said thoughtfully. "I know they'd be pretty damn proud of their kid."

Jeff had to stifle getting emotional. "Thanks, Shotgun," was all he could muster.

"And you're right," Slade continued. "Change IS coming. Remember what we talked about after we saw Easy Rider? Well, I have a plan almost set in my head that includes you, Rails, and Ed like I said before. But I'm still not ready to reveal it just yet. It's getting closer – like its gelling, man. Soon as I get everything straight, I'll lay it on all of you – when the time is right. One thing is for sure, though, at least for me. I am out of here come November and the cold weather come hell or high water. Guaranteed."

"Anybody else I'd pump for more info," Jeff offered, now over being choked up. "But I know you and your preparation thing – and your flair for the dramatic. I'll be patient and wait. I'm pretty sure I'll be hip to whatever it is. There's nothing holding me back now. I'm just a temporary factory drone. Still, not to change the subject, but there is just one other thing that's on my mind."

"And what's that?"

"What do you think about any future moves with Tina and Tress? Tress...I LOVE that name – fits her perfectly. A couple of quality women, weren't they?"

"Most definitely." Slade said scratching his head. "I thought a little about it as we left them this morning. The way I see it, we met by chance, vibed, and had a great time. You and I behaved right. We don't owe them anything and they don't owe us either. I'd for sure want to see them again if I was going to stay around here. But I know by winter, I'm gone for certain. And I expect you will be too. So...I'd say maybe meet them for lunch or something sometime between now and then but not much more than that. At least that's my viewpoint right now."

"Really?" Jeff said. "They liked us, Shotgun, and they're two hot babes. I'm not ashamed to say that I'd love to – you know – with that little Tress if the stars lined up right. I haven't had any action since I left New

175

Hampshire. But hard as it was, I'm glad I didn't make a pass at her. It would have ruined the whole thing."

"Yeah," Slade agreed. "They were nice enough to let us stay over. No way that we could have broken that trust."

"Right, but it's still tough. Being young and having like…needs. You know what I mean. Sometimes it's a bitch to carry it around on top of everything else you have to deal with."

"True, but in my case, my right hand and I do have a beautiful relationship." Slade then gave him a wink.

Jeff looked at him for a couple of seconds and then they both laughed. "Man, you have a way of putting things!" he told him. "But I kind of think maybe there's more to it than that. Five letters. N-I-double K-I. I know she rotates around your space every so often and that you stop by the restaurant to see her. I'm going to put it to you straight. You don't have to answer if you don't want to. Have you or have you not…closed the deal with her?"

Slade sat back and smiled. "Well, in the immortal words of the esteemed philosopher Larry Fine, I wouldn't say yes but I couldn't say no."

"Would you say maybe?"

"I might."

Another volley of laughs.

"No further questions," Jeff said.

Then a thought occurred to Slade. "That's all I have to say on that subject for now," he began. "But there's one other thing I'm pretty sure about."

"What's that?"

"Before all is said and done, you and Leggy Lynne Charland will do the horizontal hula. Know what I mean?"

"I think I do. You really think so? I'd die for that. What makes you so sure?"

"I live and breathe, my man, I live and breathe. I've seen the way she looks at you. Just be sure to carry protection in your wallet. I always do.

176

Even if Lynne's on the pill, double the protection. You don't EVER want that life changing surprise unloaded on you and have a monkey wrench dumped in your future."

"Oh, I know exactly what you're saying. And not that the situation comes up much – no pun intended – but I do just that. Two gizmos just in case I ever REALLY get lucky."

"You are a wise man."

They talked for another 20 minutes before the train pulled into Stiller. Then, Jeff and Slade got back to the Y just in time to catch the Boston Patriots exhibition game against the Buffalo Bills.

37.

It was Wednesday of the following week that Rails showed up back to work. The first thing he did was to go out to the floor where he found Slade. Slade noticed right away that Rails didn't look quite right.

"What went down, man?" he asked. "You look like you've been sick."

"Stomach virus I got the last day," Rails said. "But I'm over it now – just a little weak still. That was the most unreal three and a half days I ever spent in my life, dude. But there's a million things to talk about - I can't even start here. What say we have lunch on the boxes, out back around where the snake chased Beans out of the building. Away from the uninformed masses. I'll find Jeff and Ed and I'll tell them."

"Okay."

"How'd it go in Boston?"

"Dynamite. The band was great and we picked up a pair of hot sisters – really nice girls. We had the best time."

"Groovy — see you at lunch."

The others got word and assembled at the boxes at 3:30 AM sharp. The group included Beans, who learned of the plan and was interested in hearing Rails. Brown bag lunches and drinks in front of them, they settled in as Rails took a sip of coffee and collected his thoughts.

"C'mon, Steve — GO! Lay it on us," Jeff said in anticipation.

"Jeff, there's so damn much I don't know where to start," Rails said. "I'll try to piece it together in sequence. Okay...it was a nice long ride out there — six of us in the van — three college buds, two of their girlfriends, and me. You know I'm from upstate New York about two hours north of Bethel, so it was like going back home. But once we got there, it was gridlock, man. I've never seen so many cars backed up and parked to the sides of the road in my life — had to be thousands. And like...thousands more kids walking by us — peaceful — almost like on a pilgrimage to a promised land. Most of them had left their cars off the road and were walking the last mile or two. We ended up doing the same when we could drive no further."

"Cool scene, Steve," Slade said.

"Yeah, sure was, Shotgun," Rails agreed. "We walked another half an hour up a dirt road before we got to the farm where everything was all set up. Off to the sides, there were cars left all over the place facing in all different directions. It was like a big flood had just dropped them there. We came to this big meadow that seemed to span on for miles — filled with hippies and freaks from all over the country, man. Everybody in bohemian clothes — headbands — tie dye shirts — peace signs - love beads, what have you. Like a sea of color. It had to be a hundred thousand at least — maybe two bills. I've never seen so many people in one place in my life.

"Then, there at the end was one long stage, several towers with platforms on top, amps piled a mile high, and this enormous mass of people like I said, mingling around, and more continually filtering in. And behind the stage in between the trees, you could see the wide expanse of water, which I think was White Lake."

"Was you a little nervous being stuck in the middle of all those people, Railsback?" Beans asked.

"You'd think I might be, but no, Beans, not at all. Everybody was relaxed and there was no trouble. Christ – I never shook hands with so many dudes or got so many hugs from chicks – braless just about every damn one of them. It had this like...nirvana feeling to it, man – as if everybody was so mellow that nothing could possibly get off kilter. The only thing was that it was drizzling pretty steadily and the ground was wet. Bad for laying out blankets."

"It rained most of the weekend didn't it?" Ed asked.

"Yeah – I'll get to that, Ed. So a fence was set up all around earlier and there was going be an admission charge. But by the time we walked up, there were just too many people for the organizers to handle. The fence was already half way down and they announced that it was going to be a free event. You should have heard the hand that got. So we slowly made our way in closer and got a good spot near the middle. We staked out our area – the six of us, and got comfortable.

"But something became screwed up and things got started late. Somebody told us that some of the bands were stuck in traffic and others were coming in by helicopter. Richie Havens opened and ended up doing what seemed like at least an hour or two, and he was only supposed to perform maybe ten songs. He played this long, long version of 'Freedom', and then got right into 'Motherless Child'. The crowd really liked both songs. And Shotgun – the way that guy plays the guitar – tuned open upside down with rapid-fire power strums. I thought the guy's arm was going to fall off. But he played with a ton of like...passion and conviction. That 'Freedom' song felt like an anthem for the spirit of the whole thing."

"Far out," Slade remarked.

"After Havens, we saw a band called Sweetwater, Ravi Shankar from India on sitar who was really cool, and let's see...Melanie, and Arlo Guthrie, a folkie from the area I think, who looked around 16 years old. He was pretty good. I think his dad is Woody Guthrie."

"Early 60's protest singer," Slade said. "Very well known. He wrote 'This Land is Your Land'."

"I remember singing that in third grade," Jeff remarked.

"Interesting - I didn't know that, Shotgun." Rails said finishing his sandwich and taking a long sip of coffee. "So by that time, it was past midnight and all of us were pretty wet. We started back to the van. Unfortunately, we missed Joan Baez. But even with the rain, things were fine. We smoked a little pot on the way – it was all over the place - and the cops, if any were around, looked the other way. All was cool, man – with everybody."

Just then, Lynne and Melissa wandered over from the cafeteria. "Is this a private meeting or is it open to the public?" Lynne asked.

"Open forum, ladies," Rails smiled. "I spent the weekend at the Woodstock concert and I'm in the middle of painting the scene. Join us, but be advised, things might get a little – let's say edgy on the side of good taste."

"Don't worry about that," Lynne laughed. "Remember, Missy and I are both Stiller girls, born and bred. You know what they say. You can take the girl out of Stiller, but you can't take Stiller out of the girl."

"You don't say," Jeff joked looking up at her. She smiled at him.

"I'll second that," Melissa said. Then she and Lynne sat down next to Jeff and Slade.

"Okay, now that we're straight with that, where was I?" Rails continued. "So back at the van, we were right next to a grove of trees that gave some shelter from the rain. We staked out an area and got a fire going – cooked hamburgers and hot dogs. We had a couple of big coolers and brought enough chow to last us the whole three days. We shared with a couple of freaks who had nothing to eat – everybody was fine with that. It was in the spirit of the event, man. Never had to go into town once for food, not that it would have been easy. We smoked some more hay with a few other people who joined us after we ate and just hung out for a while."

"Nice and relaxed, Rails. Just the way you'd want it," Ed said.

"T'was, Ed," Rails agreed. "And the guys I was with, man – two of 'em – Kenny and Jake - are legit campers and hikers. They were always heading up to Arcadia or Baxter State Park in Maine during school breaks and I went with them a couple of times. The girls, Jenna and Marilyn, were outdoor types too. The other guy, Troy, was a real hip writer dude like yours truly – I like to at least think I'm hip. Kenny and Jake pitched a big tent like a couple of army rangers – we all had sleeping bags. All six of us all slept in it. Plenty of room for everybody and no leaks. It all worked out perfectly."

"Always better when you're with guys who know what they're doing." Jeff said.

"You got that right, bud. By Saturday morning it was raining harder, but not so bad to stop the show. We got up at around eleven, had some breakfast, and took a little walk. Beautiful area even in the rain and it was fairly warm – 80 or so. Heading back to the farm at about one o'clock, things were getting more and more...let's say unreal. It seemed like there were double the people there from Friday night. We never saw so many peace signs all in one place. And the grounds were so soaked that there were big areas of mud from all the walkers. And naked people of both sexes doing airplane slides on the mud!"

"Nude?" Lynne said. "No clothes at all?"

"Birthday suits, girl. The naked truth. Like a bunch of little kids. And nobody made a big deal out of it – no one got out of line. They were just making the best of the situation. Alive and uninhibited."

"You know what they say - if it feels good, do it," Slade added.

"For better or worse, that's exactly what it was," Rails agreed. "It was the perfect example of that line."

"I had no idea it was going to be like that!" Melissa exclaimed."

"Neither did anybody else I don't think, Missy," Rails responded. "And wait – it gets better. I'll talk a little about the bands on Saturday and then what happened before dusk. We saw - let's see – Country Joe and the Fish, Santana, and uhh...John Sebastian in the afternoon. Then we took a break for a couple of hours, ate, walked, and just jived with the crowd. We met more young people from all over the U S of A and Canada too. Some of them even had their kids with them. All in this mass of humanity where there still wasn't a speck of trouble – everybody respectful and polite. It was almost, well...spiritual might be the best word. There was even a rumor that a baby was born somewhere on the grounds."

"Groovy – oh so groooovy," Melissa said. "Did Santana play 'Self Sacrifice'? I love that song."

"Self what?" Beans asked."

"They sure did. 'Self Sacrifice' is a long instrumental, Beans – up tempo with a lot of bare-hand percussion along with the regular drums. Kind of a jazzy Latin feel with a lot of improvisation. The drummer was just a kid – maybe not even 20. He did a long solo in the middle that really got the crowd going. The song probably went on for ten minutes and Carlos Santana just killed it. That performance was one of the many big moments of the event that we got to see."

"Right on," Ed said with a thumb pointed up.

"At around six thirty, a rip roaring thunder storm moved in like it was the Wizard of Oz," Rails continued. "I was looking up in the sky for monkeys with wings. The guy on the PA flipped out and told us to get away from the stage, like ASAP! They thought lightening might strike the towers with all the power that was going on through there. But again, everybody was cool – nobody panicked – they all did what they were told.

"I think our group was one of the few with rain gear, at least in our area. The storm lasted only half an hour and hardly affected the show. But the masses got re-drenched again, man - soaked to bone. And here and there – guys, girls, everybody - it didn't faze them. They sloshed in the slop without a care in the world."

"Three days off from reality, huh?" Lynne said.

"It sure was, Lynne" Rails agreed. "At seven thirty or so, we saw Canned Heat and about half the set that Mountain did. We knew that Janis Joplin and Sly and the Family Stone were scheduled to go on at about two in the morning, so we headed back to the camp to eat supper and get some Z's. We left right after Mountain did 'Theme for an Imaginary Western' – a Jack Bruce song. Awesome!"

"You mean the bands kept going all night long?" Beans asked.

"They did, Beans. One right after the other although there were long setup breaks. But by then, I'd say ninety percent of the crowd was high so nobody really cared. We got maybe three hours rest and got back in time to hear the Dead do 'Dark Star', followed by Janis and Sly, who both kicked it, man! By that time, we were mellow and completely exhausted. It was four in the morning and we made way back to the fort. Unfortunately, we missed The Who and the Jefferson Airplane."

"Bummer," Jeff said. "Grace Slick of the Airplane is my girl. When she smiles, I melt."

Melissa tilted her head up and began to sing softly. "Saturday afternoon - yellow clouds rising in the noon - acid, incense and balloons - Saturday afternoon - people dancing everywhere - loudly shouting 'I don't care' - it's a time for growing and a time for knowing..." Then she stopped, closed her eyes and smiled deeply.

Rails looked at her with wonder. "Wow, what a pretty voice," he said. "That's beautiful, Missy. Where did it come from?"

"The song 'Saturday Afternoon' by the Airplane. I have the album it's on. I always loved the way they harmonize those lines."

"Interesting," Rails marveled. "Kind of describes what the feeling was like throughout the whole event."

"Yeah, I'll bet," Ed said. "But man, with so many groups, no way you could see everybody, huh Steve?"

"Right, dude, but we did pretty well, considering. We did get to see Janis do 'Ball and Chain' and Sly perform 'Higher'. Those two songs alone were worth the whole trip by themselves."

"I love Sly," Melissa beamed, who on this night had seemingly come to life for the first time.

"It all sounds great," Slade offered. "I had no idea it was going to be so big with all that dynamite talent. And three days of it. I'll say this right now...maybe I was wrong. Sometimes you have to drop 'cagey' and just do it. I should have found a way to go – screw the crowds. It's a good lesson for me in the future to maybe get a little looser. Well, we have ten minutes until the buzzer sounds, Steve. Lay Sunday on us."

"Sunday and even a part of Monday too, Shotgun," Rails continued. "We slept all through Sunday morning – like rocks. On the way back to the farm, we noticed that a lot of the stands had run out of food. Neighbors in the area were bringing in stuff and we even saw helicopters dropping provisions. And it was nothing to see more naked people along the way, using the bathroom in a hole in the ground, or just hanging out like it was no big deal. Behind some bushes, I'm pretty sure a couple was getting it on as we walked by. But like I keep saying, everybody was mellow. Nobody cared what anybody did so long as they didn't make trouble."

"Unbelievable," Lynne marveled.

Rails smiled broadly and continued. "Joe Cocker was on when we got back at about two in the afternoon. He did 'With a Little Help from My Friends'. The gyrations that cat makes – like borderline spastic, man! But he had the most passion of anybody there.

"Right after that, this scary electrical storm moved in, bigger than the earlier one the other day. The skies darkened like it was night at four in the afternoon and the wind ripped. The P/A guy told all of us to channel mentally for the sun but it didn't work. Everybody ran for cover and the whole production was suspended for a couple of hours."

"A lot worse than the storm on Saturday night?" Beans asked. "That one sounded pretty bad."

"No comparison," Rails answered. "Much worse, Beans. It was like a rain forest monsoon and it lasted an hour at least. We walked back to the van and decided to drive around to find a place to clean up at and change into dry clothes. Stopped at a farm to ask where we could get a shower and these great people, who didn't know us from Adam - they let us use the shower in the barn and made us stay for homemade biscuits and hot coffee to perk us up. We sat around this big wooden table in a huge
184

kitchen, man – with one of those black cast iron stoves from the 1800's, and a couple of big lazy dogs hanging out. It was like going back in time to the old west – an episode of 'Wagon Train'."

"It's does sound kind of like a movie," Lynne said. "Can't believe it really happened the way you're telling it, Steve."

"It did, Lynne," Rails said emphatically, "And I'm saying it just like it was. Who knows – maybe someday it WILL be a movie – or maybe a documentary at least. There were media people around filming everything.

"Anyway, from there, we drove back and our space was vacant waiting for us. Thank God 'cause our tent and gear were all next to it. As soon as things cleared up, we walked back to the meadow and the show continued on. Nothing could stop it. We saw...let me think - Ten Years After, a British blues band. The lead guitar player for them was this skinny kid Alvin Lee and man could he cut it. They did this song 'I'm Goin' Home' that I'd never heard before. Balls to the wall and he was in and out with searing licks - like a cobra, Jack! Shotgun, Jeff – you both would have been floored. For me, that was probably the performance of the entire weekend – at least of what we saw."

"Action packed," Ed remarked.

"You said it. By that time it was around eleven, and we were beat. The word was that the event was going to be expanded into Monday morning with Jimi Hendrix to close the show. We didn't want to miss that. So we called it a night and headed back to the camp site. But the music went on throughout the night."

"What an unreal trip, man," Jeff said. "You ought to write an essay or something on this, Rails. Submit it to a newspaper or a magazine."

"That's a great idea, Jeff. The reason I have all the details down so straight is that I took pages and pages of notes and I've read them over about 50 times. I'll consider that one, definitely."

"Let's hear about Hendrix!" Melissa cut in excitedly. "'S'cuse me while I kiss the sky.'"

185

"What's gotten into you, girl?" Rails laughed. "Did you come out from under a rock? You hardly said boo before tonight. You even have the quotes down – that Airplane verse and now this."

"I'm a big rock and roll fan," Melissa smiled. "I light up when that's the subject. I must own at least a hundred albums."

"That, plus maybe the reefer you did before work with your boyfriend that you told me about? Just might have loosened you up a little, possibly?" Lynne added.

"Could be, boss...could be," Melissa smiled, snapping her finger.

"Okay, Missy – Jimi is next," Rails said, reaching over to tap her shoulder. "On Monday morning, we got back to the farm at around nine. The place had really thinned out – maybe only ten or twenty thousand people left. And litter everywhere, man – and huge gobs of mud – almost looked like the aftermath of a nuclear bomb explosion. But now we were able to get really close to the stage.

"Jimi Hendrix walked out with his Gypsy Sun and Rainbow band. We were practically standing next to him and I took notice of his far out duds. White leather jacket with beads hanging down off long shreds like buckskin – blue jeans with a psychedelic belt all done up in hippie designs – and a red head scarf. The dictionary definition of cool. The scene kind of clicked in my mind and it was the...like, the quintessential image of the sixties and what they're all about."

"Quinter – wha'? I got to look up THAT word. But what a picture," Ed said with eyes closed.

"Yeah, man" Rails agreed. "Now at first, it seemed like a lot of the Hendrix set was just how much feedback he could experiment with. Almost like he was noodling around and searching for something. But then toward the end, he did this medley that lasted seven or eight minutes. It started with 'Voodoo Child' and then it melded into something that sounded familiar, but I couldn't figure out what the hell it was 'til he got into the main part."

"What was it?" Lynne asked.

Rails paused for a couple of seconds and then smiled. "The friggin 'Star Spangled Banner'," he beamed. "With the whammy bar going nuts and feedback and sustain all over the place. Plus he veered off into these far out explorations – just pushing the limits. Then, just when you thought he was totally gone, boom – he'd drop on a dime right back into the melody. Never heard that song done like that – ever!

"He wasn't screwing around with it?" Jeff asked.

"No – no – not at all. In its own way, it was respectful – almost beautiful. But it was done in this...totally free and expressive interpretation – creatively – another symbol of the counter culture and a whole new way of thinking."

"I gotta hear that," Slade said.

"Oh, I'm sure it will be on the radio – and soon," Rails said. "Then Hendrix finished with 'Purple Haze' and it was over. Just like it was advertised - three days of peace, love, and music, man."

Rails sat back and took a deep breath. He'd expended some energy telling the story because he was so excited that he'd been there and saw it live. There was a brief lull all around as everybody let the full picture settle in. Even the normally talkative and skeptical Beans was taken by the passion and detail that Rails provided with his description. He'd listened attentively through the whole thing. Then, the buzzer went off. Two minutes to get back to the floor.

"I hate that sound," Melissa said. They all began to get up.

"So finally, what did you come away with, Steve?" Slade asked. "What do you think like...the significance of the whole thing will be? Say in ten or fifteen years."

Rails stood up and stretched; got his trash together. He pursed his lips and looked up, but didn't answer right away.

"I'm not sure, Shotgun," he finally began. "I mean it was great – like it embodied just about everything the movement stands for. No more war – peace and tranquility – love your brothers and sisters, and so forth. Think of it – all those people. There could have been violence, looting, a riot or

187

two - all of that negative crap. But there was none. It was three and a half days of an example of how things might really one day be better."

"But you don't sound convinced," Jeff said.

"I'm not, Jeff. I'm not convinced of anything. As we were walking away, I looked back at the meadow full of slop and litter and I got this strange feeling – very strong - that it was the culmination. The end of the hippie dream rather than the beginning. I just hope I'm wrong."

38.

A few weeks went by and it got to the end of August. The heat finally let up and the nights at work became cooler and more comfortable. For several in a row, Rails was a no show during lunch and some of the other breaks. On the full moon of a clear Friday early-morning, he made an appearance in the cafeteria at the start of the 1:15 AM break. Holding a large bag under his arm, he pulled up a chair with Slade, Jeff, and Ed.

"What's in the sack, Slick?" Slade asked.

Rails looked side to side. "Just a football and a few other items," he whispered. "But let's keep it down from here on in."

"Why? What's the big deal about a football?" Ed asked.

"Well, I thought we might have a little game of one hand tag during the lunch hour – that is if you guys have the gonads."

"Where – out in the parking lot?" Jeff said. "Not a lot of room with all the cars."

"Nope. On the roof of this rickety old building."

188

"Roof? I think you smoked one bone too many out in Bethel, man," Slade laughed. "Are you crazy or did I not hear you right?" Jeff and Ed smiled at each other and rolled their eyes.

"Okay, you skeptics, just hear me out a minute," Rails insisted. "Now! I had the balls to go to Woodstock and now you all regret that you didn't go, right? Not bragging – just stating a fact."

"Stipulated," Slade agreed.

"Okay, this is a chance for some kicks and it's not really that dangerous because I've got a tight field all staked out up there with empty paint cans weighted down with rocks. The other stuff in this bag is sticks to put in the cans – the final touch. That's where I've been the last few nights, eating lunch on the roof and planning this thing. Laying out a safe playing platform. There's a long wide area where nothing's sticking up from the base – ample room for a short field. And the moon is full tonight. There's plenty of light to see the edges."

"How'd you get up there?" Jeff asked.

"The fire escape from the sixth floor. The way up is a little complicated – I'll explain it later."

"You won't have to, brother," Jeff cut in abruptly. "I'm not crazy about heights. But the main thing, Steve is...I think you've got – as they say – a bird or two on the antenna. Just maybe you do?"

"Yeah – toys in the attic," Ed laughed. "No offense, Rails."

"Very funny boys and maybe true, but we'll set that aside," Rails smirked. "But why not try just listening for once before automatically dismissing an idea?"

"Okay – shoot," Jeff conceded.

"All right. Don't you guys dig on the notion of taking on something just a little dangerous, just to be able to say in ten or twenty years to your kids that you did it? How many people have played a football game on the roof of a mill building six floors and seven stories high at three thirty in

189

the morning? At least then, when we've all sold out to society, we'll have that in our pockets from our misspent youth to yammer about."

"And you can yammer with the best of them," Ed joked. They all had a laugh, Rails included.

"How much room is there on the sidelines and end zones up there?" Slade asked, his interest stoked a little.

"The way I have it set up, plenty," Rails answered. "Like I said, Shotgun, it's a short field and safe. All we have to do is go up and down it a couple of times and we're done. It will go down in the history books."

"How many on each team?" Ed asked.

"Well, I talked to Curtis from the machine shop. He's been on the overnight the past week by himself down there. He said he'd give it a try just out of pure boredom. I figure maybe on you two and I know Eddie will do it, right my man?"

"Sure – I never turn down a challenge."

"Okay – that's five," Rails continued. "Then maybe Pete Swenson or Sharkey, the new kid for number six."

"Don't ask Ravi," Ed laughed. "He'll get us all killed."

"Tell you what, Rails," Slade said. "I'll agree to go up. I'm interested in what the view is like up there. And if it all looks okay, I'll play. But I reserve the right to back out. Fair enough?"

"We'll go with that, Shotgun. How about you, Double J?"

Jeff paused. With Slade agreeing to go up, he weakened just a bit. "Well, the idea of running my sorry ass off a roof – not appealing, Steve," he finally said. "I'll do like Shotgun said, but let's just put me down as doubtful."

"Oh, you'll relent once you get up there," Rails told him. "It's a cool feeling once you walk around and get used to it. You can see way across town, like taking off in an airplane. It's motivating, man!"

"We'll see," Jeff said dismissively.

"Okay," Rails concluded. "Let's meet outside the head on the fifth floor at three thirty. I'll find the last recruit. And I guarantee it won't be Ravi. If not, at worst, it will be two on two. And keep it just between us so that Sudden Sam doesn't get wind of it."

"Check," Slade agreed.

Rails went out to look for Swenson and Sharkey. The remaining three sat there, talking and finishing their coffee.

"He's a fruitcake," Jeff said to end the conversation. "But a good intentioned fruitcake." They all laughed as they got up and headed out to the floor.

An hour or so later, Jeff was atop his spool roller working on a machine. Simone was busy with another one down the far end and he was alone with his thoughts. He kept trying to come up with ways to get out of the football game but nothing seemed to fit. Then he felt a tug on his pants.

"What's the matter with you?" Lynne said to him. "You look like you've been kicked by a horse."

"Interesting way to put it," Jeff laughed looking down at her. "I was just thinking – that always gets me into trouble. What's up with you?"

"Oh, just counting my blessings. Right now I'm at zero."

That line struck Jeff so funny that he almost lost his balance. Lynne had to steady his roller. He got down and leaned against it.

"You're pretty clever with the quips sometimes, LC. But I can sense you've got something to tell me. C'mon, now – spill the beans."

"You're right – I do have something. I overheard Steve Railsback asking Sharkey if he wanted to play football on the roof..."

"That's supposed to be secret," Jeff interrupted. "I hope you didn't tell anybody else."

"I didn't and I won't. Sharkey said no. Steve begged him because he said he already got a definite no from Peter Swenson, who hates heights, but Sharkey didn't change his mind. But somebody did say yes. Guess who?"

"Please don't tell me it's you."

"No, not me…Missy."

"What? Rails asked Missy to play?"

"No he didn't. He even tried to talk her out of it. Melissa and I heard him asking Sharkey and she went over and volunteered. Missy played high school girls basketball and ran track. She's a good athlete. And quiet as she is, or at least used to be, she likes to take risks. She talked Rails into it."

"Wow," Jeff said. "I was trying to figure a way how to weasel out of it but I've got no choice now. I'm glad you told me. I'll keep an eye out for her."

"Please do," Lynne said. She paused and then then looked seriously at him. "And if I can change the subject, I've been wondering about something, Jeff."

"What might that be?"

"Well…about the future, I guess. I mean, a smart young guy like you – how are you looking at what's down the road? You can't be planning on staying in this place. I'm sure not."

"Oh no – definitely not," Jeff answered without hesitating. "To tell you the truth, Lynne, I had some - let's say…troubles back when I was a growing up. My head wasn't in the right place most of the time. I'm not going to go into that but in the last six months or so, I think I've matured a lot. Got a better idea of who I am. And I'm 22 years old – not a kid anymore. Slade's helped me out with some stuff and Rails has been there for me too. I'm just about sure I'll be out of here before winter. Shotgun's cooking up something pretty big and I'm going to be right on that wagon. And when that's over, I'm thinking about going back to school and doing it right the second time around. The bottom line is that I'm not just drifting around in a fog any more. I'm going to move toward something better. I'm just not yet sure of what it is or when. What about you?"

"Gosh, that sounds good, Jeff. Me? I don't know. I've got some baggage just like you, I guess. Doesn't everybody? I was kind of dropped into this place on a rope. I know I put the factory down sometimes, but I can't say

I'm unhappy here. Still, I don't plan on being a lint head the rest of my life. I'm not just another mill girl – I know I have something more inside of me."

"Lint head? First time I've heard you use that one. Not bad. Yeah, I agree with you. You have a lot of potential, Lynne."

"Thanks. The old timers call each other lint heads once in a while," Lynne grinned. "But you know, Jeff, I make good money and I guess I've gotten used to the mill life. But like you, I'm still young enough to move on to something better too. I don't have to settle for this. I just haven't figured out what I really want to do yet. At least I've been smart enough to not have let myself get in trouble and get stuck in a bad situation with a kid that I can't afford. You're a guy. You don't know how tough that can be for a girl."

"Well, I know how powerful that urge is sometimes with us guys," Jeff agreed. "And I also know what jerks some of us can be. I've been there. And most importantly, I know how good looking you are. I often wonder how you attractive women handle it. But you sound good, Lynne. You have it together better than you might think. Just keep thinking about what you might like to do and like - it will come to you. You'll find yourself on the right path. I believe that."

"Do you really think so?" Lynne said smiling broadly.

"I absolutely do."

"You know something? You're a classy guy, Jeff. I knew you were a good person from the first night I met you."

"Thanks for saying that. It means a lot to me."

Lynne took his hand in both of hers. "And I haven't forgotten – I owe you one for what happened up in Maine. I owe you one."

"I'm cool with that," Jeff laughed. "But like I told you then – you don't owe me anything."

"Oh, you'll see," Lynne said squeezing his hand and releasing it. "You'll see."

193

Then she walked off back to her machines. As he watched her backside disappear, Jeff said to himself, "THAT...is the dictionary definition of a woman". Then he thought of what Slade had said about him and Lynne getting together some day. For the first time, he realized he was beginning to develop feelings for her more than just a physical attraction. Something about her touched him inside. And it was clear that she felt something in return. It might just be there for him one day. It could really happen between him and Lynne. That idea carried his thoughts until it came time for the football game on the roof.

39.

At ten minutes past three, Slade walked over as Jeff was filling up with more spools. "I talked to Rails," he said. "If everybody agrees once we get up there, it's me, you, and Ed against him, Curtis, and do you know about Melissa?"

"Yeah – Lynne told me. She knows about the game but she said she'd keep it quiet. I don't think anybody else knows."

"Well now that Missy's playing, I think we both have to play. Not to just save face but to make sure nothing happens to her."

"That's what I told Lynne. We're hooked. How the hell did we let Rails talk us into a dumb thing like this, Shotgun?"

"He's a persuasive cat," Slade said. "But it'll be okay. I'm even kind of looking forward to it. Like he said, it's good to take a risk every now and then."

"What about Sam? What's he going to think if he walks by and doesn't see any of us in the caf?"

"He's taken care of," Slade answered. "Rails told him we're all going over to Lynne's place to eat some of the five pizzas she supposedly won in a radio contest. He explained the cover to Lynne and she's cool with it. She has to do something at her apartment at lunch time anyway, so she won't be around. It's all square, man."

"Oh...okay."

"Now about how we get up top," Slade continued. "Rails filled me in on what has to happen. We can't get to the fire escape from the fifth floor – something about a couple of bad rungs on the ladder."

"Oh, great – up to now I was nervous but that really calms my fears."

"I hear yah, man. Anyway, the doors to the staircase up to the sixth floor from the fifth are locked since the sixth is closed and off limits. I think the company has some expensive stuff stored up there. From the fifth, we have to climb up through the jay boxes and then out to the escape platform on the sixth. From there it's about 30 feet up the ladder to the roof. Rails says that part of the ladder is solid. Once we all get on top, he has all the boundaries set up. He snuck up after break and put the sticks in. See you in about 15 minutes."

Before Jeff could say anything, Dina called for Slade and he headed off. Jeff closed his eyes and shook his head. He was stuck now. The music was going to play and he'd have to face it.

The group gathered on time outside the bathroom on the fifth floor. Like a captain, Rails, holding the football, went over the plan step by step. Everybody was on board. The jay boxes were slanted wooden tunnels through which fabric rolls and other large materials used to be passed down when the sixth floor was in operation. The way up through them was slippery and dark but Rails, football tucked between his shirt and his back, had a flashlight. He went in first to light the way for the rest.

On the way up, several times someone in front slipped and tumbled back into those behind. Muffled laughs echoed through the stuffy chamber. But with a lot more effort than anybody figured on, the last person was out the trap door and they all stood before the fire escape. Reality was setting in. All was quiet as Rails stepped on to the platform.

195

"Okay," he said, placing the football down. "I think it's best if we have one person on the ladder a time – you know – just to be safe. Slow and steady to the top. And just a couple of things. The ladder is safe, but try not to look down. It can freeze you up, especially on a night like this with the full moon. You can see all the way to the bottom. Also, when you get to the top, lean forward to get on to the roof because the ladder doesn't go much above it. I'll go first so I'll be there to help. Again, if you're the next guy, wait 'til the guy ahead is on top before you start up."

"This is beautiful, Railsback," Curtis said sarcastically. "Shaky ladder, then we're going to play football on a roof. Excuse me while I pinch myself. Got to be a dream, man. GOT to be."

"I never said it was going to be easy, Curtis. But it's safe enough, believe me. I've been up and down plenty of times. You're an athlete – it'll be a piece of cake for you. And you're gonna dig that view once we get up there, dude. I guarantee it."

"I hope so."

Slade and Ed were calm and ready for whatever it was going to be. Melissa had no fear and got behind Rails to go up second, to be followed by Slade, Ed, Curtis and Jeff at the end. They all watched Rails climb strong handed and sure of himself. Near the top, he faked missing a rung and hung down with two hands for a couple of seconds. "YEEEEAAAHHH!!!" he yelled. Everybody skipped a heartbeat and then relaxed when they heard him laugh.

"Just letting out a little tension – taking the top off," he said as he went over the edge and on to the surface. Jeff shuddered and let out a big exhale.

One by one he watched the rest go up; pretty orderly with the exception of Curtis, who like Jeff, wasn't a big fan of heights. He took his time, making sure of every step. Two thirds of the way, one hand slipped for a split second and he held on for dear life. But he righted himself and finished the climb.

Jeff watched Curtis disappear over the top and his turn came. He made the mistake of looking down before he got on the ladder. It was a long way to the bottom and a chill went through him.

"How about if I take a rain check?" he yelled up.

"Feet a little cold, Jeff?" Slade laughed.

"Frozen solid," he answered wryly. "But I can't chicken out now and have to live this down the rest of my miserable life. Here goes nothing."

Jeff started up deliberately. As he got to half way, something occurred to Rails. "Damn," he muttered. Then he kneeled down at the edge and hesitated before he spoke.

"Jeff…" he said softly. "One little item we forgot. The ball is down on the platform. Nobody took it up, man. Would you mind going back down to get it?"

Jeff paused, felt a twinge go through his body, and stiffened. "Oh, I'd be happy to. You've got to be shitting me, Steve! I'm half petrified as it is – how the hell am I going to hold the ball and climb back up too?"

"Just stuff it up in back of your t-shirt like I did in the jay boxes," Rails said calmly. "I tested it out once on the ladder and it worked fine. That way, you can use both hands like normal. And try to hurry it up – we only have so much time."

Jeff said nothing more. All he wanted to do was to get up there and give Rails holy hell. But he calmed himself, stayed put, and thought about things for a few moments. He hadn't figured on going back down so soon. Rails held back and didn't pressure him.

Jeff knew he shouldn't but he couldn't help himself. Again he looked down straight to the bottom. A rush went through his body, part fear and part adrenaline to act or flee. From somewhere deep within, he summoned the courage to do what he had to do.

Carefully, Jeff descended to the platform and secured the ball under his shirt. Then he took a deep breath and started back up, with the support of a few heads peeking over the edge. Now he moved faster, surer of

197

himself, and everything was smooth until he began to feel the ball moving. He put his fear aside and concentrated on angling himself so as not to lose it.

"The ball's slipping," he told them up top. "But I think I can make it. Somebody get ready to grab it if you have to."

"Hang in there, bud," Slade said. "We're right with you."

Jeff took a chance. He reached back with a trembling left hand and tried to push the ball up a little. He got it to move an inch or two but his foot slipped. He grabbed back on the rung with everything he had. Then he started up again with a renewed sense of determination. Just as he got to the top and leaned into the reaching hands, he felt the ball go.

"Damn! I lost it! I lost it!" he gasped as they pulled him on to the roof. "I tried my best but I lost it!"

Then he heard everybody clap and looked up to see Slade do a behind-the-back flip with the ball.

"Wha' – what the…"

"Don't waste your breath – you've been through enough already," Slade said. "As you came over, I was able to get it. Luckily, God blessed me with a long reach."

"All right, gang," Rails exclaimed. "Game on!"

Jeff stood up and a bit of euphoria came over him. He'd faced fear and came out on the other side. It was behind him and there was no better feeling. There was plenty of light, the moon smiled down and the town lights flickered out on the horizon. It was spectacular and the whole group got caught up in the moment. Everybody was ready to give it hell.

Like he assured them earlier, Rails had taken care to make sure the field was marked clearly. There was plenty of room on the sidelines and in the end zones. The paint cans and sticks were easy to see. He pointed out the boundaries to everyone and the group felt pretty secure that nothing would go wrong. It was just a little hard to see the far edges of the end zones. But there was so much room that nobody worried about it.

"Okay," Rails said. "We have the all-important ball thanks to our hero, the spider, and we're ready to go. We know the sides – me, Curtis, and Melissa against Shotgun, Ed, and Jeff. Each team has a quarterback and two eligible receivers. It's going to be one hand tag, no rushes except for runbacks, and three out of four complete is a first down. Both teams get at least one shot with the ball. After that, first team that scores wins. Cool with everybody?"

"You are one prepared human being," Slade said.

"It's the only way to be, my man, just like you always are."

Rails' team won the toss and just to be safe, received a long pass from Slade instead of a kickoff. Now that the game was actually happening, everyone was leery of making a wrong move. The runback looked like slow motion but Curtis, behind a block from Rails, advanced the ball about a third of the way down the field.

Rails' team moved slowly toward the goal line, making first downs with button hooks and short slants. Playing quarterback, Rails worked the ball mostly to Curtis who was covered by Slade, but threw quick-outs to Melissa too. Jeff had his hands full with her. She was tall, rangy, and fast. In the back of his mind, he figured he was being set up for the stop and go bomb.

But it didn't happen on that drive. Rails' team stalled out at around the opposition's twenty yard line and Slade's team took over. "Men," he said in the huddle, "all we have to do is score and we're done and we can get the hell off this roof. But easy does it with everything – no accidents."

"We got it."

Slade did the throwing. Jeff ran square-outs and Ed did short turn arounds to the inside and out. They moved the ball into enemy territory, but got a bad break when a ball tipped off Jeff's hands and Missy picked it off. Jeff tagged her at the spot and the ball went back to the other team.

"Okay," Rails said to everybody. "Each team has had a shot like we said. But time's getting short and this has to be the last possession. If we score, we win – if we don't it's a tie. Agreed?"

Nobody had a problem with it. Now used to being on the roof, Rails' team moved more easily up the field. Curtis again was the main guy but Rails adeptly mixed in more short passes to Missy, who had excellent hands. On one play, Curtis would have gone all the way if he hadn't hesitated too long after the catch for fear of being too close to the edge.

Finally they went for it all. Rails pump faked left to Curtis and at that instant, Missy executed a perfect stop and go. Jeff slipped and fell down. Missy was wide open near the end zone and Rails already had the ball in the air. The pass was a little long but she caught up with it and hauled it in. Then, in a mind numbing move that no one could fathom, she forgot where she was. Missy slowed to a trot...and disappeared over the edge.

"Yeeeeooooowwww!!!" everybody heard and for a second they all froze. Jeff was still down where he fell and he felt his body tremble.

"MISSY! MISSY!" Slade yelled, and he was first to the edge. He forced himself to look down. Then, after hesitating a second and shaking his head, he jumped off too.

"Oh no – no way this is happening!" Rails said as he jogged carefully to the brink, Ed following and then Curtis. Jeff, now standing up, still was barely able to move toward them.

Then the most amazing thing happened. Slade's head appeared over the edge, and quickly after, a very - very shaken Melissa's, with Slade's arm around her shoulder and propping her up. She was still holding the football.

"Holy Jesus!" Rails exclaimed as he looked down at them, and at the four and a half foot drop to the abutting building built flush to the side of Warburton Textiles. "It's all my fault – I knew about this drop but it was so far down I never thought it would come into play. I completely forgot to tell you guys - and when Missy went off, I forgot about it myself! I don't know what else to say. Missy – are you okay?"

"I think so," she rasped. "I landed on my side. It's sore but I don't think I broke anything. But wow, I'm kind of in shock. You don't know what that felt like. I'm luh...lucky to be alive."

"Girl – when you went off, you didn't know it was just a few feet," Ed said. "You must have thought you were a goner! Can't imagine how that must have felt."

"Let's leave that aside for now, Ed," Slade said rubbing Melissa's back. "We dodged a bullet – check that – a god damn rocket! Let's just get back down and put this behind us."

"Thank almighty God," Jeff gasped.

They hoisted Melissa back up to the Warburton building roof and Slade pulled himself on too. She was still shaky, so Rails had her follow him down the ladder closely just in case she lost it. There were no issues and they all got back to their posts on time. Nobody in the factory knew anything about them being on the roof save for Lynne. After she assured Melissa them that she'd keep quiet about it, Missy told her the entire story.

On the walk back to the Y that morning after work, Jeff and Slade reflected on what happened.

"What did you think of that whole thing?" Jeff asked. "Were we nuts to do that or what?"

"Probably," Slade agreed. "And Jeff, do you have any idea how close we came to having our lives changed forever?"

"How so?"

"Think about it. If Missy went off the other side and got pancaked – was killed – we'd all be screwed. Aside from how horrible we'd all feel – like forever – we'd all be responsible in some way. She's just a young girl, man. We're all older and we should know better. The law would be all over us for letting her go up there – we'd all be fired for sure – her family would want our heads on a platter – there'd be court headaches – leeching lawyers – no end to it. We could all have faced time in the can if they got us on negligent homicide or something even worse. Significant time. We'd have been branded for life as ex-cons when we got out. It would have been a permanent horror show."

"Holy moly! I never thought of all that. There'd be no end to it is right. You know, that reminds me of a story Creech told me. I think it was during my first night in town just before I met you. Something about him almost getting his dome squished between a cab door and a tree, but he walked away from it."

"I think everybody at the grand hotel knows about that," Slade said. "Poor Creech came that close to being a vegetable or even killed. Same type of thing, Jeff – a monster in your face that you somehow slip by. The main thing is that we dodged it just like Creech did. All is as it was and we move ahead unscathed. Stuff like this happens in life, man. Some days you dodge the bear, but one day the bear might get you."

"That pretty damn well fits," Jeff laughed. "Hey…remember what Rails said about what we could say in 20 years when we'd all sold out? Now it's a better story than he could have ever figured."

"True," Slade agreed. "And just to tie it up into a neat little knot, I saw Curtis on my way to the clock and he tapped me on the shoulder. Want to hear what he said to me?"

"What did he say?"

"He gave me a smirk and then deadpanned something like this. 'After all that went down - bottom line is – Missy held on to the ball. Our team won the game, Shotgun. Don't forget it.' Then he brushed his hand across his forehead and gave me this big sarcastic grin."

"Curtis does have a slightly warped sense of humor," Jeff chuckled.

40.

September came on with the spectacular late day sunsets and a chill in the air. The time to move on was coming and everybody could sense it. Jeff was glad that his outlook had improved so much and that he'd stabilized himself. But he wondered if he might dip down again if things fell through and he had to spend a dark winter working in the factory. But no way would that happen if he could help it. Something was going to give. It had to. He was certain of it.

It was different for Tom Slade, who for what was his nature, wasn't much bothered by any kind of negative projecting. All that he'd experienced over the spring and summer had fueled his vison of leaving and embarking on something brand new and far-reaching before it got too cold. He needed to see more of the world than just the northeast. He had to have a broader perspective. And that truth – that "it". There was something – something out there. He simply had to continue to move closer to it, now in a bigger way.

Finally things came to a head and he was ready. At the end of one of his Saturday guitar teaching lessons with Jeff and Rails, Slade asked them to stay after school for a little while. He had something to tell them. They agreed, packed away their instruments, and relaxed in their chairs. Slade pulled his hands through his hair before he spoke.

"I've figured out the master plan, boys" he told them. "It involves us and Ed too. He's going to be here in a few minutes. Soon as he arrives, I'll lay it on you."

"I kind of knew this was coming, Slade," Rails said, "from the time you stoked it after we saw 'Easy Rider'. But I have to say, you took your time and kept the lid on it pretty well. How were you able to do that?"

"Just my style, Rails," he grinned. "I try to wait 'til the right moment to act on stuff. Develops patience and character, you know?"

"You sure have it all worked out," Jeff said.

"Nah, that's just it, Jeff," Slade laughed. "I like to think I'm on the ball enough to know that I don't have it all figured out. Like being smart enough to know you know that you don't know. The worst thing is when you don't know...that you don't know."

"What the hell...? I'm not even going to touch that one."

"Believe it or not, I understand exactly what the man they call Shotgun means," Rails said nodding.

Just then, there was a rap at the door and Ed walked in.

"Hope I'm not late for the party or whatever this is," he said. "Shotgun wouldn't tell me anything."

"Set a spell," Rails said. "Take you shoes off."

"Okay, Uncle Jed."

"Patience, my boy," Slade laughed. "The greatest virtue."

Slade then pulled up a chair for Ed and they all sat facing each other. "Before I get into my...proposal," he began, "let me throw out a question. Tell me what each one of you thinks you want to do when you really grow up. Like none of us is settled into anything permanent yet."

"Huh? You mean like marriage and kids and all that stuff?" Ed asked.

"No, not so much that, although for sure it's a big part of being an adult for most people. That kind of thing, you know – falling in love...more happens to you rather than charting it out – like maybe fate? At least to some degree, I figure. I'm thinking more of what you want to do in the next few years before all that – to get tuned into adult life – to set your path."

"That's easy for me," Rails said. "Experience different stuff and write about it just like I'm doing now. I'm a writer – I've known it since I was a little kid. And probably grad school for sure at some point. I need to always keep learning, man."

"I know I want to go back to college too someday," Jeff said. "But I can't figure out what field I'd want to study. Picking something out kind of overwhelms me – like I don't trust myself to make the right decision. But I am improving as far as that goes. I guess it's got to be something that has meaning for me. I don't want to get stuck in some job I hate just to make a lot of bread."

"I don't have much idea," Ed offered. "But I do get into mechanical stuff – maybe something to do with that. All I know now is that I'm 21, have my high school diploma, and I want to get the hell out of this town and away from my family. Not that I hate them or anything but there's too much damn drama. My mom's a neurotic and my father's a falling down drunk on most weekends. Going back to that house every morning is a serious drag. My older brother Wes split last year. I'd have gone with him but he moved in with a couple of jerks I can't stomach. My sister Justine just left and moved into an apartment with a couple of her girlfriends. I'm next, man, and the sooner the better."

"Okay, that covers us. Now what about you, Shotgun?" Rails asked.

"Me? I've been thinking about it and lately music is the thing I've been hearing in the end – like in the back of my head. Berklee College of Music, man – I know I've got the chops to get accepted there. Get a degree in performance on guitar – teach – have a band on the side. Wouldn't be a bad life 'cause I'd be doing something I love."

"That's a great choice - you definitely have the talent," Jeff agreed. "Okay, so what's this all leading up to?"

"Vision, knowledge, perspective, man!" Slade said excitedly. "Think about it. The four of us have been stuck in this part of the country for pretty much all of our lives. We're still young and not tied down to anything yet. Steve and I are 23, you're 22, and Ed is just 21. We're at that critical time that if we don't act now, we'll never do it and we'll be just like everybody else who just dreams and never takes action on anything."

"Act? Do what?" Rails said.

"Exactly the thing you referred to that I suggested after we watched the movie," Slade grinned. "Do an extended trip across the country and maybe even more after that. Ever since I finished 'On the Road' and we saw 'Easy Rider', it's been building in my mind. But it will be different for us. We'll do it responsibly and on the level. No drugs other than some weed of course, and we'll have respect for all the people we meet. We won't do any damage and leave a mess behind like Sal and Dean did in the book. We'll be more like Todd and Buz from 'Route 66' – you guys know that show. We'll do good things if we get the chance, help people out.

"Just think of all we'll learn on a trip like that – how much more we'll know to apply to whichever way we finally decide to go in life. And Rails, consider all the material you'll get for your books. Plus it will be something really special that we all had the balls to do together. We'll be connected forever, man."

"Far out!" Ed exclaimed. "Just the ticket I'm looking for, Shotgun, so long as I don't get drafted."

"That's the only thing that could screw it up," Slade said. "I don't know what criteria Uncle Sam uses, but if it hasn't happened by now you've probably skated it. I'm clean. I enlisted in the army after I got out of high school but I flunked the physical. I still think they botched it."

"I'm 4F too," Rails added. "Got drafted soon as I graduated from college and my deferment ran out. But they rejected me for flat feet of all things. Can you beat that? Luckiest day of my life. I just wear arch supports and I have no problem – none what so ever."

"I'm in the same boat with Ed," Jeff said. "I'm vulnerable. I wonder if me having no parents exempts me somehow."

"Doubt it," Slade said. "But that's just something we'll have to face if it comes, that is if you guys agree to what I'm selling. And another thing. I've heard rumors that Nixon's going to institute a draft lottery before next year. Could be that you and Ed will luck out and get a high number, Jeff."

"That would be great," Jeff said. "But I'll serve if they draft me No deserting for me."

"Same here," Ed agreed.

"Well, maybe you two will get those high numbers if Nixon gets that bill through Congress," Rails said. "Let's hope so. Give us some details, Shotgun. What will the route be? How are we going to travel? What we're going to do to like...finance it along the way? That kind of stuff."

"I've got all of that covered. I figure we'll leave sometime in early November before it gets too cold. That gives us two-plus months to save some extra cash. We can take advantage of the overtime Warby's offers on Saturdays. Now this mechanic I know at Maille's garage, Punt - he's got a 60 Ford Econoline van for sale. He bought it on the cheap a while back and he's done some work on the motor. It's in good shape – just needs a few more tweaks. Ed, you can take care of that. I've seen the van and I took it out on the road. It's decent.

"Punt told me he'd sell it to us for a grand. I figure we can buy it together for $250 apiece. Maybe talk him down to even less. It's a nice boat with windows all around so everybody can see the land roll out as we move along. And we can all sleep in it when we have to. We'll just flip a coin to see who will officially own it."

"Sounds cool," Jeff said. "And I can handle the $250 no sweat." The others agreed the money wouldn't be a problem.

"So...like, what's the travel plan?" Ed asked. "You know – the route. Have you figured that out?"

"Yeah – but loosely of course. First drive down to New York City and stay a few days – check out the scene. Believe it or not, I've been through it but never stayed in the city and experienced the Village or anything. Then we'll hit Pennsylvania, say hello to my folks, and after maybe move on to Maryland and visit with your brother and his family, Jeff. From there, south to Florida and then west to the Santa Fe Trail through states like Mississippi, Louisiana, Texas, Kansas, Colorado, and Nevada. We'll be pretty much dodging the winter and if we find a place interesting, we can stay a while and maybe even work a little bit. The end goal would be to move up the west coast to Frisco. There, we can hook up with Jeff's hippie connection chick and have a look at communal life."

"Great idea," Jeff said. "I still have the info she gave me. That would be no problem."

"The more I'm hearing, the more I'm liking this," Rails cut in enthusiastically. "So what after we check out the commune? You mentioned something more."

"Right," Slade smiled snapping his fingers. "It's maybe the most challenging part of the whole deal if we can pull it off. I have a cousin in Pennsylvania who spent some time in San Fran. He told me it would be easy for us to get temporary work under the table on the fishing docks while we look into getting Merchant Marine papers."

"Merchant Marine?" Ed asked. "Never heard of it. What's that?"

"Merchant Marine is a name for civilian-owned cargo ship businesses - really big cargo ships – the truckers of the sea, Ed," Slade explained. "They transport goods and equipment all over the world. They always need crew workers – seamen they call them. Think of it. If we got jobs as deck hands or whatever, we could go to places in the Pacific like Hawaii and the Far East, and get paid pretty well to do it. Plus usually you stay a while at a destination until the ship gets new orders or reloaded. You can rent a car and explore."

"That's huge," Jeff said. "How long might we be shipped out for?"

"Two – three months – maybe more. I know it's a long time and we could get stuck carrying military equipment too. That could make us a target. But from what Chris, my cousin told me, you sign on for a job – or a mission I guess is a better word – and unlike in the military, they've got you only until it's completed. Then you're free to go and do whatever you want to. So we put the van in storage in Frisco, ship out for the winter, and then we're back sometime in spring or early summer, flush with moolar. Get it?"

"This is sounding better and better," Ed added. "Then what?"

"Very simple," Slade continued. "We'll have a nice stash of money like I said. We get the van back on the road and do the Oregon Trail west back to the east coast – see the north country - states like Washington, Wyoming, Nebraska, you know…then maybe up through Montana, Minnesota, Wisconsin, Illinois, and Ohio. How cool will that be? Think of all we'll learn about our people and our nation just in general. Then, we end it somewhere in the northeast where we're all from and move on with the next phase of our lives.

"Now things won't always be easy and we'll run into some trouble for sure. But it's now or never for something like this. Now or never, gentlemen."

"You ARE a true renaissance man, Tom Slade," Rails marveled. "I can see why you waited to lay this on us. It's really well thought out. And like I'm – well – honored that I'm one of the chosen ones. I am officially on board."

"You all made the cut easily, Steve," Slade laughed. "And bear in mind, it's just a general plan, like those jazz charts I told you about. Always subject to change depending on how things go. We have a blueprint but we can play it by ear – improvise - like the way you told me you like to write."

"Oh, there is a God," Ed beamed looking to the ceiling. "I'm in. Get me out of this town ASAP. I think it's a great idea and I'm psyched, man!"

"Me too," Jeff said. "I'm buying in. Sign me up. And we've got plenty of time before we go to get it all set up. We can cover all the bases."

"Correct, Jeff. And this is the right crew too," Rails said. "We all get along and we're like-minded. And we have four guys – there's strength in numbers in case we get into any jams. I doubt anybody will screw with us anyway. We've got three tall guys and Eddie packs the killer punch."

"You KNOW that's true," Ed laughed. "And I may not be tall but I'm not short either. But what about our jobs here, Shotgun? I mean we'd all be quitting at the same time leaving Sam flat."

"I thought of that and I raised the issue with him yesterday," Slade replied. "I just brought up the possibility of the four of us leaving together in a couple of months and explained why. He was kind of impressed with what I told him. Sam said that as long as we give him at least a month's notice to hire and train replacements, it won't be a problem. 'I like you guys,' he told me, 'but you can be replaced. You're not exactly brain surgeons.'"

"He can be a glib son of a gun," Rails laughed. "But that's great. We should tell him on Monday that it's on. That gives him over two months."

"I'll do that. And he gave me his word he wouldn't bounce us before we want to leave, so long as we're straight with him. So now we're cool with that. Are we're all in, then? Are we locked in?"

"Locked and loaded," Ed said standing up straight. The others also stood and gave a thumbs up. Four hands extended out and pancaked firmly in the middle. It was a done deal.

"Okay. Then let's get the ball rolling next week and we can close on the van soon." Slade said. "Punt told me he'd hold it 'til I got back to him. This is gonna be a gas, man! Now, I don't mean to be rude, but I hardly slept last night thinking about how I was going to present this thing to you guys. And you know what a bitch it is to adjust from the overnights to the weekends. I got to crash, man – I mean right now. You guys are officially dismissed."

They all laughed and shook hands hippie style. "Peace to all," Rails said, "we're out of here."

Jeff walked Rails and Ed downstairs and out to the steps.

"Shotgun - he's something else, isn't he?" Ed said thoughtfully. "That cat is so convincing that…if he asked me to walk off a building, I'd just like…do it no questions asked, figuring it must be the right thing."

"Our own Melissa Palmer knows all about walking off buildings," Rails added. "But you're right, Ed. I've only known him what – six, seven months? But there's something about Shotgun – something outside the fence if you know what I mean. And he's honest to a fault where you trust him totally. You want to latch on to his wagon wherever it's going. As if he's the pied piper or even Jesus Christ and we're like...his disciples. Okay, maybe that's a little overboard, although with that hair and beard, he DOES resemble our Savior! But I guarantee you, there isn't a mean bone in that dude's body."

"You know the great athlete that makes all the players around him better?" Jeff added. "That's Slade. I know I'm better for knowing him."

"That IS the bottom line," Ed agreed.

41.

They settled on Monday, November 16 as the departure date, figuring they could spend Thanksgiving with Slade's family in Drexel Hill, PA the following week. Slade gave Sam notice and that part was taken care of. From that time on, they took all the overtime they could get. Luckily there was plenty of it.

After they agreed on the trip, the four got together and went to Maille's garage. They took the Econoline out for a test drive and everything checked out. It had a powerful six cylinder engine and ran great. Best of all, the van had four new tires.

They talked Punt down to $920 when they told him they had the cash right there on the spot. Deal. Jeff drew the short straw and the van was registered in his name a few days later. Now that he had access to some wheels, the notion of seeing Lynne on the outside before they'd leave began to take shape in his mind.

Ed Collins was taken with the whole thing and wound up like a top. For him, the anticipation of the trip was like getting near the end of a prison sentence where finally, he could see something better over the hills. A beautiful feeling of impending deliverance set in with him.

A trade school graduate, Ed had a background in auto mechanics and a set of tools. Per Slade's suggestion, Ed went over the motor and all other aspects of the van with a fine tooth comb, replacing worn belts, installing a used starter, and re-outfitting the cargo bay to accommodate sleeping four when they needed to. He enjoyed every minute of it. His future after the trip didn't concern him, not a bit. He'd cross that bridge when he came to it. Ed Collins was ready to take off and just go, man...GO!

Rails made arrangements for his younger brother Greg to come out to Stiller from Oriskany Falls with a friend on the weekend before they'd leave. They'd take Rails' car back home and Greg would have use of it until his brother returned. Rails went out and bought two thick blank ledgers, a battery powered lamp, and a fold-out desk he could use on the van. He was pumped and ready to write and write and write.

Jeff made his preparations in the weeks before leaving just as the others did. He dug out Crystal's Farlow's address and wrote her a letter telling her he'd be in San Francisco sometime in the next few months. Jeff asked for directions to the spread she was living on. A week later, he got them in a letter welcoming him and his friends whenever they'd arrive. They were going to get to see a real commune close up.

Every now and then Jeff would begin to second guess, but those feelings didn't stick like they used to. He plainly liked himself better than he did before and had more faith in his decision making. No way was he going to chicken out. Plus it wasn't all just on him now. He had three good friends who he trusted. Each time he did something positive for the trip, whether it was buying a sleeping bag, loading up on canned goods, or completing some other task, he got an added charge of anticipation and hope. Seeing such an extensive plan gradually fall into place genuinely excited him. Finally, he was enjoying life.

Word of the trip spread around the red brick hotel as the residents called it. Some of the long timers kidded Jeff and Slade about venturing out to seek fame and fortune only to end up broke and right back at the Y in a year or two. Shorty cautioned them to have eyes in back of their heads while walking down 42nd street in New York City. The trip was a hot topic around the building because most people living there were settled in their lives for better or worse. They weren't going anywhere any time soon. The truth was that most were impressed with four young guys with the courage to act on something of such a large scale.

211

Jeff had stuck with his regular running and lifting routine since taking up at the Y. His weight was now up to 170 pounds and he was probably in the best shape of his life. Slade often joined him on the runs and both continued to play basketball two or three nights a week before work.

For Jeff, exercise was a great stress reliever and it helped him to stay grounded. Even more now than when he first started using the track, the metronomic thumping of feet, that constant sound, gave him a feeling of a building strength and resilience. A little stronger with each run.

It reminded him of one of his earliest memories; the crackling sounds of the rapids over the stones of the Pemigewasset River in the White Mountains of New Hampshire. His parents took him and Luke there several times before his mother passed away. They rented a cabin with the stream right behind it. Little as he was, Jeff never forgot the endless repetition and power of that constant babbling flow of water, always there in the background. It was that memory that led him up to Lincoln and the job in the lumber yard before coming to Stiller.

By now, Jeff knew quite a few of the regular runners. Many times, he'd just pick up on a subject from the last time he ran along with the same guy. Creecher was one of those people. He was fascinated by the trip. During a Saturday night run, he caught up abreast with Jeff and raised the subject.

"Slow down and jog with me, Jeff," he said breathing heavily. "Let's talk a little."

"Okay."

"You and that Tom Slade – you got balls, man," Creecher began. "I gotta give you two that."

"Nah - not really, Creech," Jeff said. "It's just like Shotgun says. We're still young and if we're going to do something, now's the time."

"Easy to say but not so easy to do," Creecher offered. "I mean, don't give it a second thought, but stuff can happen – believe me. But just don't think about the negatives, Jeff – stay positive."

"Right – I'm working at living like that every day, Creech."

"No matter what happens, you always got control of that," Creecher agreed, "your outlook, I mean. So you're hitting New York City first. Ever been to the Big Apple?"

"No sir. Have you?"

"Well, my boy, I don't know what to tell you. I for sure don't know. Oh, if I were your age again – but I ain't. Myself? Yeah, I've been there many times but I never stayed for too long. Always struck me as an interesting place to visit but you better to get out quick before you get sucked down. Good looking broads – rich people driving Caddys and Lincoln Continentals – but poverty, homeless, and crime right around the next corner. Addicts, alcoholics, crooks, pimps, hookers, what have you. That's the thing about that place – the best and the worst – the lucky and the unlucky – all are mixed together in one big pot."

"Really? I'll keep an eye out for that," Jeff said.

"Keep it in mind," Creecher remarked. "But you're young like you said and you have to see things for yourself. I get that. Just be careful, Jeff, and don't give in to any vices, 'cause situations are gonna come your way and they'll tempt you. I guarantee it. Be smart and just steer clear, man. Steer clear. Take it from a guy who knows. I've been in that gutter where nobody gives a flying crap about you and you got nobody. Not in New York City, but I've been there. Just be sure to watch out."

"I get you, man. I know what you've been through."

"You don't know the half of it," Creecher gasped as they finished the run and began walking. "But let that slide. One more thing – and this is important. Wherever you go, make sure you keep on running – or whatever. Exercising regular, you know? Take care of your body – it's a temple, Jeff. I don't care what kind of shit goes down. Strong mind, body, and spirit like they say. You got to have some kind of constant in your life for the good – something that builds resilience that you continue to do no matter what the hell happens. Always stick with it. You'll stay on course and be able to handle the rough times better because believe me, you're gonna have them. Keep running and swimming. If you can't run, walk. If you can't swim, tread water. Just make sure you're always moving - doing something – anything to keep fit. I guarantee it will carry you through the tough times."

"I've kind of figured that out the last couple of years," Jeff said, "But the way you've put it really hits home. Great advice - thanks for that, Creech. You've been a real friend from day one. I won't forget it."

"That's good, Jeff. Sometimes the simple things in life are the most important. Just take a look at me for example. Twenty years ago, I had high hopes just like anybody else who was young. Now I'm 44, and as you know, I had a few bad breaks. Plus I'll admit it, I made some big mistakes. Maybe I'm living like a pauper now and I've still got some serious debt from way back. But I stay in there and I'm paying it down gradually. I'm thankful for what I have and for my health. It's not what happens to you, it's how you handle it, Jeff. Life is a state of mind, Jeff – a state of mind I tell you!"

Jeff nodded as they finished walking and got off the track. Creecher tapped him on the shoulder. "Sorry I've rambled on, but now you know it's my nature."

"I'm used to it by now," Jeff laughed. "A state of mind, huh? Hmm, I have to think a little about that one. But I do like what you said and I'm glad I heard it – really glad. All it can do is help me."

"Right on, brother!"

42.

After a shower and doing some reading in his room, Jeff went down stairs to the Television room to kick back. It was almost nine o'clock. Creecher was there along with Slade and Nikki Ford sitting to his side. She and Slade talked as Creecher read the sports page. Jeff walked over and took a chair next to them.

Off to the far end, a shabby old man wearing a scally cap sat by himself looking out the window. Jeff looked over and recognized him. It was

214

Barney Ebersol from his first night at the Y. But a sober and irascible Barney.

A rerun of the "Route 66" series came on the television. Most in the audience were fans of that program, particularly Slade. Maybe it was his favorite of all time. He'd made it a point to reference it in the trip spiel he presented weeks before.

The show followed a couple of young good looking guys travelling the country each week in a Corvette, searching for experience, knowledge, and the ultimate truth. One of the actors, George Maharas, looked remarkably like the writer Jack Kerouac. The program mimicked what was soon to come and was right up Slade's alley. Coincidentally, this episode took place in New York City.

"That's us in the very near future, Jeff," Slade laughed. "Not as cool as those two and of course, no sports car. But that's us, man — right in the middle of the big town."

"Sure as hell," Creecher remarked. "But you are correct. That blue bread box of yours is no Corvette."

"You got that right."

"New Yawk, New friggin Yawk — dat what youz guys is talkin' 'bout?" It was Barney rasping over from his spot. He had been watching the television out of the corner of his eye. He tilted the up cap to show his weathered face. The bags under his eyes drooped like a hound dog's jowls.

"Barney, oh Barney," Creecher said smiling. "You look good tonight. Are you on the wagon again?"

"Hee hee hee hee," Barney laughed. "You cahhn't put lipstick on a pig but I'm tryin'. You look good too. Who's your embaahmer?"

The whole room got a chuckle out of that.

"On the wagon? Nah, jes takin' a little break," he continued. "Drunker I get the better everything is wit' me anyways. But who'z goin' tuh New Yawk shitty?"

"A group of us, Barney," Slade said.

"Well, dat place is a fuh...friggin rat hole. I spent a winter on dose streets and near kicked the bucket back in 59. Or was it 58? I dunno - it don't matter anyways. The bigger the town, the badder the town, fellers, and dat's a fack! I got kicked in the hayud, robbed, and left for dead on dem streets. What I seen in that dump – oh – you don't wanna know. You jest don't wanna know! You don't wanna FRIGGIN know, I tell yah!"

That was all. Barney was out of gas. He coughed several times and cleared phlegm from his throat. It sounded like the rumble of death. Then he struggled to his feet and shuffled toward the men's room. Some in the group turned their heads and sadly watched him go.

"You see Barney?" Creecher said quietly poking at Jeff after he was out of sight. "Like I told you before, there's a ton of bums just like him on the sidewalks of NYC. You'll see them sprawled out right in broad daylight. People will pass by and take no notice like he said, just like they were dead rats. I'll bet old Barney spent that winter sleeping on cardboard spread over heater vents. Take it from me, pal – like I said, I know. They're all there, brother – the haves and the have nothings."

Jeff and Slade nodded to him. Nikki shook her head with sympathy for Barney. With that, Creecher tapped Jeff on the shoulder, said good night to the others and went up to bed. The rest of the room gradually cleared out leaving Slade, Jeff, and Nikki, and a few stragglers. The three sat off to the side talking quietly for a while. They were discussing Boston night spots when Jeff brought up the show he and Slade attended at Jungle Jim's.

"That place is on Tremont Street, right?" Nikki asked.

"I believe so," Jeff said.

"I used to work a few blocks down from there – in the Combat Zone," she continued.

"You worked in the Combat Zone?" Slade said, surprised. "What kind of work?"

"A candy striper," Nikki laughed. "No – just kidding. What do you think, Shotgun? You know what the Combat Zone is. I was a stripper."

"Really?" Slade said. "I knew you danced but I didn't know you stripped. How come you never told me?"

"You never asked, my dear. And I guess it's not the kind of thing a girl wants to broadcast, if you know what I mean."

"Yeah – I hear you."

"Did you have a stage name?" Jeff asked.

Nikki hesitated and smiled. "Peppermint," she said.

"Not bad," Slade offered. The three of them exchanged looks and giggled.

"Sheesh," Jeff said. "What was it like to be a stripper, Nik?"

"Well, I didn't do it very long. But it was in an upper class place and I made a lot of money. I saved and still have most of it. It wasn't as bad as you might think but I didn't want to get stuck in that kind of life. And there was too much pressure to do other things – you know what they were. I had to work hard to learn all the moves but my dancing background helped a lot. When I got them down right and actually got on stage and did it…I have to say – there was something, well…exciting about it."

"How so?" Slade asked.

"Not so much in a smutty way," Nikki answered thinking about it a little. "But I mean, picture it if you can from a woman's point of view, Tom. You feel have what it takes, you're up there, the spotlight is on you, and all those guys are drooling over you. I got a little – check that – a big rise from it a lot of times…like a feeling of power and control over them. I'm not ashamed to say that. And I was good – not to brag but I was good! I never heard a bad word said by anybody in the audiences I danced for. Not one time."

"Sounds a little like what you might have felt on stage with the band, Shotgun," Jeff offered. "You know – say stepping out front and ripping off a solo."

"Yeah – that fits," Slade agreed. "But I can't say that I'm in shock or anything, Nik. I know you're not the average kind of woman. If you feel it, you go with it and I admire that. Plus you do take good care of your body."

"Thank you my dear."

217

"You know, I haven't seen a lot of strippers," Slade continued. "But when I did see the really good ones, I always came away with an appreciation for let's say – the quality of it aside from the obvious. I remember this beautiful girl doing a dynamite routine in a giant wine glass. But set that aside. I mean I'm a big fan of the female form like most guys, and...sexy as a strip act is, there's something to it if done well, that like...rises above the flesh. It can't be denied."

"Man, you have some kind of perspective that I didn't know was possible," Jeff remarked, exhaling in wonder.

"Shotgun's exactly right, Jeff," Nikki agreed. "And if you want me to, I can give you guys a little shall we say...demonstration."

"For real?" Slade said.

"Sure. Let's go upstairs. You just get on that guitar and play something snappy, and I'll show you guys some moves. Now don't get too excited – I won't take it all off. I'll just give you two a little feel about – like what you said – the art thing of it. And no pun intended."

Slade and Jeff looked at each other and then back at Nikki. "Are you sure, Nik?" Jeff said.

"I'll be glad to do it. I've got no problem showing off my assets. Like they say, if you got it, own it and rock it."

"Then it's settled," Slade said. "Upstairs we go."

In his room, he pulled up a couple of chairs and got his guitar out of the case. From the closet, he grabbed a pair of bongos and tossed them to Jeff.

"I have to put you to work, bud," he said, "I can't do this alone. Just give me a 4/4 beat and stick to it. I'll do the rest."

"Before we start," Nikki cut in, "do you have a pair of pajamas and a robe? If I can change into something loose, it'll make for a better show."

"I don't," Slade said. "I sleep in my shorts no matter what the conditions."

"I should know that by now," Nikki laughed.

Jeff's head perked up. He looked at Slade and flashed a quick grin. "I've got both," he said. "I'll save the day. Give me a second and I'll get them." He hustled off to his room brought them back.

"Perfect," Nikki said. "Now you guys face the other way while I change."

They followed instructions. Nikki got ready and then walked to the window, covering herself with the curtain. Jeff and Slade got set in their chairs with their instruments.

"What are you going to play, Shotgun?" Jeff asked.

"Let's see – up tempo, right Nik?"

"Right."

"Okay – how about 'Love Me two Times' by the Doors. I was at a dive once and saw a beautiful girl strip to that song. It was great."

"Then by all means, hit it," she said.

Jeff set the beat and Slade got into the song with a nice syncopated groove. He and Jeff smiled at each other as Nikki strutted out from behind the curtain. She moved beautifully to the rhythm and made Slade's playing that much easier. Tall and slender like a model, she walked side to side and gyrated back and forth and up and down, as she worked the robe free and then let it fall. Jeff's jaw dropped much like it did on that night in Boston with Lydia. He had to reel himself in to keep the timing.

She began to unbutton her pajama top as she smiled with a calmness, striking different poses and doing a couple of spins before doffing it to the floor. A black bra secured what lay beneath, smallish, perfectly shaped and all woman. Slade, of course, had been with her and knew that package. But Jeff had never seen Nikki like that. She was tight, she was streamlined, and she exuded confidence.

She advanced with flowing hip and thigh movements and then backed off quickly. Darting in and out of the shadows, side to side, her long black hair cascading off her lovely shoulders, Nikki kicked off her shoes, one by one, right on cue. Inspired, Slade played with added depth, accenting "hits" on her moves whenever he felt it. And Jeff hung in there on the skins.

Slowly and deliberately, the bottoms came off she was down to bra and bikini underpants. The girl was all legs. Nikki smiled, spun the pajama bottoms and tossed them forward. They landed and draped on Jeff's shoulder. He left them there and kept the beat right on through. With a couple more twirls and a pose-on-the-dime finish, she stuck it flush with the end of the song.

Slade and Jeff put their instruments down, stood up, and clapped as Nikki retrieved the robe and put it back on.

"Why thank you, boys – thank you so much. You're such a kind audience!" she said channeling her best Marilyn Monroe. Then she went over to the side and put her clothes back on like nothing unusual had happened.

"Wat to go!" Jeff said excitedly removing the bottoms from his shoulder. "That was a great show. Not only are you beautiful, Nik, but man, have you got some slinky moves."

"Sensual and sexy," Slade added. "I can see why you raked in the dough in that Boston gig."

"Thanks, guys. That was fun - brought back some memories too. I felt like I was right in my element. And you know, like I said before, it didn't feel dirty at all. See, it's all about how you look at it. Well, I have to split – got a few errands to do before the stores close."

She got her things together and gave them both a hug. "I'm going to miss you guys," she told them. "And Shotgun, you have my address. You're going to stay in touch like we said, right?"

"Of course I am," Slade said. "And thanks for the demo, Nik – it was something special."

"I second that," Jeff said.

"Peace," she said holding up two fingers. They walked her downstairs and out the main entrance. Jeff and Slade then went back to the room and sat down. Slade opened the window and they shared a joint.

"How about that for something you'd never expect in a million years?" Slade smiled, finishing a hit and passing it back.

"Well, I've got to say…" Jeff offered taking another toke and hissing it down. "Now…I know you and Nik are friends, or maybe a little more than that. But I AM feeling this…reefer. I just have to unload what's on my mind, Slade."

"Go right ahead."

Jeff looked to the ceiling and shook his head. "I mean she shows up and brings it, man. Like I wouldn't peg Nik as a raving beauty although she's definitely well above average. But those curves – and she's so cool and well...uninhibited I guess. Sexy and sensual like you said. What a woman - I've never met anybody even closely like her."

"What you say is the truth," Slade reflected. "And the truth shall set you free. She's a slinky fox and she knows it and she loves it. The bottom line is – and I've said it before - she embraces fully what it is to be a woman."

"Agreed. And that last phrase, the way you put it, conjures up a beautiful image, man. But I'll tell you...what Nik said about it not being dirty – and you too earlier – you both were right. There was definitely something in the way she let's say...expressed it. That performance rose above the flesh and into like – pure beauty. Know what I mean?"

"Of course I do," Slade said. "The grace of the feminine figure in motion at its best. She's 25 and maybe at the height of her attractiveness. You know – in her prime. And we experienced that, man. Painters have been fascinated by the beauty and grace of the female form for centuries."

"You are so right," Jeff agreed. "Hey, so I take it you've told Nik all about us leaving. I heard her mention it."

"Yeah, I did not long after we decided on it."

"You two have kind of a special friendship, Shotgun. She's going to miss you."

"And me her," Slade offered. "You know Jeff, I can see you've figured out there's a little something more between Nik and me. I saw that look you gave me earlier. Well, we've straightened out some things and I'd like to unload a tad of history between us on you, good friend that you are. You know, just so I can kind of let it go. But keep it between us, okay?"

"You can trust me - shoot."

"Well, Nik and me, we've like...closed the deal as I know you suspected. A number of times over the past few months."

"Yeah, I thought that," Jeff said. "But I'll say you two were pretty discreet about it. Nobody around here ever mentioned it to me."

"Right – we kept it quiet and she never stayed overnight. It was more a physical thing than emotional, but you know we both like and respect each other. I mean you saw her, man, and I'm only human. But even though she was all for it with no commitment, something about the arrangement still didn't sit right with me. I mean we never even went out on a date. That one's on me. Enjoyable as it was, a little cloud always was hanging over things. I'm not sorry it happened and we used common sense every time. Both of us. I never once thought it was wrong or that I was taking advantage of her. But still, it never quite sat right. Get it?"

"Kind of," Jeff said. "But nobody did anything wrong. The worst you could say is that maybe you used each other a little but the playing field was level. Where's it at now?"

"After the four of us agreed on our plan to leave, I leveled with her about how I felt about it. She didn't completely agree, but understood my view of the situation. Considering that, we mutually decided it was time to end the physical part of the thing. That might be why she had no problem having you see her in that demonstration she did. Or me being here with watching it with you."

"I have to say, I was surprised by it."

"Me too a little, but it didn't bother me. Nik has been around the block and she does what she wants to. I get that. I knew she wasn't trying to make me jealous. She's all for free love – you know - all that hippie stuff. But she understood ending the...affair, I guess that's what it was...was the right thing for us. Nik's got a sensible head on her shoulders. I felt a lot better after we straightened things out and we were still good. And we both agreed we're were grateful for what it was and will always remember it."

"Nice. A decent ending."

"Yeah, but I don't know, sex is powerful connection, man." Slade concluded. "You just don't walk away from it easily."

"I hear you," Jeff agreed. "Nothing's ever simple when sex gets mixed up in it. And after watching that, man...wow!"

"I know what you mean."

"The main thing is, I think," Jeff continued, "that the urge for it is always there in the background even when you're just trying to be friends. It's hard wired into us guys I guess. But yeah, there's a lot that goes with it. It's no joke - like playing with fire if you're not careful and you can get burned for life. You and I know it – we've talked about it. Lynne and I have discussed it a little too. And I've heard the same sob story from a bunch of sad-faced guys around here who screwed up. I figure you just try to handle sex...as intelligently as you can and have a ton of respect for it. That's what I think."

Slade put his hand to his forehead and then dragged it across. "Phew," he said. "That makes a lot of sense. You're becoming awful 'erudite' in your old age."

"Does it?" Jeff pondered thoughtfully. "I'm not exactly an expert at this subject, you know. I've only been with a few women in my life and most times, it was let's say...not as smooth as it could have been. I don't feel like I know that much at all about it at all. I hope to one day. But one thing I have learned is this. It's always better when you're with somebody who you know a little and can relate to over and above the lust factor. Like it was with you and Nik. That I do know."

"And I agree one hundred percent."

"Well, considering the big picture, I'm glad that both of you are straight with things now. But I have to circle back to what we just observed just once more. The way she approached her...craft and rose it above dirty and porn like we said before. Nik gave it something – maybe expression is the word. Or even passion. She was like a leopard, man, and everything was so...natural. I'm still buzzed over it. I'm high, though – I know that. Am I making any sense?"

"Sure you are!" Slade exclaimed, taking the final hit from the bone and blanking it. "I know exactly where you're coming from. I'm right there, man."

Then Slade paused and looked to the ceiling. He smiled broadly. "Oh – this weed is sooooo – gooood," he marveled. He closed his eyes, tilted his head back, and for a few moments lapsed into deep thought. Then his eyes opened again and fixed back on Jeff with a gleam.

"And...wham – what you just said ignited something," he continued. "I just – I just now got a flashback – a beautiful flashback! To a freeze frame

223

moment I had a few years ago that sits forever in the recesses of my brain. Know what I mean?

"I think so."

"Okay - did you happen to feel something like that watching Nik maybe? Like a snap shot fused into your subconscious?"

"Probably around ten of them," Jeff joked. "But all kidding aside, I think I did have a couple that night with Tina and Tress in Boston. One on stage with Lydia and the other in the morning when we left the girls at North Station. You know – looking back at them from the train. I keep seeing both pictures the course of my thoughts."

"Really?" Slade marveled. "That's pretty cool. You got a few minutes, man?"

"I have all the time in the world."

"Well, I'm in just the right 'mellow' to tell a little tale – an example of one of those dynamite moments that hit me at the most unusual time. The thought that occurred to me just now. It might be on the long side and I have to set it up. But it's worth hearing."

"Let it fly, then," Jeff said with interest. "Nobody tells a story like you, Shotgun – I have yet to be disappointed. I KNOW this is going to be good."

Slade nodded, smiled broadly, and stretched out. Then he got comfortable in his chair.

"Well, see…it was a dark and rainy night," he began." Then he paused a few seconds they both broke up laughing. Jeff almost fell off his chair.

"No, no! Sorry I couldn't resist it – I couldn't!" Slade said catching his breath. "Okay – here goes. The real story. It was around six years ago, sometime in the spring. I was 17 and a senior in high school. I'd had some stupid kind of argument over nothing back home and I told my folks I needed to get away for a few days to just calm down. I walked out with the clothes on my back, a coat and twenty bucks. It was one of the dumbest things I've ever done but they didn't hold me back."

"Maybe stupid but it took some guts to split like that at 17."

"Yeah, but thought I knew it all back then," Slade continued. "I got over whatever it was – I can't even remember - fast and found my way back in

224

home in like...two and a half days. Anyway, that afternoon and night, I hitchhiked hundreds of miles all the way up to the Maine coast. Just wanted to GO, man. I got some beautiful long rides in cars and semis too. I landed somewhere at an all-night Ho Jo's along Route 1 after midnight. I didn't even know what town I was in but I think it was well north of Portland. Somewhere around Bath."

"That's far past Wells where that party was," Jeff said.

"Right – I always liked to do things big even at 17. So it was around early April and still cold – maybe about one in the morning. I'm sitting at the counter having a coffee and checking out the menu. Just twenty bucks on me and I didn't know where I was going to spend the night. I must have looked nervous."

"I'd have been a wreck."

"Well, I wasn't exactly relaxed. I glanced up and noticed these three women sitting across from me. It was one of those loop-around counter jobs. They looked to be maybe mid-twenties – one a tall red head, the middle one a short blonde, and the other one – she had a big hairdo I remember clearly. They were talking about some party they'd just left and they seemed more than a little buzzed. The little blonde was the best looking by far and we locked eyes a couple of times, after which she giggled with the other two. I smiled back over, sipping my coffee and trying to look cool. Before long, the blonde – she walked over smiling and sat right next to me.

"A bold move. Just like you did with Tina and Tress."

"You know it. I was a little shook. 'What's the matter, handsome?' she said leaning in and blinking her big eye lashes. 'You look like you're carrying the weight of the world on your shoulders.'"

"Okay, I'm warming to it now," Jeff said leaning forward in his chair. "Continue the narrative."

Slade took a deep breath and grinned. "I explained to her that I was down on my luck – no place to stay for the night I didn't want to blow all my bread on a room. I tried to look as hopeless as I could although I already figured I was going to be hitching back to Penn in a day or two. I just didn't want to sleep outdoors in some field, man. I hoped maybe they could put me up for the night.

225

"So she said to me something like, "You're a lucky guy, Sugar. My friends and I are camping out on Hermit Island. It's a ways from here but you can stay over with us. We have shelter for you and breakfast in the morning. How's that sound?"

"Talk about getting a friggin break," Jeff said.

"Yeah, but the other two looked pretty drunk and I was a little wary of what might lay ahead. But it was the only option I had, so I took it. The blonde introduced herself to me as Dawn – the name fit her just right. She reminded me of Ellie Mae Clampett with straight hair. She held my hand and brought me over to sit with the others.

"'Look what I found!' she said to them. I smiled and must have looked a little embarrassed. Everybody laughed. I sat down with them and we got acquainted. The redhead's name was Julie and the other one – I think it was Laura – no, Lanna. They were nice chicks but both were clearly high and slurring their words a little. Dawn seemed to be just feeling good – more coherent than the other two. She insisted on buying me supper - a jumbo cheeseburger with fries and a coke, which I gratefully accepted. I was starved, man. No food ever tasted so good. They joked about how cute they thought I was and about how they were going to tie me down later and take turns with me."

"I just saw about a dozen red flags sprout up."

"Nah. It wasn't like that. I got a little flustered but I could tell it was only the booze, pot, or both talking and they were just having a little fun – acting dumb as if they were guys, you know? I laughed right along with them. We finished up and they took me out to this wreck of a 57 Caddy – big as a spaceship with the fins and all - and just about riding on the ground. The three of them got in front and I jumped in back. To my surprise, I had company – a guy in a plaid shirt sprawled over half the seat. He was out cold, either loaded or spaced out on something."

"At this point, I would have been freaking," Jeff said. "I might have...absconded from that scene."

"That occurred to me," Slade remarked, "but let's just say I was apprehensive. The girls told me not to worry about Danny – that was the guy's name – like he was passed out more often than he was awake. They'd take care of him. Then before I could say anything, Julie guns the car and my head's snapped back like a whip. She was higher than I thought. We laid down rubber and were out of there like a bullet. She took us on a death ride, man - ripping the shoulders, dodging trees, and yelling "yeeehaaah…yeeehaaaah."

"Oh Jesus!" Jeff exclaimed. "What in hell did you get yourself in to, Shotgun?"

Slade paused and broke into a big laugh. "A friggin hornet's nest! My fingerprints were imprinted into the rear window, man. Before long, we were on a dirt road and she's still going 40 or 50. We're bouncing all over the place, pot holes, tree branches scraping the fenders, beating up this huge cloud of dust, and I'm praying this isn't my end. Up front, the girls are laughing like hell, and Danny – the guy flopping around beside me – he stayed knocked out through the whole damn thing! Then we come up on a clearing and wham, we skid to a stop and we're in the ocean – on a beach and right into the shore line. A flippin' wave splashed water on the windshield!"

Jeff nearly lost his chair laughing. "Oh my Gawd' stop it!" he said. "Talk about frozen moments that you never forget – you've already had about a half a dozen!"

"I know – I know!" Slade agreed rocking back and roaring. "Now that I think of it, it WAS insane. I'm sure Julie drove the car into the water on purpose just for kicks. So then she jams it into reverse and books us out just before we could have been in real trouble. Then she parked the car up on higher ground close to a pier.

"'Aren't you glad you hooked up with us, Tommy?' she said reaching back and brushing her hand through my hair. I remember that distinctly. All I could do was gulp and make like this furtive nod like I was scared to say no. It broke the girls up."

"She put you through a death ride," Jeff remarked.

"Exactly, but we survived it. We all got out of the car save for Danny, who had finally come to but hadn't sat up yet. 'Look out there,' Dawn said to me pointing out to sea. A cloud covered what little moon there was, but I could make out a dark mass in the distance. It looked almost like a miniature Skull Island from King Kong."

"Skull Island? You're not putting me now, are you Shotgun?"

"Nah – not at all. I'm telling it just like it was. I have a good memory with stuff like this."

"Okay – sorry. How could I doubt a man of your integrity?"

"No prob', bud – I like the way you put that. Now to continue, Dawn said 'That's Hermit Island where we're camped out.'

"'Cool,' I said. I had calmed down and had my head back on straight. 'How do we get out to it?'"

"'That skiff over there.'

"She pointed to a motor boat on the dock. It didn't look big enough for five people. More trouble. We all pitched in and helped Danny out of the car and down to the boat. He wasn't a big guy, but still he was just about dead weight. We dropped him at least twice, but he was so loaded it didn't bother him one iota. We planted him right in the middle of the skiff and he went into a fetal position on the floor giggling to himself."

"So things were beginning to settle down?"

"Yeah – somewhat. I was surprised that the motor started up on the first pull and the boat handled all of us without sinking. The girls seemed to sober up a little with the night air and the situation became a lot better than it was in the car. As we cut water, there was a nice sea breeze that took the edge of what had gone down earlier.

"So we got close to the island – it only took a couple of minutes - and just a slice of moon showed between the clouds. The scene took on a mystical look, but serene too. It gave Hermit Island kind of an aura – a faint glow around it. For the first time, I semi-relaxed. I even was glad that I hooked up with these nut jobs."

"I can see it," Jeff said. "Nice description, man."

"It was outstanding," Slade agreed. "Turned out to be only a five minute ride to the island. We docked and Danny straightened out some. The air did him a lot of good. He talked a little with Julie, who I think was his girlfriend, and he was able to walk with just her helping. Dawn walked along side me and asked questions about my life like she was really interested. I told her a little about my high school sports teams and the band back home. She had to be at least five years older than me but it didn't matter at all to her."

"Describe what she was like a little more."

"Well, as I said, she was petite and I'd say cute rather than beautiful. Doubt she weighed a hundred pounds. Dawn was a sensual girl with the nicest high-pitched feminine voice. When she talked, it sounded like soft music. Every so often, she put her arm around me, gave me a hug, and nuzzled her face to my neck. I'd never been with a woman that much older than me before. Somehow, she made me feel like a man more than any girl my age ever had. But it wasn't like she was coming on to me. Believe it or not, I think it was purely what she felt right then. Dawn just liked me. She was cool with whatever fate that brought us together for that moment. Even at 17, I knew that for sure."

"That's because she had lived more and knew the ropes," Jeff said. "Keep the groove going, Shotgun. You're on a roll."

"I must say I AM feelin' it. So we got to the campgrounds and a lot of tents were scattered around. Theirs was over in a corner near some trees – a full sized one. There was a fire pit and embers still live and glowing. I got some fresh wood and stoked up the flames. We sat around it and warmed up. Just me and the girls - Julie had put Danny to bed in the tent. There were others sleeping in there – we could hear some snoring.

"Dawn went in and brought this big copper pot out and brewed coffee over the fire. We drank it and shot the breeze awhile. By then it had to be past two in the morning. The girls told some of the dirtiest jokes that embarrassed the crap out of me, but they were funny, man. All the time their smiling faces glowed in the fire against the night. The vibe was just right – I can see it now just like it was yesterday. Now if you'll excuse me for a second, I have to hit the can."

"Take care of business."

Jeff sat back and closed his eyes while Slade was away. He breathed in and relaxed. He was enjoying the tale. Slade was painting the scenes like an artist. The grass they'd smoked just added to it. Jeff wondered if the freeze frame thing was going to be Slade making it with Dawn on the beach or something. "Nah, too obvious," he said to himself. With Shotgun, it had to be something more than that.

Slade returned. He refocused and continued. "So the moment of truth was near, Jeff. It came time to bed down. Dawn told me to wait a second

229

while she went into the tent. She came back out with a sleeping bag, a blanket, a pillow, and a couple of flashlights. She gave me one of them.

"'Listen, Tom,' she said. 'I'd have you stay in the tent but it's filled up – there's no room. But you can sleep in the beach wagon.'

"'The what?'" I said.

"She pointed off in the distance and I saw an old car up on blocks. Now I figured for sure it was going to happen between us and I got a little nervous. I'd only had sex twice in my life up to that point. We walked down a path to the clearing where the wagon sat. It wasn't a piece of crap. It had been gutted and set up on blocks with the tires removed as a sleeping shelter. It was clean, with the seats removed and a nice thick mattress laid down the cargo bay. Dawn explained that last year somebody abandoned the car on the beach and somehow it ended up on the island. She mentioned a narrow land bridge at the far end as to how somebody must have gotten the car out there. Whoever it was stabilized it and outfitted the back as sleeping quarters for anybody who wanted to use it."

"Hold on - let me get this straight," Jeff interrupted. "You're seventeen, you're out on some Island in parts unknown, you're going to sleep in the back of a beach wagon, and maybe you're gonna make it with an older woman you just met?"

"That's right, my man."

"Not bad."

"So she got into the wagon, laid out the bag for me, and set the blanket and pillow to the side. What a lovely behind she had. Then, she walked up and gave me this big hug, pulled away, and said something like, 'You're such a nice handsome kid, Tommy, but I have to be straight with you. My boyfriend is back in the tent – you understand, Sweetie. Pleasant dreams!' And off she went. I watched her until she faded into the darkness and all I could see was her flashlight. Nice girl and honest to a fault."

"So you didn't get lucky after all. Bummer!"

"I did not - you are correct. I struck out looking. But it was just as well - I was dog tired anyway. The wagon creaked as I got in and took my shoes off. I turned the flashlight on and stood it up on the floor. I got in the bag and propped up my head on the pillow at the end, relaxed, and thought about the events of the day. As my eyes got heavy, I noticed a handle on the ceiling and grabbed it. It was a slider. I pulled it all the way down and above it was clear glass. I turned out the light and looked up...and there it was...that snapshot that I'll never forget long as I live."

"What? What in the world was it?"

"Now...just keep in mind, Jeff, that Hermit Island is kind of cut off from regular civilization – no artificial light of any kind save for battery powered stuff, at least when I was there. And it was only a sliver of moon like I said earlier. I took a long look up and it was like Van Gogh's 'Starry Night', man. Clusters and clusters of stars painted across that huge black sky like great swarms of bees in swirls and spirals. Surreal. I'd never in my life seen so many stars together like that, like every one of 'em was alive and burning! I was stunned – I felt ripples of goose bumps.

"And then...this feeling of like...total serenity came over me – as if every good thing that ever happened to me in my life all rolled into a big ball and engulfed me right there and then. I was young, I was strong, and this huge awesome world was out there all for me to see – thoughts like those filled my head and thrilled me to my bones. I was never so excited about just being alive and having so much to look forward to. It was a fantastic and unexpected buzz, man! And I think that was the beginning of – you know – my quest and my big ideas for the future."

"Deep. Knowing you as I do now, I totally get it."

"Maybe the euphoria lasted a minute or two," Slade continued. "Then I settled into a peaceful kind of...repose I guess. I closed my eyes, and I was out like a tree stump. I woke up in the morning to this beautiful smell of salt and greenery. It was like a little pass through Heaven, man."

"What a trip," Jeff reflected. "Almost like you were on a little acid."

"Who knows? Maybe they slipped a tab in my coffee. I wouldn't have put it past them. But I don't think so. It was real, not drug induced. So I got the stuff together and walked back to the tent. I remember looking back at the tracks I left in the dew. The girls were all around the fire eating breakfast. Danny was up and two other guys too. One was Lanna's husband whose name I can't remember, and the other Dawn's boyfriend, Will. Dawn introduced me to the guys."

"How'd they react to you?"

"Surprisingly good. I don't think Danny even remembered me – he was pretty hung over. They were friendly guys, though. Probably they figured I was too young to be any kind of threat. I cleaned up in a pail of water and had bacon on cornbread and coffee by the fire. We talked a little and I filled them all in on my predicament. Will was this pretty cool kind of dude, a tall strong guy. Looked a little like Chuck Connors in The Rifleman. I told him I was headed back to Penn and he offered to help me out to get started.

"'I'll take you to shore on the boat, Tom,' he said. 'Then I'll drive you out to the main road and get you pointed south. You're about five miles south of that Ho Jo's where you met the girls.'

"I agreed to that and thanked him and everybody else for taking care of me. Will and I got on the boat and we moved out. I took a look back. They all waved and smiled. At that moment, the distinct thought occurred to me that I'd never see any of them again – which turned out to be the truth, at least so far."

"And you began hitching south?"

"That I did. It took me at least a dozen rides all told, and I slept in a meadow the following night. Luckily I had a warm coat and enough dough for food along the way to get back in one piece. I left home on a Friday afternoon and returned on Sunday night – didn't even miss a day of school. First thing I did was to apologize to my parents for acting like a jerk. They were worried sick about me but happy that I was safe – and my coming clean right away took the edge off of things. But my older sister Jodie, who is a real straight arrow, she still thought I was nuts and was mad at me for a while. You know, to this day I still don't know exactly where I was but I'm pretty sure I at least got the name of the island right. But it was one special time, man. Sometimes I think back and can't believe it really happened."

"Phew...you are a born story teller, Shotgun," Jeff said shaking his head. "Nobody can spin a tale like you – that was really good. And I knew it was going to be something different – that moment – from just a roll in the hay with that hot little Dawn. You know what? Hearing that story just might be one of those things for me, man. Not so much a snap shot deal like you describe, but something kind of special that I'll always remember."

"I hope it is," Slade told him.

That was followed by a firm hippie handshake. Jeff then retired to his room, his mind awash in thoughts of Hermit Island.

43.

The days rolled on into late October and brilliant hues of orange and gold on the horizon. Only a few weeks remained until the departure date and big change. The van was all set up and ready to go. The four took advantage of the overtime offered and each saved up enough money where it wouldn't be a problem for a long time. Everybody was psyched.

Slade spent time pouring over maps of sections of the country. Jeff made a list of lingering loose ends to tie up before he left and took care of each, one by one. Young Ed did a lot of time day dreaming about what it was going to be like, and as the trip drew closer, felt more and more blessed to be part of it. And Rails worked on organizing and finalizing all of his notes on Warburton, so as to have a fresh author's eye for all the new material coming on the long road ahead.

Back in the factory, on a Tuesday morning at about 5 AM, Jeff was atop his spool roller working on a machine. Beans approached and leaned on the side of it.

"How goes the battle, Jonesy?" he asked, head tilted up sideways. "You winning?"

"Holding my own, Beans. What's the good word?"

"Not much other than I just about had a stroke an hour ago."

"What happened?"

"Lunch was over and I was clearing out empty tubs from the floor. I started to pull on one and it was heavy like something was in it. I opened the flaps and Dina jumps out like a jack in the box and yells 'DING DONG – THE WITCH IS ALIVE!' My friggin heart stopped. She'd been sleeping through lunch in the tub and I woke her when I moved it. I never heard a broad laugh like she did."

"Oh she got you, man. I can imagine how you must have looked."

"Just about shit my pants."

Jeff shook his head and laughed. Then Beans started in on an old story about his collecting days, one that Jeff had heard many times before. Yada-yada-yada. Jeff's attention waned and he glanced across the aisle. There was Lynne sitting on a window ledge taking a break. At that moment, he remembered one of those loose ends on his list that he had been putting off. Now was the time.

"Beans," he interrupted. "I don't mean to stop you but I just thought of something important I have to talk to Lynne over there about. No offense, man, but will you excuse me a minute?"

"None taken, Jeff. Do what you got to do. I'll go find somebody else to bug."

Jeff smiled as Beans walked off. He then got down and told Simone he needed to take five. He took a deep breath and walked over to Lynne.

"What's up, LC?" he said.

"No Doz," she said. "I'm wired. You guys are getting close to D-day, aren't you?"

"Yeah – sometimes I still can't believe it's going to happen."

"I'm going to miss you – I really mean that."

"Likewise," he said, glad to hear that from her. Jeff paused and took another deep breath. "You know, Lynne, considering that...I thought it might be cool for you and me to get together on the outside – you know – just for old time sakes. Maybe see a movie or something. The van's all fixed up since you saw it last."

Lynne smiled warmly and looked up at him. "You had to wait THIS long to ask? I never thought you'd work up the nerve, Jeff. But better late than never – sure! There's a movie opening this week that got a good review in the Record American. I think the title is 'The Sterile Cuckoo' or something like that. How's that sound?"

"Consider it done," Jeff said, relieved that he got a yes. "I'd have asked you sooner but I never had any wheels. Walking dates don't usually go over too well. Saturday night?"

"That's fine," Lynne laughed. "Let's do the early show. I'll make some dinner and we can go back to my apartment after and eat. We'll make a night of it."

"It's all locked in then," Jeff said smiling broadly, drawing his fists together and twisting them. "I remember where your place is from the morning we took you home when your car broke down in the lot. I'll check the movie times and I'll get back to you."

"Great. And thanks for asking me, Jeff. I'm looking forward to it."

"Me too."

Jeff walked back to his post as if he was floating on air. He had a date with easily the best looking woman he'd ever asked out, and one he really liked. He thought back to his solitary days in the sticks up north before coming to Stiller. He would never have had the confidence to ask a girl like Lynne for a date then. He'd come a long, long way in just eight or so months. In the back of his mind, he could barely believe how much he'd changed.

On their way back to the YMCA from work later that morning, Jeff looked over at Slade from the passenger seat of the van.

"Well, I did it," he said.

"Did what?"

"I made a date with Lynne - going to take her to a movie on Saturday might. I thereby have dibs on our chariot for that night. You don't know how long I've had it on my mind, man. Once we got the van, I finally got up the courage."

"Really? That's great! How did she react when you asked her?"

"She was all for it - seemed happy and almost relieved that I finally asked her if you can believe it. It went perfectly."

235

"Not surprising. That's what I would have figured," Slade reflected. "I knew she liked you from day one, Jeff. There's always been a nice connect between the two of you. You know, with us leaving and all, don't be surprised if things – let's just say – escalate."

"Escalate? Furthest thing from my mind," Jeff said. "I've got a lot of respect for Lynne – I'd never take advantage of her. But you know what? She jumped right in with asking me to dinner at her place after the movie. She's going to cook a supper for us."

Slade's eyes danced a little. "And she'll have wine too, guaranteed," he said. "You may have to make a tough decision. Now don't be surprised if SHE tries to take advantage of YOU, my friend. Just be prepared for anything. You never know where it's going to lead to when feelings are involved. Believe me. Plus your leaving town adds another dynamic to the mix."

"Maybe so. You're pretty good at sizing up stuff like this. But Shotgun, if I get the chance for a little lip-lock action on the couch, that'll be more than enough."

"We'll see," Slade said. "But just be ready, that's all. I have a funny feeling that my...prophesy from a while back just might come to fruition."

"I'm going to try really hard not to think about it," Jeff smiled.

44.

Saturday night rolled around fast. Jeff put in extra time at the gym to feel as fit and confident as he could. He wore his best jeans over a pair of brown boots and a blue striped shirt under his bomber jacket. He felt pretty good.

At seven thirty, he picked up Lynne, who was waiting on a bench outside her apartment building. She had on a black pair of fitted slacks, a white lacy blouse, high heels, and a furry gray jacket. On her head was a black beret tilted at just the right angle. Jeff had never seen her dressed up before and looking so stylish. He was impressed big time.

"Wow!" he said as she got into the van. "Just seeing you looking so good, this is already a great night."

"Thank you, Jeff," she beamed.

"You're entirely welcome," he said as he began driving. It was a crisp fall evening and there was a chill in the air. Lynne got comfortable in her seat. As they rode along, she glanced around in the van.

"Looks like you guys have covered every nook and cranny," she said. "This thing looks like a little studio apartment."

"You know it," Jeff replied. "Ed's pretty handy. He did most of it with a labor of love."

"I can see that."

"You know, Lynne, Slade has masterminded the whole thing," Jeff continued. "The rest of us are just along for the ride – all for our own particular reasons, I guess. But that guy, he's got something about him. I don't know what it is, but like Rails says, we follow him like a school of ducklings."

"I know what good friends you two are," Lynne offered. "Did you know Slade before you came to Stiller?"

"No – only since I've been here. But we clicked from the get go. See, my room's right next to his at the red brick hotel. First night I was there, he was playing the guitar with a woman friend in his room who I'd crossed paths with earlier in the day. They invited me in and I think I've seen him just about every day since. He was big help right from the start when I really needed somebody to show me the ropes. My life has gotten better steadily since I've known Shotgun."

"Shotgun - I love that nick name. He IS sort of a special kind of guy," Lynne agreed. "I've never heard him say a bad word about anybody, or vice versa."

"That's just not in him," Jeff said. Then he paused. "You know what? I'd like to share something with you Lynne, if it's okay."

"Sure, Jeff. Go right ahead."

"Well, I don't like to talk about this much. It used to get me down, plus I don't like crying the blues either. Anyway, I think I may have mentioned before to you that I had it kind of rough growing up. See, my mom died when I was very young and my dad hit the bottle after that. He flew the coop when I was 11 and I haven't seen him since. My older brother and I got split up eventually and I was bounced around different places until I was 18 and on my own. Slade's like family to me now. I know I can count on him no matter what."

"I knew weren't a happy camper right from the beginning, Jeff," Lynne remarked softly. "I sensed you'd had hard times. I could see it in your eyes from the day I first met you."

"Really?"

She reached over and stroked his arm. "Yes. I think that's why I was drawn to you more than to Tom. We have that in common, Jeff, you and me. My mother committed suicide four years ago. She tried so hard, but she had a drug habit and was very depressed. And my dad and her were divorced a long time before that. He's remarried and lives in another state. I see him only a few times a year, but at least we have a relationship. I've been on my own since not long after my mom left us, just like you. I do have an older sister in Vermont, Terri, who I keep in touch with, though. She's actually happily married if you can believe that, and has a daughter. So our stories are pretty similar, I guess, right? You know, crazy as it might sound, I think sometimes people who have problems are attracted to other people who have problems."

"Suicide? My God...I'm sorry, Lynne," Jeff said somberly, glancing over at her. "I really am sorry. But what you say has some truth to it. Crazy as it may sound, I've always thought there's something attractive in misery – sort of a kind of beauty in desperation."

"Like misery loves company?"

"Yeah, but I think maybe it goes a little further."

They considered that for a second or two. Then Jeff broke into a laugh and Lynne joined in with him.

"How the hell did we get do damn serious?" he remarked. "Let's put our depressing histories aside - we've both overcome them pretty well I think. And things are definitely looking up. What say we just relax and enjoy a good movie?"

"Deal," Lynne nodded, and she was smiling again as they pulled into the lot. "But the main thing is that I HAVE noticed the change in you, Jeff. It's been a really nice thing to watch."

Thanks a lot, Lynne," he responded gratefully.

Jeff locked the van and they walked to the entrance. Their hands came together as if they'd been a couple for years. Jeff was heartened with how natural it felt. Inside, they bought pom-poms and milk duds at the counter. Then they took a couple of seats in the back of the theater. Jeff slid his arm right in positon around her shoulders.

"There you go," he whispered in her ear with a grin. "A year ago, I'd have had to think for an hour before I made a move like that, if I did it at all. I AM a changed man."

Lynne laughed and snuggled up to him. They watched a couple of cartoons and some coming attractions. Then "The Sterile Cuckoo" came on and it caught their interest from the start. It was a story about a wacky teenage couple attending different colleges nearby each other, who, despite their differences and hang ups, enter into a deep romance and a wild sexual relationship. Then, a possible pregnancy brings everything into reality and they have to face the truth. In the end, there's no pregnancy, but the obstacles between them are too great. Sadly, they have to part for good. In the final scene, the girl, Pookie, leaves on a bus and looks forlornly out the window at Jerry, her ex, for the last time as it slowly moves away. The film moved both Lynne and Jeff, particularly because Jeff would be soon leaving too.

"Who was the girl who played Pookie Adams?" Lynne asked on the ride back to her apartment. "She was so good. She loved that Jerry so much and it really came through."

"Her real name is Liza Minnelli." Jeff said. "I read it in a review in the Sounder. Know who her mother is?"

"No, who?"

"Remember 'The Wizard of Oz'? You must have seen that."

"I did. I loved it."

"Well, the girl who played Dorothy in it – Judy Garland – she's her real mother."

"Really? Now that I think of it, her voice sounded a lot like Dorothy's. 'Somewhere over the Rainbow' – I remember how well Judy Garland sang that song. It was perfect. I wonder if Liza Minnelli inherited her singing talent from her mom?"

"Most likely," Jeff said. "You're right – she sure can act. And the kid who played her boyfriend can too. I have to say the casting was really good. It was kind of a story about young love, I guess, and then the rough underside of it. You know, the reality of all the stuff that comes with it – all that mud you have to get through to get over the hump for it to really work. They just couldn't get through that mire."

"That's true," Lynne agreed. "But the feelings between them were powerful. I mean even though it didn't work out and maybe they never see each other again, something so strong like that – it becomes a part of you. You never forget what you felt."

"Yeah," Jeff said thinking deeply about it. "Tough as it is to leave behind, I'll bet years later you look back and say, 'I may have suffered but I'm glad it happened. I'm glad I had the experience of feeling so strongly about somebody in my life.' Some people never have that."

"That's it, Jeff." Lynne said. "That's exactly it. "

"You know something?" Jeff reflected glancing over at her. "I think we click pretty well...'intellectually' as Steve Railsback would say. I've learned some big words hanging out with him."

"Well, Jeff, now that you mention it, I did pretty well in high school even though I didn't have a chance at college. And I like to read."

"It shows over and above your beauty."

Jeff didn't know he had a remark like that in him. It warmed Lynne deeply as they pulled up to the curb, got out, and climbed the stairs to her second floor apartment. It was a one bedroom; small but cozy and spic and span clean. Jeff looked around while Lynne got a pan of lasagna she had cooked earlier out of the fridge. She placed it in the oven to heat up. Then she got some vegetables out and worked at getting a salad together.

"Your place looks really good," Jeff said checking out the living room. "Has a nice feel to it. I take it you're on your own here?"

"Yes, since last Christmas," she said. "A couple of years ago I was in a relationship and my ex moved in, but it was only for a few months. He was an okay person but one of those insecure possessive guys. I couldn't move without telling him. I had a rough time getting him to leave, but I finally did and now he's history. I was alone after that until my cousin stayed for a while and that worked out really well. But she left to move in with her boyfriend. I've been on my own here since then. I'm used to it. I may be alone but I'm not lonesome."

"And you can afford it okay?"

"Easily," she said. "I do really well at the factory, tough as it is at times. Like I told you before, I know how to run those machines and I make a lot of extra money on piecework. I have plenty of cash for what I need and the rent is low. I save money each week. It's not such a bad life."

"That's cool," Jeff said walking back into the kitchen. "I like the cut of your jib as they say. You're young, Lynne, but you have your act together pretty well and it's all on you. That's impressive."

"Jib?" she asked.

"Just sailor talk I heard somewhere," Jeff laughed. "I don't even know what a jib is."

Lynne smiled, reached out her hands and pulled him toward her. She hugged him warmly and ran her hands up and down his back. Jeff felt a charge as he returned the favor and stroked her hair, smooth as silk.

"You say nice things to me, Jeff," she said. "And I know you mean them. You don't know how good that makes me feel."

"Thanks," he said as she released him. "I just say what comes into my head and try to filter it a little bit. If it comes out right, then all the better. And I have to add – you give a world class hug."

"One of my gifts," Lynne smiled. "Want a glass of wine with the meal? I have a nice bottle of Merlot."

What Slade said about her offering him wine flashed through Jeff's mind. He had sworn off alcohol, but now, suddenly he was up against it. He had to make a decision.

"You know what?" he said. "I haven't had a drink since that party last July in Maine. But I think I'm going to go off the wagon just for tonight. A glass of wine will hit the spot."

"Oh, I'm trying to forget that nightmare. But are you sure? I don't want you to foul anything up on account of me."

"I'm okay with it," Jeff assured her. "I don't have a drinking problem or crave alcohol. It's just in a party situation that it scares me a little. You know – losing control of my, say…my good judgment. This is totally different."

"All right, then," Lynne said. "The wine will go nicely with the food."

She set out the dishes on the table and poured two glasses. Then she lit a candle in the center and tuned in some soft music on the radio console in the living room. The lasagna was hot and the aroma permeated the apartment as Lynne removed it from the oven and portioned it out in the pan. She then placed the salad, colorful in a big wooden bowl on the table along with applesauce in a glass dish. Jeff watched her and admired how beautifully she moved and how at ease she was.

"Hey, Lynne, this is terrific," he said as he sat down. "Thanks a lot for having me over – I'm really enjoying everything."

"Didn't I tell you I owed you one a while back?" she laughed. "Well, just consider this a small part of that. It's great to finally have you here live and in person."

Jeff smiled as Lynne placed a large piece of lasagna on his plate. He helped himself to some salad and a couple of big dollops of apple sauce. Before he began to eat, he took a generous sip of wine. It only took a few seconds for him to feel a little heat.

"Whew," he said, "this wine has some kick to it."

"Only the best."

Lynne and Jeff took their time and enjoyed a good meal, plus homemade apple pie and ice cream for dessert. They talked some more about the

242

movie and different things that had gone on at work. The music in the background and the candle at the table gave the apartment a comfortable level of ambiance.

"You know, LC," Jeff said, feeling the wine more as the meal came to an end. "The closer we get to the day we leave, the more I come to realize that I'm actually going to miss this town. And even the Warburton sweat box."

"How so?"

"I don't know – I mean I'm not having second thoughts or anything. I'm committed to the trip and I'm looking forward to it. But like we talked about before, I've been here – what – eight or nine months? It's actually been good for me – better than I ever thought it might be. The town took me in, the Y took me in, and the factory did too. I've met some of the best people I've known in my life and for sure you're one of them. I've actually felt like I fit in somewhere for the first time in as long as I can remember. I'm grateful for it – I really am.

"That's deep," Lynne said with some emotion. "Almost makes me want to cry. You made a good decision to come here, Jeff. You did right."

"I guess I did. I'd say from day one here, I've been better – more able to figure stuff out and to act. And Like I said, being around Shotgun and the other guys has helped me a ton. I'd have never thought I'd be able to come this far in such a short time."

"Awesome," Lynne smiled. "Now...how about the new and improved Jeff helping me to clean up? Like the way I slid right into that?"

"Beautiful."

"I'm kind of a neat-freak, I have to admit," Lynne said. "I hate the sight of dirty dishes in the sink."

"Me too," Jeff agreed. "But I just try to remember to look the other way."

Lynne jabbed him in the ribs and they had a good laugh. They cleared off the table and she did the dishes, humming along with the background music as Jeff dried them. When they finished and Jeff placed the last dish in the slot, he turned to see Lynne facing away from him pouring more wine. Without even thinking about it, as soon as she put the bottle on the

243

table, Jeff came up behind her, put his arms around her waist, and pulled her close to him.

"I hope I'm not out of line," he said, "but I'm only human."

She turned in his arms and faced him with a huge smile. Then she tilted her head up and began to close her eyes. He drew her to him and it was just the right kind of first kiss – not too hard – not too long – but with feeling and passion. As their lips drew away, Jeff held her close, stroking her hair with one hand and gently rubbing her back with the other.

"You don't know how long I've thought about that," he told her. "All those long lonely nights by myself in that creaky bed with the lumpy mattress."

The remark struck Lynne so funny that she tilted sideways and couldn't help laughing.

"Jeff!" she said with a gasp. "Sometimes you're so funny when you don't even mean to be. I love that about you! Let's go sit on the couch, have some more wine, and you know...get to know each other a little better. Okay?"

"Lead the way, my princess," Jeff said as they took their glasses and she escorted him over, both just a tad dizzily.

As Jeff took a seat on the couch, Lynne made a couple of telling moves. She took the candle from the kitchen table, walked into the bedroom and placed it on the bureau. Then she went to the radio back in the living room, adjusted the volume a little quieter, and left just one dim light on. She was setting things up for romance just like Jeff might have if the tables were turned and it was his apartment. He drank some more wine and felt primed. He was ready to cruise.

Lynne sat back down next to him and snuggled up close. For a few minutes, they just held and stroked each other, not rushing into anything, but simply experiencing and enjoying moments that both had often thought of. Then Jeff gently began kissing her neck, caressing her hair, and moving along into a smooth make out session. She was the most passionate kisser he had ever been with.

"Where'd you learn to work it like that?" he said softly to her. "I feel like I've been infused with electric current."

"The more I like somebody, the better I work it," she came back with. "Hey, you know what I'd love right now? A little back rub. Think you can do it?"

"Oh – I think so – definitely," Jeff laughed. "I actually learned how to give back rubs in a health and fitness course in college. You won't be disappointed."

"Start right here and if you're really good, we'll move to the bedroom."

"I'm at my best under pressure...well, at least I like to think I am."

Lynne gave a little chuckle. Now Jeff knew that chances were high that they were going to make it together. But to his surprise, he wasn't nervous about it. The wine had taken care of that somewhat. Besides that, he'd known this girl for a while and was comfortable around her. He had feelings for Lynne. It was a good mix to calm any nerves. If it did happen, all was going to be fine he told himself.

Jeff got behind Lynne on the side of the couch and began to massage her neck, softly but with some easy pressure.

"Oh, just like that," Lynne said with a little murmur of pleasure. "That feels so good."

"I'm going to improvise a little," Jeff said as he began to unbutton the back of her blouse. "Just tell me if you think I'm going too far."

Lynne didn't say a word. He got to the bottom and pulled the ends aside, exposing her silky smooth back. Then he went to work on either side of her spine with thumb pressure and circular palm motions – slowly – down to her waist and back up to her shoulders, then side to side on both arms. All the important points were covered. In between, he kissed her neck, brought his hands around her waist, and gradually moved them around her bra and experienced her breasts. His body lit up like strobe lights; he'd never felt anything so perfect. But Jeff reeled himself in and made sure he was gentle and loving. Lynne buried her head under his chin and let herself bask in the attention of a guy she really wanted to be with.

Before long, they were both naked from the waist up and the living room light was out. The only illumination came from the candle in the bedroom. Things moved along more and more and soon, decision time hung over them. Lynne hugged Jeff tightly and whispered into his ear.

245

"Let's head to the bedroom, honey," she said. "I mean it – let's go – right now. If it happens, it happens. And when I feel like this, it usually happens."

"You're sure, right?" You know in a few weeks I'm going to be gone."

"I'm sure." she said. "I know the big picture. Don't worry - I'm protected. I just want us to have this to remember in case we never see each other again after you leave. I've thought about it and I feel right about it."

"I do too," Jeff agreed. He picked her up and carried her to the bedroom.

"Welcome to the boudoir," Lynne grinned looking up at him.

Jeff smiled and released her. He slowly removed the rest of her clothes. Then she helped him with his. For a number of seconds, both stood naked facing each other by the flickering light of the candle. Jeff was stunned at how spectacular Lynne was; her long hair draping softly over her breasts and his eyes moving down to drink in her feminine curves and honey thighs.

"You are something to behold, Lynne." he said softly bringing her to him. "You are a beautiful woman. Lie on your stomach now and I'll finish your massage."

"You're looking awful good too, Jeff. I can see that you work out," she said admiringly.

"Just about every day. Keeps me pointed forward."

"Well, it's paying off."

"I'll say it is – in silver dollars."

Lynne knew what she brought to the party and had no inhibitions about being naked. She got prone on the bed. Jeff got a condom out of his wallet from his pants on the chair he'd tossed them over. He broke it open and placed it on the bed table. Then he got on the bed and kneeled to the side of Lynne.

"Have your way with me and finish my massage, please," she said softly with a smile.

"Gladly."

246

Jeff worked the lower half of her body, down her buttocks and all the way to her toes. Then he gently turned her over. Now Lynne took the lead, laid him down, and gently loved him all over. She was a young woman but with ample experience. She knew how to get it done. Jeff had never been with anyone who made him feel like Lynne did just then.

Finally it got to that point. Jeff paused and slid on his condom. He didn't even fumble with it like he thought he might have. Lynne remained silent, closed her eyes and breathed in deeply. Slowly but surely, they became fully engaged and Lynne let out a beautiful moan. It was a sound that would be imprinted in Jeff's brain for the rest of his living days. He almost let it all go right there, but was able to hold himself back. He wanted her to have the same feeling he knew he was soon going to have.

And it came to be. After a several minutes of easy going, Lynne let out another moan. It was a clear indicator of a climax of pleasure and he knew. Jeff picked up the pace and not long after, he felt a release from some far-away place that lasted and lasted. He let out an extended sound of gratification different than any he'd ever made before.

Then, silence. Jeff and Lynne basked in the surreal realm of satiation. By pure coincidence, "Time of the Season" by the Zombies played on the radio in the background, with the repeating motif, "It's the time...of the se-ee-ay-son for lov-ing." They lay there together, Jeff on his back and Lynne on her side, her head nuzzled in his neck and her arms around him.

"That was other worldly," he whispered to her, "I feel like I'm on the moon or something. For me...the way things developed and went down just right – I'll never forget this night. Nothing could have been more perfect."

"I feel just like that, Jeff," Lynne said softly stroking his hair. "It was meant to be. I may be just a mill girl, but I've learned a little about making love in my life. That's 'making love', not having sex. It's best when it's an expression of something...deep and real, you know? If you're lucky enough to be with the right person. And I am."

"Right, I get it," Jeff said. "Me too. I think we handled it pretty well, don't you?"

"Sue we did. That's why we feel so good now."

"I most definitely DO feel good."

"We'll always remember this night, just like you said," Lynne told him. "Always...no matter what happens."

Jeff kissed her and they lay back together. Before long, both were asleep. Although they were used to being awake all night for work and struggling to adjust on weekends, it had been a long day and a full evening. Jeff and Lynne slept soundly through the night.

In the morning they had an encore experience. Then they took a shower together, a first for Jeff with a woman. After that, Lynne made coffee and cooked up a tasty breakfast, which they enjoyed between the Sunday morning rays running through the kitchen window curtains. After breakfast, they sat in the living room a while and talked over more coffee. Then Jeff felt it was time to leave and get himself squared away for the coming week.

"Well, guess I'll have to split now," he said getting up and putting his cup in the sink. "I don't know how to thank you, Lynne. That was the best night...and morning of my life."

"Same with me," she said, walking over and hugging him tightly. "And listen, I want to say this because I mean it. It's almost 1970 now and not the fifties any more. I understand our situation and we don't owe each other anything. All I ask is that if you will, stay in touch with me with letters. Let's keep up a friendship at least. And who knows, if in a year or so or whenever, if you come back to the area, I might still be around and unattached. Maybe we could make a go of it, Jeff."

"Man," Jeff sighed, "after all this, leaving isn't going to be as easy as I thought. But it's set in cement and I have to do it. I know you understand that, Lynne. The way you look and the quality kind of person you are, I expect - I figure you'll get involved with somebody else. And you should. But you never know in this life. If it's meant to be between us, it will happen somehow. Sure I'll write. You can count on it. And I'll look forward to hearing about what's going on with you too – regularly I hope."

"Then it's a deal," she said extending both hands and holding Jeff's firmly. "And something good has come up that I haven't told you about yet. Remember that night at the factory when we talked of our plans for the future?"

"Sure."

248

"Well, I've thought a lot about that since then. See, I've always been interested in sewing and dress making – you know, tailoring. I learned about it a little in high school. Starting next Saturday, I'm going to be working with my aunt – not Hattie, her sister Mary. She's a seamstress."

"What? You're quitting Warbs?"

"Oh no. It'll be only for four hours on Saturday afternoons. She owns her own dress shop and is really nice. Aunt Mary's going to teach me the ropes and I'm going to get paid too. Maybe someday I can have my own shop and leave the mill life for good. I know I have a talent for it and I want to do it."

"That's great!" Jeff said. He pulled her close and rubbed her back. "You've got a lot on the ball, girl," he continued. "I knew it from the day I met you. You're not going to waste away in that mill like some of the old timers have. It's going to work out and you'll have your own business someday. You have too much going for you for it not to."

"Oh - that's JUST what I need to hear!" she beamed, stepping back. "Support from somebody like you goes so far."

"Thanks," Jeff said. "Thanks a lot." Then something occurred to him.

"Hey Lynne," he said. "There's one other thing that's been in the back of my head. I have to ask you this. Remember after what happened in Maine, you said something about owing me one and I'd see what you meant? Were you thinking about last night maybe developing back then at some point? You don't have to answer but I kind of got that feeling. I'm just wondering if I might have been right."

Lynne paused and grinned. "Well, let's just say I had a few ideas. And if the situation, let's say - presented itself, that was in the mix. The rest is history now. But don't consider it payback. I wanted it just as much as you did."

"Okay, that satisfies that," Jeff laughed, hugging her again and kissing her on the cheek. Then, with a twinkle in his eye, he added, "You know, I always admired you from the beginning, but remember that time you told me you liked the Three Stooges?"

"Yes?"

"I think something special happened then."

249

Lynne paused and then they both broke up laughing. "You are too much, Jeff!"

"Okay...well, guess I'll be going. I'm a loner and loners have to be alone, right? See you Monday night."

"See you then," Lynne smiled giving him a shove. She walked him out to the van and Jeff was off back to the Y, his thoughts focused on so far, the most memorable experience of his life.

45.

As Jeff walked up the steps and into the building, Creecher was coming in the opposite direction.

"Creech," he said, "have you seen Shotgun around?"

"I walked by his room and I heard him practicing on his guitar. At first I thought it was the record player. He plays that good."

"We call him 'the Natural'," Jeff told him. "Thanks."

Jeff hopped up the stairs and headed toward Slade's pad. As he approached the door, he stopped and listened. Slade was playing a new song that he hadn't heard before. It was so pretty and harmonic, that it sounded like Slade had somebody else in there playing along with him. Jeff waited until he finished and then rapped on the door.

"Door's open. Enter and sign in please," he heard Slade say.

"Paper boy," Jeff said as he walked in. There sat Slade and his guitar, music stand and ledger book in front of him, and nobody else there. Jeff grabbed a chair, faced it backwards and sat down.

"What was that song you just played?" he asked. "What a rich sound. It's a new one, right?"

"Right. I just figured out how to play it today. It's an instrumental by Tom Rush called 'Rockport Sunday'. I saw him perform it last summer on the Cape and then again in the fall at Club 47 in Cambridge."

"Rockport Sunday?" Jeff said. "Interesting title. It does kind of sound like the tide and the sea."

"You are very observant, my friend. I remember how he described the song before he played it. He said something like…'This song is about the feel and sounds of the ocean on a Sunday morning in a seaport town. You know – seagulls, church bells, and the rugged shore crashing on the surf.' He made the mistake on the last phrase just to get a rise out of the audience."

"What a memory," Jeff marveled. "How do you get it to sound so full, though – like you're playing a 12-string?"

"You don't know how I struggled with that. I fooled around with it in standard tuning but I couldn't get that full ringing echo effect with all six strings that Rush gets. I figured he must use some kind of open setting with harmonics. I experimented around and finally settled on an open C tuning. You adjust the strings so that when you strum them all and don't fret anything, you get a C chord."

He demonstrated it and Jeff was intrigued. "I didn't know you could do that," he said. "You never showed us."

"That's because you and Steve haven't gotten that far yet – that's somewhere down the road. Anyway, it all locked in after I hit on that – the full chording, the harmonics, everything. It's actually not a hard piece – only took me an hour or so to work out a complete arrangement. Did you hear the bends in the middle?"

"Yeah – I really liked that."

"Supposed to sound like seagulls calling over the rolling waves. Works, doesn't it?"

"Yes, really well," Jeff agreed. "When you think I'm ready, I want to learn that song."

"It's a winner," Slade. "I got a thrill the first time I played it through and it sounded right. If these artists only knew what their great stuff does to people – how it affects us. Maybe some of them do. Anyway, you have to

251

get better with barre chords first. Remind me in a month or two. So I noticed you didn't come home last night. I take it things went pretty well with our lovely and talented Miss Charland?"

Jeff rocked his chair back, closed his eyes and smiled. "Other than it was the best night of my life, not bad."

"Hmm…sounds interesting," Slade smiled. "Lynne's a first rate person and she cares about you. I kind of knew it was going to be special."

"Special isn't a strong enough word. I have to respect her privacy so I won't go into any details. But you were right about your prediction. I've never felt like that with any other woman in my life, man. It couldn't have been better."

"That's great," Slade said. "Both of you deserve it. But after it was all over and done with, reality must have set in at some point. How does she feel about you leaving? Did you talk about it?"

"It did come up. Like you said, she's top notch. She made it a point to tell me she's cool with the deal before I left her place – only asked that I write to her regularly. No strings, man. Not even a thread. But she kept the door open to us getting together again someday, and I'm taking that very seriously."

"And you're going to write to her, of course."

"Oh, most definitely. I care about her. I think I have feelings for Lynne like I've never had for another woman. At one point, I almost dropped the "L" word but I was able to keep the lid on that. I sensed she maybe came close too. I'll definitely miss that woman and I told her how it was going to be harder to leave than I figured. Shotgun, she touches something in me like no other chick ever has."

"Deep. Any second thoughts?"

"No – I'm locked in totally."

"Well, then just remember this," Slade projected. "If one day we're having breakfast, and you look down at your eggs sunny side up, and you see her eyes, you'll know you've REALLY got it bad." Then he poked at Jeff and laughed.

Jeff smiled and looked at him sideways. "Where in hell did you ever think up that line?" he asked incredulously.

"Heard Barney Fife say it the other night on Andy Griffith and I filed it. But all kidding aside, man, that's groovy. On a similar note, I got together with Nikki last week and we talked about things some more. But no action. Although we ended the physical part of it mutually like I told you a while back...still, I felt we had to close things right, you know what I mean? Anyway, I'm glad we talked again. We got all the loose ends out on the table and now everything's squared away between us."

"That's cool. Nik is one of the most interesting females I've ever crossed paths with." Jeff said thoughtfully. "I think that was the one and only personal strip tease demonstration I'll ever get, that's for sure. But you did the right thing, Shotgun. No good leaving any unfinished issues still dangling out there, man."

"Right on. I'll stay in touch with her but it probably won't be like you and LC, which I know will be more regular. Nik and I weren't deep like the two of you. You can share with Lynne what's going on with the group in those letters. And make sure she saves them. It will be a good record of our travels."

"I will," Jeff said. "You know, I'm still on cloud 9, Shotgun – make that 10. You don't know how many nights I lay in my bed thinking about her but never figuring I'd have what it took to make a move – to take a chance. Remember back when I said she was too much woman for me?"

"I certainly do."

"Well, she was then. But I've come a long way since. I handled it and kept my cool the whole way through. It feels good. Like your TV hero Cheyenne would say, 'mighty good'.

"Of course. The one and only Clint Walker. He was and always will be...'The Man'. Too bad that show isn't on any more – I really liked it."

"Me too. He might have been soft spoken, but he always got the job done."

Slade smiled and tapped Jeff's shoulder. "Just like you and Lynne did, dude – just like you did."

46.

The month of November took hold with frost on the grass in the early mornings. With their departure date closing in, the group felt like short timers at Warburton, as they anticipated their release and freedom. Nothing much would change around the place after they were gone. Replacements were being solicited and things continued to roll along as usual. It would be the same for a time and then one day the big green doors would close for good. In New England, textiles were now a sunset industry and the sun was half way down on the horizon. The remaining mills in Stiller were on their way out. The workers knew that in the back of their minds but most avoided thinking about it. What would be, would be.

During the afternoon before their last night of work, the four made final preparations. They got the van washed and their packing completed. Each arranged to have their last paycheck and lingering mail forwarded to a post office box in Slade's home town that he had arranged for them. They'd pick it all up on the way south through Drexel Hill and then make further arrangements directed to San Francisco. The plan was to rest up over the weekend, get accustomed to sleeping nights again, and then hit the road south on Monday morning. All systems were go and the anticipation level was over the top.

It was cold and misty outside during that final night of work. Most of the crew knew they were leaving and there were many handshakes and good luck wishes. Beans was particularly affected. He'd grown especially close to Jeff and talked at length with him most every night.

"Hey Jeff," he said to him as he walked over to his work area. "I just want to say that a lot of people are going to miss you guys around this place...I know I will."

The way Beans looked up at him after he said that struck a chord in Jeff. It was an expression of the young man Beans once was, wishing he could go too but knowing he couldn't. There was an underlying sadness about it. For a couple of seconds, Jeff got a lump in his throat.

"Thanks, buddy," he said, shaking Beans' hand and patting his back. "I know it wasn't easy for you to say that. I'm going to miss you too, man – you've been a good friend. Your jokes and stories made the time go by in here a lot smoother. Thanks for all you did for me, Shotgun, and Ed."

"What I did? Really?" Beans said. "Sheez, I don't get many compliments – I'm not used to it. But thanks. I'll remember what you just said."

"Well, it's the truth. Ask anybody around the mill, Beans. They might kid around with you, but they wouldn't if they didn't like you. You add a lot of color to this place and believe me, it needs it."

Beans put his hand to his chin and thought for a couple of seconds. He was touched and uncharacteristically at a loss for words.

"All I can say is that it's a tough life, but I'm livin' it," he finally mumbled staring down at the floor. "My dad told me that a few days before he kicked the bucket. He was a tough old basted." Then Beans looked up and smiled widely. "I try the best I can, Jonesy – what more can a guy do?"

Jeff nodded and smiled.

Then looking Jeff in the eye with conviction, Beans added, "I just wish I was young and I could go with you guys, but let's face it, I ain't. I got my wife and my daughter and that window closed for me twenty years ago. I'm going to die right here in this town. But if you can do me one small favor, Jeff, it will mean a lot to me."

"Just name it."

"Every once in a while, send me a postcard from wherever you are with a picture of the place on it, and tell me what's going on. No letters – just cards with pictures. Not much – a few sentences – that's all I need. It will mean a lot to me. See...that way it will be like I'm there too. I'll even give you some dough to cover the postage."

"Consider it done and your money's no good here," Jeff said. "Just give me your address. You'll be getting regular postcards – I guarantee it."

"Thanks," Beans smiled. He got out a pad and wrote down the information. He handed it to Jeff.

255

"I can count on you, right?" he said.

"Don't ask dumb questions."

"And keep this in mind down the road," Beans concluded as they shook hands and he walked off. "The truth has a loud voice."

That remark intrigued Jeff as he watched him disappear down the ramp. Then Simone dispatched Jeff to the cafeteria for coffees. At the far end of the floor, Slade was taking a break at one of his machines and Rails was talking with him. Dina walked over and faced them.

"What are we going to do without you two tall handsome guys?" she said. "And Jeff and Eddie too. This place will never be the same."

"Oh, you'll adjust," Slade smiled. "You know how it is, Deen – nothing is forever."

She saw Ed coming up the aisle and waved him over. He joined them.

"Well, just let me say that you boys added a lot to this place," she continued. "Even you, Steven with all your weird ideas and note taking. Just be sure to make me look good in your book or I'll sue your sorry ass and I won't look back!"

That broke them all up.

"But seriously," Dina added, "I just want to thank you guys, and I'll tell Jeff too when I see him. Thanks from me, Simone over there, and all of us in this place. You did a great job and we all had fun working with you. You're four special people. And I will never forget the night that snake chased our poor Lew Masterson out the fire escape. That is one for the ages."

"We appreciate it, Dina," Rails told her. "I can say for all of us that it was an experience working here and we'll all take it with us on the road. That's for sure."

"And, blunt as you could be sometimes, Deen - and I liked that...we all thank you for being straight up with us," Slade added. "You always said what we needed to hear."

Dina smiled widely and hugged each of them. Then she wiped a tear from her eye. "I hate good byes," she said. "Now you keep young Eddie here out of trouble, Tom. You have the most common sense in the group."

"He won't have to, Dina," Ed laughed. "Being around these guys, I'm growing up real fast."

Jeff returned with the coffees. He and Simone walked over to the group and Simone wished them all the best. Dina gave Jeff a long hug. Then it came time to get back to work. A couple more hours passed quickly. The morning light filtering through the great windows brightened the floor as quitting time approached. For the final time, the four air-hosed off the lint from the night's labor.

At the punch clock, most of the third shift crew waited. All encouraged the soon-to-be travelers. Then Sam walked over with an envelope and presented it to Jeff.

"We all collected a little gas money for you guys," he said with a smile, "comes to around fifty bucks. The four of you were assets to the company and we appreciate what you did here. And as long as we're up and running, you're welcome to come back and work here any time you want to."

"Remember that," Beans said jabbing Jeff. "You never know when you might need it."

"Thanks Sam, and everybody else – for all of us," Slade told them. "We'll put the fifty to good use."

Everybody clapped. Finally, Lynne and Melissa gave their hugs and good byes. Missy made sure to thank Slade again for being first to help her after her fall on the roof. Lynne spent an extra few seconds with Jeff.

"Now don't forget me," she whispered in his ear, "and I'll see you in my dreams."

"I won't. Me too," he whispered back with a smile.

With that, they punched out and their time at Warburton Textiles was over. Down the creaky flights of stairs the four stepped deliberately. As they got to the bottom, Slade stopped and took in a big whiff of air.

"That smell – that unmistakable aroma," he said. "Every night I walked into this place it hit me. I never got used to it so I didn't notice it any more. I remember it like I was hitting a wall the first night I walked through the doors – like stale old paint with some bad molasses mixed in."

"Add a dose of turpentine," Ed said. "That dye odor."

"Right. And it still hits just as hard now nine-plus months later. I will never forget it."

"Sure as hell," Jeff added.

Rails took his note pad out and scribbled something down. "Good material, guys," he said. "That smell will find its way into my book. You can bet on it."

"Well, we got a nice sendoff and the people all turned out to be great. But I'm glad to be done with the place," Jeff said as they passed through the doors and into the morning. "I was always afraid in the back of my mind that I might end up stuck at Warbs. Now it's over and it's on to the next chapter. Big part of life, man – how well you move from the old to the new."

"Just like a good book," Rails agreed. "You keep turning the pages of the seasons of your life. Yesterday is gone and it can never be changed. You must always look ahead no matter what, my boy."

"Don't' get too philosophical on us, Steve," Slade laughed as they got a distance away, "but I like the way you said that. Now let's all turn around and give the old structure one more look. Then, when we think back about it, we'll start with that picture. I always do it when I leave a place for good."

They all flipped into reverse and did as Slade suggested. And as they eyed the old building, alive in the morning sun and framed by the blue sky with the river rapids singing in the rear; for the first time, it looked oddly beautiful. It was the place had taken them in and looked after them for a time. And now, it was sending off the four it had adopted, stronger and smarter for the experience.

47.

The group took it easy on Saturday. Each one relaxed individually in his own way. They got together and went candle pin bowling on Sunday. Rails made three strikes in a row, the first time ever for him. It was a good time and a nice further bonding experience outside of the mill and work. In the evening, they got the van completely loaded save for their overnight bags and Jeff's guitar. All was ready to go.

That night in his room, Jeff relaxed and played his guitar for half an hour before turning in. He sounded unusually good to himself and was pleased. Then he turned out the lights and got into bed.

Not yet used to sleeping nights, Jeff was keyed up and stayed wide awake for at least an hour. He remembered the spider from the spring and looked to the corner of the ceiling where it used to be. It was long gone now, just as he soon would be. Eventually, everything would fade away he thought to himself. A year ago, that notion would have stuck in his brain and he might have obsessed over it. Not now. He'd made it over the hump. The goblins residing up in the attic were now in handcuffs. They no longer ravaged him.

"Wonder what became of that black bug," he pondered. "Why did it leave? Not enough little insects to eat? Some other bigger bug killed it? Died of old age? Or just maybe it just knew the time had come to move on. Could be that it just knew, like I do now. Nothing's permanent in life – all is temporary. You come to get a handle on that. It's all in how you adjust – especially when it doesn't go your way."

Repeating that last sentence over and over, his eyes became heavy. Before long, he was out and in a deep sleep. The next thing he knew, a few knocks on his door woke him.

"It's open – come on in," he said drowsily.

"Rise and shine, my man," Slade said. "The time has come and that yellow brick road awaits us."

Jeff sat up and ran his hands through his hair. "I slept like a rock, Shotgun – I meant to get up earlier," he said. "I must have forgotten to set my clock. Give me like twenty minutes to get a shower and make sure I have everything straight."

"Take your time, buddy – no rush. Rails and Ed should be downstairs by now. Meet us when you're ready. We'll be at Shorty's."

"Will do."

Jeff got cleaned up and dressed. Then he put on his bomber jacket, picked up his guitar case in one hand and his carry bag in the other. He took a last check around the room to be sure he hadn't forgotten anything. Lastly, he glanced in the mirror. Jeff remembered the drawn uncertain face that stared back at him on his first night at the Y. Now, with the fear and uncertainty all but gone, he smiled and had to admit to himself that he looked pretty damn good.

Downstairs, he hooked up with the group and had toast and coffee. There was a lot of talk, good lucks, and positive vibes. Shorty even got a little emotional. Finally, all of the salutations were over and the group was out the door and down the steps. It was brisk and clear; a good day to start a trip. They made way over to the van. Slade stopped them for a final word before they got in.

"Okay, guys," he said earnestly, "this is it – the bottom line. We worked hard, we saved, we got ourselves a dependable vehicle and we're in good shape. Most important of all, we have each other. The life we knew before is over now and we're moving on to something brand new. Different people, places, situations and challenges. We'll handle them all together – as they come – one by one. Agreed?"

"You got it, Shotgun," Rails answered with enthusiasm. "That's the most important thing. We have each other's backs and we stick together."

"Right, Steve...and I have to add this little item. Like my old Pop has told me many times, no matter what we face, let's always look on the bright side.'"

"Cool," Ed said. "The bright side is where it's at."

Jeff had nothing to more to contribute. He just looked ahead down the road and smiled.

Slade, Ed, and Rails had been to the van earlier while Jeff was upstairs and loaded the last of their gear. His backpack already on board, Jeff stowed his bag and guitar. As they departed, he glanced back at the building that had been home since early spring. From one of the windows, an old man in a shabby coat, with his signature black scally cap angled down low looked out straight at him. It was Barney Ebersol, peering out with eyes of deathly sorrow, framed in red brick.

48.

Slade drove. Jeff sat up front with him with Rails and Ed in the back. Before long, they were out of town and on the trail pointed south. The van was in excellent shape. It hugged the road strong and solid.

"Can't believe it," Jeff said. "The day finally is here and we're on our way. This is like a dream come true, man – a dream come true!"

"I don't think I've ever felt so good," Ed added. "And like Shotgun said earlier, we busted our asses and paid our dues. That's one thing I think I learned from boxing and my trainers. You show up every day, put in the work, and even if you get knocked out, at least you know you did your best to be ready."

"Right on, Ed," Rails said. "The thing of it is, there are no guarantees, man. You control only what you can control. But you have a hell of a lot better chance of things going right if you put in the time, right?"

"Just common sense," Slade added. "So much in life is plain common sense."

As the sun rose higher in the sky, they rambled on into southern Massachusetts, through a series of towns running one over the other. They talked and talked and talked; about what they were seeing, what lay ahead, pretty girls in cars they passed - everything. All conversation was spiced with anticipation and wonder. It was a high that felt like it would never wane.

On the road for over three hours, the group closed in on the outskirts of New London, Connecticut. They were getting hungry and decided to get off the highway to look for a place to eat. Just into the city, a roadside sign in the distance beckoned. It said DAISY'S PLACE – GREAT HOME COOKING.

"That joint looks like it's for us," Slade said. The rest agreed and he pulled the van into the front lot. It was a railroad car style diner with an addition built on, painted bright red with a black and silver checkered roof. Beneath the windows were flower boxes filled with hardy yellow mums. The building glistened in the early afternoon shadows.

They took four seats together at the counter, directly behind a middle-aged man at the grill. He was brown haired and broad shouldered; his golf cap positioned backwards, agile on his feet and nimble with his hands, juggling multiple orders on a row of slips in front of him.

"Laura," he yelled in a small window that connected to a second grill in the back room. "I need two dropped on wheat and a spinach and feta cheese omelet – pronto! Daisy!" he shouted down the aisle. "I got your grilled cheese workin' and I owe yah two sides of frenchies."

"Calm down, Dad – I'll get to it – I'll get to it!" Laura yelled from the back sharply. "Gawd!"

"Gotcha Big John," Daisy shouted from aside a booth.

Big John turned to the new four at the counter and flashed a big smile. "What's up guys? My daughter back there," he smirked. "Day out of school and she doesn't want to be here. I'd love to kill her but I just haven't figured out the right way yet. Nah – she's a good kid. Daisy will be with you in a minute."

Everybody in the area had a good laugh. "Dad, please!" they heard from the back.

At the far end, Daisy cleared a table with clanks of dishes and the tingles of silverware before she began moving toward her new customers. In the meantime, the group had a look around the place. There were a bunch of autographed photos on the walls, some of notables posing with both Big John and Daisy. One included Bobby Darren, another Dean Martin, and one more with James Brown. The restaurant had been around a while. It had a reputation and a rich history.

Finally, Daisy zoomed in front of them as if she were on roller skates. "Hi yah' boys – how's it goin', boys? Sorry about the delay, guys but one of my girls is out sick today. I'm Daisy and that big lug to my right is my husband John, fellahs."

"He's a big, big man," Rails said. "Sorry – I couldn't resist it."

"Big in stature and huge in personality too," a man with a crew cut wearing a visor interrupted. He was sitting a few seats down.

"Thanks, Dentist," Big John laughed. He then winked at Slade and jabbed his arm. "Only he isn't really a dentist. Know why I call him that?"

"'No idea, Big John."

"Well...see, I golf with him and two other guys every Friday afternoon. We'll be out there 'till it snows. His real name is Dave and he's a good player – always drive's the ball right down the middle. Down the Middle Dave – DMD for short – the Dentist – get it – get it?"

"And we call the chef Zig Zag and I don't have to tell you why," Dave said sarcastically. "How's about getting the dentist an order of liver and onions, master of the short orders?"

"You're a brave man, Dave," Big John shot back. "A very brave man!"

"Can I get in a word edgewise or are you going to blab – blab – blab all day?" Daisy said with her palm on her hip. "These boys came here to eat – not to listen to your boring stories."

"Okay, okay woman," Big John laughed turning his attention back to the grill. "This place is named after you – we all know who the boss is 'round here."

"And don't forget it!" Daisy laughed. "Now that that's over with, you want coffees boys?"

They nodded. In a flash, Daisy plunked four cups down and filled them. She was something special, 35 or so, lean, strong shouldered, pretty and in fine shape. Her frizzy auburn hair was alive with her spirit and she had about as genuine a smile as God could draw up. Her red and white uniform had "Daisy's Place" sewn on the collar and a daisy flower next to it. It fit her perfectly; not a wrinkle to be seen.

"Nice to know both of you," Slade said, introducing himself and the others. Daisy dealt out the menus and the silverware. Clink, clank, clink, clank.

263

"We serve breakfast all day and home fries and beans come at no extra charge, boys," she told them. "Need a couple of minutes, fellahs?"

"Not me," Jeff said. I'll go for a couple of scrambled eggs with ham – and we'll do the beans and fries. And a large glass of OJ."

"Meatloaf dinner and a coke for me," Slade said.

"I'll try the hot turkey sandwich and a cherry coke," Ed added.

"And blueberry flapjacks for yours truly," Rails finished with." Plus a glass of iced water."

"Sure, boys, sure!" Daisy said looking more interested than she had to. "You guys are easy!" She scribbled it out and clipped the slip on the queue for Big John.

"Take special care of these gentlemen, Johnny," she said. "They're personal friends of mine."

"Oh, I'll take care of 'em all right," Big John laughed. "Where are you boys from?"

"Stiller up in the Bay State," Ed said. "You kind of sound like you're from around Boston, Big John. Am I right?"

"Close," John answered. "Winthrop, right next door to East Boston. We're mostly Italian there, we all talk like me, and everybody knows everybody else's business. Like a sea full of front porches. Get the picture?"

"Oh yeah."

Daisy brought them their drinks. She spilled the iced water a little but didn't bother to wipe it up. This was an informal establishment. Then she hustled down to the far end. Daisy had such a presence that it was like a spotlight was on her wherever she went.

"Your wife sure gets the job done, Big John," Rails said.

"You got that right, Stretch" John agreed. "I may kid around with her every now and then, check that - all the time. But she's tops. Ten years ago, Daisy had the idea for this place. She was twenty six and I was just turned thirty - we'd been married around seven years. It was a big risk and we had to borrow a lot of dough, but she never had a doubt we could make it work. Daisy had more drive than I ever did. Now, here we are doing pretty damn well. Some days I look around and still scratch my head."

"Well, the place has a great atmosphere, no doubt about that." Jeff added.

"Thanks," Big John said. "We live for compliments like that."

Slade, Jeff, and Ed sat back and breathed it all in. On the grill in front of Big John sat half a dozen eggs, an omelet, slabs of ham, a steak, bacon, hot dogs and hamburgers on the side. Everything sizzling. Toast popped left and right. It was laid on the hard wood counter and quickly slabbed with butter. Then it was taken up in a flash by Daisy or one of the other waitresses and framed on a big plate before it could even begin to get cold.

The prototype short order cook, Big John was in full control of the ship. The other girls scooped up dishes of piping hot food, plopped them four at a time on big round trays, and carried them off on their shoulders to the customers. The place was all action, noise, and laughs.

An older man struggled through the doors. He walked to a stool one empty spot down from Ed and climbed up on it. Once he got situated, he looked at Ed sheepishly, reached over and tapped his shoulder.

"Nice day out there, ain't it pal?" he said. "I reckon, huh, ain't it?" Then he looked down as if he didn't expect an answer.

"Sure is," Ed said. "Warm for a November afternoon. There won't be many more like this, buddy."

Surprised, the old man nodded and smiled. Daisy then spotted him from the other end.

"Hi yah, Hank – how you doin' kiddo?" she yelled down the counter.

His face lit up like a Christmas tree. "Now that I seen you, Daisy, fine!"

"Oh, you're too kind, honey," she laughed. "Be right with yah!"

Daisy dumped some dishes into a bin down below with clanks and rattles, scooped change into her apron pouch from the counter, and sauntered down to Hank with a sympathetic smile, hips swaying left and right.

"What's it gonna be today, honey?" she asked, leaning to the side and balancing herself on the point of her toe, pad on the counter and pencil poised.

"Lemmee see," Hank stammered, holding her wrist with a trembling right hand. "Don't tell nobody, Daisy, but I got my pension check today and I dodged my landlady. Cashed it myself. Usually she takes care of it and gives me an allowance, which is why I'm always tight on cash. But today's diff'rent! How's about a blue plate special and a root beer, beeyewteeful?"

"Whaddayah mean, allowance, Hank?" Daisy demanded. "You tell that landlady to give you enough money so you can come over here and have lunch every day. Least she can do for a nice old timer like you, Toots. And if she doesn't, you let me know. I'll go straight over to that boarding house down the street and the three of us will have a little talk. And I mean it!"

Hank's face lit up again. "Thanks, Daisy – I'll do that – I'll do that!" he said gratefully, even though he, Daisy, and everybody nearby knew he wouldn't. He just needed to hear it from somebody and to think it even for just a few seconds. Daisy gave him special attention because she knew it would help keep to keep him going. Hank was feeble and couldn't do a lot for himself any more. He was lucky to have his landlady controlling what little money he had and looking after him. Even he knew that deep down. But still, he needed just a little ray of hope every once in a while that things might one day be different. Daisy provided that sunlight gladly.

The food came and the group dug in. It was hot, tasty, and there was plenty of it. Even the beans were good. They conversed with Big John throughout the meal. He was a born talker, full of anecdotes and observations between juggling all of his orders. His friend Dave got right into it too. Like Big John, he could also gab up a storm. Slade, Jeff, Rails, and Ed all felt great just being in the place. It was a memorable start to going cross country.

Dave finished up and paid his bill. "Gotta hit the road, John," he said. "I have sales appointments this afternoon. We're swinging clubs on Friday at two, right?"

"I'll be there, DMD – I'll be there – at two sharp. Me, you, Pete and Tommy."

Ten minutes later, after more coffee and talk, the group was done and ready to go. They left a generous tip for Daisy and thanked her and Big John. Both made them promise they'd come back whenever they were in the area again. As they walked out the door, they heard once again from Daisy.

"So long, fellahs – thanks, and have a great day, boys!" They looked back and waved.

"Was she something or was she something?" Ed asked excitedly as they climbed into to the van.

"Pure America, man – Americana," Rails answered with a smile. "The hard working mom and pop of the greasy spoon diner in Any-Town, USA."

"Down home, no frills place," Slade added. "Honest work, getting it done, and people from all walks chowing down and taking a break from the grind."

"And that Daisy," Jeff remarked, "she was the total package. Had it all, man – like she was born to run a humming diner."

"Right," Ed agreed. "Just what I was thinking. I couldn't take my eyes off her and she could be my aunt or something. But not like that, you understand. It was just that the room lit up every time she walked by."

"It's called charisma, my boy," Slade said. "Charisma – either you have it or you don't – and she's got it in spades. Dig how she sacrifices a little femininity to do a tough job day in and day out. Rolls up her sleeves and earns an honest buck. That's character, guys – character. "

"And don't sell Big John short, Shotgun," Rails added. "That dude had a cool edge. Perpetual motion - and the man had star quality. He's the perfect foil for her. I'm glad we happened into that spot. Once we get rolling, I'm going to sketch the whole scene out in my notebook and I'll choose each word carefully for sure."

As they pulled out, he got right to it.

49.

They began to close in on New York City. The traffic thickened with rush hour fast approaching. From outside of Bridgeport, they got their first look at the immense skyline; skyscrapers, one next to the other stretching across the horizon. Only Rails had stayed in the city before, but still, he was as awed as the others in seeing it once again.

"Damn, look at that mass of construction," he marveled. "And every one of those buildings is heated, air conditioned, and has toilets that work on every floor. It never fails to amaze me just what mankind is capable of."

"You are so right, Steve," Jeff agreed. "Just awesome."

As they got on to the Henry Hudson Parkway, a female hitchhiker appeared ahead.

"She looks interesting, Shotgun," Rails said. "What say we give her a lift?"

"Why not?" Slade said. He pulled to the shoulder ahead of her. She was very thin, with bleach blond hair and dark roots. The woman wore kind of a built in frown and took her sweet time getting to the van.

"Going into Midtown," she said as she settled in back with Rails and Ed. She checked side to side and hesitated for a few moments. Then she looked straight ahead.

"Any of you guys want a date?" she asked softly. "Ten for a blow job and I can do it as we roll."

All was quiet for a couple of seconds as the group kind of froze. Then Slade spoke up.

"No thanks, Miss. We're just four small town boys – not looking for any action. But you mean Manhattan, right? We're going your way and we'll be glad to help you out."

"You serious or are you putting me on?" the girl asked.

"My friend speaks the truth," Rails said.

"Well that's a switch," she said sarcastically, crossing her legs which were like two sticks, "but I'm easy - we'll go with it."

About 30 seconds of silence passed. Then Rails spoke up. "So I take it that you're a lady of the evening?" he asked boldly. "Nothing personal, but I'm a writer – always looking for fresh material."

"A writer? Okay...then why not just call it what it is?" the girl answered, not the least bit insulted. "I'm a prostitute – a hooker – or if you want to go bottom line, a street whore."

The group took on a surprised hush. None of them had ever heard a woman speak so openly about selling her body for a living. But after a short pause, it was Ed's turn.

"Have you got a pimp?" he asked.

"I've had a few in my time," she answered somberly, "but I've been working solo the past year. It's better this way. You get a bad pimp and he'll kick your ass if he even gets the slightest drift that you might be holding a little money back. And most of them cheat the crap out of you and you can't say a fucken word. I got away from the last guy I was with and now I'm done with that scene forever."

"If you don't mind my asking, how did you get into the business?" Jeff said.

"Well now, how old do you think I am?" she asked.

"I don't know – 25, 26?"

"I just turned 21 last week," she said lighting up a cigarette, taking a drag, and blowing out the smoke from the side of her mouth. "See what the streets do to a girl? Well, guys, let's just say I was born into a bum deal. I was dealt a bad hand. I come from a town up near Albany. Don't even know who my father is and neither does my mother. She was a bar tender at a dive and slept around with customers for money on the side – got knocked up with me and had no idea whose baby I was. Maybe she didn't even want to know. Some faceless john – that's my father. It's a miracle that she saw things through and I'm even here."

"That's tough – that's really tough," Slade said, shaking his head.

"Oh, there's more," she continued. "When I was around 11, she hooked up with this piece of crap pervert who moved in with us. He was a good looking guy but a closet psycho. When he got horny and was tired of my mother, he'd come into my room and...you know what he'd make me do. Until one night when I was 15 and bigger. I kicked him in the balls as hard as I could and held a baseball bat over his head. Told him I'd find a way to kill him if he ever touched me again. It scared him and he left me alone after that. Soon as I turned 16, I quit school and ran away. Anything was better than that fucken arrangement.

"Man!" Ed sighed.

"I spent a year or so on the streets in Yonkers," the girl went on. "You don't know what that's like in the fucken winter, man. But I started turning tricks and I survived – I didn't know anything else. I finally ended up here in the city – best place for somebody like me. Once they know you, the cops look the other way. Some even become customers. There's plenty of action. I'd never tell you I'm happy – I don't even know what that is. But I got a decent place to live with a couple of other working girls. I have food on the table, and two friends I can trust. No pimp, no kids, and I'm not an addict. So many of the hookers have habits and are totally strung out and dependent. I'm proud that I'm not one of them. For what I do, I think I got my shit together pretty fucken good, guys."

Slade was particularly taken aback by her description. The others silently turned it over in their thoughts.

"What's...what is it like to go out on the streets every night?" Rails finally asked. "I mean – you must get hit on by some really scummy guys."

"Yeah, that's just something you learn to deal with – goes with the territory," the girl said, warming more to the conversation. "And because I've seen a lot, I can smell trouble in a couple of seconds. I bolt before anything goes down and if I can't, I always got my backup."

"What's that?" Ed asked.

She smiled, went to her pocket, and in a flash flipped out a switch blade.

"Nice shank," Jeff said.

"All I gotta do is show it and it stops them cold," she said. "They know I mean business. I've had to do it a few times but I've only cut one guy on the arm. You should have seen him run. I'd never be without it. The only thing better is the great equalizer – the one-eyed widow maker. I'd love to get my hands on a snub nose 38. Easy to hide and will stop any dirt bag cold."

"Serious heat," Ed agreed.

"What about the future?" Slade asked. "Do you think about it at all? Like maybe someday leaving the streets behind?"

"Future?" the girl laughed sarcastically. "What's that? No - not much. Sometimes I see stray cats hanging in the alleys and I think I'm just like them. You know - living day to day, scraping and surviving. But I'm not depressed or suicidal or anything. With all that's gone down with me, I still like being alive. I do want to live."

Slade looked back at her and then to the road. There was hurt in his eyes. He heard her say "I do want to live" over and over again in his mind and it affected him. The girl had touched something deep within.

"What's your name?" he asked.

"I go by Sunshine on the streets, but my real name is Nora."

"Nora - that's a pretty name. And you're a nice person," Slade said softly glancing back at her. "It doesn't matter what you do to make a buck, Nora. Just don't ever give up on striving for something better. You have guts and it took plenty for you to tell us your story. No matter what you face, you can handle it. Never give up."

Nora leaned back in her seat and looked out the window. She was moved and a tear or two trickled down her cheek. Rails looked over at her and for a few seconds, she was the pretty young woman she should have been.

"Thanks," she finally said, the edge gone from her voice. "You guys have been really nice, I have to say. I knew you were good people soon as I got in the van. I'll remember what you just said, driver."

"The name's Slade, Nora."

"Okay, Slade."

"And we'll remember you too," Rails smiled reaching over and gently clasping her wrist. For the first and only time, Nora smiled.

271

50.

It was getting later in the afternoon as they moved into Manhattan. Nora got off at 23rd street and faded off into the distance as the three watched from the van.

"We went from a Daisy to a Sunshine – check that – to a Sundown in the matter of maybe an hour," Rails said. "Like the north and south poles."

"And we'll probably never see either one of them again," Jeff said. "That always gets me. You cross paths with somebody, talk for a little bit, maybe about personal stuff like we did with Nora. Then you never see them again."

Slade paused and thought about it. "And why do you think she shared her background with us like that so matter-of-factly?" he asked.

"I think I know," Jeff answered quickly. "Maybe...just because she knew she'd never see us again, she laid it all on the table – held nothing back. I'll bet it helped her to get it out."

"Right. She unloaded and I saw her cry just a bit," Rails cut in. "What you said got to her, Shotgun. Who knows? It could be a turning point for Nora. Sure as hell, she's going to remember it."

"I couldn't say it any better," Slade agreed. "You guys put it just the way I was thinking of it."

"I learn something new every day with this group," Ed added shaking his head with wonder.

Driving slowly along 23rd street, they watched the herds of people fast-stepping up and down the sidewalks, eyes locked forward as if they all were wearing blinders. Everybody seemed intent on getting someplace else and all were in a hurry. Professionals, blue collar types, hot babes in mini-skirts, young studs, tall people, short people, fat people, skinny people, sad faced dogs, feral cats, opportunistic rats; everybody and everything locked solely into what they were about and where they were headed. What the next thing was. Nothing else mattered.

And here and there were psychos, winos, and just plain bums lying right on the walks, just like Creecher said they would be. Nobody paid much attention to them, if any. Pedestrians absently veered to the sides of the homeless; one or two even stepped right over them. For all they cared, the bums could be dead and cold.

Looking to the left side of the street, Jeff's eyes focused on one of the street urchins standing against a building. He was a tall middle-aged man and there was something vaguely familiar about him. Jeff felt a twinge go through his body.

"Hey – that guy over there by the pole...he looks kind of like my fah...nah – couldn't be – could never be!"

"Couldn't be what?" Ed asked.

"Nothing, Ed," Jeff said looking away. "Just forget it."

"Check that out," Rails said pointing to the other side. "A dude and a chick in clown suits on roller skates and nobody even looks twice. Anything goes in NYC."

"They all have some kind of angle." Slade said. "They'll do whatever it takes to get noticed. But they're just people in the end trying to get over to the other side".

"Yeah," Rails agreed. "Whatever faraway place that might be."

Further into town, they got into a district of porno theaters and peep show sex stores. As they sat in a traffic jam, they noticed a disturbance up a side alley. A prostitute in a low brimmed fedora was rammed up against a building by a heavily tattooed man. He had her by the collar and his knee was between her legs. It looked like he was threatening her as if maybe she owed him something. The woman was silent and strangely calm. People walked by. Some looked curiously at them but not for long. No one stopped. Nobody thought to intervene. It was nothing they hadn't seen before.

273

"Man!" Ed exclaimed. "That guy might hurt that broad and nobody does anything. Think we ought to pull over and get him off of her?"

"Better that we don't, Ed," Slade said, looking ahead again as the jam began to clear. "This isn't that small New England mill town we came from. See, we're in Rome and you do as the Romans do when you don't know the ropes. If we go over and hassle that punk, who is probably a pimp, it's OUR throats might get slit. And for sure he's got iron inside that vest. One of us could easily get wacked just trying to do the right thing. It's sad, but this the big time, you know? We've got to watch our rear ends first. Leave that kind of stuff to the police."

"Plus I'll guarantee you she's a pro just like Miss Sunshine was," Rails added. "Don't worry about her, Ed. She's street wise and she'll handle the situation just like Nora probably would. Just look at how cool she is about the whole thing?"

"Yeah...you guys are probably right, but that still doesn't make it right," Ed said forlornly. "But I agree - we stay put and move on."

"Unfortunately, that's the score." Jeff said. "We live and learn."

The jam lifted and they put some distance between them and that scene. For a while, they drove around the blocks and made a few inquiries on places to stay, double parking with one guy running in and out. Finally, they settled on an upscale Hilton Inn just for the night. Rails convinced the others that they deserved at least one night of luxury. They'd start fresh in the morning to look for cheaper digs. The plan was to hang out in New York City for the next few days and soak up the scene.

They parked the van in an underground garage. On the way up the staircase, Slade tripped and fell, banging his knee hard on the sharp edge of one of the cement steps.

"You okay, Shotgun?" Rails asked.

"Damn," he said as he got up and rubbed it. "That hurt like hell and I'm gonna have a nice bruise. But we'll hold off on the lawsuit for now."

Slade was limping as they checked in at the desk. For forty dollars for the night, they got a top floor suite with twin beds. It was a big room and the hotel would provide a couple of cots within an hour or two. The clerk gave them the key and said they'd have use of the weight room, whirlpool bath, sauna, and a heated indoor pool on the top of the building.

Their room was large and modern. It was much classier than any of the four were accustomed to. At the far end were glass doors and a deck looking out over the city. Ed walked into the bathroom and noticed something on the toilet.

"Check this out, Jeff," he said. "Must be a brand new unit – the seat still has the wrapping on it."

Jeff looked in and then laughed. "Did you grow up on a farm in Cow Hampshire or something, Ed? I mean I never stayed in a swanky place like this either but at least I know a sanitary wrapping when I see one. They scrub the commodes and put one of those down every time somebody checks out, dude."

"Oh, is that right?" Ed laughed. "Well, now that I know that, I guess I'm just that much more...what's the word, Rails...so – FIS – tic – ay - ted?"

"I think that's the perfect word, Edward."

"Let's set that jive aside," Slade said. "I'm tired from all the driving and my knee is aching. I'm going to lie down awhile and maybe take a nap. You guys do what you want to. We can go out and get something to eat later.

"Okay, Cap'n," Jeff said. "I'd like to go over and have the pool experience. After all, we're shelling out ten bucks a piece. We might as well get our money's worth. Anybody else up for it?"

Rails gave a thumbs up and Ed said to count him in. Since he'd planned for the group to stay occasionally in hotels along the way and to spend some time in Florida, Slade suggested beforehand that everybody go out and buy a pair of trunks. They did and now they would come in handy. Cut-off shorts wouldn't fly at this place. They changed and headed to the pool area.

Up a set of stairs and through French doors, Jeff, Rails and Ed walked on to a spacious patio with a stone waterfall in the middle. It was encircled by canals of running water. Tropical fish swam around darting in all directions. Further down was the full sized pool. The entire area was enclosed by a big dome of tinted glass.

275

"How about this place?" Rails said as they approached the pool side. "A little more dough gets you some luxury, doesn't it? Think the poor mill rats back in Stillborn will ever get to see something like this?"

"No with a capital N," Ed sighed. "They're still wasting away as we speak."

On the patio were glass tables set up with wicker chairs. Several couples sat around, sipping mixed drinks and talking quietly. A striking woman with jet black hair was at a table by herself with a cocktail, reading a magazine. She looked like a movie star, dressed in a leopard mini-dress with stilettos, and sitting in a provocative pose.

The woman was stunning and Jeff looked a little too long at her. She glanced up and their eyes fused for a couple of seconds. Jeff felt jolt and was almost unable to look away. The woman then took a sip of her drink and fixed her gaze back on her magazine.

"Wow, that was weird," he whispered to Ed and Rails as they stopped at some chairs.

"What happened?"

"That hot babe over there – she caught me looking at her and zinged me. Know what I mean?"

"Yeah – that happens to me sometimes," Ed said. "Christ, Jeff – she's so hot, she must get a hundred stares a day. Man, she IS sexy."

"No – this was different – almost like what you feel when a black cat flashes you. I got a searing vibe, man...almost like she's a harbinger of some bad thing to come."

"Really?" Rails said. "That's strange. Hope you're wrong but we'll have to keep an eye open for it. I don't take stuff like that lightly."

"Well, I seriously felt it," Jeff repeated, a little shaken.

"By the way," Ed said, "not to change the subject, but do you guys get the feeling that we don't exactly fit in here?"

"You're absolutely right – we don't," Rails said. "But we are what we are. Screw it – we can hide in the pool."

And that they did. The water was warm and soothing. It felt great after a long day on the road. For the next hour, they were in and out of the pool and the whirlpool next to it.

Back in the room, Slade slept unevenly. He tossed and turned with pain up and down his leg and into his side. In a flash, he woke up, or at least he thought he did, feeling woozy and needing fresh air. His knee throbbing, he felt down and it was swelled up like a balloon.

Slade carefully got out of bed. He limped through the glass doors and out on to the deck. The sun was setting over the skyscrapers and it sat between two billowy clouds. Slade leaned on the railing and his eyes fixed on that frame for a few seconds. He breathed in deeply with long exhales. Gradually his head cleared.

Slade looked north up the street at all the blocks of spectacular buildings and opulence. Then he looked south down the crossing avenue, and not too far in the distance, he could see slums and trash. "Opposite ends of the spectrum, yet so close to each other," Slade thought to himself. Daisy from the diner popped into his head with all her energy and positivity. Conversely, he thought of Nora the prostitute with all her baggage and troubles. Then his eyes shot back to the sun between the clouds, which were now positioned as if they were lovingly embracing the bright mass afire in the sky.

Suddenly, Slade felt the pain leave his leg and his body lightened. He felt a warm with a glow. His head now crystal clear, a notion slowly came to him. "The center, the center – the beautiful pure center," he whispered to himself.

There it was. He said it over and over again and then began to expand on the thought. "Capitalism, socialism, communism, all the isms – even the counter culture," he reflected looking above to the red sky. "Titles, concepts? Just words. The center rises above all that stuff. The center! Nobody's ever completely right or completely wrong. No zealot ever really knows for sure one way or the other. No black – no white...it IS all gray like old Beans said. The cherry in the middle of a chocolate candy...the pure center! That's the ticket. Seek it. Strike that balance. Look to the center no matter whether you're way up or way down. That's it! It's as simple as the old saying, 'The TRUTH lies somewhere in the middle.'"

Tom Slade basked in this feeling of enlightenment and bliss. He experienced an inner peace so gratifying that he now felt weightless, as if he floated back to the bed. He lay on his back and slowly closed his eyes. Gradually, he fell into a deep sleep, deeper than he'd ever slept in his life. In a dream like none other he ever had, in vivid technicolor, he was in motion moving through fields of spectacular enormous flowers, all drooping toward him as if they were smiling and full of love.

"Come to me – come to me." He couldn't be sure from where, but he heard those words spoken softly; from the flowers or maybe from somewhere beyond them. Then, in the far distance, a brilliant golden light appeared, and it rained diamonds all around it, as it drew closer...closer...closer.

51.

Jeff, Ed, and Rails had been gone over an hour. They returned to the room invigorated after their time in the pool.

"Look at Shotgun," Rails said quietly. "Out like a light on his back and so peaceful. He looks like a young stiff."

"He's in dream land all right" Jeff whispered. "Let's keep it down and let him rest a while longer. He drove the whole way here and banged up that knee on top of it."

"Right," Ed agreed. "How 'bout we rest up a little while too. Then we can wake him up and go out and get some chow."

"You got it," Rails said.

The cots hadn't been delivered yet but the room had a couple of big easy chairs. They changed clothes and then flipped a coin for the other bed. Jeff won and he laid down adjacent to Slade. The other two collapsed on the chairs. They crashed for the next hour-plus. Then, they all roused at about the same time, except for Slade. Rails looked over at him.

"That's strange," he said. "Shotgun hasn't moved since we got back. Wake him up, Jeff."

Jeff stepped over and nudged Slade's shoulder once, then again harder. "Shotgun, wake up," he said. Nothing. Jeff didn't like how Slade's body flopped back. A bolt of adrenaline seized him and he became alarmed.

"Steve – come over here – I think something's wrong with him," he said, his voice fluttering slightly. "Ed - you too – c'mon over here."

They bolted to the bed and the three of them surrounded Slade.

"Shotgun, Shotgun, wake up," Rails said quietly, trying to be calm, leaning over and shaking both Slade's shoulders. He shook them harder and then also became alarmed. Rails put his ear to Slade's chest and could hear no heartbeat. He looked at Jeff and Ed with a fear in his eyes that neither had ever seen in him.

"Check his pulse! Check his pulse!" Ed said excitedly.

Jeff fumbled around with Slade's wrist, waited, and then looked at them in desperation. "Nothing! Nothing! He's flat lined. God no! He can't be dead...he can't be dead!"

"Not if we can help it!" Rails said, his voice soaring. "Get on the phone and call an ambulance. I'm gonna try to revive him!"

Rails got on the bed and began feverishly performing CPR. Jeff tripped over the coffee table and dropped the phone once, his hands shaking, but he quickly got through to the police and the ambulance was on the way. Ed stood by the side dumbfounded for a few moments, and then tried to help where he could.

The next few minutes were pure hell as the three of them tried to revive Slade but could get nothing out him. Finally, the EMT's hustled into the room and took over. They worked on him for a bit. Then Slade was quickly secured on a stretcher. In what seemed like a blur, Jeff, Rails, and Ed were in the van following the ambulance to the hospital.

For a while, they were in a state of shock and there was a long silence. Then Jeff willed up the strength to say something.

"I don't believe this – this can't be happening," he murmured softly at the wheel, trying not to lose the ambulance. "My friggin head is about to explode."

"We've got to steady ourselves, man," Rails said having regained some control. "We have to be ready for the worst. We all know what the truth is likely to be. He was dead when we came back in that room from the pool and it was at least another hour later before we tried to rouse him. That's right. I said it. It had to be said. He's probably gone to us. Better that we face it now."

"Let's just hope for a damn miracle," Ed said forlornly.

"I can't even talk about it – I don't want to think about it," Jeff said, his voice cracking.

All was quiet the rest of the way. At the hospital, they sat in the waiting room for what seemed like forever but wasn't actually very long. Then, a couple of doctors came through the doors and sat down with them. By the looks on their faces, it was clear what the news would be.

"We're very sorry," one of them said. "Your friend didn't make it. We did everything we could to get him back but it was far too late. He was technically dead on arrival."

Rails put his hands to the sides of his head and looked down. Jeff and Ed both closed their eyes. None of the three could say anything even though they'd all suspected the same thing. Had they been standing, all would probably have dropped to the floor. Hearing the unthinkable rendered them numb. They just sat there, jaws hanging, looking off into space.

"Wha'...what caused it?" Rails finally managed to ask. "The guy was a top athlete and in great shape. What the hell happened?"

"A blood clot from his leg went straight to his heart and caused a massive blockage," the doctor closest to them said. "We noticed a deep bruise on his knee. Did he have a fall recently?"

"He did – he did," Jeff said coming out of his trance. "A few hours ago. He fell on some stairs and banged up his knee."

"And did he have any history of circulatory problems?" the other doctor asked.

"Not that I can think of," Jeff said. "But I do remember him mentioning about his legs tightening up and falling asleep sometimes. Wait a minute – phlebitis – he told me he flunked the army physical because they detected phlebitis. But he always blew it off and said they were wrong."

"Think that's what did it, Doc?" Ed asked.

"Most likely," the other doctor agreed. "He may have been having an episode of thrombophlebitis before the accident but didn't say anything about it. If so, the fall was tragically unlucky. It was most surely the catalyst for the clot. The only good news is that Mr. Slade probably didn't suffer. A death like his happens very quickly."

Jeff looked at the doctors and then to Rails and Ed. He took a deep breath and tried to stay composed. "Here today, gone tomorrow," he said in a whisper, bowing his head with his hand over his eyes. "He wasn't just another guy – he was everything to us. Myself – I don't know how I'm going to make it now – I just don't know how."

Rails put his hand on Jeff's shoulder from one side and Ed did the same from the other. "We'll see it through, man," he said somberly. "Together we'll see it through just like Shotgun always told us."

"Steve's right, Jeff," Ed added. "I know how close the two of you were. But we'll figure out a way to handle this...somehow."

All Jeff could do was look side to side at them. Then he explained to the doctors what he knew of Slade's family, which wasn't much. The doctors said that they had his wallet from the EMT's. In it were the contacts to make if anything happened to him. They assured them they would phone the family in Pennsylvania, explain the situation, and then turn the wallet back over to them. The family could then make arrangements for transport of the body. Before they left the hospital, Jeff, Rails and Ed got the wallet and thanked the doctors for all they did.

The drive back to the hotel was a nightmare. All Jeff could say was that he was glad they didn't have to tell the family, considering none of them had ever even met them. They all were so knocked out that they agreed to let it all settle in and talk about things later when they were ready. It was just too much, too soon. Nobody wanted to think about...what now? No one wanted to jump to any conclusions. The task at hand was just to try to accept what happened and to get their heads on straight again. They'd get a night's sleep and talk in the morning.

Back at the room, they straightened up Slade's belongings. For a while, they did go back over what happened just a little. It was impossible not to. But for the most part, they stuck to the plan. They needed quiet, just peace and quiet.

With the television on softly in the background, Rails took the bed opposite Slade's. Although he won the coin toss earlier, Jeff wasn't going near either bed. Nobody was going to take the death bed. The cots had come while they were away at the hospital and Ed chose one. But Jeff didn't take his. Instead, he grabbed a blanket, walked to the far corner of the room, and sat down on the floor. Rails and Ed watched him but neither said anything. They understood.

Jeff curled himself into a ball, covered up, and put his head in his hands. It was something he used to do as a teenager after his father deserted him, when he was by himself after he'd been moved to a new foster home and he was afraid. This was the first time he'd ever done it since he was on his own. He was afraid now. As frightened as he'd ever been in his life.

 They finally got some sleep and got up late the next morning. And although all slept in fits and woke up several times during the night, the rest did them good. At some point, Jeff got off the floor and went to his cot. Now his head had cleared a little. He was ready to talk.

"God help me," he said to Rails and Ed as he pulled on his shirt. "I know how bad you guys feel, but for almost a year, I practically lived with the guy – saw him every day. I knew him as well as I've ever known anybody. First my mother, then my father, now this – the closest friend I ever had. God help me."

Rails and Ed held back from saying anything for a few moments. Jeff's words, so sad and mournfully sincere, just stopped them cold. He was right. He was a lot closer to Slade than they were, especially with no parents to lean on. Both of them fought back tears.

"I hear you, man, I hear you," Rails finally said, his voice bouncing up and down. "But life is a crap shoot, you know? We're all young and maybe we think we're indestructible but something like this brings it all home. Nobody knows what's going to happen – nobody knows."

"He was...he was the best of us," Ed said sadly. Jeff and Rails nodded.

"Well…we have to be strong and be able to handle the next few days without freaking out," Rails said more steadily. "One thing at a time."

"I'm still kind of in shock," Jeff said. "I can't think straight – I don't know where the hell I'm at. What do you figure we have to do?"

"First things first," Rails said after a pause. "Let's not even talk about the future until we get Shotgun's wake and funeral behind us. By now, his mom and dad know the story. We have to call that number the doctors gave us – his folks – and get the information we need. Slade was from somewhere around Philly, right?"

"A town called Drexel Hill," Jeff said, "maybe ten miles outside of Philadelphia."

"Okay…then we have to get moving out there and find a place to stay the next couple of days," Ed said. "Shotgun's body is probably on its way as we speak."

"That's an image that stops me cold. But you're right, Ed," Rails agreed. "We'll get settled and then one by one, we'll do all the things that we have to do. Like I said before, one step at a time. If we get too far ahead of ourselves, this whole thing will swallow us up and we'll be toast."

"I know, I know," Jeff lamented. "I should be the one. I'll make that phone call."

They checked out of the hotel and hit the road to Philly. On the way, they stopped at a service station. Jeff went in and got a roll of quarters. Then he made the call from the booth outside. He struggled to explain who he was to Slade's mother, but she was surprisingly calm and helpful. She knew all about him, and Rails and Ed too. She explained that Slade called the family regularly and kept them up to date on his travels and friends. His mom even suggested an inn not far from the funeral home where they could get lodging. Several times Jeff told her how sorry the group was and each time, she thanked him graciously. He was greatly relieved when he got back into the van.

"It went okay, I take it?" Rails said at the wheel as they resumed the trip.

"As good as it could have," Jeff said with big exhale. "I spoke to his mother. I didn't get any inkling that she held anything against us at all. She sounded really nice and I got all the info. She even directed us to some digs."

"Groovy, man – that's a relief," Ed said. "First break we've gotten since this all came crashing down on us."

"It'll all shake out okay," Rails said bringing the van up to 65. "We'll get through this and the sun will shine again."

It was a solemn ride the rest of the way to Drexel Hill with the enormous void of the empty fourth seat staring them in the face. But it had only been a day and they weren't even close to processing the situation yet. It would take a lot of time before they would be.

In Drexel Hill, they got a room at the Post Road Inn, the place Slade's mom had suggested. The next couple of days were like a dream; like they were happening but somehow they really weren't. It was as if all would eventually be erased, Slade would be back, and things would again be like they used to be. They all felt this and Jeff even mentioned it once. Rails sighed and nodded as Ed also did. Then Rails raised a finger and said, "Classic coping mechanism – it's got to be...in that all of us are thinking the same thing."

Slade's wake was a big production. The expansive parlor at the funeral home was loaded with flowers, including the beautiful spray his three friends had ordered for him. For four hours, the line never stopped and the room percolated with talk, laughter, sorrow and tears. There was a big board of pictures of Slade growing up, many with his sports teams showing him in action. There were also shots of Night Hawk performing at different venues, Slade on guitar in his sideman role.

Slade's parents stood by the coffin, his dad tall and square jawed and his mom slender with an air of elegance about her. Next to them were his sister Jodie, an attractive young woman of 25 with a strikingly similar face to her younger brother's. Her solemn husband stood closely by her. Down the line were his grandparents and other relatives. Jeff remembered Slade talking about Pop and all his sayings. He knew immediately which one he was.

And finally, lying in state before them all, was the body of their friend and companion Thomas "Shotgun" Slade. A picture of him in life smiling and sitting with his guitar sat atop his black coffin. He was as handsome a young deceased man as there ever was, with an ethereal expression on his face.

Jeff, Rails, and Ed took it all in transfixed. They were stunned by their first look at Slade in a casket. Ed, standing in front of Jeff in line, was particularly shaken. Jeff noticed and patted his hand on his shoulder. Ed turned back to him with a deep look of sorrow.

"That's not Shotgun, Ed," he whispered. "Just his empty shell like you find on the beach. He's moved on from there. Just think of it like that if you can." Ed nodded somberly.

One by one, they knelt before Slade and prayed for his soul. Then they paid their respects to the family. Jeff was so full of grief that he could hardly speak. He barely managed to get out "I'm sorry" to each member he consoled. And although Jeff, Rails, and Ed knew no one in the room, they stayed until almost all of the mourners had left. They didn't discuss it beforehand, but each felt they had to talk to the family as a group. There was no way they could leave without doing that.

The end of the waking period neared as most of the mourners cleared out. Slade's mother, father and sister were sitting near the casket as some people they were chatting with said their good byes. As soon as they walked away, Jeff, Rails and Ed looked at each other and nodded. They then approached the family.

Jeff took a deep breath and then another one. "Can we sit and talk with you a minute?" he asked.

"Of course, Jeff," Slade's mother said.

They sat down and looked at each other again. Jeff sensed he should be the first one to speak. He paused a few seconds to collect his thoughts, willing himself to stay calm and get it all out right.

"Well first of all, Steve, Ed, and I want to thank you for recommending the inn," he began. "They've taken good care of us over there."

"We know the owners," Slade's father said. "We called them and told them to expect you. They're very nice people."

"They sure are," Ed agreed.

"Umm…I just need to talk about Slade – I mean Tom - and a little about how much he meant to us," Jeff continued. "Early last March, I came down to Stiller in Massachusetts from up north in New Hampshire. I was alone and I didn't know a soul. I was nervous and I'll admit that I was lonesome too. I happened to luck out and got a room right next to Tom's at the YMCA. I think he knew right from the get go that I needed some help and he was there for me from the first night I met him. I've never had a friend like him in my whole life. I had some of the best times of my life when I was with Shotgun.

"I think he kind of mentored me too without ever saying it or telling me what to do. Tom was always positive and he had such an easy way about him – and he led more by example than anything. I have to say, being around him every day – he was so full of hope and excited about life. And he set a good…framework I guess, of how to act in the right way. It was contagious and it changed me - almost immediately. I went from this…negative untrusting guy to somebody who came to like himself, have some confidence, and the will to take a risk. Tom was behind all of that – believe me. I hope I'm not rambling on – I just need to get this stuff out because I feel it so…strongly about it."

Jeff paused and choked up just a little. He fumbled a handkerchief out of his jacket, coughed, and dried his eyes. Slade's parents and his sister were clearly moved. Jodie reached out and put her hand on Jeff's shoulder.

"Thanks so much for sharing that," she said, as her husband sat down next to her.

"And one other thing," Jeff added. "Tom told us he was locked in on to applying to Berklee College of Music up in Boston after we got done with our trip – to become a professional musician. Believe me, he had what it takes and then some. He'd have gotten in easily."

Rails and Ed nodded in agreement. Slade's parents looked at each other and smiled.

"Ed and I also worked with Tom," Rails added. "We didn't see him as much as Jeff did but we still were around him a lot. He had the exact same effect on us. Tom had it all – smart, good looking, great athlete, funny - all that good stuff that draws people to you. He could play the hell out of the guitar. And Shotgun could tell a story better than anyone I've ever known. He had a way of really putting his heart into everything he did."

"Everything," Ed agreed.

"A while back," Jeff remarked, "Shotgun told me the story of the weekend he spent on Hermit Island in Maine when he was 17. It was the perfect example of what Steve just said. The descriptive way he related it – with dialogue and everything...I was floored. It was like I was there with him the whole way."

"Yes, he was the best at that," Rails continued, "But you know...he never bragged about anything or flaunted his talents. Tom had a kind heart and was more apt to want to help others than to think about his own thing. He got Jeff and me started on guitar and gave us an hour lesson every Saturday. We wanted to pay him but he would never hear of it. Tom told us just to practice each day and get better. That was all the payment he needed. Not many people are like that. He was a quality person all the way. And the main thing was, like Jeff said, he had this hugest regard, respect and fascination for life itself. It definitely rubbed off on all of us. I just wish it hadn't been cut short."

"A class act who never talked bad about anybody," Ed said leaning forward. "I can't remember him saying one negative thing – not one. You know I'm just a small town kid. I'm not much of a talker and I have a lot to learn in life. I'll be first to admit that. But I do know a good person when I see one and Slade was that. Like with Jeff...and I'm sure with Steve too, he gave me hope to look ahead to something better. I was blown away that Shotgun thought enough of me to include me on the cross country trip. It was like a booster shot to my confidence. I'd have followed him to the moon."

Slade's family were thoroughly impressed and grateful to hear all of those sentiments. For a few moments, they all just sat back and thought. His dad shook his head in wonder. His mom and Jodie wiped tears from their eyes.

"That was wonderful, boys," Slade's mother finally said with the deepest sincerity. "We all loved Tom so much. It's very comforting to hear how he influenced his friends in such a good way in his travels. I know he wanted to do that."

"He did, Mrs. Slade," Rails said, his voice cracking. "He most certainly did. And there's something else I've thought about a lot since we lost him. Let me see if I can say it right. I'm only 23 years old and hopefully I have a lot of life ahead of me. I...we got to be friends with a guy who had that special gift we've been talking about. Some refer to that thing as 'it'. He had 'it'. Most people are never that lucky in life – to be around somebody like that, I mean. But the three of us were, and I know we were hugely affected by it. Permanently. Tom's sense of wonder, his inspiration, and most importantly, his spirit will be with us as long as we live. And the three of us will always be connected through it."

Jeff and Ed nodded emphatically.

"Beautifully said," Slade's father responded. "And that goes for everything else you guys just shared with us. I don't know what else to say other than that Tommy sure knew how to pick his friends. Hearing all your sentiments, straight from the heart comforts us all greatly. Thank you, thank you! It means more than you could ever know."

Slade's mother, overcome with emotion, nodded as her husband reached over and held her.

"Thanks so much, guys," Jodie added, tears streaming down her face and her husband's arm around her shoulder. "My dad's right - what great friends my brother had!"

Everybody got up, shook hands and exchanged hugs. Rails made arrangements with Slade's father to return Slade's belongings before the funeral the next morning. He, Jeff, and Ed had gotten their chance to pay their respects in the personal way they wanted to. And because they felt so strongly, nobody stumbled. It was something that was very important to each one of them. It needed to be done and it had gone well. They walked out of the funeral parlor with just a slightly lighter step.

52.

The next morning they got ready to witness Shotgun's final stand. Jeff was last to get a shower. As he stood under the spray of hot water, he thought

288

of Slade's smile the first night he walked into his room and of all the good times they shared together. Suddenly the enormity of the loss shook him to his soul. He began to make mournful wails that he'd never heard himself do before; sounds that he had no idea that he was even capable of. They were quiet and with the noise of the shower, the others couldn't hear him.

The wails were the rueful song reserved from deep within the soul for only the most intense sadness and loss. They were so plaintive and true that their sounds fascinated Jeff as he listened to himself make them. They were highly personal utterances, and nature's way of helping him to cope. Somehow he knew that. After he got out of the shower, dressed, and joined the others, he didn't mention a word to them.

The funeral took place on a crisp November day with a few scattered clouds. Ed joked that Slade had probably ordered it that way. The church was filled with family, relatives and friends. It had a large section of glass built into the ceiling; an atrium to let the light shine in. The setting was so beautiful that it dulled the sad aspect of the situation and led more to a feeling of celebration of Tom Slade's life.

His uncle Bill, who coached him in basketball, gave a beautiful eulogy. Then his grandfather Pop, who he loved and often quoted, spoke briefly and straight from the heart. Jodie gave the final words about her brother with such intensity and feeling that there wasn't a dry eye in the church.

"Let's not remember Tommy for the way he left us far too early," she ended with, "but for the wonderful way in which he lived."

Near the end of the service, the choir performed a soaring hymn. During the middle part, they sang "Alleluia" in threes as the Reverend spoke in between:

"Alleluia...Alleluia...Alleluia"

"Blessed are they who Thou hast chosen and taken unto Thyself O Lord..."

"Alleluia...Alleluia...Alleluia

"Their memory is from generation to generation..."

"Alleluia...Alleluia...Alleluia..."

"Their souls will dwell amid good things..."

"Alleluia...Alleluia...Alleluia..."

During the time all of that took place, the clouds had given the sun the stage and it shone directly through the ceiling glass, warming the church and giving it an aura. It was a powerful moment for Slade's three friends, sitting together and consumed by the present as if time had stopped. All felt the presence of something huge, all powerful, and eternally loving and good. Right then, right there.

At the cemetery, a throng of over a hundred mourners surrounded the grave site. After the Reverend concluded his closing prayers and remarks, one by one, each person placed the single rose they had been given atop the casket. Jeff, Rails, and Ed waited until everyone had finished before they approached. Their roses were the last three laid down before the casket was lowered into the ground.

They attended a dinner given by Slade's family following the burial at a local restaurant. Rather than a somber affair, it was very upbeat with wonderful stories from the past and plenty of laughter. The three sat at a table with a group of Slade's former high school sports teammates. Leon Choate, the MVP of their state championship team was there all the way from Cleveland.

They heard many tales of Slade's basketball and baseball accomplishments that he had never talked about. In addition, three former members of Night Hawk told them about some of the great gigs they did with Slade, and what a dynamite rock guitarist he was. The dinner was the best way to relieve some of the sorrow and begin to move on, with the memory of good times taking the forefront.

On the way back to the inn, they stopped at a restaurant for coffee. Now had come the time to talk and all three of them knew it. They sat in a booth, sipped coffee furtively, and looked at each other. Surprisingly, Ed was the one to start it off.

"Well, what do we do now?" he asked placing his cup down. "We lost our point man – the guy with all the ideas and the master plan. It's like our main sail got ripped to shreds. Where do we go from here?"

There was about twenty seconds of silence. Ed looked out the window. Jeff glanced to the ceiling and closed his eyes. Rails just stared straight ahead expressionless. Then he reached into his pocket. He pulled out several pages of notes, unfolded them, and placed them on the table.
290

"I found these last night as I was getting the last of Shotgun's stuff together for his family." he said. "I held off showing them to you guys until now. Have a look."

Jeff took the papers and skimmed over them as Ed leaned in. "Man!" he exclaimed. "He detailed out the whole thing from Stiller to San Francisco – where to stop – what to do – everything."

"That dude was so organized," Ed said. "Soup to nuts, he covered it all. He left the blueprint for us!"

"He sure did," Jeff said excitedly. Then he looked up and put his hand down on the table with conviction.

"You know, guys," he began firmly, "a year ago, this thing would have shattered me to pieces and I'd have been a wreck. I probably would have dropped out, gone off on my own and sulked somewhere for a long time. But not now. Shotgun injected me with a ton of adrenaline...and curiosity too. I've just got to know what's over that next hill, get what I mean? What's out there in the great beyond like Slade was always after. We HAVE to go on and do this thing just like he envisioned it. We're three losers if we don't!"

"I'm with you, – I'm there - all the way!" Ed exclaimed.

Rails leaned back and smiled broadly. "I couldn't have put it better, Jeff," he beamed. "Then it's settled. I agree with you guys a hundred and ten percent. And I'm really glad to hear you sum it up it like you did. We'll follow his plan and Shotgun's vibe will be right there with us every step of the way, just like it is right now. Oh, it's here all right! And like I said to his folks, his passing creates a bond between us that will never be broken. Just as Slade told us before we left, whatever we have to face, we'll face it together."

Elbows went down on the table and three right hands clasped tightly. It was cast in iron.

"As the great Sal Paradise professed in 'On the Road'," Rails concluded, "there's nowhere to go...but everywhere!'"

"Right on!" Jeff and Ed said at the same time.

They rode back to the inn and checked out. It was about three in the afternoon when the group got their gear together and once again, were

291

on the move. The gloom had lifted some and all eyes were pointed forward. Ed took his turn at the wheel, Rails next to him, and Jeff in back.

"Before we leave this all behind, there's one more thing I think we need to do," Jeff said.

"What's that?" Ed asked.

"Stop back to the grave once more now that everybody's gone. There's something I want to do."

"I remember how to get there," Rails said. "I'll direct you, Ed. We'll probably never be out this way again, you know? Good idea, Jeff."

In fifteen minutes they were back at the cemetery. They parked the van and made the slow walk to the spot. There was no stone yet, but the hole was filled in and all of the flowers were in a pile on top. The three looked at each other but said nothing. Then, they knelt, put their heads down, and prayed; as sincerely as they'd ever prayed. There was no crying but all three wiped away silent tears when they were done.

Then Jeff stood up, scanned the flowers, and found the ribbon with OUR CLOSE FRIEND written on it that they had included with the spray they bought for Slade. He carefully removed it and placed it aside. From his jacket, he pulled out a pouch and filled it with dirt from the grave, He then tied the pouch securely with the ribbon. The three of them stepped back and contemplated the scene.

"I had to have something to take with me from here to remember Shotgun by," Jeff said somberly.

"Amen, my friend," Ed said, tapping the small of his back. "Amen."

"You know, guys," Rails added, "this is the time when you know they're really gone to you forever. When you go to the grave after all the stories and tributes are over and you see all those flowers left behind. I'm glad you thought for us to stop by, Jeff. It was the right thing to do."

"Sad as it is, I feel better," Jeff said. "It's time to move on, guys. Like the old saying, 'there, but for the grace of God, go us'."

"But for the grace of God," Ed repeated. Rails nodded looking skyward.

Before they got into the van, all three turned and looked back at the grave. "Be good, Shotgun," Jeff said softly. "It's just a shame you can't be with us."

They pulled out of the cemetery and headed south, putting all that had happened over the past few days in the rear view mirror.

"After getting through all of this, I think the three of us became adults," Ed said from behind the wheel. "It's never going to be like it was before."

"That's about as good as anybody could put it," Rails agreed. "You're really getting there, Ed."

"Thanks, I appreciate that."

"Turn on the radio, Steve," Jeff said from the back. "We need a little music to liven things up."

Rails tuned into a good station but set the volume low. It seemed like the respectful thing to honor Slade's memory.

Jeff turned around and took a look in back of the van. He noticed something and shook his head.

"Do you know what's back there with our instruments, Rails?" he said. "Slade's guitar - we forgot to return Slade's guitar."

"No, Jeff – that's not right," Rails said.

"What do you mean?" Ed asked.

"This morning, before the funeral, I met with Shotgun's dad to return his stuff while you guys were busy helping with the flowers. He told me he wanted us to keep his guitar and he wouldn't take no for an answer. He said the family was so moved by what we said about him, they all agreed that Slade's guitar had to come with us. That's the way he would want it."

"For real?" Jeff exclaimed. "What a cool thing. I can just hear Shotgun saying it's the next best thing to him being with us."

"Far out," Ed beamed. "That guitar was his baby – his fingerprints are all over it. Man!"

"And it won't be played again until one of us gets really good and is worthy, right, Rails?" Jeff said.

"Yeah – you know it, dude."

Everybody relaxed and smiled.

"Hey, guys," Jeff added. "I've been wondering about something. Remember how Shotgun used to talk about that thing he was looking for – you know – that universal truth to live by or whatever it was? Do you think he was reaching for the stars or do you figure he really believed there was something like that out there?"

"Oh, it was legit," Ed said. "I have no doubt he did. Maybe WE can find it."

"I'll tell you this," Rails said seriously considering the notion. "There was a look about him on the bed before we knew there was something wrong – like all the questions had gone away and he'd found some kind of peace. I sensed it and I'm pretty keen on things like that. I wouldn't be surprised if some form of revelation came to him – maybe even just before he died. But we'll never know."

Nobody said anything for a time while they turned that over in their thoughts. Then a familiar song came on the radio. Jeff's eyes opened wide.

"'Green Onions' – that's 'Green Onions'!" he gasped.

"What of it?" Ed asked.

Jeff put his hand to his forehead, dragged it down his face, covered his mouth, and then pulled it away.

"The first night I got into Stiller and checked into the Y," he began, "I walked by Shotgun's room on the way to mine and I heard him playing the guitar. The door was part way open. Nikki Ford, the waitress at Joey's was with him and I'd met her earlier in the day. She called me in and I met Slade. We talked awhile and then, after she left, Shotgun and I shared a roach. I asked him to play something on his axe right after that. He did that number – 'Green Onions'. I remember it like it was yesterday because he played the song so well and I really liked it. We talked about it a little when he got done. He told me the title and that it was by...Booker T and the MG's. The title and group – they just like...froze in my brain."

"Well, then that's him!" Rails said. "That's Shotgun from the other side – a sign as clear as could ever be. Whatever he was seeking, he found it, man – I guarantee it!"

"Wow!" Jeff and Ed said together.

A period of quiet followed after that and all was neatly resolved. It was now truly a done deal. Nothing further needed to be said. They eased back and continued south on course, secure in knowing that everything was going to be okay no matter what they encountered. His spirit right there with them, they would see Shotgun's vision through, wherever it led them.

EPILOGUE

They spent Thanksgiving in Annapolis with Jeff's brother Luke, his wife Penny and their young daughter Rebecca. They stayed on for a couple of additional days, giving Jeff the chance to bond with his niece, who he'd seen only as a baby. After what he'd been through, Jeff felt closer to his brother than ever before. It was a great visit, as Luke and Penny warmed to Rails and Ed. They made them feel like family. Before they left, Jeff vowed to keep in touch more regularly with his brother than he had in the past. Luke did likewise.

From Maryland, it was south down the coast through Virginia and the Carolinas as the sun became stronger and the weather warmer. Then it was into Georgia where everybody was friendly and talked as if they were singing. They spent a few days in Savannah where they admired the young belles and soaked up the southern hospitality.

Continuing south with Florida the target, they picked up a hitchhiker along the way. He was a young guy named Tony going to Port St. Lucie. He said if they took him all the way, he could get them temporary work with him on an extensive beach cleanup project that he'd already been hired on. It sounded good and they agreed to it.

For two weeks, they stayed with Tony and his girlfriend in a shack along the ocean shore, slept on the floor, and worked the beach detail. They added more money to the coffers and in their free time, enjoyed the spectacular Florida birdlife, tangerine trees, and warm weather.

As he'd promised, Jeff sent off a letter off to Lynne and one to Beans too. In them, he explained about Slade's passing. Jeff also posted a note to the Stiller Y informing them. He'd continue to keep Lynne up to date with letters, and Beans with the post cards he requested, regularly throughout his time away.

Jeff also thought of Nikki not knowing about Slade's death. He spent a lot of time on letter to her explaining it and also describing what a beautiful sendoff Slade was given. He mailed it in care of Joey's Restaurant hoping it would find her.

With the cleanup completed, it was west in Florida to Lake Okeechobee where they stopped and spent an unseasonably warm afternoon at the beach. They rented a canoe and were out on the water for a few hours of peace and relaxation. From there, it was a couple of days north to the panhandle and then west through Alabama and Mississippi, during which they picked up several hitchhikers along the way. They were all characters in their own right with funny stories and observations. Every word they uttered had the unmistakable lyrical flavor of those born and raised in the deep rural south.

When they got to the Mississippi delta and New Orleans in Louisiana, Jeff, Rails, and Ed knew they had to spend at least a couple of days in The Big Easy. They got into town on Christmas day and celebrated with a baked ham dinner at a local restaurant and inn, at which they got a room. The three had a blast mingling with the people in town and listening to live jazz and blues in several clubs. None of them had ever experienced any place like New Orleans before. It was an eye opener, especially for Rails, who fast-handed prose sketches on his note pads left and right.

From there, they moved on through Texas, on highways so straight that it seemed like forever before there was a bend in the road. In some of the towns they passed through, they saw the oval faces and winning smiles of people of Mexican descent. Outside of Odessa, approaching an expansive cattle ranch, the van sprung a leak in the radiator hose and overheated. They had to pull over and stop. One of the ranch hands, a real life cowboy, approached on a horse and said he'd ride back to the main house and get what was needed to seal it up. He returned with some sealant tape and a couple of jugs of water. In a few minutes, he had the leak repaired temporarily and the van was up and running.

The group stumbled on more good fortune in that the ranch owner was repairing fences along the big spread and needed extra hands. It was another opportunity for extra money. He set them up in a bunk house and the next morning they had the van hose replaced in town. For ten days, they worked hard on the fencing under the Texas sun and experienced a little bit of what life on a cattle ranch was like. That, in addition to the genuineness and hospitality of the people of the Lone Star state. They even did a little horseback riding in their time off. By the time they left, they were referring to the place as "The Ponderosa". As Slade would have said, it was the balls.

From Texas on toward New Mexico, they had an interesting encounter with a hitchhiker long after dark. She was a young hippie girl by herself headed to Roswell. Rails remembered reading about the UFO crash that happened there in the forties and told the others about it. It was on the right track. They agreed that they might as well head there and have a look at the town.

The girl had an exotic look and the unusual name of Orianthi. Most likely she was of Italian or Greek lineage. Her hair was a mass of tightly curled jet black ringlets which cascaded all the way down to her waist. She was olive skinned and very pretty, with full lips and a smile that lit up the van. A cerebral type of girl, Orianthi spoke slowly and softly, carefully choosing her words.

They talked for a while. Then she noticed Slade's guitar in back and asked if she could play it. Before anyone could say anything, she had it out of the case and was tuning the pegs. After warming up with some cascading runs up and down the neck, Orianthi got into the Joan Baez song "Jesse Come Home". She played a beautiful fingerstyle accompaniment that women always seem to do especially well. Slade's guitar became alive in her delicate and knowing hands. Orianthi had the voice of an angel and articulated the somber lyrics with intense feeling. Her audience was dumbfounded.

They clapped enthusiastically when she finished, Rails taking both hands off the wheel to join in. Jeff mentioned how much Slade would have liked it and they demanded an encore. But the girl just smiled shyly and said that was all she had for now. She put the guitar back in the case, sat back and closed her eyes. She slept for the next few hours before they reached Roswell shortly before sunrise. It was another special brief encounter. Again, with the godly vibe the girl emitted, they wondered if Slade was behind that too.

In town, they let Orianthi off at a bus stop. Then they found a shady spot and slept in the van until the early afternoon. They spent the rest of the day checking out Roswell, and bought some alien mementos in a gift shop before they left.

From there, they continued west into Arizona and spent a day at the Grand Canyon. The three hooked up with a guided tour and descended to the bottom. There, they learned a great deal about one of the Seven Wonders of the World. All agreed that it was the most amazing thing they had yet seen on earth.

Then, after many hours of driving through desert and saguaros into the deep night, a yellow fire ball appeared on the horizon, getting bigger and bigger as they got closer. It was Las Vegas; that mass of casinos, sky scrapers, and neon out in the middle of nowhere. None of them had ever been there before and the sight of it looming ahead blew them away.

They got a room at a Ramada Inn and spent a couple of days in Vegas, playing the slots occasionally and some black jack. But mostly, they observed all of the fascinating gamblers from all over the country. Surprisingly, there were many wrinkled old ladies and men, smoking cigarettes and intensely playing the slots. Most everybody they saw was involved and focused like they were panning for gold, looking to make that one big hit.

During the next few days, they moved on up north through Nevada and then into California. They bisected part of the Mojave Desert and then travelled out to the old cowboy town of Barstow, where they spent a night. From there, it was on through the Rocky Mountain passes where they saw hang gliders soaring so high in the sky that they looked like condors. Further north, they encountered the cliffs and canyons of Big Sur and the Salinas Valley, the setting of many of John Steinbeck's novels. Rails gave the others lecture on the great writer of "Travels with Charlie" who was one of his inspirations. Finally, after being on the road for close to two months, they reached their destination. The hills and winding streets of San Francisco.

For a couple of days, they explored the city and spent a considerable amount of time experiencing the activity in the Haight/Asbury district. It had deteriorated since the Summer of Love in 1967 and there were addicts, homeless people and crime all over the place. Whatever vibe it had back then had long since flamed out. Rails took it all in and began to lean more toward the idea that the hope and passion of the 60's was indeed fading away.

From there it was seventy miles north to Calistoga in the wine country. And then ten miles west to someplace way out in the wilderness. After a few wrong turns, and finally a few miles down dirt roads, they found it. Crystal Farlow's commune. It looked like something out of the old western frontier: shacks, tents, lean-tos, a clearing with a fire pit, bicycles, a motorcycle and two old pickup trucks. There were about 25 members in the community. The longhair guys and the braless women all looked like dictionary definition hippies. There was a scattering of young children playing around too. It looked a lot like the scenes the group remembered in "Easy Rider".

Jeff, Rails and Ed stayed there for three days and got a taste of communal life. They were treated well and chipped in with the chores, but it was clear there were many problems. Having enough food was a constant issue and some of the members looked dirty and unhealthy. Crystal had gotten thinner since Jeff last saw her and her face was drawn and lined. It seemed as if she'd lost some of that spirit that so impressed him when he rode with her back in the spring.

One couple in the commune had journeyed 500 miles north six months before to join, from a similar settlement west of Los Angeles. It was in a far out-of-the-way place called Chatsworth. They'd lived on an abandoned movie ranch there with around 30 other people. The couple talked on and on about a weird guy named Charlie who was the leader and called the group his "family". The two described all kinds of drugs, orgies, dumpster raids for food and the eerie hold that Charlie had over the group, especially the girls.

Ultimately, they sensed big trouble brewing and decided to bolt. They had a rough time getting out but made the break late one night. Now they were relieved that they had moved on to a better scene. With the arrests of Charles Manson and other members of that former group on murder charges just a few weeks before, they'd learned just how lucky they were to exit when they did. Their story got the full attention of the three visitors.

Although everybody generally got along at the commune and there were few spats, it was clear to Jeff, Rails, and Ed that this wasn't going to last. Throughout their stay, Crystal and some of the others tried to talk them into joining up. They did it in a nice way with no pressure, but nobody even considered it. They came away educated for having seen a functioning commune but it just didn't sit right. It wasn't for them. It was an idealistic dream with the best of intentions. But in their opinions, it wasn't going to stick.

Back in San Francisco, they found a cheap rooming house along the docks. Just as Slade said they would, they got temporary work as laborers loading cargo ships. In their spare time, they acted on securing their Merchant Marine papers and in a few weeks had them. It took a little time, but by the end of February, they got hired as seamen on the crew of the 998 foot merchant vessel SS Golden State. Jeff and Ed were designated as deck hands and Rails as a cook's assistant since he had kitchen experience from working in his college cafeteria. They were beside themselves with excitement when it was all locked in.

Going to sea was the most challenging part of Slade's vision and here they were actually putting it into operation. All totaled, it would be three months or so out of the country in an environment they'd never experienced. But nobody was overly nervous or apprehensive about what was ahead. It was the next item on Slade's docket and they had complete faith in his plan.

Jeff took a picture of the Golden State and sent it to Beans. He also wrote Lynne a long letter describing in detail what had happened in California and what they were about to do. He thought of her daily and missed her more and more as time moved on.

Before they shipped out in the first week of March, the group found storage for the van and the things they couldn't take along. Everything would be there for them when they returned.

During their time at sea on the Golden State, Jeff, Rails, and Ed's perspective on things changed greatly. No longer free to do whatever they felt like doing or going wherever they wanted to, they were subject to the rules of the ship and whatever Captain Jonas Ingraham dictated. It wasn't easy. He was a hard-ass and they had a scrape with him and one or two with other superiors. Plus there were a few crooked crew members they had to deal with. There were some rough soul searching times but they stuck together and overcame those issues.

In time, they earned the respect of the crew and became friendly with many of them. Even the gruff captain, who the seamen jokingly referred to as Wolf Larsen, came to like them for their resilience and work ethic. Gradually, as they toughed things out with an undying resolve, Jeff, Ed and Rails gained an admiration and an affinity for the vast ocean and the seagoing life. Rails of course, was going to be a writer, but Jeff and Ed began to think of maybe carving out some kind of future working at sea.

The Golden State made cargo deliveries and pickups first in Hawaii, where they were docked for four days. The three were able to go ashore and get a little feel for the warmth and beauty of the Aloha state. From there, it was west on the long haul to Sydney, Australia and then south to Melbourne, where the ship was docked for 10 days waiting for cargo coming by train from Perth.

Taking advantage of that extended period, which included regular leave passes from the ship, Jeff, Rails and Ed used their time off to explore the area. They got to experience the beauty of the city on the bay and the friendliness and hospitality of the people of Australia. The three rode the city trams and played some pickup basketball with welcoming Aussie athletes at Albert Park in downtown Melbourne. They hung out at Flinders Street Station in the heart of the city and watched the natives go about their daily routines. And they visited the spectacular botanical gardens in the Melbourne suburbs.

Later, they rented a Mini Minor and toured the mystical Dandenong Ranges in the bush outside of the city. There they saw thousands of gum and mountain ash trees growing out of a thick undergrowth full of enormous ferns. It was pristine and looked prehistoric. They were awed by it. Before they shipped out, they made it south to Phillip Island. At dusk, they watched hundreds of fairy penguins emerge from the ocean for their evening waddles up the beach to their nests.

From Melbourne, there was a stop at Port Arthur, Tasmania, where they were docked for three days. In town, they toured the closed prison facilities that formerly housed criminals from the United Kingdom. They walked in chambers where the prisoners used to be kept in 23 hours of darkness with just one hour in light outside for exercise.

Before leaving Tasmania, they explored a small part of Russell Falls National Park for a day on a guided tour. There, they got a feel for how much uncharted frontier remains on the fabled rugged island at the bottom of the world. From the guide, they heard an interesting item about the Tasmanian tiger, thought to be recently extinct. He talked about hikers traversing deep within the sprawling park recently claiming to have sighted a live animal, plus the fact that tiger tracks having been found.

Then it was back out to sea, east to Wellington, New Zealand, which was the final stop before they headed home to the states. They were there only for two days and never got far out of the city. However, they still got a taste of what an interesting place New Zealand was, so far out in the ocean by itself, and sheltered in many ways from the greed and prejudice of the rest of the world.

It was early June of 1970 when they docked back in San Francisco and their commitment with the Merchant Marine was completed. It came to a total of 92 days at sea. They'd survived the ups and downs and grew miles from the experience. Now, all three felt they'd changed and significantly matured. They talked about it many times. Their perspective was in the stratosphere from what it had been before. And they were flush with money; the hitch had been very profitable.

Finally, some good news greeted them back home with regard to Uncle Sam. Jeff and Ed learned of the new draft lottery and found out that both had numbers in the two hundreds. There was practically no chance of them getting drafted.

They got the van out of storage and took it easy for a few days in Frisco. Now the final leg of Slade's plan was left; to travel north and then loosely follow the Oregon Trail west. As soon as they were rested and had their bearings, the three got back to the place where they the felt most comfortable. Moving on to new places and new experiences.

They made their way up the California coast into Oregon and Washington State, amid the forests of spectacular sequoias and redwoods. From Seattle, they headed west through Idaho and Wyoming. Outside of Cheyenne, they hooked up with one of Rails' college connections. They stayed with him in his cabin for several days, taking it easy and soaking up the spirit of the American west.

Then they then headed north through the Bad Lands of Montana, south to the corn fields of Nebraska, and back north to the higher country of Minnesota and Wisconsin. They hung out in Beloit to rest for a few days, and then toured a portion of the Cheese state up north through Madison and Green Bay.

From there it was on to Chicago, Cleveland, and around Lake Erie to Niagara Falls. Then up to the friendly city of Buffalo where they hung out briefly before embarking on the last leg east. Finally, they moved on to the New York Thruway from Buffalo upstate to the village of Oriskany Falls near Utica, Rails' home town. There they spent the fourth of July with his family before Jeff and Ed parted ways with him to head east back to Massachusetts.

It was no surprise to them that this was the end of the line for Rails. On the way to New Zealand, he decided it would be time to get on with the next phase of his life and informed them. Rails was accepted in a master's program at New York University in Journalism after he graduated from Boston University, but he'd put it off now going on two years. He already had a ton of material for his writing. It was time now to go back to school to gain more knowledge and to work on his first novel on the side.

Rails would stay with his family the rest of the summer before heading to NYU and graduate school in the fall. He'd go on to complete his Master's degree and that first novel about the mill workers, which he titled "The Factory". It would eventually be accepted by Viking Books.

Before they left Oriskany Falls, Jeff and Ed settled with Rails on his cut toward the van. All made solid promises to keep in touch. It was an emotional scene before they left, with handshakes, hugs, and even a few tears. The three had shared something that could well go down as the most significant thing each would ever do in life. And as Rails told Slade's parents at the wake back in November, they were surely forever bonded.

Jeff and Ed made the drive back to Massachusetts. Their first stop was at Stiller to reconnect with Lynne and their other friends. It was a joyful reunion, as Jeff and Lynne had kept up their communication during the eight months he was away. That had further strengthened their

303

relationship and feelings for each other. And to Jeff's surprise, she wasn't involved with anybody else. She'd waited for him.

Jeff and Ed checked back with their friends at the mill and the Y. Beans was beside himself to see them again as was Creecher. They also tried to look up Nikki Ford, but were told at Joey's that she'd left town months ago with no forwarding address. Joey did tell them that Nikki got Jeff's letter. Jeff felt sorry that he didn't have the opportunity to speak with her further about Slade. But he was glad that at least she knew.

Now, it was off to the final destination; the old seacoast town of New Bedford, Massachusetts. Through the duration of their time at sea, Jeff and Ed further solidified their bond with the ocean. The notion to live by the sea and work on it took on a firm hold. They talked about it many times, and after learning of Rails' future plans, discussed the idea of getting an apartment together in a seacoast town.

With that idea in mind, Ed wrote a letter from New Zealand to an uncle in New Bedford about finding him and Jeff an apartment there. The uncle made the arrangements and a unit was waiting for them to move into, right on shore of the fabled whaling port. It was a second floor apartment in a rickety old Cape Cod shingle building. It fit their needs well.

With their experience with the Merchant Marine in their hip pockets, Jeff and Ed easily found jobs in the New Bedford fishing industry. They got full time work with the FinestKind Lobster and Scallop outfit which operated six boats. They learned the ropes and the nautical information they needed to know, and also got experience in operating the boats. It felt right to both of them, working off shore on the mighty blue Atlantic.

Ed went out and purchased a used car. Jeff bought out his share of the van to have it for himself. He began driving up to Stiller to be with Lynne when he had time off. Before long, she was spending weekends with him in the New Bedford apartment.

By the time August rolled around, Ed could see where it was going between Jeff and Lynne. He began to feel like the third wheel. Ed had an idea about what he wanted to do next and sensed it was a good time to move on.

When he, Jeff and Rails were in Port St. Lucie for those two weeks in Florida, Ed made a connection with the owner of a deep sea fishing outfit. The man liked him and was interested in his mechanical background. He

304

told Ed that he could set him up with a job working on one of his vessels if he ever came back to Florida, and he'd teach him about boat engine mechanics on the side. The man gave Ed his phone number. Ed was intrigued by the idea. He saved the number and never forgot about it.

Now, he decided to take advantage of the opportunity if it was still there and made the phone call. He got the job and was blown away with enthusiasm. Ed loved the idea of relocating to Florida, which he really enjoyed for the time they were there. He'd take his brother Wes with him as well, who although older, had no direction and needed his guidance. In a few weeks, Jeff and Lynne saw them off. Again, they promised to stay in contact.

With Ed's departure, the separation of the group was complete. Because he was closest to Slade, Jeff was left the keeper of his guitar. That had already been decided before hand by Rails and Ed. He set it up in a prominent spot in the living room on the wall. It was there as a symbol, in memory of the most important friend he ever had, the catalyst who changed the direction of his life for the better.

As if guided to from above, Jeff went out and found a music teacher. Playing the guitar regularly and always trying to improve would become a constant of good karma for him for the rest of his life.

Not long after Ed left, Jeff and Lynne decided to live together. She moved in with him at the New Bedford apartment. They'd talked over their situation many times and came to agree it was the right thing to do. Jeff and Lynne had cultivated a deep and respectful love for each other. They needed to be together. In time, their commitment and support for one another would help both to make further peace with their troubled pasts.

Lynne found employment as a seamstress in town for a good salary. By now, through learning with her aunt, she was skilled at wardrobe alterations and dressmaking. Lynne loved finally being out of the confines of the mill and the having the freedom to create that her work afforded her.

Jeff continued working on the lobster and scallop boats, adding to his sea going knowledge with each week. In early September, he finally decided to take that shot at furthering his education that he never forgot about. He got lucky. With the aid of his Merchant Marine experience and his good college grades in the year he attended, he was accepted at

Massachusetts Maritime Academy in Buzzards Bay on short notice. It was to begin study in an evening program toward a degree in Maritime Transportation and Materials Moving. He'd be able to keep his day job and also work toward a better future.

Jeff's goal was to one day be a deck officer on a cargo ship and maybe even captain his own vessel. It gave him a great feeling of satisfaction that he was acting on his vow to return to college, and in a direction that genuinely excited him.

In the end, Jeff, Rails and Ed were fueled by the spirit and idealism of their departed friend, the man they affectionately knew as Shotgun. And they were also inspired by the same spirit and idealism of the American counter culture movement of the 1960's. Nobody sold out. In their time together, all three learned to be true to themselves. They came to act not on what society dictated to them, but on what rose from within their souls.

Made in the USA
Middletown, DE
06 August 2017